In the Middle of the Journey
A Novel

ROBERT SHANKS

authorHOUSE®

"In The Middle Of The Journey of our life,
I came to myself in a dark wood where the
straight way was lost."

THE DIVINE COMEDY
Canto I
Dante Alighieri

AuthorHouse™
1663 Liberty Drive
Bloomington, IN 47403
www.authorhouse.com
Phone: 1-800-839-8640

First published by AuthorHouse 6/9/2011

ISBN: 978-1-4634-0499-4 (e)
ISBN: 978-1-4634-0498-7 (dj)
ISBN: 978-1-4634-0497-0 (sc)

Library of Congress Control Number: 2011907085
Printed in the United States of America on acid-free paper.

To Linda Finson; Monica Ryan and Cynthia Cornwell:
Gratitude for their devoted preparation of this manuscript.

Digital Graphics Production by Ghislaine Pitt of W.J. Blueprints,
Pittsfield, MA; plotting@wjblueprint.com

Permissions:
2 lines from the poem "The Second Coming" by W. B. Yeats is reprinted by permission of MacMillan & Company.
3 lines from the song "Light My Fire" Words and Music by The Doors © 1967 Doors Music Co. Copyright Renewed. All Rights Reserved. Used by Permission. Reprinted by permission of Hal Leonard Corporation.
1 line from the poem "I See the Boys of Summer" by Dylan Thomas, from THE POEMS OF DYLAN THOMAS, copyright © 1939 by New Directions Publishing Corp. Reprinted by permission of New Directions Publishing Corp.

Anboden Press is a privately-owned limited catalogue publisher. AnbodenPress@gmail.com

Library of Congress Cataloging in Publication Data
Shanks, Robert
In The Middle Of the Journey.

For Ann, always

Also written by the author:

Fiction

Love Is Not Enough, a novel

Non-Fiction

The Cool Fire
The Primal Screen
The Name Is The Game, with Ann Shanks

Plays

S.J. Perelman In Person
When Jefferson Dined Alone
No Cure In Sight

Television Movies

Drop-Out Father
He's Fired, She's Hired
Good-Bye Super Mom
Once Upon A Beverly Hills
The Darwin Games

IN THE MIDDLE OF THE JOURNEY

CHAPTER 1

Lately, Gardner had taken to carrying a knife. It was not a very impressive-looking knife, but rather oldish really and rusting slightly. The blade extended perhaps four inches. The bone sides were dark and yellow, and a small piece even had been chipped from one of these.

Gardner was not at all sure where the knife had come from, but, just to settle it for himself, he had decided finally that his son had acquired it, in school probably, or along the way – a fair trade for three baseball cards – or in the dry riverbed of a gutter.

Somehow it had turned up in the apartment one Sunday morning when he had been cleaning out papers and back magazines from his desk and the bookcase which lined one wall of his bedroom. But of this even he could not be certain, since he had malingered so that day – his eyes slow-chewing blocks of type, grazing on every letter, theatre program, tourist brochure or magazine that he picked up; slovenly feeding himself an anarchy of ideas and yesterday's alarms and personalities, before he would assign each of these remainders to the throwaway pile or through a slow shuffle back to one shelf or another for a later – what?

And too, that day, there had been other distractions, he remembered: music, loud from the stereo in the den, which his wife had turned on; television noise from the living room; and overall, the clavichord voices of his children—thin strings constantly striking. Probably too, he had been hung-over. He nearly always was on Sundays.

Now, in the twelfth floor apartment where he lived along Central Park West in New York City, in the bathroom of the master bedroom where carpeting covered the tile floor, Gardner stood shaving. He had a towel wrapped around his waist and his pelvis was pressed against the sink to the left (there were two sinks side-by-side here). He was swishing the razor through the soapy water to clean the blade that was advertised to last

1

fifteen shaves (he had designed the ad layout for it), but which never got him through five.

It was April. The 26th. And it was Saturday. At 6:30PM. Outside, darkness was coming onto the city – cool, but unchaste. It was Gardner's birthday and he was 43.

Why should I be carrying a knife? he thought.

He picked up the filter-tipped cigarette (he had designed the ads for it too) which had been suffocating in the ashtray on the glass shelf just below the sliding mirrors of the medicine chest. I've got to stop smoking, he thought. The ashtray was a clear glass object and etched into it were the words, "Ritz Hotel, Paris." He and his wife had stayed there for a week the previous September. When they were leaving the Ritz, Gardner had packed the ashtray in his bag, along with two towels, soap, shampoo, a shower cap and a lot of swizzle sticks from the bar for his children. Gardner and his wife had two children, a boy, 9 and a girl, 5. His wife was pregnant now in her seventh month. All went or would go to Dalton. All our kids were conceived on vacations. "Dr. Harris tells all couples who are having trouble getting pregnant to do it on vacation," he remembered his wife saying.

As he inhaled, Gardner could smell the overburn of the cigarette. One side of it was scorched and the paper was unconsumed. He inhaled again, carefully, leaning farther forward, but the paper re-ignited and fell into the shaving water. He couldn't catch it.

Gardner looked at the paper in the water. Dead flesh. Ugly. Disgusting. Out of place. Suddenly he felt unable to control things. Vulnerable, Mortal. Nothing. Quickly, he lifted the charred paper from the water and threw it into the wastebasket. He took another deep breath through the cigarette and put it back into the ashtray. The center cannot hold, he said to himself.

He jutted his chin forward stiffly, Mussolini-fashion, and brought the safety razor up to meet it. That did it. It didn't hurt nor was it bleeding yet, but he knew the blade had missed its proper angle and had cut him. The center cannot hold! What was that from? Auden? Yeats? Eliot? I can't remember. Anyway, that says it. I'm halfway home – at least – and feeling lost. From Norma. From myself. From everything.

Garner looked into the mirror, certain, for the second, that his face would disappear. Instead, he saw the cut begin to bleed. He reached over, tore off a piece of toilet paper, wet it and pressed it against the blood.

"Harry," she said, "look."

Gardner looked into the mirror and saw Norma standing behind him.

"What?" he said.

"Look."

She stood, unnaturally, he thought, as though in a pose, but blurred for all of it, since he didn't have his glasses on.

"Are you looking?"

"How's our time?"

"You're not looking. Look, Harry. Not through the mirror. Turn around."

Gardner turned around and squinted at his wife.

"Well?" she said. "Where are you glasses? Can you see?"

Gardner moved towards her. He saw.

"What's that?" he said.

"A body stocking."

"Swan Lake?" Gardner laughed. "With a knocked up swan?"

"It's the latest." She put her arms around him.

"What ever happened to saddle shoes and bobby socks?"

Norma pulled out of the embrace and looked at Gardner.

"You're bleeding," she said.

"Stigmata. It's a sign."

"You? Religious?"

"You Jane."

Norma stepped back and sat down on the edge of the tub.

Gardner turned around and picked up his cigarette. He inhaled and looked at the cut in the mirror.

"You look pretty good still in just a towel," Norma said. "You been exercising?"

"I have a pot." Gardner patted himself below the waistline.

"I didn't marry you for your muscles – or your hair."

"Damn – it is coming out – isn't it?"

"You're like a girl about your hair."

"Oh, don't start that again."

"Well, you are. Doctor Wein–"

"I don't want to hear what Harpo has to say."

"That's another thing–"

"Do we have to take marital inventory now? We'll never get to the damned party!"

"But your stone-age attitude about psych–"

"Norma, please. It's my birthday. What're you going to do with your old bras?

"I'll make ear muffs for the kids. I thought you'd love the new no bra look. All those bouncing boobs on parade."

"Not me. I was breast-fed."

"You look. I see you."

"I said 'fed' – not 'dead'."

"You're always telling me you want other women."

Once. He had told her once.

One night about a year ago (it had come up a lot since then), Gardner had tried to convince Norma that it was unnatural for a man to confine himself sexually to one woman. They had been at dinner – drinking and being good with each other. After that, Norma had started going to the psychiatrist three times a week and Gardner had started drinking more.

"What happened? I thought you had to have everybody?" Norma said.

"The discussion was hypothetical. Intellectual."

"It was a lot farther south than your intellect. You still want them."

"I didn't say that – ever."

"Look, Norma, honey," Norma said, mimicking Gardner, "I've got this wonderful plan, see? I'll go out once a week and get laid – okay?"

"It wasn't just – to – get laid," Gardner said.

"Oh, it was to, though – when you could. Aren't you a little old for the sexual revolution?"

"It was – very complicated. More than just – what you're saying. I suggest we drop it."

"—What was I supposed to do? Say wonderful, go, yes – have a horny holiday. Send a postcard. 'Having a wonderful time. Penis on a pogo stick. Glad you're not here.'"

"Are you feeling insecure about the party?"

"What am I supposed to feel? I look like a kangaroo shop-lifting. And what are you trying to prove? Running around putting your penis into every God only knows – does that make you feel like a big man? The great conqueror? Some conquest! You'll break it off trying to service all the girls who spread their legs in this town!"

"Oh, Christ, Norma." Gardner looked at himself in the mirror and began singing to the image of himself, "Happy Birthday to me, Happy Birth–"

"So, it's your birthday. All right. I'm sorry. I just came in here to get a little reassurance about how I looked. If you liked my new – if it pleased you."

"I told you, yes."

"Why I care to please a bastard who only worries about himself and his own IMMATURE NEED, I don't know."

"Cause you can't live without me."

"You bastard," Norma said and she smiled. "Give me a cigarette."

"Should you?"

"I'm just going to hold it."

Gardner took up the pack from the glass shelf and shook out a cigarette for Norma and a new one for himself, and lit his off the one he had been smoking. He handed Norma her's. He went back to shaving. He looked at Norma's face reflected in the mirror. He couldn't see her clearly without his glasses, but he knew her face by memory. Dark, wide, angular. It's an extraordinary face, he thought. Alive, urgent, energetic – a constantly changing transparency of her feelings. Not the death mask most people wear. Not like yours, he thought, looking at himself in the mirror. You have one smile, one frown and mostly a kind of neuter nice look that says you'd like to be liked. But not Norma. He looked at her face again.

"She looks foreign," they had said, out in Indiana – remember? Yes, and I remember liking her even more because of it. And remember guessing right – the first time you met her – about the possibilities of that large mouth? You've come away from it since then a thousand times in a thousand different ways, shuddering and piecemealed and consumed. And her eyes. Brown, running to black – like two visible souls of very good people. Saints even, if they can be trusted for goodness, good enough to match her eyes. And her strong jaw – that made you think you could trust her in a crisis, which you've learned you could. And her hair. Surplus thick and dark and good for clutching and hiding in. She has a good body, too. Full. Strong. I know it's out of fashion now, but it's the kind I learned to love in Correggio. A body that knows what bodies are for.

Norma was still sitting on the edge of the tub. Gardner walked to her and got down on his knees in front of her. He spread the fingers of his hand gently over her swelling tits.

"Oh, Harry," Norma said, softly.

She leaned over and kissed him on top of his head. He looked up at her. She kissed him on the mouth. Their mouths went open. Easily Gardner brought Norma down from the tub rim and onto the floor, while their mouths stayed against each other. He lay over her, gently, because of her swollen belly where the baby was, and stretched her full on her back. He held her securely in his right arm, which formed a cradle for her back. In his right hand he continued to hold the cigarette, which in fire, was nearing its filter-end. His left hand stayed on her breast, his fingers moving softly over the nipple. He continued kissing her and their mouths were open. But as he kissed her, he could not keep from thinking that it was true. That is, about his plan for one night out a week. It <u>was</u> so he could be with a woman who wasn't Norma. Even now, kissing Norma like this, and enjoying it, he could think about it, about wanting other women, and not feel that it was not true, but still not wrong. You've got to admit the honesty of the feeling at least to yourself, he thought. Wasn't that the whole point of psychoanalysis? Or at least a big point? You have to admit your feelings before you can try to understand them. But then, of course, at least with these feelings – the analyst – (old Harpo) – was society-bound to patch you up enough – adjust you – to function within the public proprieties – whether they jibed with your deeper baser motivations or not – and which probably were what confused and shot you down in the first place! And shot down – up – fractured – fractioned – splintered is what you've become!

Gardner's thoughts began to pick over the whole medicine chest of pills he knew he had invented to cool the hot water that had come to boil in his stomach, and which increasingly had lost their potency to help him pretend.

The sweating and crashing boy-men who meet Saturdays in the touch football game in the Sheep's Meadow in Central Park (run, sheep, run) – games which get very rough and the rougher they get, the more you enjoy yourself, and how in the huddles you always ask for the assignment to block the biggest member of the opposing team and refuse to play end or catch passes, which on your high school team had been your position and your special talent. That was too easy! And how, instead, you urge yourself into each bruising and bashing piling-up to guarantee coming home – bone-aching and emptied-out beyond knowing responsibility to any drive you might have for your IMMATURE NEED! So much so that you're too tired to make love even to your wife – even when you want to – and she you!

Gardner thought about the handball pill and the gym-at-the-Y pill and the tennis-before-work pill and the skiing-in-the-winter pill and the hard-ocean-swimming-in-the-summer pill, which was a hard-to-swallow pill especially, because of the young, strong, near-naked bodies of the girls on the beach and for whom, to over come, to blank out, he would go to the swim-too-far-out-pill, the too-far-for-safety-from-unknown currents-and-certainly-for-his-own-stamina-as-a-swimmer pill.

Out there, there were days truly when you were barely able to bring yourself back to shore, when your arms felt like dead penguins and you'd think those birds would pull you down and you would think you were going to die by drowning from your pill; and yet, when you would finally flatten out in the shallow – body touching the bottom – and cork about, breathless in the breaking waves, able to lift only your eyes to the beach – your eyes would look and find a bosom, or a butt, and your sack would fill with grain and your groin with pain – beyond the exhaustion, beyond what you knew was your physical impotence at that point. Even beyond all this, there was still the longing to have her. To go into in her. How can you pretend against such feelings? Pretend? Impossible! Contend almost the same. With <u>that</u> power? Deny that force? With some sniveling 'thou shalt nots'? Thou canst not help was truer. Sure – you try, especially for Norma, since you know it hurts a woman for you to want other women, especially to talk about it. So you remain faithful – against yourself. <u>What faith demands faithfulness against yourself</u>? And so you try to put out the fire in your bag and belly with make-shift, with pills – swilling gin and smoking and successing and sweating bang-on into the man-boys in the park! And you see how the others try – to deny it, put it off, out, away – with Playboy and dirty jokes, harder porn and God-fearing and TV commercials and erotic dreams and paid whores and bets on pro football games, and sometimes (you have also – be honest) by ending up in the bathroom, jerking out the scalding pearliness from yourself in a mixture of embarrassment and displacement and defeat. Is there anything sadder than a married man masturbating? Still – you try – for Norma. Cause you know – even if you don't want to – she can't let you have <u>wanting</u> in your way. That hurts her in her heart and feelings – so much she has to think you're unnatural – a pitiful creature – some carnal Caliban! With this – this IMMATURE NEED! A regressions-boy created by Mom or Dad or some fetching sixth grade teacher!

But that couldn't be true, Gardner thought, not the whole truth of it. It wasn't just Mom – "be a good boy" – or Dad – "do the right thing, son" – the full extent of Gardner's sex-ed 101 -- or the unattainable Miss Mitchell in that slippery rayon kind of dress sliding over her hypnotizing behind with a hissing sound and hiding the join of those legs, so muscularly perfect, and strong enough to snap you in two, of the whispered secret of

7

her silk stockings rubbing together – "swit, swit" – as she walked, or the explosive, searing joy caused by her exposed garter snap, sneak-seen when she would sit and her dress would hitch up. Oh, my Sigmund, the near-faint and ecstasy for that poor eleven year old boy of me when I would see her stocking top – or song of songs – a lightning flash of flesh just above. Holy Sigmund, maybe it was Miss Mitchell afterall! That sweet love never known. She young; me infantile, practically. Oh, Sigmund, the tender pain of never touching that backside at her blackboard.

But no, that was too simple. It came in you at birth. The power. Haven't you seen your own son when he was a baby fondle his fellowhood in his crib and smile from the feel, from the pleasant force of that good touching? It was always there. From forever. It was there when that some mossy-moist pre-man thing first slunk from the sea to the beach. (Didn't sperm and love-making smell of fish and the sea?) It was all you needed to know to believe in evolution. It was always there! To learn it, to track the source was not the souring process. To unlearn it, to cage it was the rabies. To harness the hard-on, bend the erection in the direction of marriage, Jesus, the office and the boss. Wall Street. War.

With that comes the frustration and the beginning of death. The pressure in the hide and head and hot rod so insistent that – you – Harry Gardner – could believe in the reality of your physical coming apart – could believe in becoming a scorched, shattered self lying literally in pieces for a dust pan and broom to wisk away, good and anonymous nuisance.

Dearly Beloved – Here, in a film of dust, lies what's left of Harold Crist Gardner, known as Harry, who yearned for nearly all women and who, with a tenderness and love that was all consuming – being allowed to touch them not, died in a fountain of fleshing fragments; demolished by the warm, moist sheaths not sworded, the soft, wet lips not pressed, the buttocks not clutched, the calves, the inner thighs not traced by hand, the tongue pirouetting about the clitoris, the breasts not kissed, the heart of darkness, the capital of the universe, the Maude not made, the Sally, the Joan, the Laura, the May, the Madelyn, the Sue, the Beth, the Mary Jane and Sarah. The WAC at headquarters, the girl on the bus yesterday, the Homecoming Queen, the life guard at the state park, the cheer leader, the model in the bathtub in the TV soap commercial, or in the bra and panties ad in the New York Times Sunday Magazine, or the stewardess on the night flight to London, or the baby sitter, or the high school girl on the other side of the building, or his college roommate's stepmother, or his wife's best friend, or his best friend's wife – or his wife. Her too! He wanted them all.

Gardner was convinced. Anything imposed – anything – brought repression and deviation and perversion. The rules against him had brought lies and Jesuses and inquisitions – and slaughtering wars – the sensuality of combat – and had tied sex like a dirty tin can to the tail of love. Sex only with love was a lie, and its child-lie – love with only one person – outgrew its parent. Sex was possible – necessary – without love and with more than one, because it was the big one – the I. (Of course, you could love without sex – an idea even more suspect in our time). Are there any sex offenders in the animal kingdom besides humans? Sade but true.

Sexuality is the kingdom and the power and the glory. It's the meaning of being alive. That's what proves it and sustains it. It is life. Limp there, that yardstick never gives you certitude of your existence, but up – out, erect, throbbing, powerfully veined – you know you're living. Are life! And life-giver!

"Oh, Harry, Harry – My God, Harry. Unnnnnh. Harry."

Gardner heard Norma's voice from over a long distance and remembered finally where he was. He felt her body twisting beside him, partly under him, on the floor. He felt her hand on his penis, which was full and pounding. She was kissing him and groaning. He felt himself feeling good – great, glorious, full – grown. His arm was asleep though – from its position under Norma. He shifted the arm slightly. Glorious, great, full going –

Hisssss.

Gardner heard the curious sound and felt Norma jerk away.

"What the hell? Oh Christ, Harry, you burned my hair." Norma sat up and swiped at her head with both hands. Gardner heard the phone ring, once, twice.

"Oh, damn – you and those cigarettes!" Norma said.

Andrew was knocking at their bedroom door. "Mama, it's for you," Andrew said. "It's Mr. Rosen."

"Can I call him back? I'm busy now," Norma said.

"Yeah, call back," Gardner said.

"Says he's got to talk to you, Mom – he's going out."

"Oh damn," Norma said. She started to get up.

"You can't go now," Gardner said.

"What am I supposed to do?" Norma said.

"What am _I_ supposed to do," Gardner said.

"You coming?" Andrew yelled.

"Yes – alright, Andy – I'm coming," Norma said.

"Who isn't?"

"Later – okay?" she said to Gardner.

He nodded.

Norma got up, arranged herself, put on her husband's robe and went into the bedroom to answer the phone.

Gardner rolled over on his back and tried to let go, but the wires between himself and the plunger were fixed. He was ready to explode.

After a moment, he got up and tried to calm himself. He rearranged the towel around his waist. He changed the water in the basin and finished shaving – miserable. He dried his face and put his glasses on. My balls are killing me!

He walked into the bedroom and saw that Norma was off the phone and had her dress on.

"What'd the sonofabitch want?" Gardner said.

"Where was the UJA release was all," Norma said. "I'd given it to Harris and he forgot to tell Rosie."

"Jesus."

"Button me," Norma said.

Gardner did. The dress she wore was of satin material and had a column of satin buttons up the back. It was the color of raspberry sherbet and was cut in an A-frame style from the neck, full to the knee. It was very pretty, Gardner thought.

"How do I look?" She said.

"Beautiful."

"Do you like the dress?"

"Yes."

"Really?"

"It's very elegant."

"Well, don't get rhapsodic about it."

"Prick tease."

"You'll get yours – no complaints up to now, are there?"

Gardner finished buttoning her, patted her on the ass and walked to his dresser. He opened the second drawer and took out clean boxer underwear pants and a T-shirt. He dropped the towel from around his waist onto the bed behind him. Naked, he looked at himself in the mirror over the dresser. Not bad, he told himself. Could be taller. Nice smile. Hair. Oh, sure, hair – cause you arrange it to cover the bald spots. At least I've got enough to do that! But there's lots of grey. And those lines from your nose to your mouth are really getting deep. And your mouth is turning down. That's what old people's mouths do. I'm not old! Then hold in your stomach. All right! All right! Hello, modest cock. Hiya, boss. Boss! You're the boss, you little prick.

Gardner pulled a shirt out of the dresser, and a pair of socks. He sat on the foot of the bed. He put on the socks, which were black stretch and elastic and which, when on, came nearly to his knees – and of which he had no other kind, since he did not like to see his exposed calves when he was seated with his legs crossed. Gardner put on the shirt and pinched his neck with the top button. He walked to his closet and picked out a tie. It was wide and silk in burgundy red. When he had tied it, the back piece was longer than the front. He untied it. He took down the new suit he had bought at Bonwit Teller's. He looked to see where Norma was. She was fixing her hair. That'll take an hour. He put on the pants. They were very tight. Gardner owned seven suits from Brooks Brothers, but this one was a Pierre Cardin. Navy blue. It had a flared waist and bell-bottom trousers, and he felt a little funny in it. Maybe it was too young for him. You've let your hair grow, too, sport, he told himself. A real peacock, ain'tcha?

Gardner re-tied his tie, though it still came out wrong. This time he left it. He put on his shoes – mod black boots – and came back to his dresser. He turned on the radio on top of the dresser and – trying to find music – heard, "Viet Cong and North Vietnamese troops ambushed a Cambodian –" Dial. "An attempted coup by Haitian naval –" Dial. "Do you prefer acting on stage or in films? –" Dial. And Gardner found music, a Beatles song: "I heard the news today – oh, boy."

He looked at himself again in the mirror. He touched at his hair – here and there, pushing it forward.

"Oh, God, you're going to drive me crazy," Norma said. "That's the fifth time you've fixed your hair."

"If you were ready, I wouldn't have to stand around."

"That's why I never wanted to marry a handsome man. I hate your looks. That's part of your problem. You depend on them – like a starlet. Where are you going?"

"To get a drink. Just a little one. So we don't walk into Billingsly's alone. You want one?"

"No, I – oh, God, okay. I may as well."

Gardner walked to the door of their bedroom and undid the lock on it. He came out of the room, along a hallway and into the foyer of the apartment. He went to the bar there and lifted out two glasses. From a locked cabinet just below, he took up a bottle of Johnny Walker Black Label Scotch. He poured it into the two glasses. More in to his own.

He could hear the sound of the television set in the living room and supposed the children were in there watching. From the noise, he knew it was tuned to one of those filmed situation comedies which has no comedy. He could hear the laugh track, its disembodied shrill bearing no true witness to the words and events it was supposedly laughing at. It occurred to him that probably many or most of the people whose laughs were recorded on the track were long since dead. <u>Lazurus laughter</u>. Gardner didn't go in. He didn't want to see the children until it was time to go. Instead, he headed for the kitchen to get ice and water for the Scotch.

At the door of the kitchen, he bumped – body to body – into the baby-sitter and nearly spilled the Scotch.

"My God!" he said.

"Mr. Gardner – I'm sorry."

"That was close. How are you, Patience?"

Patience was English and she dressed – fantastically, Gardner thought. Right now, she was wearing a mini-skirt. Very, very mini, Gardner saw. She had long, straight, blonde hair which fell below her shoulders and she had a puckish and pretty, though plane-less English face and a pouty, pale-lipsticked mouth. Reedy legs you couldn't stop looking at. She was 22 or so, Gardner supposed, and she had been in America six months. During the week, she worked as a receptionist for a television production company. Week-ends and evenings, she baby-sat. She was saving up to make a trip across America. Gardner had most of this information from his wife. He barely spoke to Patience, except when they got home and then only to ask her how much he owed her for the evening. He thought often about her sexually. Once or twice even, while making love to Norma, he had pretended she was Patience – and he had liked it.

"I didn't hear you come in," Gardner said. He could feel himself tuning up to "polite" – <u>that good fraternity social training</u>.

"The children let me in."

"I was shaving. I didn't hear the bell."

"You cut yourself," Patience said.

"Yeah. This is to kill the pain."

"Oh, yes, quite."

"Good for wounds of all sorts."

"So I've been told."

"I was just getting some ice. Excuse me."

"May I help?"

"It's all right."

Gardner moved past Patience and went into the kitchen. They touched as he went by. She followed him.

"You probably smoke pot or something," Gardner said.

"I have. It doesn't do anything for me."

I'd like to do something for you, Patience! Gardner laughed to himself. I wonder if she thinks I'm attractive? That'd be nice.

Gardner took an ice tray from the refrigerator and walked to the sink to remove the cubes. Patience was looking at him – and she was smiling. He smiled back.

"That outfit's great, Patience. Really good."

"Do you like it – really?"

"A lot."

"Nothing much, actually."

Gardner smiled, looking at her legs. "Yes."

"I meant – not fancy."

"You have, um, um –" and he continued to look at her legs.

"Thank you. Great sense of freedom you know. Symbol of liberation and all that."

"Are you liberated, Patience?"

"Rather," Patience laughed.

"Can I fix you – something?"

"No, thank you, sir."

Damn, Gardner thought. I could live without that "Sir." Maybe she said it cause she's English. They're taught to say "Sir" and "Ma'am" to their betters as well as their elders. Well, not "betters" – But, well, hell, I am her employer.

"You live in the village – right?" Gardner said. He was trying to keep his voice low and calm, but he thought it sounded higher and pinched.

"I do, yes," Patience said. "West 10th Street. Very pretty, really. Scads of trees. Not at all Bohemian."

"With a roommate I suppose."

"Oh, never. I wouldn't dream of that, would you?"

"I might – but my wife won't let me."

"Oh, Mr. Gardner. I meant – I'd have no privacy." (Soft i.)

"I know. Lot of girls live like that though – because of the expense."

"I'd work the street first. Not that I'd fancy it, mind you – I hate to walk," she laughed. "But I do insist on my privacy, if you know what I mean. Think of it."

Oh, don't worry, Gardner thought. I'm thinking of it, all right. My God, Harry – She's practically inviting you!

"I know what you mean," Gardner said. "Well – cheers, Patience."

"Bottoms up, Mr. Gardner."

Bottoms up!? Yes –

"Those are marvelous trousers, Mr. Gardner."

"They're – new."

"They fit – snugly."

Gardner's intestines knotted and he felt as though his bowels were dissolving. She's looking right at my crotch.

"Uh – thank you," he said.

"You're very trim."

Gardner could feel himself sucking in his stomach. "I swim a lot – and play tennis."

"Mrs. Gardner told me you have a house in Easthampton. I love the Hamptons. Frightfully expensive, isn't it?"

Suddenly, Gardner got a picture of himself and Patience running along the beach, hand-in-hand and laughing in slow motion. Nothing's too expensive for you, he thought.

"Yeah – and horrible traffic. You come back Sunday night worse than you went out." Gardner re-filled the ice cube tray. He put it back into the freezer compartment and spilled some of the water. He always did, but especially this time.

"I go to Fire Island a lot," Patience said. "It's awfully gay."

"Some parts more than others."

"Oh, I didn't mean that sort of 'gay'. I meant – everyone's so attractive and well-off-looking."

"Do you go with a friend?"

"I haven't got anyone steady – if that's what you mean. I certainly don't want to get married. I'm having too much fun the way I am. Mr. Gardner – you look so pensive."

"Harry?" Norma called from the bedroom.

"I'd better see to the little ones," Patience said.

"Coming," Harry said, calling to Norma.

Patience started for the living room, but stopped and turned around and stared at Gardner. "Taurus is very good for me," she said, and she came back to Gardner and, going up on her toes, she kissed him on the cheek. "Happy Birthday." She hurried away.

Harry blinked and felt some kind of acid burrowing through his intestines. My God! He said to himself. Forget it, Harry. No, I don't want to. Look at her, Harry. She hasn't even got an ass on her. You can't get involved with that.

"Harry," Norma said.

Gardner pulled in his stomach and headed back towards the bedroom.

"What took so long?" Norma said.

"Was it long?"

"Longish."

Gardner had come into the bedroom. He closed the door behind him, kicking it with his foot, and he handed Norma her drink.

"Here."

"Did you see the children?"

"They're fine. Catatonic in front of the TV. Patience came."

"Oh, good. I was wondering."

"Cheers." Gardner took a long swallow from his drink.

"Happy Birthday, Harry. How does my hair look?"

"Great," said Gardner, half-looking.

"Did you really look?"

"Yes, it looks very pretty. I like it full that way." This time Gardner studied her hair and saw that he had answered sincerely. He did like it this way. He went to her and touched her hair. He felt suddenly that he might cry.

"I've got on two pieces. That's what fills it out."

"S'hhh – I don't have to know that."

"Nobody has hair this full, naturally."

"Let me fantasize," Gardner said, as he stroked her hair. His heart was galloping. He kissed Norma lightly on the mouth. "Don't worry, I didn't disturb the lipstick," he whispered.

"Oh, Harry, my God – I love you. I really do. When you're the way you can be – I'm the happiest woman alive. I'm sorry we didn't make love. You know I never say no. It's just – you've made me so uncertain lately."

"I love you."

"Do you?"

"Yes. You know I do."

"Oh, God, I want you to."

"And I love that you love me."

"I don't know why sometimes. You don't seem to need me really. Sometimes I think you'd be better off not married."

"But I am and I love you."

"You really are a bachelor, but that good middle class background holds you to me. I know that."

"No, I love you, Norma."

"More than anyone, I think – you do – though it's hard for you to."

"I do."

"I know, Harry. Just be kind. That's all I need, honestly. With that, we can work out the rest."

"I – I try, Norma."

"I know you do. I guess it's harder for you."

"We'll be all right."

"You always say that."

"I believe it."

"I wish I did."

"Well, don't worry, sweetheart. We'll be very old people together. You can push my wheelchair, and change the hot water in my intertube. We'd better go. You ready?"

"Yes, just let me fix my bag."

Norma put her cosmetics, comb, mirror, driver's license and a twenty dollar bill into a small matching satin evening bag. She had been taking a twenty dollar bill with her every time she went out with a man or boy since she first began dating in high school. Her father had suggested the idea originally and he had given her the first twenty – "just in case, they try any monkey business, you bring yourself home – in a taxi." Norma had needed the money only once and that had been with Gardner, within the past year. He had refused to leave a party, deep in the night, long after she believed it was time to go, and she had left without him.

Gardner finished off the Scotch and he could feel the liquid doing its inside job of coaxing his senses to sit back. He felt a little better. He walked to his dresser to get his wallet and change and keys. He saw the knife lying there. He was surprised by the feeling he got when he looked at it. Up quick, it was – spontaneous – though somehow fully prepared. Like a banished, opportunistic cat waiting for you to forget about opening the screendoor too wide and you do and it's in. Fear. I can feel it. Nothing large. Just true. Lightly turning stomach screw. Premonitional.

An anonymous, but threatening crank letter to my intestines. A kind of creditor's first nasty notice.

Now Gardner felt bound to the knife – <u>committed</u>? – <u>terminally</u>? – like an accomplice in some kind of crime. <u>But what</u>? <u>Why</u>?

"You ready?" Norma said.

Gardner nodded. He put the knife in his pocket and adjusted his tie again.

"Do you have your glasses," Gardner said, "and gloves? Try not to leave them this time."

"I won't," Norma said. "Don't you leave yourself."

CHAPTER 2

Downstairs, the doorman got them a cab and Gardner, realizing what he was doing – in the manner of a man buying future grace – gave the doorman a dollar.

The cab driver they got rodeoed the taxi – consumed inside with the sweet smell of leaking fuel – away from the curb and bucked it down to 72nd Street, where the light was red. He hurt the cab to a stop and Gardner and Norma snapped forward against the front seat. They straightened themselves and looked at each other in harsh knowledge.

"I know," Norma said.

When the light changed, the driver, like some crazed anesthetist, gassed the car and jerked it into the park drive, throwing Gardner against the door.

Gardner pushed down the lock button on the car door and straightened himself – bracing for the ride.

The cab driver reached back across the seat and pulled the button up.

Gardner, surprised, pushed it down again.

The driver, continuing to drive, reached back and pulled it up again.

"Don't do that, hunh, Mac?" he said.

"Why?" Gardner said.

"I don't like it."

"I don't like the way you drive. That's what they're put there for. You push them down and the door won't open."

"The door's not going to open."

Gardner pushed down.

The driver pulled it up.

"You aren't going to fall out for Christ's sake, mister. Nobody falls out of my cab."

"You're lucky anyone gets in," Gardner said. He pushed the button down again.

"Leave me be, mister. What the hell does it matter to you? Those buttons. They break. The door jams. I'm out of work for a day." The driver pulled the button up.

"I want it down," Gardner said.

"You're a big boy, you won't fall out," the driver said, loudly. He pulled the button up.

"I want it down!" Gardner yelled, so intensely he felt his throat hurt.

"Harry!" Norma said.

The driver jerked the car to a stop.

"Don't yell at me! I can't stand people yelling at me!"

"Then – <u>down</u>," Gardner said, quietly.

"Get out – get out of my cab!"

"I'm staying and the button stays down and if you don't like it, get a cop – No. 67-8A."

"Harry, please," Norma said.

"I'll get you out of here, you bastard." The driver swung open his door and grabbed up a hammer off the front seat. He opened the back door of the cab on Norma's side and shook the hammer at Gardner.

Gardner felt no fear, but instead a kind of sudden definition of himself, an elation. The man had 2nd day whiskers, Gardner saw, and he appeared tired and enraged like a badly shot animal. Gardner felt sure he could take him easily, even with the hammer. His hand dug into his pocket and gripped the knife. He felt really good.

"Get out, bastard," the driver said.

"Try me, 67-8A. You can kill me but you can't get me out of this cab."

"Harry, stop – stop, the baby," Norma said. "Driver, are you crazy? I'm having a baby. Put that hammer away. Harry, Jesus!"

"Yeh, come on, pal. Put the hammer down. Get ahold of yourself." Gardner said.

"Leave my button up. Don't push my button down!"

"Look," Gardner spoke as though to a child, "I'll put the button down now and then when I get out I'll pull it up, okay? Isn't that nice and fair?"

"Don't mock me, mister, bastard. I'm not kidding. I had a lousy day. Now you. I'm in no mood. Christ, have some concern."

"Harry, stop. Leave the damn button up," Norma said.

"I got ulcers without you," the driver said, "and bad feet."

"What difference does it make?" Norma said.

"Up or down, I agree," Gardner said, "so, down."

"Lady, get him out of my cab or I will," the driver pleaded and he shook the hammer again at Gardner.

"Sir, you're crazy," Gardner said.

"You're a dead man,"

"Harry," Norma said. "Stop, stop – look out! Stop, both of you. I'm getting out." Norma pushed the driver away from her and he receded easily. She ran past him, around the cab and onto the sidewalk. Cars swooshed past her honking and veering. Not slowing. Like great animals migrating.

"Norma," Gardner said. He jumped out of the cab on his side and chased after her.

"You're a goddamned freak, mister – and your wife knows it – and your baby'll curse you for it," the driver yelled after Gardner, who did not hear anymore.

"Norma, baby, wait," Gardner said and, catching up to Norma, grabbed her from behind by the shoulders. He saw the cab – a yellow metal spasm – go by him, the driver's middle finger out the window held erect and shaking.

Norma pulled away furiously.

"No, I'm going home!"

"Norma, you can't."

"Watch me."

"Norma, no."

"Oh, yes. You're a madman."

"Norma, please, I'm sorry, wait." He still struggled with her, she trying to walk away.

"You're crazy."

"What about him and that goddamned button?"

"He's a cab driver," Norma stopped and faced Gardner. "He earns shit and probably has an I.Q. of 108. Don't compare yourself. If he wants his button up, let him. We'd have never seen him again after five minutes. Why do you pick fights with people like that?"

"I'm paying for the ride. I wanted the button down."

"Do you hear yourself? You're like him. Worse."

"Well, am I right?"

Norma looked at him. "Oh Harry. What gets into you? You've got a – brain tumor or something. You scare me. You do. You're crazy – and, God, I loved you so."

"Crazy?"

"Insane. Truly."

"I'm insane? He's got a button fixation and I'm crazy. That's wifely loyalty."

"He doesn't count. You'd never have seen him again. You're – an educated man. Look at us. Stuck in the middle of the park and, oh, Harry, goddamn it, what's become of you?" Norma began to cry. She put her hands up to her face and walked over to the row of benches lining the sidewalk. She sat down and slumped over.

Harry looked at her for an instant, then he came over to her and sat beside her. He put his arm around her.

"I – I don't know, Norma, what's wrong. I'm – I'm just trying to keep from vanishing."

"Oh, Harry, Jesus, Jesus, Jesus," Norma said and cried harder. She pushed his arm away. She slid away from him down along the bench and tried to get control of herself. She threw her head back and she jabbed into her handbag for a kleenex.

"Who the hell is vanishing, for Christ's sake?"

"I—am." Gardner said.

"Have you looked at my belly lately?"

"I don't mean that. Me. Personally. What I am."

"I wish to God we knew what that was!"

"I used to."

"You keep saying that!"

"I did."

"Kid dreams? Fantasies? Still rooting for the goddamned Chicago Cubs?"

"They weren't dreams, just. Ideals. Ideas. Meanings. I knew myself then. All sorts of definite things."

"Why the hell didn't you stay in Indiana and leave me alone? I'm sick to death of you – always pouting and living in the past. Oh, God, what's the use? I wish, Harry, you'd get some help. I wish you'd see a doctor or something."

"Is that your only and always solution to everything?"

"What's yours? Picking fights with cabdrivers? Sitting stuck in the park in party clothes and pregnant? Are those your brave, defiant answers hurled back at <u>the indifferent universe</u> you're always droning about? If that's it, count me out."

"Psychoanalysis is a mythical experience. To get you back in line with the accepted mores of our culture."

"My God, you really are crazy. You almost get your head hammered in and you start lecturing."

"I thought we were trying to—if you're bored—"

"Oh, it's fascinating, I'm sure. Save it for the party, though, why don't you? I'm sure there'll be some little thing there who'll plotz over it."

"I was—just trying, Norma. For us. That's all. I've been trying for a long time now." Gardner took out a cigarette and offered Norma one. She shook her head no. He lit one for himself.

"What does that mean?" Norma asked.

"Just – trying – that's all."

"Is there anyone else?" Norma asked, after a pause.

"No, of course not. I—must it always be another woman? There's more than that."

"Not very much, Harry. Not for women. Not for me anyway. My children, maybe."

"For a man, there's more," Gordon said.

"Himself? That's all you think of. Really. You're the most self-centered person I know."

"I'm – I'm sorry."

"Which means you want to cut off talking altogether. I know you. You're never really sorry, are you, Harry? I mean genuinely contrite, the way people are? Are you?"

"Of course, I am, lots of times."

"I don't think so. You always just seem to use being sorry the way you use everything else. To ease things for yourself. Emotions and manners are commodities to you. To get your way. To keep people out. I've noticed that. For a long time, God, how I regret marrying you sometimes."

"Do you mean that?"

"With all my heart – and sense of meaning."

"Norma."

"It's what you've done, Harry."

"Norma, I love you."

"Say the magic words, sooth the sick and wounded. Sugar down the sucker and never give him an even break. Relief is just a swallow away." Norma smiled, kind of. "Well, I thank you for the love-pill, Harry. I thank you for bothering to make the effort still, but I don't think I can give you one back – just now. Not this minute anyway. I've been so battered and stolen from by you this last year I don't know what I feel. I was the happiest, proudest, most contented woman alive with you those early years. I'd never known such gentleness and quiet strength and good manners in anyone. And your – charm. You were the most charming man I'd ever known. And fun and sure of yourself, in the nicest way. And the love-making. No woman was ever made love to so well and – I don't know. I don't know what happened. Do you, Harry? What spent itself? Or does it always happen this way?"

Gardner shook his head. "I don't know. I get – intimations. But not really. I'm not sure really. What do you believe in, Norma?"

"Us. Living."

"God – how marvelous that sounds."

"What'll we do, Harry?"

"Go to the party."

"Can I trust you?"

"Go to the party, go to bed, get up, get older, die."

"You make it sound so – little. Why are we having another baby?"

Harry shook his head. "I apologize, Norma, that I have to say I do not know."

Norma looked at him and then at her lap and then was silent for sometime. They both were.

Gardner suddenly felt the frightening power of the rush of automobiles, coursing by on the park drive towards mid-town. He turned and looked south at the buildings, a huge jeweled Giant's bed of spikes. All those people down there, he thought. With so much power – and ignorance, and anonymity. He could make no decent connection with any of them.

"We'd better go," he said.

Norma nodded.

"We're not far from Tavern-on-the-Green," he said. "We can get a cab there."

CHAPTER 3

The cab pulled up in front of the townhouse on Beekman Place, which is where Gardner's boss lived. Gardner poked awkwardly into the pants pocket – the pants were very tight on this new suit – for money to pay. When he finally had the money he paid the driver and overtipped him.

Gardner's boss called himself Buzz Billingsly and he lived in his Beekman Place townhouse with his wife Janelle and two children, Kirk and Tracy. Kirk was 14 and enrolled at Alan Stevenson School; Tracy, who was 12, went to school at Brearly. Also, in the household were a Great Dane, Madison, (for Madison Avenue), and a cook, a maid, a nurse for the children and a butler-chauffeur. Three days a week a man came to see to the basement, tidy the garbage cans out in front of the house and tend the stone, mostly sooty, garden in the back. Additional service people came as required, which was frequently.

Buzz Billingsly was the president of the advertising agency formerly known as Ingersoll, Barker and Esposito which was now named Ingersoll, Barker and Billingsley. Ingersoll was dead and Barker was chairman of the board. Esposito, an artist, and a very good one, who brought much business to the company in the beginning with his work and his ideas, spoke with a Brooklyn accent and knew almost nothing about corporate life. Except for his talent, no one had every really wanted him, especially on the letterhead, so Ingersoll and Barker were both very grateful when Billingsley got rid of him.

Ingersoll was the man Billingsley used for his climb. Ingersoll was David Ingersoll and his family was related to the watch people but made its own money in a medium-sized rolling steel mill. He lived in South Orange, New Jersey all of his life except for four years at Princeton, where he had helped write the Triangle show his senior year; he had drifted into advertising after a vague hope that he might write fiction; he failed at fiction but was very good at the fictitious realities of advertising; thereafter he played golf every clear Saturday and Sunday for the entirety of his life. That's how Billingsley met him. As his caddy. That was in 1940, when Billingsly was nineteen, and a sophomore at NYU, still living with his parents in Newark, and had only recently stopped being Bernard Bernstein. In fact, in some places, he was still known by that name such as in the NYU files. (You can't change a name in a yearbook). He did change his name to Billy Billingsley when he applied to the country club for the caddy job. Ingersoll liked Billingsley-Bernstein, who didn't look Jewish, and gave him a part-time job in the agency until he finished college. Ingersoll was always saying Billingsly-Bernstein was like a son to him. The next year he advanced the money for Billingsly to take a one year business administration course at Harvard. It was at Harvard that Billingsly got the name Buzz. He was so eager, so affable and articulate, so enthusiastic and insensitive to insult – and there were many – that someone dubbed him Buzzy. It was in his nature to have been pleased rather than offended, though he did work at and succeeded in getting it shortened to Buzz. Nowadays, Billingsly went to all the Harvard football games and gave the school money every year. He was listed in Who's Who in America as a graduate of Harvard with an MBA. No donations for NYU and no mention of it.

In 1942, Esposito was 29 years old and in good health and got drafted. Billingsly, at the same time, at 21, enjoyed very good poor health – a rheumatic heart (an employee once quipped he was pleased to hear he had any kind of heart at all) – and stayed on the home front and climbed for the presidency.

"It is a pretty house," Norma said. Bricks and shutters.

"For the 3rd division of hell," Gardner said.

They went up the three front marble steps and Gardner pressed the brass bell button, then hit the gold eagle mounted on the front door, in the stomach, with the gold knocker. After a moment, the door opened.

"Good evening, Mr. Gardner, Mrs. Gardner," Gregory said.

Gregory, a voting Socialist, who owned shares of stock, was the butler-chauffeur and was married to the cook. He and his wife had worked for Billingsly since 1953. At a New Year's Eve party two years ago, Gregory, drunk, had bragged to Gardner that after the first week on the job he had spit, without fail – colds, viruses and all – every morning into Billingsly's coffee which he poured and served from a sideboard in the dining room in a silver carafe. Since then Gregory had always been reserved and distant with Gardner, because, Gardner supposed, he was afraid he might be given away. Don't worry, Gardner thought. I cherish our little secret. It's a nice psychological edge with a boss to know somebody's spitting in his coffee every morning.

"Hello, Gregory," Norma said.

"Gregory," Gardner said.

"It's very nice to see you again."

"You too," Norma said.

"Happy birthday, Sir," Gregory said.

"Thank you, Gregory. I hope Clara's well," Gardner said.

"She is. Thank you."

Gregory closed the door and led Gardner and Norma along the entrance corridor to the elevator at the back. The corridor floor was black marble. The walls were covered in white linen and hung with original drawings by Braque and Chagall; and a painting by Larry Rivers and another by Georgia O'Keefe – a vaginal flower.

"Here we are," Gregory said and he opened the elevator door.

"Thank you," Norma said and so did Gardner.

Gregory smiled and nodded as the Gardners entered the elevator but he would not look them in the eye. The elevator door closed and as the machine ascended, Norma and Gardner, hearing music, looked at each other.

"My God, he's put stereo in the elevator," Gardner said.

Norma smiled and whispered, "S'hhh, he's probably got a microphone too."

"I wouldn't put it past him."

The elevator stopped, the door opened and Billingsly, a martini in his hand, stood facing them.

Billingsly had a full head of hair, black, mixed with just so gray, which he wore in a modified long cut, low in the back, but neat, there, and around the ears. A man named Tony-From-Rome who told dirty and tasteless ethnic jokes, mostly about Italians, came to the office every second Monday to trim and shampoo the hair, which was on the curly side, so he straightened it as well. Billingsly's body, six feet tall, was trim and erect and always standing at attention for the Star Spangled Banner. He went three times a week to a gym and steam bath, and on week-ends played tennis or golf, tennis mostly. His face was tanned—always. He took many vacations in sunny places and when he did not, there were lamp treatments. His face had no interesting planes, but was rather roundish really and full, except for a good, straight nose (he was very proud of this) and a clean jaw line that kept him youthful-looking, or at least, vigorous-looking. Billingsly's eyes were hazel – or gray? – Gardner guessed, but he never could be sure; even now, staring, it was hard to know. They certainly were not lively and did no service to the cunning quickness of the inner man. Maybe it was the contact lenses he wore. The one signal feature about the face, Gardner thought, came through in the ever present tightness in it as it leapt in and out of smiles, smiles in which the teeth flashed like a Times Square ad. Although they were, Billingsly denied that his teeth were capped.

His clothes were hand-tailored (English) and cost from $750 to $1,000 a suit. They were always in wool, the winter ones, and in the latest style, though quietly. He had not gone for bell-bottoms or love beads. Tonight he was wearing a dark gray, double-breasted, six button, high lapelled suit – a wide maroon tie – and rust-colored shoes, suede. His nails were severely polished and manicured, and he had dabbed himself with a ponderous, and irritatingly-present cologne. Gardner knew the odor since he had coined the name himself, designed the lay-out and written the copy for it – all one Sunday while watching football on TV. "PRO BALL…Cologne for the Player!" The idea, as with so many American ads, was to infer that the man who bought the product could get laid all the time by all the girls. Of course, he hardly ever did – and usually it was his wife who bought him the stuff. Pro Ball! Jesus! Gardner said to himself. And the stuff had been a runaway success.

"Harry, heart of mine – come in, old boy," Billingsly said, thrusting his hand forward to shake Gardner's. Gardner hated Billingsly's "look-him-in-the-eye-and-shake-firmly" shake. Gardner figured Billingsly had gotten the handshake out of a book he'd once read on how to succeed. Firm's bad enough, Gardner thought, but the bastard does you sideways at the same time and throws you off balance.

"How's my fellow birthday boy? – feeling creaky, I hope. I am. Norma, Darling – you're an angel, a Madonna. Look at you," Billingsly said. He moved into Norma, as close as he could get and kissed her on both cheeks. Norma felt him pressing against the baby and she recoiled lightly. Billingsly stepped back and placed his free hand on Norma's stomach and patted it. Norma blushed. Get your hand off her – you sonofabitch, Gardner thought to himself.

"Little Mother. You're a cornucopia!"

"Not bearing fruit, I hope," Norma said.

Billingsly threw his head back and laughed – too loudly, Gardner thought. He was always so damned affable!

"Jesus, that's a good one. Good thing Duane didn't hear it."

"Hear what, Buzzy?" Duane said from the room inside.

"Janelle – look who's here. The other birthday boy and his witty wife. You've got a very funny wife, Harry, old heart."

"I've stopped him laughing from the diaphragm," Norma said, patting her belly.

Billingsly laughed again. "Jesus H."

"What's the 'H' for?" Norma said.

"Hadassah," Janelle said. She walked up clutching a drink in her hand, Gardner saw. It was vodka on the rocks, always.

Janelle Billingsly was tallish, thin, elegantly-boned and flat-chested – though not unsensual, Gardner knew. She was wearing a white pants suit with an American Indian motif and a see-through blouse. Her breasts were small, but her nipples were good, Gardner thought as he looked at them now. The material was crepe and a feathery fringe extended off the arms and from a belt of discs with Indian designs, which hung on her pelvis like John Wayne's gun belt. One eagle medallion rested just low enough to cover the pubic area. On her head, she wore a beaded band and a huge black-hair fall that came down to her waist. On her long, narrow, East Side feet were some kind of jazzed-up moccasins. She wore rings on several fingers, and a bracelet on her upper right forearm. Janelle Billingsly was beautiful, in the way of an expensive restoration of a classic auto, Gardner thought, and her clothes, like this outfit tonight, stayed always at the cutting edge of fashion. She wore all the outlandish dreams of every effete or arrogant designer with a grace and naturalness that transcended and tranquilized the shout of the original idea. Not that you didn't notice; you noticed a lot, Gardner knew, but she just never looked like a costume party freak, as so many others did dressing this way.

She was an Anglo-Saxon from Madison, Wisconsin and her father owned a fountain pen company which floundered when the ball point came along. Her beauty was the best of the Anglo-Saxon kind. Left to her own color, she was blonde-haired, though tonight, the wig and fall she wore were crow black. Her nose was high and straight. Her eyes, vivid green, alert and – when they focused – were what people called "penetrating." Too, underneath, always, they were puffed – from the vodka; but not unattractively. She had come to New York originally to be an actress and she had succeeded as a fashion model. She had been a good one, though indifferent in her ambition; and, for which Gardner was grateful, she had none of a model's stock dead looks or postures. Just the opposite. Janelle's face, fronting for a very good brain, was mobile and constantly busy expressing the quick intelligence inside. Her body too. Energetic. She had been educated – in theatre and literature – at the University of Wisconsin and at the Royal Academy of Theatre Arts in London.

"Harry, you've knocked her up again, poor thing. All right, you're virile. You don't have to be Puerto Rican about it," Janelle said.

"We do live on the West Side," Gardner said.

"God, won't you and Pope Paul ever come around?" Janelle said.

Janelle put her cheek up to be kissed by Gardner.

"Is that the best you can do, Jose?" Janelle said. "I wonder."

Gardner reacted to this allusion and hoped it didn't show on the outside.

Janelle kissed him back. "I won't bite you, for Christ's sake. Well, what the hell, maybe I might. Ah, forgive me. I'm half-pissed already. Course, I'm always half-pissed, you and your bride are probably thinking. Well, so what? You'd better get drunk too, if you want to get through the evening – and you have to get through it, don't you?"

"Janelle," Billingsly said. "I'm a very democratic boss."

"You and the Greek generals," Janelle said. She kissed Norma on the cheek. "How are you, Normal? Welcome to Heartbreak House."

"How was Europe?" Norma said.

"Full of foreigners – and fornicators," Janelle said. "Come on." They moved into the main room and the eight people there stopped talking.

"All right, everybody," Janelle said. "This is Harry and Norma Gardner – alias Ken and Barbie. Harry's our sexy creative director, whom I personally dig the very most diggable – and Normal suffers from chronic pregnancy."

"Hiya, Gardner. Happy, happy, Harry," Duane Lissner said.

"Hi, Duane," Norma said. Gardner nodded. Duane was an art director (the best after Harry, Harry thought) at the agency. His hair was dyed blonde and styled carefully and sprayed, you could tell, and he wore large glasses – tinted lightly, and when he took them off, his eyes were dewey-looking; he vaselined them. He always wore pants that showed off his privates. His nails were long and polished and he seemed to Gardner to be the cleanest person he had ever seen. Janelle enjoyed picking on Duane; that's why he was always invited to their parties.

"This is Cleve English – from the boob tube you know," Janelle said,

"And Nancy English. She's been telling us about séances – she spoke to Bobby Kennedy just last Tuesday – isn't that right, Nancy? That's Madelyn Shoaly, who writes those terrible, trashy, juicy dirty books. She belongs to the beard over there – which belongs to Garve Shoaly, the ultra-famous photographer. And this is Toni Carpenter, the infamous recording star..."

"Hello."

"Hello."

"How are you. Hello."

"And this – is Ralph Wright, from Cincinnati. Our guest of honor – birthdays not withstanding. And his great and good friend, Honey O'Hara, actress-model and social worker."

"How do you do, folks," Mr. Wright said. He and Gardner shook hands. "Are you a celebrity too – everybody seems to be."

"Here you are, birthday boy," Billingsly said. He offered Gardner and Norma the two martinis he had carried over from the bar, which was set up in the near end of the room. Behind the bar stood a black waiter in a white jacket.

"I'd had a Scotch at home," Gardner said.

"One won't hurt you, old boy; you can switch off. This is my own recipe. You've got to try it," Billingsly said, pushing the drink at him.

Norma and Gardner nodded and did not resist. As he took the first sip, Gardner saw Norma looking at him, pleadingly. He knew what she was asking: Please do not get drunk tonight, or make a scene. Please. He told himself he would not. He never had here, though increasingly he had everywhere else; and a lot of people didn't invite him anymore. What do I care? Gardner thought. I don't like them anyway. Still – I better not give one of my performances in this house. Too much is riding on it. He smiled at Norma and tried to look relaxed and reassuring. Ralph Wright, that's the new account Buzz was courting and wanting me to meet, Gardner thought.

"Cheers, Darling," he said.

"I hope so," Norma said. They sat down in two white chairs with plexiglass backs and no legs. The chairs were supported by white metal bases and they were uncomfortable to sit in. One had slogans, graffiti-like, inscribed in the plexiglass: Don't trust anyone over 30. Hugh Heffner is a lousy lay. So is Helen Gurley Brown. I am a human being; do not fold, spindle or mutilate. Love, with a Robert Indiana angled O. Save Lincoln Center. Black is beautiful. Mao can't swim. The other chair had horoscopes on it. Buzz and Janelle's. The room (Janelle and Buzz called it their "Playroom") had a very high ceiling and a sky-light, floor to ceiling, at the far end, which had a door in it, which opened onto a terrace, which overlooked the East River and Welfare Island, which tonight did not show. Hung from the ceiling, and throbbing, was a large Calder mobile. The room was cluttered with lean, modern furniture and there were lots of stainless steel everywhere and big pillows. The couch before the fireplace was long and low and was covered in an American flag design. In one corner, a George Segal paper mache man sat wearing a real black fedora on a real park bench reading a real Jewish Daily <u>Forward</u>. The walls of the room – white – were put upon by Warhols and Rauschenbergs, a contraption by Oldenburg, a Klee and an Indiana. A huge new Otis Price Poster of the Nixon family—a kind of hallucinogenic American Gothic—was pasted billboard-style on one wall. Gardner liked the art but thought the room was an anxious, noisy bleat. He took a heavy swallow of the gin. From the stereo Ray Charles mourned with dignity, <u>"I got a losing hand."</u>

"Norma, you look absolutely divine," Duane said. "Never knew you were <u>encient</u>. I loathe most preggy women—they look like 5 Mexicans slipping into California—but that's <u>so chic</u>, honey."

"Thanks. It was on sale at Good-year--$39.75."

Gardner began to listen to the conversation.

"John-John goes to Collegiate," Toni Carpenter said. "My lawyer's kid is there."

"Garve knows them both—Ari too. He Was at Scorpias for the wedding, even. For <u>Life</u>," Madelyn Shoaly said.

"I did a portrait sitting of her last month," Garve Shoaly said. "You should see that diamond he gave her for her 40th birthday...40 carats."

"Shazam," Duane said--"That's a carat for every year."

"If she'd known that," Norma said, "she wouldn't have lied about her age."

"Not to mention the $20 million last year," Gardner said.

"Must be tough to make ends meet," Toni Carpenter said.

"Specially his and hers—from what I hear," Madelyn Shoaly said.

"All the same, she got his Callas removed," Janelle said.

"Are her feet really that big, man?" Toni Carpenter asked.

"What are you working on now, Garve?" Norma said.

"He's going out to do a big piece on Barbra Streisand for <u>Vogue</u>," Madelyn said. "Through history—dressed as all the famous women."

"Is it true," Norma said, "she's playing The Godfather in the movie version?"

"Here's to the new little creative director," Billingsly said, who has gone back and picked up a new martini for himself. "And to the lucky parents. What a blessing."

"What'll you name him?" Madelyn Shoaly asked.

"They just number them now—there's so many," Janelle said, as she came up and sat on a high pillow on the floor.

Mr. Wright had turned around and was listening now. "Oh, that's nice. I'm from a big family myself, you know," he said.

"We only have two others, actually," Norma said.

"Oh," Mr. Wright said, "I was the seventh of eight myself."

"How marvelous," Garve Shoaly said. He and Madelyn had a Yorkshire terrier.

"You're very brave, Norma, what with pollution and ABM's—and Nixon," Janelle said. "Or careless."

"A good sport," Norma said.

"Did I hear someone take Mr. Nixon's name in vain?" Mr. Wright asked.

"Janelle was joking, Ralph," Billingsly said. "You know we're behind him a thousand percent."

"He is doing a good job, isn't he?" Wright said, in a wistful, reverential, rhetorical tone. "Don't think he'd care much for that poster though."

"Mr. Wright is President Nixon's friend," Garve Shoaly said.

"So you're the one." Janelle said.

"Ralph," Billingsly said, jumping in, "Harry here is the boy who's going to sell the Wright Company the right way, if you give I. B. & B. a fair chance of it."

"Oh, Zat so?" Wright said. "You like Mr. Nixon, I hope; most artsy folks don't seem to," Wright said and laughed. Gardner figured that he supposed he had made a witty remark.

"He loves Nixon," Billingsly said. "Don't you, Harry? Harry's my genius in residence, Ralph. Great artist, great writer—idea man. God knows, he ought to be—with what we pay him."

"I was going to have him ask for a raise tonight," Norma said.

"He's creative director of I. B. & B. I stole him from Thompson," Billingsly went on.

"Well now," Mr. Wright said.

"And feet on the ground as you can see. Good family man," Billingsly said.

Janelle said, looking at Norma's belly, "He didn't do that with his feet on the ground."

Duane giggled.

"And from the mid-west like you," Billingsly said.

"You don't say?" Wright said.

Gardner saw Wright's face warm-up and now Wright was facing him directly. "Where would that--?"

"Indiana. Near Indianapolis," Gardner said.

"Well, isn't that something?" Where near there?" Wright asked.

"Lancaster," Gardner said.

"Sure, I know Lancaster. Been there many times. Lancaster. Nice little town. Good people. Isn't that nice?"

"So nice he couldn't wait to get the hell out." Janelle said.

"Janelle has a typical New Yorker's prejudice against the rest of the country, Mr. Wright--" Billingsly said.

"Because I'm from Wisconsin," Janelle said.

"Just ignore her," Billingsly said.

"Is your family still in Lancaster?" Wright asked.

"Yes, they are. I get there about once a year—around the holidays," Gardner said.

"Rosh Hashanah and Yom Kippur," Norma said.

Duane giggled and everyone else laughed; except Billingsly, Garve Shoaly and Ralph Wright.

"What?" Wright said.

"You go out for Christmas, don't you, Harry?" Billingsly said.

"That's right," Gardner said.

"Why'd you leave, Mr. Uh—Gardner? Wright asked.

"Well, Harry's always been interested in advertising—since he was a boy," Billingsly said. "And the opportunities in our business are in New York. Didn't mean he didn't like the mid-west, did it, Harry?"

"No," Gardner said.

"You can't help but like it. Not if you've once been there. Indiana's a wonderful place," Wright said.

"Mon Dieu," Duane said. "I haven't been any place but New York and California—and nearby Connecticut, as they say, I feel so out of it in my own country."

Wright looked at Duane, Gardner saw, as though he could not possibly believe that he and Duane were citizens of the same Republic.

"I was in Indiana last week—Indianapolis--promoting my book." Madelyn Shoaly said. "They have this old movie star there—what's her name, Garve?--she does a local interview show and she's half-drunk right on the air and she kept asking me if I knew Irving Thalberg and a lot of people like that who've been dead for ages—and I said 'just how old do you think I am, Darling' and well, anyway—my sales there are just fabulous. They can't keep the book stocked."

Madelyn Shoaly had written two very successful dirty books. Gardner had met her a long time ago, when she had worked as a booking agent in her father's theatrical agency. The agency too had been very successful, because, it was said, in the beginning, the father had signed up nearly all the good Negro acts who could not get work, especially in the Depression. He booked the acts for CCC shows, in the Catskill Mountains—where he underbid agents who handled white performers; and, it was reported, he had even turned a good dance team into a couple who copulated for parties for the rich on Long Island and in Palm Beach or in tenement apartments especially rented for the purpose over on 10th Avenue. Gardner had seen this couple recently on "The Ed Sullivan Show" and had wondered if it were true and he had tried to imagine them that way. He had not been able to since they had looked so old now and fragile and nice.

In the days when he had first met Madelyn Shoaly, and he had never, even then, known her well, she was big-hipped, big-busted with an unignoble ugly nose. She talked loud and with a skin-prickling New York accent. She had shown a lot of tit then and had worn spike heels and an ankle bracelet.

Later, after her first book, when he had seen her on a television talk show, he had had trouble recognizing her. She had lost lots of her weight, had suppressed her boobs, and had had her nose fixed. In fact, Gardner thought, the whole face now looked re-worked. It looked so new and unnatural, like something they might do to patch up a soldier whose first face got blown away by a grenade. Too, she must have taken speech lessons, because her accent was gone and now she talked like Maggie Smith. But he had been able to recognize her finally, because of something in the eyes—right in the pupils of them—and again around the mouth, that was a mutt expression of anger and street knowledge that taught you that everybody was a shit and out to kick ugly dogs like you and that you might as well bite as many of the bastards as you could. Oh yes, her teeth were capped too now. She looked like a used car, Gardner thought, all shaped-up and simonized on the outside, but whose insides wouldn't give you 10 miles without trouble. Though shining bright, you just knew she had a cracked engine block.

She was wearing a very expensive dress that was sequined and awful, Gardner thought, and was floor length, which was to hide her thick ankles, probably. Gardner remembered they were thick because of the bracelet which always drew your eye there. She had on a heavy fall of hair, not her own of course—suddenly he got a picture of a lot of poor Sicilian girls standing around in a pen, like barnyard animals bred for this purpose and waiting to be shorn—and she had so mascared the fake lashes she wore that you could hardly see her eyeballs. (Was it true they were putting shoe polish on them these days.) But they were in there, Gardner knew, the pupils—hating in on you.

Still, the whole package, as grotesque as were the individual parts, was not bad, Gardner thought. Seen quickly, she looked glamorous, even attractive—like some circus girls if you didn't sit too close.

About her husband, Gardner knew little, except that he had been a combat photographer for <u>PM</u> in Europe and later, after his marriage to Madelyn, had switched off to shooting fashion lay-outs and celebrities and had become very popular after a picture book he had done on Jacqueline Kennedy when she was First Lady. He was shortish, with silver hair (you knew he did something to accentuate the color) worn in a pompadour and he had on mod checkered pants which were too tight and showed that he had to work hard at not getting fat; and a jacket which did not match and a kerchief instead of a tie. When he spoke, his English sounded Middle European.

"You know, I was born in Indiana," Wright said. "Sure is a pretty place."

What a lucky break for Billingsly, Gardner thought.

"Now that settles it," Billingsly said. "I knew I felt good vibrations bringing you and Harry Gardner together. God, I've got to get out there someday—see that part of the country. You can get so busy and cut off in New York. Maybe when I visit you in Cincinnati, Ralph. Harry, you know who this Ralph Wright is, of course? He's <u>the</u> Ralph Wright, the 3rd—from Cincinnati. The Wright Company?"

"I was in Cincinnati too—I've been #1 there for 8 weeks already— even before publication," Madelyn said.

"Oh, yes," Billingsley said, Gardner hearing the enthusiasm fake up through his throat.

"Then you make Wright shampoo?" Norma asked.

"That's right, Mrs. Gardner—with a W," Wright said. "That's how we started anyway. 'Shampoo the Wright Way'?"

"Yes, I know. It's a good slogan," Norma said.

"It's a classic," Billingsly said.

"Movingly simple," Janelle said, quietly, "like 'Malice towards none and charity for all.'"

"Now—Buzz--let's not forget who introduced you to Ralph Wright," Garve Shoaly said. "Please."

"Credit where credit's due," Billingsly said. "Garve got us together. He did a lay-out on Mr. Wright—Ralph--a kind of day-in-the-life-of-a-business-dynamo—for Fortune. Brilliant coverage. Great insight. I badgered Garve into introducing us. And he did—thank God—over lunch last Tuesday."

"At Lutèce," Garve said.

"I haven't been the same since." Billingsly said. "Had to get him up to the house—really get to know him. Incredible."

"Did you hear the story about the Texan who sent his daughter to Radcliffe so she could learn to say incredible instead of bull shit?" Janelle said, as she got up and went to the bar. The line was a bit thrown-away, though Gardner had heard it clearly. He wondered (believed really), the others had also heard it.

"He's got," Billingsly continued, "some of the most damned exciting ideas I've ever heard. Revolutionary."

"Well, I just try to use the old noggin'," Wright said.

"Hell, Ralph, you don't have to be modest in this room. These people are talent. And they know the worth of talent in other fields. What's wrong if a good man knows he's good?" Billingsly said.

"Exactly," Shoaly said.

"Fraid Mr. Billingsly here's too nice," Wright said.

"He's not nice at all—he's just honest," Shoaly said.

"I'll subscribe to that," Cleve English said, in a pleasant, authoritative voice. Gardner looked at him. English was an ex-disc jockey who now had a successful talk show on the Continental Broadcasting Company.

"I've used Wright Shampoo ever since I was a little girl," said Honey O'Hara, speaking her first words since Gardner and Norma had arrived. She had a little girl voice and had trouble with her "L's" Gardner heard.

Everyone looked at Honey oddly, since what she had just said would have related about three minutes earlier, but now came from nowhere.

Honey's eyelids were blue and the lashes had been made to cluster in about five groups, looking like lashes on clowns and some dolls. Her own eyes were blue. Her breasts were well-defined but not large. Her legs were thin. They reminded Gardner of his own legs, as a pre-pubescent boy, at age 12. Gardner did think such female models were now in fashion, because of the pedophilic fantasies of so many mainline designers. Honey's hair was long too and straight and truly blonde. She took the ends of it into her mouth a lot or twiddled them with her fingers. Her nose was small, straight in the bridge and snub at the end. She wore very pale lipstick and her lower lip was full and pouty. She had rings on all her childlike fingers. The nails were polished blue.

She had, over-all, the eye-catching good looks of a fashion model but when she spoke, Gardner was tempted to pull the string in her side—like a Chatty Kathy doll. Jesus, is she really that old pecker's date? Wonder how she'd be in bed? It was clearly beyond question that she was ignorant as a dustball.

"I really have," Honey said. She had made the whole speech as though she were in a television commercial and being paid. Well, she probably was, Gardner decided.

"Well, now," Mr. Wright said and smiled. He patted her hand. "You're all just too nice. I don't take any credit for myself. It's just using the noodle our Maker gave us."

"Here you'll need this, for the harpooning." Janelle said, handing another martini to Gardner. He started to say no, but took it when he saw his first was empty. He wanted the drink anyway. They're really greasing up Wright for the kill, he told himself. And on my birthday yet. Ah, money trumps sentiment.

"It's just—men nowadays don't live like they had to face the Maker at the end," Wright said.

"I don't think many people really believe they're going to," Norma said. "Do they?"

"Well, we are, Mrs. Gardner, sure as we're sittin' here," Wright said. "Sure as shootin."

"Sure as <u>what</u>?" Duane asked.

"I believe in Heaven and Hell," Wright said.

"As actual physical places?" Norma asked.

"You betcha."

"So do I," Nancy English said.

"You believe in everything, Nancy—from UFO's to unborn lamb urine injections for staying young." Janelle said.

"Well, Heaven and Hell are real places—just like Cincinnati," Nancy said.

"I know which one it is," Janelle said.

"Will you stop?" Billingsly said. "Mr. Wright is serious. We all are."

"Well, maybe the ladies would rather change the subject," Mr. Wright said. "My daddy always told me two things never to discuss in polite company were religion and politics. I never listened too good. Fraid both religion and politics are my weakness."

"Tell him about yours, Duane," Janelle said.

Duane laughed. "You're outrageous."

"Maybe the astronauts'll find Heaven" Gardner said, and wished he hadn't.

Wright turned and looked at Gardner sternly.

"I'm serious, Mr. Gardner. I don't know where Heaven and Hell are, but I believe in them."

"I meant no disrespect, Mr. Wright," Gardner said. "Religion's very serious for most people and I understand the necessity—in some form or other."

"I'm a Christian," Wright said. "A Protestant. A Baptist."

"But, even so," Gardner said, "There is room for honest doubt—when you consider America's only 200 year's old--(He knew as he talked that he should be dropping this whole thing immediately) and Christ two thousand. And the 'God' we describe is about five thousand years old—roughly. That hardly seems eternal. Not when you consider the earth is 5 billion years old and the Universe older still and--"

"I thought God died," Janelle said. "Didn't I read that in <u>Time</u> magazine? 'Do we not smell the divine putrefaction...for even Gods putrefy.'"

"Scuse me, Mrs. Billingsly," Wright said, "I'm a deacon of my church."

"Janelle, please," Billingsly said.

"I was only quoting," Janelle said. "Nothing personal."

"I'm surprised at <u>Time</u> Magazine," Wright said.

"It was Nietzsche," Janelle said.

"Well, he shouldn't be on that magazine," Wright said. "I'm going to tell our advertising people."

CHAPTER 4

"The Gallup Poll says 98% of Americans believe in God," Cleve English said.

"I believe in UFO's," Nancy English said. "I don't care what that report said."

"Creatures of God if they are. That part doesn't change," Mr. Wright said.

"I know the Air Force knows about them. They're just afraid to tell people," Nancy English said. "Cleve knows a man who worked in Colorado on that government report that investigated them."

"Of course, a lot of it's from crackpots, but they do have things they can't explain," Cleve said. "Real sightings by flyers and sheriffs—policemen, responsible people."

"I think they're much more brilliant than us—and they're what's going to save mankind," Nancy said.

"Save Mankind," Janelle said. "Again? 'And what rough beast, its hour come round at last, slouches towards Bethlehem to be born?' This time?"

That was it, Gardner realized. The same poem as The center cannot hold. And it was Yeats. "The Second Coming."

Maybe we can save them—Mrs. English," Wright said. "If and when they land—or we get where they live. That's more likely, with our know-how."

"My Lord," Janelle said, "I hadn't thought of it. You mean the Church is going to convert all those two-headed little darlings to Christ? Cortez in a bubble helmet? Well, what the hell. I guess if that's your business, all you're really doing is expanding the territory."

"Do you believe there's life on other planets, Mr. Wright? Do you believe in UFO's? Nancy English asked.

"Well, I sure don't disbelieve in them yet, Mrs. English," Wright said.

"I believe in all the miracles in God's Universe. Old Testament, New Testament and Future Testament."

"Adam and Eve?" Norma asked.

"It's better than coming from apes, Mrs. Gardner," Wright said.

"You don't believe in Darwin's theory?" Norma asked.

"I don't not believe in it especially. But if I think about it, there's nothing there that leaves out God. Fact is, I do sort of believe in natural selection. I see it in business every day. The best win out."

"I just can't believe I came from an ape," Honey O'Hara said. "I've never seen a blond one."

"I'm with you, sweetie," Duane said. "Creepies, we're both much too pretty."

"It is hard to think about folks like us that way. Our kind." Wright said.

"What do you mean?" Norma said.

"People like—such as ourselves, I mean" Mr. Wright said.

"Whites, right?--Mr. Wright?" Janelle said.

"Well, I suppose, yes, more or less, you could say that," Wright said.

Janelle nodded and walked back to the bar.

Nancy English said, "I heard the cutest story today; did you hear the one about the colored man who had diarrhea and thought he was melting?"

Mr. Wright laughed sincerely.

"Oh," Honey O'Hara said, "I just love jokes. I don't always get them."

"Here's one. You know why Polacks never commit suicide?" Cleve English said.

Honey O'Hara shook her head, as though she were really supposed to consider the question, Gardner noticed.

"It's hard to kill yourself jumping out a basement window," English said.

Honey O'Hara laughed out loud. "I don't get it, but it's funny."

"You know how to tell the bride at a Polish wedding?" Toni Carpenter said. "She's the one in the clean bowling shirt."

Honey O'Hara laughed again.

"What's the one, Cleve, about recognizing Alitalia planes?" Nancy English said.

"They have hair under the wings." Cleve English said.

"You folks are so witty," Wright said. I just can't keep up."

"Me too," Honey said.

Garve Shoaly said, "I want to hear more about the Ralph Wright story. Shampoo's only the beginning."

"Tell them, Mr. Wright, about the other aspects," Madelyn Shoaly said.

Gardner got the strangest feeling that everything said by the Shoalys and the Englishs was scripted and rehearsed, written and directed by Buzz Billingsly. And it could be practically, he knew; he had been a co-conspirator himself in a lot of these kinds of conversations-for-gain.

"Call me Ralph," Mr. Wright said. "Well, I--"

"Ralph's too modest. I'll tell—I don't need coaxing," Garve Shoaly said. "I'm a fan. Strange for me—as a photo-journalist--(Shoaly had not taken a photograph which could be defined as photo-journalism in at least fifteen years, Gardner thought)—and a damned serious and successful one, if I may say so myself. And photo-journalists are a pretty rough breed—cynical, very skeptical—all of that. And usually very snobbish about businessmen. (My God, Gardner thought, they're going to make pate out of this guy!) I have to confess that's the way I always felt too—till now, that is. I always thought businessmen lacked compassion—sensitivity for one thing. But as you can see tonight, that's not true here. Ralph Wright, I found out, knows people—their needs—real needs and frailties—and--and this is the most unique part--(It can't be _most_ unique, Gardner said to himself. Himself answered, "Oh, yes it can when you're dressing a steer)--

"Garve, in all humility, you do me too proud—and this is a sociable get-together. What could be more dull for a lot of sophisticated New Yorkers than hearing about a little midwestern businessman?"

"I think of you as a big businessman," Honey O'Hara said.

Mr. Wright smiled broadly and patted Honey O'Hara's hand.

"You may be prejudiced," Mr. Wright said.

"I hope so," Honey said.

"It's been my experience," Cleve English said, "that if you scratch a New Yorker – chances are, underneath, you'll find somebody from the Midwest. I'm from there myself, originally."

"Oh, I know that, Mr. English," Wright said. "We've heard you mention it on the air. Missouri."

"Yep, that's right," English said. "Raised. I was born in Cleveland. That's how I got the name. I've always been grateful for my childhood there. I believe, essentially, the middle-west _is_ America."

"Zat so? Well, that's sure how I see it – no offense, folks," Wright said.

Norma said, "What do I know – I'm from the Bronx."

Gardner had been looking at Garve Shoaly when Norma spoke. Shoaly reacted as though she had said "fuck."

"My wife's from the mid-west too," Cleve English said, quickly. "Illinois. Born and bred."

"White bread." Janelle said.

"Seems to me, friends, having Cleve English here, stead of talking about me we ought to be finding out what <u>he's</u> really like."

Everyone smiled.

"Are you a fan of the show, Mr. Wright?" Nancy English asked.

"One of the biggest, Ma'am," Wright said. "I sure do admire this husband of yours."

"Cleve's a phenomenon of our times," Madely Shoaly said. "Quite incredible."

"Radcliffe," Janelle said, softly.

"Well, we sure do like you back home," Wright said. "And the things you stand for. But where you get some of those weird people with those scarey ideas, I just don't know. Tiny Tim, for one."

"We have to shed light on all kinds of opinions and people," English said. "I don't agree with everybody I have on the show or even like them."

"I'm sure," Billingsly said. "Ralph – and I'm sure Cleve agrees – we'd rather hear about you and some of those ideas you were telling me about. What you're doing is what drives America – gives it shape and substance – what'll put the stamp on our culture – the dynamic energy of creative force coming from a man acting by his own talents in our free enterprise system."

"I'm sure we'd <u>all</u> like to hear your ideas," English said.

"Yes, we would," Nancy English said.

"Come on now, don't make us coax you, 'cept a little," Honey O'Hara said.

"Well, -- " Mr. Wright said.

"Let me start," Billingsly said, "if you're shy. Ralph's company has come up with an absolutely amazing new product. It's revolutionary. It'll change women's lives."

"How?" Madelyn Shoaly asked.

"If I can get a good name for it, that is," Mr. Wright said.

"What is it?" Nancy English said.

"A new vaginal deodorant," Billingsly said; and, Gardner thought he said it as though he were announcing the Easter Show at Radio City.

"Does it come in flavors?" Janelle asked.

"It does as a matter of fact," Mr. Wright said. "Raspberry Risque, Cherry Jubilient, Miss Mint and Lemon Libido. Buzz thought of that one."

"He also coined the phrase," Janelle said, "if you can't join 'em, lick 'em."

Billingsly said, "It's a very humane product. It's like Pasteur inventing the Papp test."

"Or Papp inventing pasteurization." Janelle said.

Billingsly looked annoyed and said, "Oh, you know what I mean."

"How does it work?" Toni Carpenter said. "Roll-on or spray?"

"Insertion," Billingsly said; "It's a soft-fiber tube with holes in it. You squeeze it and this oil – emits."

"Then you leave your husband for it," Norma said.

"All we need's a name," Mr. Wright said. "It's very difficult."

"There's Right Guard –" Duane said. Why not call this – Middle Line Backer."

"Are you a football fan"? Wright asked. He looked very surprised.

"Only when the quarterback leans over the center," Janelle said. "How bout calling it Channel 5?"

"Or Stick Ball," Norma said.

"I've got it," Toni Carpenter said. "Twat-Not".

Duane laughed until he realized how silent everyone else was being.

"Uh – another drink, Ralph," Billingsly said.

"Yes, please," Wright said. "I'm sure it seems funny, but women do need..."

"What was it again?"

"Rye and ginger," Wright said.

"Well – Harry, what do you think?" Billingsly asked.

"What about S'hhh-Fem?" Gardner said.

"What'd you say?" Billingsly said.

"You could call it S'hhh-Fem."

Billingsly said, "That's it, man! S'hhh-Fem."

"Good, Harry," English said. "It has a ring – and it's in good taste."

"My gosh, I like it," Wright said. "Darned if I don't."

"I told you he was a genius," Billingsly said.

"S'hhh---Fem—not a whisper," Norma said.

"Perfect, Norma," Billingsly said. "Good Lord, it runs in the family."

"Golly, this is exciting," Wright said. "I've never actually watched creative people work before. S'hhh-Fem is awfully good, isn't it?

"Ralph, this is only the beginning," Billingsly said. "Our meeting was made in Heaven. We're going to do big things together." Billingsly put his arm around Wright's shoulder.

"You want another martini to celebrate?" Janelle said to Honey.

"I don't know if I should –" Honey said.

"You may, if --," Mr. Wright said.

"Sure, you may, Honey, honey. Tonight is history and you're gonna be part of it – later, no doubt," Janelle said. "We've breached the Vaginal line. No more odor south of the border."

"Well, all rightie," Honey said, and giggled. "Just a teeny one."

"I'm flying now," Duane said.

"You always are, Peter Pan," Janelle said. Duane giggled. "Here's yours, lover," Janelle said. She handed Gardner a drink and stared at him as she leaned over him. Norma noticed it. Janelle broke the stare and returned to the bar. Honey O'Hara, Billingsly and Ralph Wright followed her.

"Where'd you get "S'hhh-Fem," Norma said quietly. "Did you know about the product before?"

Gardner shook his head. "It was just – a throwaway."

"A damned good one – considering," Norma said. "Probably mean a whopping raise."

Gardner nodded. "Yes. Isn't that awful?"

"What awful," Norma said. "Why was Janelle staring at you that way? You didn't encourage her, did you?"

"Norma, please, of course not."

"Of course not – you lie so truthfully."

"I'm a product of my time."

"In the time of products."

Cleve English approached the Gardners.

"Janelle asked me to deliver this message," English said. He handed Norma a Martini.

"Thank you," Norma said.

"How are you, Harry?" English said.

"Hanging in there," Gardner said. "And you?"

"Tip-top. Couldn't be better. Say, S'hh-Fem was a stroke of genius."

"Thanks," Gardner said. "It just – seemed right."

"W-r-i-g-h-t?" English said.

"Yes," Norma said. She laughed, politely.

"It's a pleasure meeting you, Mrs. Gardner. Harry's a very lucky man."

"He is, but I'm lucky too," Norma said.

"All our dreams of joy seem to come true," Gardner said, singing it as in the song.

"I hope you won't mind, Mrs. Gardner, my saying how – radiant – you look," English said.

"I don't know any woman who'd mind a man telling her that," Norma said.

"I mean it. I believe a woman's never more beautiful than she is when she's – well, in your condition. There's an added glow. The well-spring of motherhood, I suppose. 'Nature's proxy is motherhood', someone said," English said.

Gardner observed English selling Norma on himself – as though he were a new product. Gardner thought it would be appropriate if English held up a little doll of himself the way he held up commercial products on his television program.

"Mrs. Gardner," English said, "you know your husband is the best in our industry. You can't know how I appreciate him. He never – never asks you to say a thing in his copy about the product that isn't true. Did you know I test all the products I endorse?"

"What are you going to do about S'hhh-Fem," Norma asked.

English laughed and said, "I wish all ad people were like him. But, mostly, not all, mind you, but, mostly, I think, the simple rules of ethics are just cast off, forgotten about. It's very difficult for people like me, whom the public trusts, to maintain their integrity in this business. The pressures are immense. But as I keep saying, or it's my feeling anyway, the only way I can be – there are rules. I always say it – 'Gentlemen, there are rules – commandments.'"

"Would that be the Big Ten?" Norma said.

"Fortunately with the help of men like your husband, I've been able to withstand." English said.

"He doesn't snore either," Norma said.

As Gardner watched and listened, English continued the commercial message of himself to Norma.

Cleveland English, Gardner believed, was what people used to call a very good boy, a real nice fellow. He had been born in Cleveland and his father had been a traveling salesman for Standard Oil. His mother had won ribbons at county fairs for preserving canned fruit. English had gone to high school in St. Louis when his father was transferred and he became a disc jockey there. He looked younger, but was 47. Not that he tried to look younger, Gardner had to concede – as Gardner did; there was just nothing going on in his brain, Gardner thought.

He had known English to talk to for about two years and he disliked him intensely, despite respecting him as an effective television communicator. I can't stand that safe, well-fed, Anglo-Saxon face of his – Gardner said to himself. Nothing but pleasant smiles or pleasant frowns. I wish, just once, I could see that mug without the mask. He hasn't got a single line in it! Just a kind of slow, bring-down of gravity. Like a creek bank, muddy-softening. Especially there beneath the eyes and along the jaws. I wonder if he can even feel real feelings? Let along show one. God, he must exercise such rigid control over himself. Imagine it. All these years of oozing to the top.

And another thing, Gardner thought. It's impossible to pin English down. He's always saying things like, "it seems to me," "I would only suggest," "I'm only saying perhaps," "Don't you think?" "I couldn't say absolutely," "On balance," "I wouldn't want to be held to it." – Unless he's shilling a product – then he's Saint Unequivocal. And yet, Gardner knew, the way he uses his voice – and his use of words – most people think he's forthright, thoughtful, honest. Intellectual, God help us.

The Sonofabitch never reads books – and never meets the people on his show away from the program. His producer scribbles questions out for the bastard while he's on the air – on an art pad, while he's interviewing. He's a goddamned vessel. A copper wire. The only thing I ever heard him get excited about is golf!

Gardner knew also, from his business dealings with English, and through confirmation from others who had had the same experience, that English used his position of power and public-ness to promote, gain and confiscate anything – money or goods or favors – that he could lay his white hands on; all the while making pious speeches on the air as to his personal incorruptibility in a corrupting business.

English had, Gardner knew, furnished a townhouse and a country house on the induced generosity of commercial clients who vied for his services, prayed for his conversational endorsements on the show and counted themselves actually blessed if he and his family flew <u>this</u> airline, packed <u>that</u> luggage or stayed at <u>this</u> hotel or island. All the while, English promoted this free furniture, the cars and clothes, the vacations – all the trinkets of modern materialism, with a somnambulant innocence. These were, afterall, merely the just rewards for a man like himself.

English's wife Nancy, who had worked in a dime store when she was a teen-ager, it was said, had a habit of telling you the exact retail price of every item they owned. If you admired her dress, you got the cost. "How was your trip?" Plane fare followed – first class quote to be sure. Since it's all free, Gardner reflected, this quirk of hers, must take a lot of time for research and/or comparison shopping. Course, I'm sure it sweetens the pot considerably to know exactly what it doesn't cost you to have something – if you're Nancy English.

Thus Gardner thought – Cleve English: A reality which any good mother in the United States might pray in the night that her own son would become.

"Wright's really a good sort of chap, I think, don't you?" English said. "Solid type. A refreshing change."

"In what way?" Norma asked.

English's face shifted from the pleasant smile to the pleasant frown. "Well, I feel, in his ideas, it seems to me."

"Another vaginal deodorant?" Gardner asked.

"Well, that's not a big thing, I suppose, but on the other hand, it'll give security to – to – I mean if you can discover a new or better way, don't you agree, that's something?"

Billingsly, with Wright by his side, walked up.

"Ralph's really impressed, Harry." Billingsly said, "You came up with greatness on the spur of the moment."

"I'm sure I couldn't, if I'd stopped to think about it," Gardner said.

"No time for modesty," Billingsly said.

"Or irony?" Norma said.

Shoaly, Gardner saw, moved in quickly, like a man who didn't believe in the right of assembly unless the assembled included himself.

"Ralph, you still haven't announced the big news, have you?" Shoaly said.

"Oh, the uh, well, no. I'd almost forgotten," Wright said. "In the excitement about S'hhh-Fem."

"Forgotten?" Shoaly said. "An idea that'll revolutionize the cosmetics field and benefit millions of women – and you've forgotten?"

"Well, Garve kinda exaggerates…" Wright said.

"What's your other idea?" Norma asked.

"Well," Mr. Wright said.

"One of his many other ideas. Go on, Ralph," Shoaly said. "Listen, everyone." He raised his voice to get the attention of everyone in the room.

"Well, you understand," Mr. Wright said, "it's only in the planning stage. I'm working with Mr. Billingsly here on it. It needs some fleshing out. I'm for it mind you, and I expect to go ahead. We'll just have to iron out a few wrinkles. Oh, I didn't mean that as a pun. It just came out –"

"Just tell it like it is, Ralph," Billingsly said.

"Well, okay, it's – The Wright Company is going to give scholarships to deserving medical students, who want to be plastic surgeons – on the condition that each of them give "$5,000 worth of free surgery a year for four years after he graduates."

"Tell about the contest," Shoaly said.

"Oh, yes, yes, the contest," Wright said, "Well, women all over America'll be able to apply for free plastic surgery on every $25 dollar purchase of Wright products. If they tell in 25 words or less, in a sincere, convincing manner why they want their nose fixed or their face lifted or – other things."

"You're kidding," Norma said.

"He's not," Billingsly said. "We've worked night and day on this. Your husband's not the only one with bright ideas!"

"But," Norma said.

"Go on, Ralph," Shoaly said. "It's really great."

"Well, I guess," Wright said, "That's about all?"

"Not all, not at all," Billingsly said. "Tell them the title, Ralph."

"Can only women enter the contest?" Duane asked. He wasn't kidding, Gardner heard.

"What?" Wright said.

"Nothing, Ralph, nothing – go on," Billingsly said.

"But, did – he, uh – have a question? I'd like to –" Wright said.

"The title, Ralph," Billingsly said, "tell them the title of the campaign – er, the plan. That puts the whole project into focus."

Wright took a somber pause, Gardner thought; looking for all the world like a man who felt the grateful respect of posterity about to settle its warm mantle on his shoulders. Joffre at the Marne, Ike on D-Day. Wright surveyed each person in the room, Gardner saw, trying to look into the eyes of each. Then, he smiled broadly and said, "Americans, The Beautiful."

"Amen," Billingsly said.

"It's glorious," Shoaly said.

"Great," English said.

"Fantastic," Madelyn Shoaly said.

"Very touching," Nancy English said.

"Wow!" Honey O'Hara said.

Gardner looked around for Janelle. She – silent – was at the bar, with her back to the others in the room. That bitch, he said to himself.

"What a kicky idea," Duane said.

"It's sublime, Ralph, simply sublime," Billingsly said.

Janelle turned and came towards the group.

"Go ahead and cry if you want to, Buzz, nobody'd blame you," she said. "The whole thing is so goddamned philanthropic and patriotic. So uplifting. She handed another martini to Gardner. He took it and tried to find her eyes. She looked at the floor.

"What do you think, Mr. Gardner?" Wright asked. "You're the genius in this department."

"Genius knows Genius," Billingsly said, speaking quickly before Gardner could say anything, for which Gardner was grateful. He knew he couldn't move his tongue or mouth and he could not believe his ears.

"He applauds you, Ralph," Billingsly said. "We all applaud you. Don't we applaud him?" Billingsly began to clap his hands together, and everyone else, knowing that Billingsly expected it from them, joined in.

Gregory entered, a bit much on cue, Gardner believed, and said, "Dinner is served." The whole thing was so pat, perfect, rehearsed, unreal! Gardner thought.

Billingsly took Norma's arm and led her towards the elevator. Wright and Honey O'Hara followed. Then came the Shoalys and the Englishes. Duane and Toni Carpenter walked behind. Janelle came last. Gardner did not, could not move.

"The damned thing is full," Janelle said. Cleve English and Garve Shoaley started to get off the elevator to allow Janelle and Toni Carpenter to get on, but Janelle motioned them back.

"We'll walk down," Janelle said. "All right, Harry?"

"Us too," Duane said.

"I won't steal him, Norma," Janelle said. "But if he gets fresh in the stairwell, I won't holler. Wouldn't that be fun, if he did try to kiss me?"

"I don't know, Janelle, I've never tried kissing you." Norma said. The elevator door closed.

"After you," Janelle said, indicating the stairwell to Toni and Duane. "Oh, Harry, be a darling. I left my cigarette case on the bar."

Duane and Toni Carpenter started down the stairs. Gardner stood where he was. Janelle walked back to the bar and picked up her silver cigarette case.

As Janelle joined him she said, "Shall we, darling?" Gardner grabbed her upper arm, hard.

"Damn you," he said, "Goddamn you!"

"You're hurting my arm." Janelle said.

"I'm gonna break it." Gardner said. "You didn't even change the fucking title!"

CHAPTER 5

"Oooo, we are angry, aren't we?"

"You bet your ass I'm angry."

"Now, now. The title's the best part, Harry. <u>Americans, the Beautiful.</u> It's perfect. Everyone thought so."

"It was satire, goddamn it."

"Ralph Wright's whole life is satire, baby – and Buzz's and yours."

"My painting! Just pissed away."

It wasn't all that good, darling. A couple of nice devices, but not –"

"Does Buzz know it's my idea?"

Janelle shook her head.

"Jesus."

"By now, he's forgotten <u>I</u> ever gave it to him. He's convinced it's his very own pearl. Is that what's bothering you?"

"You really are a bitch."

"Oh, didn't you know? Just because I didn't give you credit?"

"A stainless steel bitch."

"Look, Love, Buzz needed an idea to get Wright's account and his money. I need Buzz to get money. I had an idea. Yours. Idea to Buzz, Buzz to Wright, Wright to Buzz, money to Janelle. Tinkers to Evers to conspicuous consumption."

Gardner could feel the sink in his stomach and in his legs; and his head was pounding.

"It'll be all right, Harry, you'll see. Come on, give a kiss." She moved closer to him, teasingly.

"I'd rather kiss a toilet seat," Gardner said. He turned and walked down the stairs.

"Oooo, you lovely bastard." Janelle started after him.

Gardner took the steps two at a time and almost tripped from his forward momentum when he got to the first floor landing. When he walked in, he tried to compose himself, before he entered the dining room. He looked at Norma, who was looking hard at him. The others were just beginning to arrange themselves to be seated. Harry tried to smile at Norma. She did not return it.

"You're over there, Harry, next to Janelle, I think," Billingsly said. "Across from Toni."

Janelle entered the room. "I stopped at the little girls' room. My God, those martinis. Come on, everyone, sit. Find your little place cards and sit your little asses."

"Janelle, please," Billingsly said.

"Are we waiting for Grace? Say Grace, Duane," Janelle said.

"Kelly or Coolidge," Duane said. He and Janelle laughed.

Everyone sat. Gardner did not help Janelle with her chair, but he did assist Madelyn Shoaly who sat on his left side. At the head of the table sat Buzz Billingsly; at the end, Janelle. Clockwise from Billingsly sat: Honey O'Hara, Garve Shoaly, Norma Gardner, Cleve English, Toni Carpenter, Janelle, Gardner, Madelyn Shoaly, Duane Lissner, Nancy English and Ralph Wright.

Gardner did not look across and down the table, as he did not want to catch Norma's eyes staring at him (which he felt sure they were), not at least for a moment or two, until he could get his insides settled enough to be sure that he could control his outside. Norma knew that this idea for AMERICANS, THE BEAUTIFUL was contained in a huge canvas he had painted and while she would not necessarily know – how could she know at all – that the first among these outsiders to know about it was Janelle, she would be wondering how it had got full-grown into Wright's head, without any mention of him, Gardner, in connection with it. He supposed that she would think he had given the idea to Billingsly, who for some reason had not wanted to give Gardner credit. But she would soon start wondering why he hadn't told her before and why, in any case, he would give away an idea which he knew she knew had meant something of value to him. Though mostly, she would, he believed, be furious about Janelle's attentions to him. Soon, she would sense everything, he figured; her instincts were that honest and good.

Gardner was beginning to feel his drinks, but even so, he was wishing that he could have another one. He did not like what he was feeling and he did not like being forced to remember his involvement with Janelle

Billingsly; but now as he sat, punched by his anger and remorse, he could not stop seeing how it all had begun.

He wished that he had not felt so dead-out that day, finished off, emptied, pointless, as he had been feeling for so many days during the winter and before – (if he were honest with himself), for he had felt the same in the summer of the year and in the spring before. There had been so many erasures outside himself to keep on blanking him – Nixon's win, Chicago, Bobby Kennedy cut down and Dr. King; Czechoslovakia, and, on-going over it all, the Vietnam killing, as oozily routine as manufacturing soft ice cream. Even before all that it had been there in him. It had been there when President Kennedy went skull-blasted down in Dallas (or had it been so bad before that?) – some vague-shaped, unnamed beast, half-slumbering, half-ready to pounce on his sense of well-being, coiled to spring and tear away at his safety and certainty about himself and the world. In fact, it was hard for Gardner to reach back to a time before the beast had entered – to remember definitely when it had not been there, in the way that it was always difficult with pain when you were in pain, to recall clearly what it felt like to be in the absence of pain. When had it been? The coming of the beast. Korea maybe? Hungary? Or way back – those pictures of British bull-dozers pushing bodies of bony Jews into a communal grave? Certainly, by the time of Janelle, the beast thing was at home in him for sure and living off his innards.

In November, following Nixon's election, to escape his beast or to keep it more sleeping than awake and eating, Gardner had signed on for a painting class at the School of Visual Arts and had rented a small studio room on West 64th Street near Lincoln Center in which to work.

The idea for the form of his painting had come quickly and naturally out of his experience as an advertising art director. It was in a format of what is called a "storyboard." That is, individual panels of art which were static, pictorial representations of what a commercial on television would look like when it finally moved, frame by frame, on film or tape; a kind of comic strip presentation. The idea of its content surfaced more slowly.

It was total, but scattered in his mind; representational and fragmented all at once. Linear, motion-picturey, headliney, and audible even. Snatches of dialogue were in it. Remembered faces. Dead family, and-might-as-well-be dead; and other figures he had seen, or experienced – in school, in the army, on a train, at a theatre, in a passing car. Bodily forms, real and newsreely; read about and factually touched. He wasn't aware of it always, but it was always there, as though you were in the dark and it was storming and there was thunder, then a flash, and you would see the someone or something you had not known was there or had forgotten was there in the dark, until the dark was lit by the lightning; and after the lightning it would be dark again of course, and it would disappear, but it would not be gone, you know, because it stayed just beyond, in the threatening powerlessness of your blindness in the dark, and you were afraid of it and your battering heart would threaten to ram through its own doors; and you would want, as you had at your grandmother's house as a child, to run and hide your head in the feather bed until the storm and the thunder and the lightning that revealed these familiar objects in their true terror were over; and you would promise these haunting figures promises you would not keep and which they did not expect you to keep; and you would vow vows to a God whom even then you were beginning not to believe in. (What God would humble so humble a creature)? But still you vowed – what else was there – (Gin now, but God then) and prayed for Him, It, Something to spare you, want you, forgive you, vindicate you, hold you (so snapable) to just put some distance between your fright and the night, between the day and the swaying stalk of your vulnerability, between your wonder and your no-wisdom; to grant you the gift of saying, of reaching out, of touching with, "I know, I understand; s'hhh, it's going to be all right: and to mean it really and to be answered, "Yes, so do I, I know. I know." With everyone – with <u>anyone</u>. But then later, when you were what was named "grown up," you tried to learn how not not-to-be-afraid, but just finally not to expect things; to live without appeal, to finally not to try, not even to want to see the faces or hear the pleas from yourself or from all the others; all of the others whom you know or the millions you saw or the billions you realized were living but that you would never see. So many people! The unknown ones especially, you learned to shut out, off. Close-up was difficult enough you know. But with what did you replace the real beliefs of your head and heart and senses and intuitions about life? What did you use to blank those out, anesthetize them, forget them? What sustained you, gave you some mythology to live by. "Bong, bing, bung." – NBC. The National Broadcasting Company and M.G.M and <u>Boy's Life</u>. "Lux Presents Hollywood." "Jello, Again, this is Jack Benny." Pretty color pages, slick with big cars with wondrous women draped on them, and refrigerators and clothes washers and cigarettes being smoked in smart rooms with head waiters in tails and all the people looking like you when you looked in the mirror. And all this made the real things go away. It got easy not to tell between Lana Turner and life, between

Life and life, between Look and looking. Between your real father and Spencer Tracy playing your father. Clips and clatters of station breaks, and FORGET–inducing dulcet radio voices and film flicker-fantasies and bill-board blurring by in the family car. Burma-shaaave----Ask The Man Who Owns One. Time to Re-tire. "We, The People," It's Your "Hit Parade" "Double or Nothing" – even you might win. "The Shadow Knows." "Kid, I won't let you go up in a crate like that." "Let's get this one for the Gipper." Security? "Buy Mom a Hoover." "Drake (Errol Flynn) may be a Sea-Dog and a pirate but he's saved England." "Frankly, Miss Scarlet, I don't give a damn." "We'll (me and Gary Cooper) cut 'em off at the pass." "Tom, (George Brent), I (Bette Davis) can't go on like this." "Get those wagons moving!" – by music to match the mountains. Westward Ho strings and tympani by Alfred Newman, Franz Waxman and Dimitri Tiompkin. (Poor Midwest boy, how could you know they were European Jews who had just fled from the gathering gangrene of Hitler; men who know more about Mendelsohn than Matt Dillon; Brahms yes; Jim Bowie, no).

The painting formed up out of all of this, out of this city dump of experience which cluttered your mind; this litter of litany which could be said to be forgotten, but which participates in every action, every attitude of your present – that frail, pale ounce of existence which lays between having been and becoming, or becoming-not, which you're afraid is more precise. Gardner thought he knew that that's all he was: These shards of broken experience, swept up in the dust pan of his brain like cheap glass dropped on a tile floor. No sure form in daily life (success, maybe? Money? Popularity?) no ritual, no rules (any boy could be President), lots of instruction, but no education – no continuity – nothing understood, no roots. No, that can't be true! He told himself. I do have roots. I'm not one of the rootless Americans, transferred from branch office to branch office! I can find my way back to the Revolution and Virginia mountain men who fought with Lighthorse Harry Lee and who came through the Cumberland Gap to Kentucky and the Ohio Territory and who might have known Tom Lincoln or Daniel Boone. I know both of my great-great-grandfathers by name! They both owned farms in Ohio and both came from the same town as William Tecumseh Sherman; and one of my great-grandfathers fought with the 117th Ohio Volunteers in the Cumberland, and at Chickamauga and Reingold, Georgia, and at Atlanta and marched to the sea, and, when the war was over, pushed west to Illinois and served in the same state legislature as Abe Lincoln had once.

And a great-great-uncle died at Libby, the Confederate Prison at Richmond, and he had written sad, soldier poems that I still have somewhere. And later on, one of my grandfathers published a newspaper and another engineered a train and both had been mayors of their towns, and my own father fought in World War I and served on the draft board in World War II and he sent me, his only son, off to the Army. I have roots in America! Still, with it all, you've never had a certain sense of yourself, Gardner thought. Have you? You're not those men in your family. You're made of something else. You're all the print ads your eyes have seen each day since childhood; more the shape of the metallic pleas of the radio and television, the movies and the billboards and the matchbook covers: Buy, Be happy, Offend not, Be popular, Brush, spray, splash, comb and gargle till you get the girl. Solve things quickly, simply, violently without completion, fulfillment or wonder. Only sex satiates you and that's mostly nervous, harried and deceitful. You cork along on your polluted sea of persuasion and illusion – of prism sights and noise and things, things, things! Moses has become money; mystery falls out through a test tube; and as for the heart – it no longer even was a well for transcendence, but shown up as a pump merely, which when faulty could be traded-in for a transplant. Gardner knew his senses were as worked away as the words "I love you," written in sand and gone with the tide.

And it was not just the advertising messages that made him up, he knew, or the movies or radio shows of his youth; now it was the hard news of life too, as presented in the news programs on television and in the daily barrage of suffering in the newspapers. TIME FOR MURDER AND RAPE FROM HOME AND AROUND THE WORLD. No plane crashes anywhere that you don't have to see it on the 11 o'clock news. No madman pulls a trigger in Texas or Tokyo that your newspaper doesn't have to banner it full on the front page. No flame of killing fire, no flood, no quake of earth, no volcano, hurricane, blizzard of snow, no untracking of train, no burst of dam can be kept from its clicking dance on the wire service teletype and from there to you. You, it is thought, in the name of communication, have to know it all and thus you, in order to survive at all – fragile thing you are reminded you are – finally, have to learn to know nothing. The real death has to become as indifferent a consideration as the Hollywood script death, when there is so much of it. Events real have to be absorbed unrealistically; hidden away, swept into the under-the-carpet of the unconscious. Otherwise you could not go on. But what does that do finally to a person? Who needs all the horrible knowledge?

Death next door had a dignity, Gardner remembered from his youth, weight and an awesome presence, and you couldn't escape participating in it. It concerned flesh which you knew the name of and you knew what the person was like. The local rapist, the local embezzler, the local hero, the local old person who aged and died were touchable and always something of you and made you ponder. And each in his agony or triumph had a oneness about him that lent importance to you all. One killer in your hometown was worth a million megatons in anguishing the heart and steeling your resolve to do better, to be better. Computers don't bring forth compassion or contrition. A serial number gives no succor. The human heart's a vessel—goddamn it—and it can only hold so much! Even the brain, in all its wonder, can't make order out of all the ordeals of all men! No wonder we feel so helpless.

A few of everything, even the worst of things, might make some sense or be borne and give you strength but the surfeit in our time crushes sensibility. Mass consumption consumes the sense. That's why the drugs maybe—it's a cry, a try to find the ancient, amorous gift of our senses. And what have we created, produced? What's the bounty of our age? The sick joke, the Chinese commune, starvation with food surpluses, the gas chamber, Hiroshima, the child with napalm scars, 38 wax witnesses to the knife-dicing of one screaming girl; Black encounters, guns in the hands of madmen killing off our few wise men? God, Gardner thought, in our time "Turn the other cheek" means turning it away—so as not to hear, to smell, to see, to feel, to touch, to get involved. Pretend everything is important; fragmentize, mass produce till there is so much that finally the only thing you can do to live is to believe nothing is important. "Survive." "Do your own thing." "Cool it." Smile during coffee breaks but never look up or sideways when you go to the subway. Avoid the drunk, mumbling, shouting curses like some deranged Tiresias, a blind (blind-drunk) seer of now, who mocks your cool and shouts his obscenities at no-one in particular, except that you know it's a last slobbering signal from the heart, a slurred prophecy of extinction which you hear, then quickly unhear. Who the hell has time to save himself even?

Thus, did Gardner think about his painting. America was the re-ordering of reality, he concluded; visions without seeing, hearings without listening, science and thinking without feeling. Dying—but looking chipper. How could he paint that? Synthesize it? Americans, the Beautiful was how he tried. It took shape in a large canvas, 4' by 6', in individual panels with text painted under each panel, and the whole describing a national contest for people to write in in 25 words or less why they would want a face lift, and it announced, as it might in an advertisement, that young doctors (beautifully pictured in a Norman Rockwell-style) would perform these good works free because they had been put through medical school on scholarships provided by a famous cosmetics company, which Gardner called in the painting, "The Famous Cosmetics Co." He kept the painting in his studio on 64th Street and worked on it on weekends and during one or two evenings on week nights. In his office, Gardner kept several rough sketch-pad-size versions of the painting. He had been working on these, he recalled now, on the day Janelle Billingsly had come in.

It was a week or so after Nixon's inaugural; a sullen day in a week of unwashed blackboard skies, when the sun, he thought, seemed a bulb burned out forever. He remembered feeling so soft that day. A flaccid, thin-haired mediocrity in good suits.

He didn't notice her until she spoke, although later she had told him she had been at the door watching him for quite a long time.

"Hello, DaVinci," Janelle said.

Gardner looked up and there she stood...she was dressed in a leopard coat, sable-trimmed, and she was wearing a sable hat. She was wearing over-sized, yellow-tinted steel frame sun glasses too, and he was struck physically by her appearance—by her looks and by his astonishment at seeing her there. She looked not so much beautiful, he thought, as striking, imposing, a form in nature shaped by weather. He felt unsettled, as though someone had actually jostled him.

"Janelle." Gardner stood up.

"I think I just brought you back from a moon shot."

"What—oh—I was just—doodling."

"Doodling? Buzz'd die if he heard that, with what he pays you. No kiss?" He kissed her on the cheek quickly, and retreated.

"Uh—what brings you to the valley of the Philistines?"

"Insufficient Funds! I think is the polite term the bank uses. January, it turns out, not April, is the cruelest month."

She just stood there staring at him, Gardner realized. He found himself staring back and beginning to see her and feel her inside himself as desirable.

"I—uh—think you should be grateful there's someplace you can come to get more. I'm always broke." His voice was clotted, he could hear.

"Oh, I am. God bless Buzz's greedy little raisin of a heart." Janelle closed the door behind her and came farther into the office. "I don't know what I'd do without him. Or him me, back at the beginning." She sat down. She put her gloves and bag on the desk. She took a cigarette out of her purse.

"Got a light," she said.

"Uh, sure," Gardner said. He fumbled about in his center desk drawer for a pack of matches and, finding one, lit her cigarette. He felt nervous suddenly about her being there and about the closed door.

"Want one?"

"Okay, thank you."

"I'd ask about your family," Janelle said, "but families bore me. I see you have the obligatory portraits. I wish I could be more hypocritical. Let me see your doodles."

Gardner reached to try to save the sketches from Janelle but she picked them up quickly.

"They aren't really work on any--" he said.

"What the hell kind of campaign is this?"

"It's not actually—a campaign."

"It's a storyboard. My God, it's hilarious. Who's 'Famous Cosmetics"!?"

"Nobody. I made it up. It's—it's just a sketch idea for a—uh--a painting."

"A painting?"

"Yes."

"An oil painting?"

Gardner nodded.

"Yours?"

He nodded again.

"You paint? Where? Where is it?"

"In—uh--a studio."

"You have a studio? Where?"

"Nothing much. Just a—sort of a room really."

"God, a real painter. You mean your work here doesn't satisfy your soul?" Gardner shrugged. "Every third person in this brothel has a secret novel or something. Now you too."

"It's just a—hobby really."

"Money, major medical and a pension plan aren't enough?"

"Maybe when I'm sick, dead or 65."

"That's treasonous talk, Mr. Gardner. We'll have to ship you off to the re-education camp." Janelle's voice was imitating Buzz's, Gardner realized.

"Don't tell me we have one."

Janelle smiled. "Not yet. Though it's been suggested. Where's your studio? I'd love to see the painting."

"Oh, it's way over. By Lincoln Center. 64th Street."

"Will you take me there?"

"Well,"

"Will you?"

"Oh, you mean now?" Gardner felt himself getting increasingly uncomfortable.

"Yes."

Gardner studied her face. She was still staring at him unblinking. He began to be conscious of his sex.

"Do you mean it?" he said.

"I mean everything I say."

"Well, God, Janelle, I—I couldn't now. I'm working. I--"

"I thought you were not working. I've got your doodles to prove it."

"Well, yes, but, no, God, I couldn't. I just got back from lunch. It's almost three and I haven't done a thing."

"The least you can do is buy me a drink."

"But I've got to do some work."

"I'm work. I'm a stockholder. You can tell them I want to re-do my kitchen and I asked you to help me with some design ideas. Come on. You can't reject the boss's wife."

Gardner was frightened of the invitation, but suddenly he realized that he was feeling that there was nothing he wanted so much as to go with her.

"Well, what the hell," he heard himself saying.

"Not exactly said with the abandon of Modigliani yet, but it's a start. Where do you want to go?"

"I—I don't know—where--" Gardner felt very confused and could not think of a single bar and felt embarrassed that he could not.

"Come on. I know lots of places," Janelle said.

Gardner followed her command and was grateful for her sureness. He got his coat and they came out of his office. He saw Kathleen, his secretary, staring at him like, he thought, some grand god-damned Catholic Inquisitor or East Side apartment doorman. He could feel sweat coming on his brow and under his arms.

"Kathleen, I'm—uh—going out for a few minutes—oh, Kathleen, this is Mrs. Billingsly—uh, this is my secretary, Kathleen. I won't be long, uh--"

"Hello, Mrs. Billingsly," Kathleen said. Janelle nodded and half-smiled.

"Where can I get you?" Kathleen said.

"What? Oh, uh—well, I'll just be awhile--"

"Jerry Novack called three times, I told him you'd be back after lunch. What'll I say?" Kathleen's voice sounded wounded and warning, Gardner thought, like a hurt mother. Mother Superior.

"Tell him to shove it," Janelle said.

Gardner laughed—too loud—he realized—from his nervousness—and he saw Kathleen bleach out white as a dead Swede.

"Yes, tell him that," Gardner said, "He's a pain anyway."

"In the ass," Janelle said. "Come on, I'm thirsty. Good-bye, Kathleen. Give my best to Jerry."

"Okay," Kathleen said, stretching out the word in that way she had of saying "you'll be sorry."

"I'll be right back," Gardner said and felt as though he wanted never to come back. Suddenly, he felt lifted and free and powerful and Kathleen could go fuck herself, he decided.

CHAPTER 6

Coming out of the building, which was the Time-Life Building at 50th Street and the Avenue of the Americas, Gardner and Janelle Billingsly stopped in the narrow plazaway by one of the plain and now-empty fountains. The sky was the color of cremation left-overs and the cold stabbed Gardner. He felt, at first weakened by it and lessened in his resolve to go with this woman, a resolve which he had been gaining in the ride down in the elevator and he felt the wind razor up against him, hard and scrapping.

"It's cold. You want to go to La Fonda? It's right here. We could even go back inside the building and go--"

"I hate it," Janelle said. "And everybody from upstairs'll be there."

"How bout 21 or Shor's"

Janelle shook her head.

"There's a new place—Pip's."

"There's a cab," she said. "Let's get it." She signaled for it. "Taxi." The cab stopped and she got in. Gardner followed her in.

"Where're we going?" Gardner said.

"The Ginger Man," Janelle said to the driver, "it's on West 64th, just off Broadway. Go up Broadway."

The driver turned the cab into 6th Avenue and headed uptown.

A Daily <u>News</u> lay on the seat—Gardner looked at the headlines: "Model mauled by Lion" Jersey fire kills 3."

"Janelle, I've got to get back sometime today, you know," Gardner said.

"I know."

"Couldn't we just stop along here—anywhere."

"I like the Ginger Man."

"So do I, but--"

"Relax."

Gardner felt a chill from having been outside and then having gotten into the over-heated cab. His glasses steamed up. And, he thought, the chill probably also came on from what was happening. And what, in God's name, was happening, he asked himself. Suddenly, he felt fearful. But he could not deny that what was happening was making him feel awake and alert. His self-pity and softness were going. He was suddenly very aware of his body. He was feeling very good about seeing her leopard coat out of the side of his eye and the cut of her good shoe and the arch of her foot which he stared at. My God, he said to himself, I've never seen such a perfect arch and perfect heel tendon. He also knew that he was feeling as though he had to go to the bathroom. The Ginger Man was very close to where his apartment was. Norma lunched there often with her girlfriends, he remembered. My God, what if she should be here? Or any of her friends? Or any of the people he knew. Many ABC people and agency people lunched there. He was sure to meet someone he knew. Still, he didn't want to think of a way to get out of the cab or away from this woman. My God, stop staring at her arches. And stop thinking what you're beginning to think about her and yourself. She doesn't want you, he told himself; and how can you even think of wanting her? Billingsly's wife? That's suicidal. She's too tough, too metal, too dangerous, he told himself. But then, he remembered, there were those stories about her. Everybody spoke about her. About her trips to Europe. Everybody said it was for rendezvous with lovers. Everybody made jokes about it. Even he and Norma had seen her a few times in restaurants around New York dining with men. But even so, he told himself, even if she did want him, he would have to be crazy to have anything to do with her. He was not that far gone. Oh, Christ, why do I think every woman who treats me decently or kindly wants to go to bed with me? You do, he told himself. You do think that way. The slightest smile or kindness from a woman's enough to get you thinking she wants you. Ridiculous. She doesn't want you. A married square block of a man with two children and living from pay check to pay check? Billingsly probably put her up to this. Take out the little creative director for a drink and let him cry on the boss's wife's shoulder. Give him a pat on the head. Tell him how much he's loved and needed and shouldn't go around feeling depressed and so forth and so on and etc., yours truly, best regards, sincerely, signed, office morale.

"Jesus," Janelle said, "why do we stay in New York at all in the winter time?" Janelle leaned over and slipped her arm through Gardner's. Gardner squeezed down on his colon because he was so certain for the moment that he might shit. He could feel his heart stutter.

"It is freezing," Gardner said, and he was angry about the shakiness he heard in his voice.

"I feel like those statues look in the New York State Theatre," Janelle said. "My hands are ice." she took Gardner's right hand between her two hands and rubbed the three of them together. He had not noticed before then how large her hands were, though he did not think they were coarse or ugly; just the opposite, that they were perfectly formed and strong, like the hands of a woman in a sculpture from the Renaissance. When the cab stopped for a red light, he looked out and saw they were at Central Park South and 6th Avenue and he wondered if he knew any of the people who were moving along the sidewalks and in the cars and across the street in front of the cab or if any of them knew him or could see him riding in this cab with this woman and that if they could see him could they also see his hand in hers? Just then a bus pulled alongside and he looked up and saw the face of a woman who was looking down—into the cab—and he knew she could see that Janelle Billingsly was stroking his hand and had her arm through his and he felt his intestine tighten again and he pulled his hand out of Janelle's two hands and he knew he could no longer trust his voice to sound like his voice.

"I thought my secretary was going to faint—our going out together." He tried to sound light, jocular, he hoped.

"Does it matter?"

"Well, no, I suppose," Gardner said. He felt embarrassed that he had seemed to care. It suddenly seemed very—what, he wondered—middle-class?

"Unless you're sleeping together."

"What?" Gardner did not notice, he was so taken with the impossibility of sleeping with Kathleen (an idea he had considered and rejected), that the cab had started again and had turned into Central Park South and was heading towards Columbus Circle. The flags on the immense hotels were whipping in the wind and the people walking arched along concave, looking as though a huge, invisible ball had just hit each of them in the stomach. Marcel Marceau was everywhere.

"Well Harry, don't sound so shocked. Half the men in New York are sleeping with their secretaries."

"Not me."

"You need a prettier secretary for openers."

"Janelle, even if I had a pretty one--"

"Oh, Mr. Clean. I forgot."

"Not Mr. Clean. I just don't think it's--"

"Let's get you a pretty one and see what happens. Kathleen is no test." Janelle took Gardner's hand again, but this time not to stroke, but to clutch; the fingers of her right hand enmeshing hard into the fingers of his left. And she pressed her right forearm against his ribs. He was conscious of the slight flab just below his ribs and he sat up higher and pulled in his stomach and leaned to his right to tighten his left side. He made an attempt to pull his hand away, but she made a more definite move to keep it there.

"Relax," Janelle said, and she looked at him, with sureness but with warmth too, Gardner felt. He looked back. The metal was gone in her, he believed, except for the strength in her hand, but even that was tender, somehow, and her eyes seemed moister, softer. He felt elated and miserable.

"Do you like what you see?" Janelle asked.

"You're beautiful."

"My God, how marvelous."

"What?"

"That. What you said. And so easily. So honestly; it sounded like anyway. I thought you'd never allow yourself to say anything like that to me."

"I just meant—well, you are, it's a fact."

But you didn't say it matter-of-fact. You said it like you meant it—for yourself. Not for a professional judgment. Not for an ad."

"Janelle. Look. Shouldn't we be--"

"Please." Janelle clutched his hand even more firmly.

Gardner could feel himself getting even more nervous. But, she is beautiful. It's what you feel, he thought. There is no harm in saying that—is there?--Lying Harry? Harry asked himself. He knew the harm.

"You're very beautiful."

"My God," Janelle said, softly, Gardner heard, and as though with great finish and relief. "You're so nice, Harry. And gentle."

She gently leaned her whole body closer in towards his. Gardner suddenly thought, what if Norma should call the office and I'm not there? What would she do? What would Kathleen say—that virgin typist nun? She'd probably say it right out. "I don't know, Mrs. Gardner. He left here about an hour ago with Mrs. Billingsly and they wouldn't tell me where they were going. They told Jerry Novack to go shove it and they both were laughing and seemed very nervous and everything. I don't know what to say but it looks just terrible and you such a lovely wife and mother and what is this country coming to and what can you expect from men, they're such beasts!" Whoa, boy, whoa—don't panic! Kathleen never said over ten words to Norma in her life and even if she did say that you had gone out with Janelle Billingsly, so what? You can cover that easily enough. Why, Janelle was re-doing her kitchen wasn't she and she just wanted to consult you about designing ideas and we just went into the neighborhood for a quick drink and (neighborhood! What were you doing at The Ginger Man then? Sylvia said she saw you at the Ginger Man. That's hardly the neighborhood! I meant our neighborhood. Janelle was dropping me off at home and we stopped in on the way. I wasn't feeling so well so I was going to leave the office early, oh, damn). and—my God, that's the excuse Janelle had made up—that about the kitchen decoration—and you were already using it. For a creative type, you're not very creative. Anyway, calm down. Norma never calls at 3:30 in the afternoon—unless—unless one of the children is sick or something or gets runover by his school bus. Holy, God, man, get ahold of yourself! What school bus ever runs over the kids who are riding in it? Well, not run-over then, but hit or stranded in the bus. Remember, it poured once and water flooded the tunnels in Central Park and a school bus got stranded in one of them and the kids had to be pulled out by a police emergency squad and it was very dangerous and, my God, it's 20 degrees and no rain and no snow and the kids are fine and stop panicking. Could they freeze to death if the bus stalled? Act your age, Gardner told himself, show a little "cool." Suppose though one of them got hurt in a fight or something. Oh, shut up. So what? You'll worry about that when the time comes. Stop worrying. She'll feel it.

"Are you all right?" Janelle said.

"What?"

"How are you?"

"Fine, fine. Shouldn't I be?"

"Yes. You just seem—tense."

"Isn't that part of the fun—when you're playing hookey?"

"Hookey?" Janelle laughed, tenderly. "Harry—you're like finding a copy of Boy's Life at a lake cottage. Does your secretary love you?"

"What's the fascination with Kathleen?"

"I just think if I were your secretary I'd be in love with you."

"Well, thank you, but I'm sure Kathleen doesn't feel that way."

"I'll bet she does. One way or other. I could tell by the way she looked at me. She was very possessive."

"She thought I was goofing off and she's very conscientious about the work."

"She was jealous."

"Well, if she was, it's kind of transference. It has nothing to do with love."

"Then she's a stupid girl. If I were her, I'd love you – unashamedly."

"Here we are," the driver said. Gardner was relieved that they had arrived. It gave him a chance to break off the conversation which was pleasing him more than he wanted to admit. He paid the driver and overtipped him. Gardner and Janelle got out of the cab and went into the Ginger Man. It was semi-dark and Gardner felt grateful for that and for the fact that the room was almost empty. Three young people, two men and a girl, sat at a big round table in the front under a Tiffany lamp, and two young men were at the bar. He did not recognize any of them.

"The bar?" Janelle said.

"No," Gardner said. He knew there was a table immediately behind a partition which separated the main room from the front aisle which paralleled the front window and the sidewalk and street. This table would be partly hidden from street view and from anyone in the room unless they came around into the main room. "Let's take a table." Gardner took Janelle's elbow and steered her to the table he had in mind. He was very happy to see that it was vacant. They sat down. Gardner helped Janelle off with her coat and pulled his own off, which he left on his chair behind him. He did not want to get up to hang it up because he did not want to be seen.

"You're so sweet," Janelle said. "But you're very uptight."

"How so? What would you like to drink?"

"You don't do things like this, do you, Harry? You never really have, have you?"

"What things?" Gardner fidgeted from the things Janelle was saying and of course he knew very well that she was right, but he pretended to be looking for a waiter.

"Go out with other women. Make <u>trysts</u>."

"Well, I wouldn't say that. I'm not—"

"You're not what? Not that it matters. I think you're marvelous."

A young man, with a contrived-casual shock of brown hair hanging down his forehead, and wearing a butcher's apron, came up to the table. "Yah, what'd you like?"

"What'd you want, Jan—to drink?"

"Vodka martini."

"I'll have a Scotch on the rocks," Gardner said, and then he thought. Scotch would give him breath when he got home. "Uh, I'll have a Vodka too—a Screwdriver, please."

"Why didn't you finish saying my name? Didn't you want them to hear? No names, please, huh?"

"What? When?"

"Just now. You started to say my name and then you cut yourself off."

"I did? I don't know."

"You can give me another name if you want. Call me let's see—what can you call me? Uh, you can call me Ginger in honor of this place and our first date."

"Can't I just call you by your regular name?"

"But you didn't want to—and I don't blame you. The CIA's everywhere these days. Let's see, what'll I call you? You've got to have a name too. Did you ever have a secret name for yourself?"

The young man brought the drinks and put them down hard. He spilled a bit of the martini, and without wiping it up or saying anything, he walked away.

"Cheers," Gardner said, and he lifted the glass to his mouth quickly, eager to get some of the alcohol inside of him to calm himself down.

"To us," Janelle said, "to Ginger and—Henry."

"Henry?"

"Henry Fonda. You look like him. Younger, but—"

"You're crazy."

"Well, you do—enough. And, what the hell, you've got to have some name. It's good. I like it for you."

"God, Henry. I hate Henry."

"Then you think of something."

"Anything but Henry."

"What about Sam—we'll pretend we're Humphrey Bogart and Ingrid Bergman in Casablanca."

Gardner took another long sip from his drink. "Sam was the piano player. Anything is better than Henry."

"Then Sam it is."

"Ginger lives a very rich fantasy life."

"And Sam can learn to."

"Sam does not exist."

"That's what Harry thinks. We'll let Sam speak for himself. He will."

Gardner drank again and then lit a cigarette for himself and looked at Janelle full in the face. He smiled when she looked directly at him. She smiled too.

"May I have one?" she asked.

"Of course, I'm sorry." Gardner gave her a cigarette and lit it. They continued to look at each other. His face felt warm and he was conscious of the blood pulsing through his head and especially a new pressure drumming behind his ears. All the vessels of his hands he could see were swollen but the knots in his stomach and intestines were loosening. Her eyes were very powerful, Gardner thought, and they really worked into you.

"Have you got lots of paintings?"

"No, just a couple. I've mostly worked on that one since I started working."

"Do you despise advertising?"

"No, not altogether. It's not just advertising."

"Does painting give you what you thought it would?"

"It's a release."

"I'm all for that. What do you want from painting?"

"U'mm, it's difficult to say."

"Look—what's heard in a saloon is as privileged as the confessional—or the couch."

"Most analysts I know spill everything about their patients."

"They write things down. Drunks don't. We have more integrity. Fewer scruples maybe and more dead brain cells, but more integrity."

"What are we doing here?"

"I want to know about you—and I'm sure the painting is very important. And I love to hear you talk. I like your voice. I care about all that. Now tell me what you get release <u>from</u>."

"Melancholy. Do you ever get it?"

"Get it? I import it, I use so much."

"Well, <u>that</u>. And—I feel so impersonal most of the time and impotent."

"Sexually?"

"Spiritually—and as a factor of power. I never feel as though what I do makes any difference or changes anything. Not myself even. And the painting, or with the act of painting, I feel as though I get to be the cause of something as least—something singular—like my tree on the plain."

"Your what?"

"Oh—Tree on the plain. It's a memory of mine. A kind of personal symbol. Out west—in the mid-west—sometimes the fields or prairies reach as far as you can see with nothing to interrupt them—nothing at all. When I was a kid I used to think about views like that as people—me especially—and that nothing in me stood out. And probably never would. But there was one place—near my grandfather's hometown—out a country road from town—where the fields ran to the horizon like that, just like the other fields—except for one huge tree—about half-way along to the edge of the earth; it rose up against the sky like the nervous system of a giant man—the foliage part looked like a huge brain. It seemed the most singular dignified, most magnificent living body I'd ever known. Like the tree Nebuchadnezzar dreamed of and told Daniel about. It was just the most damnest beautiful thing you could imagine. I think Franz Kline must have had something like that in mind to learn how to make those masterful one and two black strokes against a stark white canvas. There's so much power in something like that daring to impress itself against a void. I used to go out that road and sit down by—lie down really—just up on my elbows from the earth—along the slope of the culvert which ran beside the road, and I would stare for hours at that—supreme tree. It made such a majestic mark. And other times; when it was cloudy—or even more so when the whole sky boiled and you thought it might rain hot melted lead—and when it would lightning—the tree shone like an old King Lear or Horatio. Of course, I knew, even as a boy, that someday the tree would die, but that didn't bother me because until then, it would stand like nothing else ever had, anywhere, ever before. Nothing could eliminate that in the consciousness of the universe. And I would think about wanting to be like the tree and I would sometimes think I was the tree. And that it would be possible to be some-<u>one</u> and to stand out."

"Whew," Janelle whistled softly.

Gardner smiled. "Yes, I know. Don't worry. I haven't thought that way for a long time."

"Did you actually sit out there outside in the lightning?"

"No. That was later. In a car. High school kids used to park along that road to neck. That's when I'd see the tree in storms."

"That must have made you some kisser—the way you felt about that tree. Who was the lucky girl?"

"Oh, nothing serious. Just a nice girl—in my grandfather's hometown. Her father owned the hardware store there."

"Did you make love to her?"

Gardner laughed.

"Did you?"

"You ask very direct questions…on one topic."

"I'm curious."

"I guess I'm yellow."

"Well—did you?"

"Yes—after a fashion."

"My God. Can you believe it? I never made love in a car."

"You must be the only woman in Wisconsin who --"

"How can you do it?"

"Awkwardly."

Janelle smiled. "God, I'd love to try it."

"Uh, would you like another?" Gardner said, nodding towards Janelle's empty glass.

"I would."

Gardner looked back over his should and caught the waiter's eye, whom he imagined was looking at him knowingly and condemningly. He waved him over to the table.

"We'd like two more—please," Gardner said.

"Yeah," the waiter said.

"They're really very warm here, aren't they?"

"All the waiters in these places want you to know they're better than just being waiters. They'd die if they thought you thought they were here more than temporarily—before they become famous actors or writers or whatever glamorous god-damned thing it is they want to do. Do you believe there's a universal consciousness? You did use that expression didn't you?"

"Yes."

"That sounds like a friend of mine—Nancy English. Not a friend really, but I know her. Cleve English's wife—the TV guy. Do you know him?"

"Yes."

"She believes in that kind of crap. Oh, I'm sorry."

"It's all right. I don't believe in 'that crap' now. I used to, I guess, as a kid. I used to feel—I don't know—connected, I guess, you'd say, with—things—it. Not now. It's easier I suppose when you're young and sitting by the edge of a field that runs forever and seeing a tree like that."

"Are you religious, Harry?"

"Not really."

"You sound very religious."

"Sentimental is all, I'm afraid. Movie house emotions."

"You seem to know the Bible. Nebuchadnezzar's tree and dream and all."

"Not really. That stuck with me I guess because of my tree."

"What happened in old Nebby's dream?"

"He dreamed they cut the tree down."

"You know what Freud would say about that?"

"My Lord, I hadn't thought about it that way."

"Little old castration complex or cut your you-know-what off."

"You're right, of course. I just never…"

"What'd they say in the Bible?"

"Daniel interpreted the tree as Nebuchadnezzar's kingdom and that God ordered it cut off to show the king there was a higher power than himself and to humble him."

"That would do it."

Gardner laughed. "You're right."

The waiter brought the drinks, without comment.

"Thank you," Gardner said. He took a swallow from his drink. "You know, my tree isn't there anymore."

"Don't tell me. Inside, you mean?"

"Yes, that—and really too, I mean."

"What happened? Lightning?"

"No," Gardner said, "a thruway."

"Jesus," Janelle said. "And America settles in the mould of its vulgarity."

"What?"

"Just a piece of a poem."

"You know lots of poetry. I've noticed at your parties. You're always quoting."

Janelle took a sip of her drink. After a pause, she said: "Why don't you quit? Be a painter."

"I couldn't. I'd be too embarrassed."

"You mean it?"

"Yes."

"Why?"

"It's too remote a thing for me to do."

"You should. Jesus, anybody should do what he wants."

"Is what anybody <u>wants</u> always that clear?"

"I know what I want. That's all I care about."

"What's that?"

"Comfort. Fun. A good time. Feelings of pleasure."

"What's feelings of pleasure?"

"Poor boy. You never seem to have any, do you? I've noticed that. You're always so earnest. You have a nice—a very good, in fact—sense of humor, but you don't have any fun. You're very mid-western that way. You have no joy in you."

"We were discussing you. What's your big fun?"

"Travel. Clothes. Pretty, interesting, famous friends. Good food. Danger."

"Do you have friends?"

"Some. People I know, meet; acquire, I suppose is a more precise way of putting it."

"What else?"

"Wine, martinis, gambling, all Ritz Hotels, silk sheets, Courtier dresses, Ray Charles records—making love."

"Are you happy?"

"Next you'll ask me if I'm happily married. That's always the prelude, isn't it, to try to get me into bed."

"I hadn't even thought about that."

"Thanks. That's flattering."

"Well, yes, actually, I had thought about it, Janelle. I didn't mean—you're not attractive. You're very attractive. You know that. You don't need me to tell you."

"Oh, dear boy, I do."

"I just never—never considered—well—us."

"Why not?"

Gardner shrugged and looked down. He felt embarrassed and unworldly. He thought she was playing with him—turning him on. He took two quick swallows of his drink.

"Isn't Mr. Clean interested in sex?"

"Very."

"De Sade said 'you may have and I may have absolute rights over each other's bodies—temporarily, at least." Janelle finished off her drink. "What have you heard about me? May I have another, please?"

Gardner signaled the waiter, who was watching them. This bothered Gardner. Had he ever seen the waiter before, when he had been in here with Norma, he wondered. Worse still, did the waiter recognize him or know Norma?

"What have you heard?" Janelle said.

The waiter stood over them. Gardner looked down. "Two more," he said, "please." The waiter took Janelle's empty glass and Gardner quickly lifted his, which still contained some liquid, off the table to prevent the waiter from getting it. The waiter left. Gardner felt a loathing for him.

"About what?" Gardner said.

"You know. What's your impression of me or the rumors you've heard?"

"I don't pay attention to—"

"Then you have heard things."

"I didn't say that."

"Yes, you did. Oh, it doesn't matter. None of it matters. I know you've seen me with other men. I've run into you and Norma in restaurants."

"So?"

"Didn't you ever wonder? You must have. Or Norma?"

"Not really."

"I don't believe that."

"Can't your ego accept—no, it isn't true, you're right. We did wonder—and talk about you. Not to outsiders, I don't mean. Just to each other."

"You and Norma Goodwife discussing my sex life. Isn't that groovy?"

"Don't make Norma out a fool, Janelle. She's s—"

"Of course, you decided I was having affairs."

"It seemed logical to consider matters that way."

"Jesus, Sam. You sound like a lawyer—or the New York Times. I'd hate to gossip with you. Well, I was. Lots."

He said nothing, and tried to show no outside change. He determined that he would go easy on the next drink that was coming.

The waiter put the drinks down, harshly, and stared at the one, almost empty which Harry held in his hand. Gardner realized that the waiter was staring at the glass, and, abruptly, surrendered it. "Oh, here." The waiter took it, and smiling at him, contemptuously, Gardner thought, departed.

"Aren't you going to ask me about them?" Janelle said.

"I don't see that I—"

"That's not very gentlemanly. A girl is willing to give up her girlish secrets and the man doesn't even seem to want to hear them."

Gardner recalled that once he had seen Janelle with a famous black actor and he wondered if--.

"The Negro too," Janelle said. It shook Gardner that he must be so transparent or predictable that she could read his way of thinking. "Does that shock you? And all my trips to Europe too and Sun Valley and Jamaica—not black there, only the one black. Token, you might say."

"What do I say? Congratulations?"

"I expected something more creative."

"Okay, so you're the Joe Namath of nookey. I don't know."

"Creative, not crude."

"Janelle, what do you want? I shouldn't say anything and you shouldn't tell me anything—like you have—why tell me—why me?—and hell, we shouldn't even be here."

"Why not?"

"You know why—oh, hell, what's the difference." Gardner took a long swallow on the orange juice and vodka. He could begin to feel the drinks now. He felt looser, bolder, more certain that what he said would be what he felt, without its going through all the filters of worrying about its effect. "But I'm not your shrink, you know, and I don't want to be. And I don't want to go to bed with you." Gardner said.

"Don't you? Have you ever had an affair," Janelle said, "since you were married?"

"It's none of your affair—business—if I have or not."

"Have you?"

"I told you. You're got no right to—"

"Of course, you have, you must have—how long have you been married?"

"Twelve years. No, eleven. Twelve in August."

"Then, of course, you have."

"What, 'of course'? for Chr--. What gives you the—"

"Every man in this town like you has had at least some kind of affair—or new piece of ass—God, especially after 12 years."

"I hate to disappoint you."

"Not once?"

"No."

"Not even one time? A quickie? Not a hooker? Nothing?"

"No."

"A fag maybe?"

"Oh, hell, really, Janelle. The whole thing's just a big put on to you."

"That must be some kind of goddamned national record."

"My father's been married 30 years."

"So? You think he's never strayed?"

"I'm sure of it."

"How do you know?"

"He just wouldn't."

"Holy God."

"That seems unimaginable to you—square, I suppose?"

"Well, doesn't it to you?"

"Yes, a bit. It's just—I don't know. Maybe for my father it was fear of hell or lightning bolts or of what people would say if they found out. Maybe that's all that kept him faithful. I don't know, but I just know he was—he was in everything. If he believed in something, he lived it or if he made promises, they were kept."

"You sound like the <u>Saturday Evening Post</u>—in its heyday."

"And now it's dead."

"Small wonder—hearing you talk."

"Look—I love sex, Janelle, and before I married I had a lot of it with a lot of different girls and, by God, I'm no prude. All that was great and we all helped each other and gave a lot to each other. One thing in a small town—at least for me—there was plenty of sexual freedom. I never had the sexual inhibitions I read about in other WASP Americans. There were about thirteen of us. Five guys and eight girls—all very big in the school. Honor roll and awards and all that—and all of us—by graduation—had slept around with each other—all five boys with all eight girls. Nobody leered about it. We just did it. In cars and in fields and in the city park. In barns and on hay rides. It was all very natural. And beautiful. And we liked each other. And later too. College. The Army. When I first came to New York. I've always loved sex and girls and been respectful of both. But when I married Norma I just felt—loyal—loving, if you will—and that I'd ruin that somehow, if I made love to any other woman. God, so much else is crumbling in the world, that, I don't know, it just seemed that this was something I could control and maintain."

"What if things deserve to crumble?"

"I'm not sure yet."

"Wow, they really got their teeth into you, didn't they?"

"Who did?"

"People like yourself now. The 4th of July orators. 'The American Dream' hustlers."

"Don't you believe in it?"

"My God, you really do, don't you?"

"I don't know. How could we be so different? You're from Wisconsin."

"Poor Harry. You've got a lot of Candide in you. And at your age?"

"The best of all possible worlds, huh?" Gardner said.

"Why do you drink so much?" Janelle said.

Gardner had, at the moment she asked, been starting to take a drink from his vodka and orange juice.

"What?" Gardner said, and he put the drink down. "Who says I do? Oh, you mean today?"

"I mean everyday—the last year or so—from what I see and hear."

"What do you hear?"

"And the way you do it. The whole office talks about it. Did you know you were referred to lovingly as Dr. Jekyll and Mr. Hyde? Mister nice guy sober and a hostile, belligerent sonofabitch when you drink. Why? Do you know?"

"I don't. I guess—the more successful I get, the freer I feel about behaving the way I wanted to."

"Like that? That's your true nature?"

"I guess so."

"You get pretty hairy, Harry."

"So I'm told."

"Course Buzz doesn't mind. I think he enjoys it, in fact, cause you're usually on target and you say all the things he's thinking. And I love it."

"I feel bad about those who have to take it cause they work for me. I just can't seem to get through to them, nicely, during the day. Or not nicely really—honestly is what I mean."

"Well, who the hell can keep up with your ideas? It does them good to get chewed once in awhile. I've never heard you be wrong drunk. Rude yes, but not wrong. From what I hear there are a lot of places now where you don't get asked back."

"You're right."

"There are other ways, Harry."

"None works as well for me. I can't be direct. A, it's not my nature and B, it wasn't my upbringing and C, booze—if you get to work on time and do your job—is an accepted outlet for aggression in our society—at my level. People grant a lot of forgiveness with it. What the hell, he was just drunk and didn't know what he was saying. How many times have you heard that?"

"Plenty. I've been every player in the game."

"And there's something sporting and cavalier—masculine, about men who drink in our class. It's a virile kind of act men think. Of course, I go way beyond the code. I get savage. I do it with a vengeance. I don't know why, for sure, always."

"You know, I don't think success has gone to your head. You know what I think it is?"

Gardner shook his head no, and took another swallow from his drink. He felt Janelle's knee under the table touch his, and it did not pull away after the contact. He pressed back against her knee with his, ever so gently, but certainly.

"I think it's your homelife," Janelle said. "Sex."

Gardner took his knee away. Then, he thought, what the hell, and he put it back.

"On, no, Janelle," Gardner said. "You're way off there. My drinking's caused trouble at home, but it's not home that causes it."

"Are you so sure?"

"Positive."

"Don't tell me you really are big-headed about your job?"

"Of course not—not at all. Just the opposite, if anything."

"You've never gotten over being a Puritan, have you?" Janelle reached out and put her hand over Gardner's, which was resting on the table. She stroked the veins of it, tracing them from his wrist, along to the fist knuckles and then she took her forefinger and felt along each of the fingers of his hand and he could feel it and he liked the sensation and he watched her hand and the moving finger of it and he saw the hairs flair up on his hand each time her finger passed over. She did it over and over and over and did not stop even then.

"How do you feel?" she said. "I feel fabulous. My whole self feels fabulous. Warm and fabulous."

Gardner watched her mouth each time she said the word "fabulous." It arrested on the first consonant sound "F," as though she might say "fuck" or "fly" or "freedom" and her upper teeth would show slightly each time and get stuck in the soft flesh of her under lip and then the whole remainder of the word—"fabulous" would run out like a small, furry animal scurrying from it's hole.

"I feel like I'm swimming in very hot, soft water," Janelle said, "under a roof of sunlamps, and still all steamy."

"I feel high—very," Gardner said.

"Good." Janelle said.

"I'm not sure."

"You never are. You can't help speeding with the brakes on. Self-doubt in a kind of double-breasted hair shirt, taken in at the waist, to be sure."

"I wish I had your cool."

"I'll teach you. Hey, look, why don't you get the check and we'll go see your painting. How bout that?"

It suddenly occurred to Gardner why Janelle had chosen the Ginger Man. It was five doors from his studio room. Gardner admired her premeditation and decided he would take her up to show her his work. Take her, yes.

"I don't know," Gardner said. "What time is it?"

"Time to see your work of art, baby," Janelle said softly. "Feel yourself let go. See your hand relax? See how steady and loose it is?"

"Waiter," Gardner said. The waiter came and Gardner gave him ten dollars. The drinks came to six. The waiter made change at the table. Gardner left a dollar for the waiter, who said nothing, and Gardner and Janelle got up and walked out, on sea legs.

Outside, in 64th Street, the wind hit Gardner but this time it did not hurt him or make him feel smaller as it had before when they had come out of the office. Just the opposite. He felt younger and stronger and better because he had this natural force to resist. He took Janelle's arm and with resolution aimed her down the block towards his building. It entered his mind that he might be seen and seen especially holding her arm, but now it did not seem to matter so much as before and this, he knew, was the soothing song of the vodka which put his intestines to sleep and the more Prufrockian clerks of his brain, it roused in him instead the Hemingway guys and Errol Flynn flashes of buried image and stance. He strengthened his grip on her arm and he believed he could feel strength throughout his body, new and nice and necessary for his well-being. They reached the granite stoop of the building which contained his room and they mounted the stairs quickly.

"Hurry, I'm losing my steamy feeling." Janelle said.

Gardner jerked around in his pocket once or twice, got past his knife, and came up smoothly with the keys. His eyes were not focusing cleanly, he knew, but he was operating on the confidence of the booze and he hit the lock with the first thrust of the key and they got inside fast.

Gardner had forgotten how dark and badly in need of paint the building hallway was.

"It's not much of a building," he said.

"I love it. Look, marble floors and steps."

"Just up to the second landing," Gardner said. "Come on, it's a long climb." They made the five flights with surprising speed. Gardner did not even feel winded, which he always did otherwise.

"Here we are," Gardner said. Again, he was lucky with the key and thought of this as an omen that this adventure would go well and be worth it.

"So this is your little hideaway," Janelle said. "My God, what a delicious skylight. I didn't know they existed anymore. It's perfect. The whole place. It has just the perfect stench for a $200,000 a year starving artist."

"Yeah, it is absurd, I guess." Gardner said. He flopped himself down on the old modern couch he had brought here from his apartment.

"Not a bit. It's f---abulous. Show me the painting."

Gardner got up and went to the large easel angled across the way which held the covered canvas, facing the north light. He took the covering away and there was AMERICANS, THE BEAUTIFUL. He looked at it and suddenly hated it and rejected the whole notion of his painting seriously.

Janelle came closer, missing a step as she came, but recovering beautifully. Her tripping was like an Astaire step, Gardner thought. She looked at the painting for a long time and in a very serious way, though very naturally, in the manner of a person who is used to studying painting and cares about them. He stared down at her leg tendons.

Finally, she said, "It's good, Harry. It's really good, you Bastard. Rich. Alive. Very solid. Very, very good."

Gardner could feel something drop in him and gently break and coat him warmly—like the ball in Times Square at midnight filled with Pepto-Bismol or something, he thought; he felt fabulous himself now, he decided, and suddenly saw nothing but virtue in the painting—all the virtue which he had seen upon other occasions when he would look at it alone and critically.

"And it is funny—very scolding and ironic. You're damned good, old boy."

"Thanks, Janelle. Thank you. I'm really glad you like it."

"It's okay. But I'm sure painting gets to be as crappy as everything else after awhile, so don't quit your job just yet."

"I hadn't planned to."

Gardner looked at his painting carefully—examining each detail of the canvas and he was absorbing himself in it in the way that he could with his knife, so that he and it—the painting—were beginning to go away on a long journey of great psychic distance when he felt Janelle touch him and call him back.

She had reached over and taken his right hand with her left hand. Now she came around in front of him and, not loosening the hand she held, took his left hand in her right hand and she stood between him and the painting and she took a step towards him and she caught his eyes with her eyes and she would not let go and finally she touched her belly against his and he felt his cock swell in one gush of blood, as though his blood had been blasted from a seltzer bottle, and he felt it reach out for her and he felt her react to it, recoiling for just an instant and then even more forcefully coming back in towards it; her underbelly and his cock locked on each other. Pressing and pressing. Her mouth dropped open and it aimed up towards his face and, staring into it and seeing its redness and wetness and wanting, he could not help bending his own mouth to it and going into it, onto it, mounting and consuming the lips of it, until he had overcome these and was charging in on her teeth and tongue and pallet. His heart was thumping against his chest cavity, he could feel, and he could hear her groan and then, so did he, and their bodies ground against each other hard, and began to rock, just so, back and forth, and his hands, unlocking her hands, trap-closed around her back and waist, then slipped down her spine to buttocks, which were just a handful for each hand, he could feel, almost like a child's, small and firm, but pliant; and her tongue forced his tongue back and hers followed it, hungrily, into his mouth, and for a terrifying moment, he thought that he might come right there, right then.

CHAPTER 7

"Janelle, my God!" Gardner said, and he broke off the kiss and the embrace and he dropped his hands from her ass and he bolted to the couch, where he threw himself down and with his hands readjusted his cock which was clubbing its way against his shorts.

"Oh, Harry, come on," Janelle said.

"I—it's ridiculous," Gardner said.

"Why—why is it?"

"I don't—you know why."

"No, I don't. I want you and you want me. I felt you. You can't lie about that. I felt it."

"What's that? Of course, I want you. You're—Jesus, I'm half-gassed and you're beautiful and, hell, that's not the point."

"What is? What is? You knew we would when we came up here."

"I—don't know."

"Then lets have it. Something. I want you." Janelle twisted her face into a smile which did not show her teeth and she moved, slowly and certainly, walking towards Gardner. He watch her and felt that she was using all she had learned as a model about walking sensuously and gaining attention for herself. He was not at all sure he could resist her. He tried to hate her to himself and to find something negative about her, like thinking her walk was calculated and unnatural, but this did no good, as his body wasn't taking no for an answer.

"Come on, old sad face," Janelle said. She was standing over him now, thrusting her pelvis towards him, till it almost touched his face. He turned away and felt in his jacket for a cigarette.

"Janelle, cool it, will you?" Gardner said. He found his cigarettes in his upper handkerchief pocket. He pulled one out quickly and lit it. "Just cool it—for a minute. God. You want one?"

Janelle shook her head. She just stood there, looking at him. "I want to fuck you," she said.

Gardner had never heard any woman use that word for that act. He felt himself falling apart.

"Just—just like that?"

"What's wrong with it?"

"Well, nothing. Nothing. It's just so cold."

"Cold? Did I feel cold?"

"It's so sudden—and direct."

"And comfortable."

"You back to that?"

"I never leave it. Who says life is linear?" Janelle sat down beside Gardner and she pinched his cock, so that it hurt, just a little, though he jumped more in surprise than in pain.

"Hey."

"That hurt, didn't it?"

"What was that for?"

"Don't worry. I'm not sadistic. Just trying to help you understand my philosophy."

"Thanks a lot. Buy a pointer."

"Did it hurt?"

"Well, no—sure a little."

"And now, that I'm not pinching it, it doesn't hurt?"

Gardner shrugged.

"And how does it feel now?" Janelle said. She took his cock, through his pants, into her hand and began to rub it up and down.

"Janelle, uh--." He did not take her hand away.

She tucked her left leg under her right leg, which touched the floor and this pushed her left knee against his right leg which forced her legs to part slightly and Gardner saw the line of her inner thigh and he could feel her. She put her left arm along the back of the couch, so that part of it touched Gardner and, with the fingers of her left hand, she began playing with the hair at the back of his neck along his collar line. She turned her body so that she faced Gardner and she leaned in and began kissing him on the ear and along the side of his neck and now the control of his body was becoming untenable, he knew, and the good sensations which Janelle was causing surged up and down his body and they caused his face to contort, and his back to arch and loosen, arch and loosen, and he could feel his skin burn and tighten and he felt his cock go bursting into hard, harder, hardest. Once more, the pounding started in the back of his head and his eyes went half-shut and he turned his face to Janelle and found her mouth and kissed it and kissed it and kissed it, opening it, closing it, opening, closing, opening, closing with his lips and tongue and chin and never losing it and he turned his torso to her and their upper bodies met and he could feel her small, tight breasts flatten out on the crush of his chest and he felt her ass begin to stiffen and soften in a powerful, consistent rhythm and he felt his own body and ass take on her beat and he moved his right arm in at the small of her back between her and the couch and his left arm enfolded her from the front.

"Um, Harry, Harry," Janelle's tongue said against his own tongue and teeth in the joined cavity of their open mouths, and, suddenly, Gardner felt Janelle's hand reach over and clutch his zenith stick, squeezing and stroking the erection through the fabric of his trousers and, as she did it, from far away in the dungeon of his own throat came the constricted moans of a long term prisoner who sounded as though he believed that at last he might be being set free; and though the voice did not resemble his own as he was used to it, Gardner knew that it was his own, since he could feel the fists of it pounding against the bars of his larynx; and the voice groaned louder with each stroke Janelle made, as though they were footsteps of the turnkey coming along the cellblock corridor and the voice shouted down and out to unhearing the other voice which had been talking at the same time—the cool, cultured, measured tones of his brain—that judge who had sentenced him to imprisonment in the first place and who had denied to him ever since every subsequent appeal—and then another stroke and another—and the cell door was unlocked and the prisoner rushed out and stumbled till he reached the high bench of inhibition where he pulled down the judge of his conscience (Gardner knew he was both these men—prisoner and Chief Justice), dragging him from the bench to an open pit where he flung him in and began to thrown down on him soft, warm, fleshy-moist-and-thick soil that he gathered up in his bare, hungry hands, until the honored juror fell and was finally buried, "Die, you fucking righteous sonofabitch," Gardner heard himself silently scream and then, Gardner knew—now that the judge of himself inside himself, who was in the pit, could be seen and could resist no more, that Gardner-as-the-other-man, standing on the edge of the grave, exhaled the halitosis of fetid jailhouse air and, letting go, and breathing deeper than ever he had since incarceration, felt the painful sting of fresh, highly oxygenized air enter his raisined lungs and after the first shock, rejoiced and felt transcended and he submitted to the result of his action and certified the sanctity of his flesh, which the burial rite had consecrated and, at that moment, some ancient honorable freedom in him began to rouse from slumber and he could feel himself almost grown whole, except still not completely—though he knew now that that was coming too—when he had merged himself into this feminine part he pressed and moved and kissed against—not until he could close with that, go through into her, would he be at one for certain and united in his own body and touch and taste and odor and history. Then he would be meaningful, would be meaning, existence, present tense—alive, alive, alive! Exclamation point in extremis! In Excelsior extremis—penis! Bright, alive and shining!

Just then, the fingers of one of Janelle's hands pecked away at his fly, as though they had formed themselves into the beak of a foraging bird, and when they had undone the zipper and pulled out the throbbing worm of his cock, they changed themselves into the petals of a night-closing flower seen in a stop action film, and clutched him with a gentle crush.

"Um, Harry," Janelle said, pulling her mouth out of his mouth.

Gardner believed from what he now felt that he must be dying, since he was being pulled so far away from the things which made him recognize, in a usual way, his sense of being a living thing, but before he could perish, he realized what had happened, and he lifted his head and opened his eyes and looked down into his lap and saw all that he could see which was the top of Janelle's head, burrowing into his middle and, from beneath it, he could feel his penis being sucked and tussled in the mouth of Janelle and nipped at by her teeth. His left hand dropped down and clawed into her hair pulling it towards him until he could feel the skin of her scalp stretch and he heard the prisoner in him, in his escape to freedom, yelling "yes, yes, yes," and he knew the prisoner knew he would not be shot for killing the judge or for breaching the prison wall and thus would not enter the realm of death, but would instead stride full and sure from the false womb of those suffocating chambers out into the sunlit brightness of a second borning.

"Janelle, Janelle, oh, God, Janelle," Gardner called to her and to himself from across the wide plain of observing-perception as he watched his prisoner-self step back from the grave and stretch outfull from feet on floor to top of couch with shoulders, With his right hand, Gardner reached around Janelle and took her breast, like a softly-tossed ball caught into the web of a first baseman's mitt, and he kneaded its hardened, insolent nipple with his fingertips, The breast felt just like that of a good female swimmer he had known once in college, he remembered. The fingers of his left hand traced down along Janelle's face now until they reached her distended mouth and to where there he could feel the conjunction of her lips and his pulsing prong, which felt like some thermometer made of smooth, hot skin, which was reaching into the cave of her face to gauge her fever and he heard old lines boiling up from the back burners of his brain—"Keep it under your tongue, now. Don't talk. Mustn't talk till we get a reading. Is it under your tongue, child?" and then his whole body spasmed to the feeling of Janelle's tongue darting around the head of his dick like a mother bird feeding its young, and he knew the rising bird of himself would be an eagle soaring soon up and out of the nest of himself. With her feeding tongue inside and the motion of her lips chomping and chewing him outside, Gardner felt it was like being the victuals and the devourer at the same time. He concentrated now on being eaten and loved the meal she was making of him and he pretended he was a smaller animal being consumed by a larger one and he felt a new exhilaration at being food and wondered (believe actually) if it were just possible that the animal being eaten in nature could feel this joy of being a gift of nourishment to another living creature. Could the eaten be just as elated as the eater?

He was loving the ecstasy of this exercise and his thoughts on it but finally he needed something else. He needed to become the hunter stalking his own hunger's quarry which he knew lay trembling in the shadows of that dark hole just over the ridge of her belly, and so, he lifted Janelle's reluctant head off the head of his penis and he hurled himself onto the floor, sliding down off the couch like a body being buried at sea and where, here, his ocean was a paint-spattered tarpaulin, he bottomed out. He pulled her down on top of him.

Helping each other, they came out of their outer clothes as quickly as the caskets out of the flags of those same funeral-at-sea ceremonies.

Janelle was full on top of Gardner, clad only in flower-patterned silk panties and a bra of the same design. He was in his shorts and their two middles were milling away at each other like two grain stones. Janelle lifted her upper body and stared at Gardner, her power strong, but her eyes beginning to unfocus, like a fighter's who's just taken a good first punch and is trying to shake it off. She bobbed her head back and forth and up and down and examined Gardner's body—all of it she could take in—and she said, in a voice cooler than Gardner would have thought possible, "You're beautiful."

"You're really beautiful," Janelle said. "I thought you would be, but you're even more so. You're really, really fucking beautiful. Look at your arms, And the hair on you. It's all in just the right places. You're perfect."

Janelle slid down his body, snaking him as she went, and making him know from the pressure of her body that she wanted him to stay flat. She took his shorts off as her hands passed them and as she kissed him all along, and she and the shorts continued down the length of him until they were off.

"I'm glad they're boxers," Janelle said, "I hate jockies. I was so afraid you might wear jockies when we were in the office and Ginger Man."

Gardner felt Janelle's hair and head at his feet and felt her mouth nipping at them and at his toes, then at his ankle bones and then back to his feet and toes, toes and arches and feet and he remembered her arches and she was then up—at the muscles of his calves, with her mouth mobilizing every cell in his nerve ends, then south again, while her hands reached north and grabbed the pole. His body was rolling and turning and twisting in many directions at once. Muscles kept moving into each other, against each other. Tensing—then loose—tensing, loose—tensing, loose, tensing, loose, tensing, loose. Moving. Burning. Twitching. Hot. Ripple cold. Hot. Cold. Chill. Surge. Recession. Breath, breath, breath.

Gardner felt himself about to explode in coming and he cursed that he could not hold it longer, but Janelle sensed it, he felt, and he felt her dig her fingernail into the swollen duct of the underside of his swollen penis and he felt the sperm stop and subside and at the same time he felt his entire body wrench just as though he had come, and he groaned and spasmed in his breath and limbs and felt everything in him letting go, except the juice of himself, a phenomenon which stunned him, but he could feel in the same instant that he felt the explosion, that he was still on-going and erect and not spent, but wanting more.

Janelle was working him over like a carion bird until Gardner reached down and taking her under the arms pulled her up towards his head and he heard himself saying from far away, "What are you doing to me? What are you doing? It's fantastic. Fantastic."

Janelle halted herself at Gardner's penis and sucked it in full. At this, he dropped his head against the floor, bang, then made it hit against it bang, bang, bang, while her mouth moved up and down on him, furiously, but not paining.

Janelle said, "Don't think of things a thousand miles off."

"Don't talk with your mouth full," Gardner said.

"Don't be vulgar," Janelle said.

"I was always taught that,"

"New manners here. And don't think about the army or a baseball game. Don't be a martyr. Think your cock. Think right in it. Yes. I'll hold your come back. Yang and Yin."

How did she know guys thought of other things, non-sexual, during sex, so they wouldn't come so fast? He had been thinking not about the Army or baseball and Woody Allen but about an account at the office, in order to slow his excitement, but at her command, his brain drained into his hard-on and that was all he thought and all he felt.

"Don't be a martyr," Janelle said again. "Feel it. Feel it."

Now Janelle let go of him with her mouth and moved north and with her hand guided his cock into the hot, wet center of her womanhood. Gardner shuddered, but felt her groan aloud and he knew he had her pleased and he felt glad and he began to move his ass so as to move this mount who rode him well and regally and he pretended he was a great stallion about to take his mistress over the jumps. Janelle clung to the saddle of him as though they were one and she worked her ass in time with his, forward and backward and, at the same time, pushed down on his groin so that his horn hit to the hilt of her vagina. "U'mmm," she yelled.

Through it all, Janelle kept a hand reached behind her buttocks and onto Gardner's penis, down low near the testicles, working him like a riding crop. She was working everything, fantastically, and in a little while, Gardner felt her come and he was glad and he was glad she had fucked him this way first, her-on-top, because he could sustain himself better in that position, although he knew now that she had brought him new staying power with her new trick, or old trick new to him.

Janelle came lots—fully. She came as emphatically as he did, usually, Gardner thought, and he heard her good screaming and he was pleased, but he was very surprised. He had figured her for a colder one. Now he knew he had not experienced any such demonstrative release in any woman except Norma, whose comes were colossal and freer even than these of Janelle's now. Oh, Norma, God! I love you, Gardner said to himself. I do. But I'm liking this. Really liking it, Norma. What can I do? What am I?

"U'mmm," Janelle said, aloud. "You're so beautiful."

Gardner started to move her some more, but she fell over on top of him with her upper body against his, though without losing him out of herself and she stopped him.

"Please, Sam, Honey, give me a minute. I really came. Give me just a minute. U'mmm, that's so beautiful. You have a beautiful, big penis."

"It's not so big. I think."

"It's perfect. It's big and just right on your body. U'mmm. I can feel it."

"You're fantastic. What did you do to me before?"

"Did you like it?"

"You know I did. I was going crazy. I am."

"You came without coming. Yang and Yin."

"What?"

"Yang and Yin. Equal forces. That's what we can be."

"I know Yang and Yin, but—"

"Buddha. It works in sex."

"I know from Buddhism. But I never thought about it here."

"Why not? Why should one partner dominate here anymore than anywhere else in nature? We can be equal. We'll get very good at it. I squeezed off the duct of you, so the come couldn't come. Still, you felt the sensation. It's Oriental, of course. So the man can keep enjoying himself without distraction—or exhaustion."

"Not so inscrutable after all, these Orientals."

"I wouldn't know. I never actually scruted one."

"You didn't learn that in a Charlie Chan movie."

"I don't mean to embarrass you."

"You're not. If this is Women's Lib equality—count me in."

Janelle kissed Gardner and began rooting her pelvis against him again.

"Umph," Gardner said, "fantastic," as he began to move again also.

Once more, Janelle—the rider—took him—stallion—over the jumps and around the whole course and together they were winning the race—all the races—until finally she jumped him completely over the railing of the track and she galloped him off across country, over cut meadows and fences, through talking creeks and up and down hillocks and through woods where the branches stung and lashed across his face, but still he carried the lady powerfully and without pause. He felt the forefingers of her two hands push hard into his mouth and he considered them to be the shafts of a bit and this drove him on even more furiously. But, still, here, the horse was as much the master as the mounted one and his ears brought to him the sweet agony of his rider's throaty noises, her voice was charging through all the octaves—like a power saw whining its ways through thick trunks of trees—screaming out its heat and friction.

Then the voice formed words, "Oh, God, now," she cried. "Now, now,

now." And he knew she was coming again and—now, now, now, now! She dropped onto him and squeezed him to her full and he felt the spurs of her nails driving into the flesh of his back.

"You're beautiful. Beautiful, Oh, God, such beaut—beauty. Beauty." She said.

"Oh, take it, take. Take it!"

"Oh, you make me come so."

And, in that moment of her crying, trembling convulsion, the great horse of himself foamed saliva at the mouth and he reared up, unable to take the next jump and with a great pain ripping through his testicles as though they had not cleared the last barbed wire, he could hear himself shouting and he could feel the liquid flame of his semen burst up and out of his penis, a throbbing bundle of flesh and blood-choked veins and it charged into her like a pack of hot hound dogs in pursuit of a wet fox scurrying up into the darkness of her cunt. Twitch, scream, twitch. Twitch, scream, twitch. Every muscle in him spasmed. His intestines coiled in electric shock. She was the same, he could feel it. The jerk and cry, jerk and cry consumed them both. Jerk and cry. Jerk and cry. Jerk and cry. Then—she fell over on him, as though dead.

"Hold me, hold me," she whimpered, but otherwise she did not move. He held her, as he was able. He embraced her, though his arms were weak as willows and the two of them, she, Janelle, he, Harry, were being carried along without power to resist, like two fallen leaves wetted together on the determined current of a clean, clear stream of human liquid, and he held her and drifted and never feared drowning, so thick and buoyant was the stream of their juices. They went a long way like that. A long way. Searching for the sea.

"Jesus, Harry—Sam" Janelle said, at last. "I never guessed you'd be so—so goddamned good. You seem so restrained most of the time. You're really good. Jesus. Great."

"And you're fantastic."

"Did you think I would be?"

"I don't know. I never thought about you."

"I don't believe it. You mean you never once wondered about me in bed?"

"No, I have. I did."

"What'd you think?"

"I thought you'd be cold. And full of wise-cracks. I figured you put men down."

"And now?"

"Yang and Yin?"

"Yeah, yang and bang, thank you , M'am."

"Are you—all right?"

"Holy God, yes. I'm so spent, I may have used up a year's supply."

"Oh, no. You'll see. You do come a lot though. I can feel it. But you'll come again."

"How are you?"

"Unbelievable. I've come six or eight times. That's incredible; the first time especially. The first time is usually so awkward and boring and unsatisfying."

"I know. I always used to dread it. I used to come in a second and spent the next half hour apologizing."

"You needn't apologize today. You were beautiful. Absolutely fucking beautiful."

"Thanks to the wisdom of the East."

"Are you sad—I know so much?"

"Lord, no. Why should I be? Look how good I feel."

"Sometimes—men—resent too much knowledge."

"You are showy—formidable."

"Does it bother you? You can teach me things."

"No. Anyway it doesn't bother me now—that you know so much. I'm glad you were so bold. This is the first time I've—I've strayed since my marriage and--'strayed'. Goddamn all those words sound so silly and old-fashioned. 'Strayed', 'cheated', 'been unfaithful'. They're ridiculous. I always feel like George Brent saying them. I always feel like those kind of movie people. George Brent or Robert Young. Never Bogart or Gable or any of the new anti-stars. They wouldn't say those words. Jesus, I really am so square."

"Was this the first time?"

"Yes, in eleven years—twelve in August."

"Hadn't you wanted to?"

"Oh, yes."

"Why didn't you?"

"It didn't seem—I don't know."

"How do you feel—now?"

"Fine. Fantastic. As though I had put down a huge weight and had drunk till my belly hurt, from a cold stream along the road. And now, I'm lying in cool grass, looking up, but with my eyes closed, and I'm feeling the sun warm on my face. I feel very relieved and happy. Yes, really happy."

"Oh, good, good, I'm so glad. I want you to. I want you to enjoy me. I loved loving you. Really—for yourself. It's such a good feeling."

"You sound surprised."

"Yes. I am."

"Why? What'd you expect?"

"I expected. You won't be angry?"

"No. I don't think that's possible in my condition."

"I expected to exalt over you. Over seducing you. I figured it was your first time, that you hadn't had anyone but Norma since your marriage. I wanted to break that. I hated the perfection of that. You two always seem so damned perfect. While the rest of the world was moldering and decaying and going its rotten way to cataclysm, you two went right along making everything seem just the way it was in the rule books. I hated you for it and wanted to destroy it."

"Why?"

"Why should you be the only two to have it? But I didn't count on the way I feel now. I thought I'd have you and you'd pant and groan and get your gun off and I wouldn't even be moved. You'd be just something to ball and conquer and bring down to the level of the rest of us humans. Then I could relax about you."

"And what do you feel now, instead?"

"Sated, loved, filled—vulnerable. Conquered myself. Feminine in a way I'd almost forgotten about. Harry—Sam, please don't be angry at me. Or feel remorseful or guilty. I love what we've had. It really means something to me."

"I'm glad for it to, Janelle. I'm not sorry at all. Not now anyway."

"Do you like me?"

"I told you—you're fantastic."

"I mean. The way I look. My breasts aren't very big."

"They're very pretty. Very defined. Sculpted."

"I wish they were bigger."

"It doesn't matter. They're good. The nipples too."

"Do you like my body?"

"Yes. It's very—feelable. Lean and feelable. I can feel it against me everywhere. You have a good little ass."

"I'm too skinny."

"No, you're good. I can feel your body."

"How can you like Norma's body and mine? I'm much thinner."

"It's possible to like both."

"That's a wrong answer. I want you to like mine only—or best."

"Both are likeable."

"Is she a good lay?"

"Not a good question, Janelle."

"Why? Is she? I'll bet she isn't?"

"She is—very."

"Shut up. I don't want to hear it."

"Then why'd you ask?"

"I thought—she wouldn't be. I thought you'd say that. I still think that. You're just protecting her and yourself."

"That's what you want. I told you the truth."

"Screw the truth, you bastard. There is no fucking truth."

"Are you going to turn sour?"

"I can."

"I know. I wish you wouldn't."

"What do you care—one way or the other—about me?"

"Why do you want to destroy the good things you just came through feeling?"

"That always feels good."

"Always as good as today?"

"You want a horseshoe of roses, stud? I think you think Norma is suffocating you. That's why you're unhappy—drink. You just hate to fucking admit you're not perfect. That your marriage is a grip around your throat. That you're not all those fucking virtuous people in those families in those Maytag ads."

"Drop it, Janelle. Don't psychoanalyze me. You're wrong anyway."

"Am I? I don't think so."

"It doesn't matter, really, what you think."

"Probably not. That's true. There you told the truth. You don't give a damn about me, so why would you give a damn about what I think or why tell me the truth."

"Does it matter whether I like you? I do care about you."

"Will you please stop talking that legalese shit. Talk straight. Yes or no."

"I loved this today. I've very excited by you. I'm also torn-up as hell about it. It's going to take some getting used to."

"Why? You'll never see me again after today. I'll bet on that. I know you. You'll be so fucking guilty about it. You'll be doing penance the rest of your life."

"I'm not so sure. I'm not a priest, for God's sake. No, I don't think I will feel so guilty. I've been waiting for signs of that. But they're not there."

"Listen to you—they'll come. There's an incubation period and you're half-stoned. Wait'll you sober up. Too bad. You're a good lay. But—well, I'll just have to find somebody else—not so fucked up."

"Janelle, do you have to talk that way? Can't we be decent to each other?"

"Will you be—to me—tomorrow?"

"I'd like to be. Then and now. I feel decent towards you. It you'll let me."

"This sure as hell isn't the first time you've fucked around since your wedding. I know that."

"You don't know that. And if you did know anything about me, you'd know it was the first time. The first time in real life. I've fucked myself crazy in fantasy. God knows. Constantly. Agonizingly. Every woman I know."

"Me?"

Why, yes, of course, he had, Gardner realized for the first time. Yes, he had fantasized fucking Janelle. Not really often, though, he recalled quickly. She had not been a big favorite. Not even Top 40.

"Yes."

"Really?"

"Yes."

"How was I?"

"Okay," Gardner lied, since he could not really remember, "but not as good as today."

"I hope not. Jesus, that makes me feel better again. You really pretended to have me, huh?"

"Yes. More than once."

"But you really never had anyone else—really—besides Norma all these years?"

Gardner shook his head no.

Janelle sipped at her drink. "You don't have to pretend with me. I don't judge."

"I'm not pretending."

"Good. That's something. Okay. Give me a cigarette."

Gardner looked around. He saw the pack on the couch. He reached up and took it and shook out two cigarettes. He gave one to Janelle and he lit them both.

"What about you? Do you keep a scorecard on your activities?"

"Yes, I do—mental. But I'm not telling you. I don't have to tell you anything."

"No, you don't. I don't want to know even."

"They why'd you ask?"

"I don't know. To get the subject off me."

"Does it disgust you—that I told you I slept with so many?"

"That you did, or that you told me you did?"

"Don't joke now. Do you feel degraded sticking it in where so many others have. I'm serious. Do you?"

"Do you?"

"I'm no whore."

"Thou sayest."

"What's that mean?"

"That's what our Lord said when they asked him if he were King of the Jews."

"What the hell's that got to do with anything?"

"You are what you tell me you are, I believe."

"I'm not a whore, goddamned you!"

"I said fine, I believe as you believe."

"What the hell are you—some kind of watered-down closet faggot, that you never had one outside screw in twelve years?"

"You're out of line, Janelle. Stop it."

"I want a drink." Gardner did not move but looked, as steadily as he was able, right at Janelle. "Oh, piss off," she said, and she pulled herself up. "Over there," Gardner said, and he indicated with his head, a white enamel metal wardrobe that stood against the far wall. She walked to it.

Gardner studied her as she went. He liked her stretched-out body and the compact curve of her ass like fruit, fresh and full on the limbs of her long legs. Opening the door of it, she reached up to the top shelf and pulled down a bottle of Johnny Walker Black Label Scotch.

"I don't have any glasses," Gardner said. "You'll have to use paper cups."

"Any ice?"

"No, it'll have to be neat."

"Neat is better than nothing."

Janelle took down the paper cups from the shelf and poured out a good measure of the Scotch into a cup for herself and into a second for him. As Janelle returned, he concentrated on the ringlet curls of her blonde pubic hairs. He thought about them as the stuff they wrap fragile Christmas presents in to keep them from breaking. Excelsior!

"Here." Janelle said, handing him one of the paper cups. "Does it bother you? Please tell me. The other men? So many?"

"Have there been so many?"

"Yes."

"It may. Not now though. I think it freed me even—when we started just now. It made it easier, you know, for me. I didn't have to feel---"

"Responsible?"

"Yes, that's right."

"It's not always good or pleasant you know. I mean it hasn't always been so great. I don't like it always. Sometimes I loathe it. Not like today— hardly ever. It's—today was special. When I feel like this—when it's special when I make love, I'm absolutely absorbed by it—consumed, Harry, and made innocent again. Unconscious—or in a state of Grace of some kind. Better than any trip on Mary Jane or LSD. I've tried those. They're shit. With this, with you, I forget Buzz and Viet Nam and all the rest of our screwed up human doings. They just simply, literally do not exist anymore. There's just left the one good feeling and a feeling of life, of being alive. Most lovers are such grubbers. Pawing and slobbering and impatient. Like people eating at a World's Fair. Stupid and brutish. You've been good and gracious and gentle and exciting. Will you learn to make me innocent? To sanctify me? I need it, Sam."

Before Gardner could answer, Janelle took a swallow from her drink and then spoke again.

"Do you remember your first? I always like to ask people about their first time," Janelle said.

"I remember."

"How was it?"

"I remember the first few. In fact, I guess I remember fairly vivid details about each time."

"How was the first one?"

"Stuttering, clumsy. Depraved too. Pretty awful scene, though I didn't think of it that way at the time. I knew it seemed a bit strange and unusual and I was very compelled by it, but I wasn't scared or put off or anything.

It seemed very natural. And, God, I guess it was the first and last orgy I ever took part in."

"How old were you?"

"31."

Janelle laughed. "Be serious. I really want to hear."

"Twelve."

"Ummm, a good early bird start."

"There's not much else to do in Indiana."

"Tell me."

"The thing I remember most vividly is a new necktie I had. My first tie really. In fact, it wasn't even really for me, originally. My Dad got it for his birthday and—I don't know—I guess he didn't like it. That was it probably. Anyway, I said I did, and I did, and he gave it to me after I begged him for it, and he and mother had a big fight about it and she screamed I was too young to wear ties yet, and I was still just a baby, and he said there were no babies 12 years old, and that I wanted it so, and she shouldn't mother me so and finally he won, and for the first time in my life I buttoned the top button on my dress white shirt and I put the tie on. Dad showed me how to tie it so I could do it myself. And. My God! It was bright red—a wool one."

"That's what you remember about your first lay? Jesus, you really are a WASP."

Gardner smiled and nodded. "I remember cause I didn't take the tie off or my shirt. Just my pants and underpants."

"You didn't do it with your shoes on, yelling, today I am a man—with your voice cracking."

"No, I took off my shoes—and my socks."

"Sensualist."

"A craven satyr."

"Well, tell me about it. I don't want to go out whistling the wardrobe. What about the performances? What was depraved? You said there was something depraved about it?"

"It was a family next door at the lake. At Indiana Beach—it's called now. On Lake Shaffer. There were four or five kids in the family. Four, I remember for sure. They were there one summer renting the cottage next door. We owned our cottage and we went there every summer, but they rented the one next door and these rental kids and I played together all summer. There was a girl—oh, fourteen, I guess, and a boy about fifteen maybe and another sister about my age—little younger really. I was twelve that summer. It was late in the summer, the week before going home I think, just before Labor Day."

"Had you passed puberty?"

"No, just GO and collect $200."

"No, really, had you?"

"Like a crocus—I had constant erections. And that's why the tie becomes important."

"Those were the Days, My friend," Janelle sang.

"Yeah—you're right. Anyway, there was a younger brother, ten or so, and always talked dirty—a whole string of dirty words, like he'd say shit, piss, fuckbastardsonofabitchasshole. Like that, I remember, fast, all run together. And he'd just say it over and over every time he was angry and then the others—his brother and sisters—would laugh at him and that'd make him angrier and he'd swear even faster and louder and longer. And he had great energy I remember. Never sat still a minute. And this one day I went over there to play, like usual, and it was all quiet when I went through the screen door and nobody was downstairs at all and I saw their car was gone and I was disappointed because I wanted to show them my new tie. I was just wearing it right then for the first time and I didn't think anybody was home to show it to and I was leaving when I heard the little brother swearing upstairs. And I called up then and they asked if it was me and I said yes and they said come up and I did and they were all there— naked—completely—and the sight of them really stopped me. That was the first time I'd ever seen anyone naked but myself—well, guys in gym class and at the swimming pool bathhouse but, and never a girl—and here were two girls naked and the big sister had hair where her legs joined and that I never imagined ever, and I didn't even have that myself. And she had breasts. And they said hello just as though they would say it anytime and the little brother kept on swearing and finally I could act natural too, at least pretend to, though I couldn't keep my eyes off the older sister's breasts and crotch and the younger sister said when I asked why was the little one swearing she said because he had such a little ding-dong and he couldn't put it in anything and everybody laughed and I laughed too—though I didn't quite get what I was laughing about—and the little one went off cussing even stronger."

"Come on, sissy, screw him," the older sister said, indicating me. "Let me do it to you first," the older brother said, and his little sister threw herself down on a mattress there that was on the floor and the brother's thing was sticking out hard and I felt mine getting hard too, watching them. He said, 'have you ever fucked anyone, Harry?' to me and I said, 'Sure, what do you think?' and they all laughed and I couldn't tell if they were laughing because they believed me and enjoyed that or because they thought I was lying and bluffing. I didn't even know what "fuck" meant. I'd never even heard the word. 'I'll bet he can do it just good,' the older sister said and, God, I'll never forget the way she looked at me. I was scared to death, but all worked up, excited at the same time. 'Not as good as me,' said the older brother and then he got down on top of the little girl and he started to put his thing in between her legs. I thought I was going to faint, looking. I thought even, I shouldn't look or wouldn't, but I couldn't take my eyes off of them.

"'Don't jam it in, you jerk,' the little sister said. 'Easy, darn it, it hurts.' 'Aw, shut up,' the brother said, 'if you weren't such a little green cherry cunt it wouldn't hurt. I'll get you stretched out, but good.' 'Ouch,' she said, 'ouch.'

"Then the big sister said, 'you do it to me, Bowe, and let Harry stick it in Inez. He won't hurt her I bet. He's so nice.' I was petrified. I didn't know what to do.

"'Okay,' Bowe said, and he jumped off his little sister and onto his big one, who had lay down on the mattress too, right next to the little sister. Big sister spread her legs and her brother's thing disappeared into her middle and she said,'umm'mm, that feels mighty good, Bowe,' and Bowe moved up and down on her four or five times and then he stopped and looked up at me. All three of them did. They were all looking at me. The big brother and the two sisters—the little brother too, probably, though I don't remember that for sure. He had stopped cussing—I know—I do remember that. 'Close your mouth, boy, less you're catchin' flies,' Bowe said to me, and they all laughed again, not meanly though, really, just—good-natured, naturally, free and for fun. I had the feeling they all liked me, really. I closed my mouth.

"'Well, come on, Harry,' the big sister said, 'put it in her. Put your whatchamacallit in her thingamajig.'

"'Punch her in Poontang,' Bowe said.

"'He don't know how, I betcha,' the little sister said and she just stared at me—she was defying me now—and she spread her little legs wide and put her hand on her vagina and a finger in it and she began stroking herself and going in and out of herself. 'He ain't never fucked anyone.'

"'How would you know,' big sister said. 'And don't say ain't. It ain't polite.'

"'I know. He's a goddamn cherry. Harry is a cherry. Harry is a cherry. Harry is a cherry.'

"'Are you virgin, Harry?' Bowe said. They all laughed again.

"'Like hell I am,' I said—and was dying cause I didn't know what Virgin meant. What could it mean?

"'Round yon Virgin, mother and child,'

"'Virgin territory,'

"'The Virgin Queen' – flashed through my mind at that moment. Never used. Not even once—I figured it meant that. Something like that. I didn't have much frame of reference in those days.

"So I started ripping off my shoes and socks and pants and underpants--'I've done it lots'--'more than any of you'--'you'll see who's who'--and there I was suddenly—with a maximum erection-- for me—naked on down from the waist. And the older sister I heard saying, 'Hey, Harry's got a cute little dong,' and she reached up towards it though she couldn't quite touch it and I didn't move. I was frozen.

"'Come on, Harry,' Bowe said, 'Let's see you fuck Inez.' 'Show him how,' Inez said, 'he don't know,' and Bowe rolled off his big sister and onto his little sister and he pumped his penis back into Inez—as much as he could. 'Ouch, you shit jerk. Get off! Come on, Harry, you do it. Fuck me,' Inez said. 'It's easy as pie. Nuthin' to it,' and I was onto her like a trap shutting, pushing Bowe off, and I felt her fingers guide me into her inside and I just pushed once and was in and I felt myself coming, though then I hardly knew what it was that was happening or what it meant and I didn't know the word <u>coming</u> at all. I just knew the feeling seemed the most profound, terrifying thing I'd ever had happen to me, and I thought I'd done something to myself—hurt myself, you know. I thought I was gushing blood and I pulled myself out of her and then I saw the stuff spurting out of me and I heard my voice crying out like in pain and I saw the stuff spasming out and all over everywhere and shooting mostly onto my new red necktie. I rolled off Inez and fell face-down and flat into the mattress and writhed and almost cried and I heard the little sister saying, 'Shit, that was sure fast. What kind of lightning fucking is that?'

"'That <u>is</u> his first time, I betcha,' I heard the older sister say, 'that's all. It is your first time, hunh, honey? Hunh, Harry?' She reached over and ran her hand through my hair and her voice sounded soft as rain on tree leaves and I—I loved her. I just loved her—and--after a moment—or several—I don't know really. Anyway, finally, with her still rubbing my hair, I did turn over and face her and she smiled at me and I smiled back and I felt a little more settled and not so torn-up and she said, 'first time, aren't I right?', and I nodded <u>yes</u>, and she said, 'You'll be okay. Now do me.' And my penis went hard again instantly, like one of those toys you can make limp or erect by pulling the string inside the little wooden pieces. She pulled my string good.

"It was very nice with her, I think I remember. While I was doing it inside her I remember looking around and seeing the little sister masturbating her brother Bowe and he had his finger in her and the little brother was fondling his own soft goods and she—the sister I was doing—put my hands on her breasts and then warned me to pull out when I felt myself coming or she might just have a baby from me—and I didn't even know what <u>coming</u> meant, I mean that, but I could tell from her tone and from what I'd just experienced before—what the feeling was she meant and—Holy God—do you know what I just now realized—that that was the first time I ever heard that babies came from—from <u>that</u>! God, I actually didn't realize that till just now, telling you. Jesus. Anyway, I pulled out and again the stuff got all over my shirt and tie.

"'I got stuff all over my neck-tie,' I said. 'It's new. It's a new tie.' They all laughed.

"'You shoulda got naked,' Bowe said.

"'Don't worry,' said the older sister, 'It'll dry—and then it'll look just like ice cream stains or something. Just say you spilled ice cream on yourself if anyone's to notice. Hey, that's a good idea. Let's walk down to the dairy and get some.'

"We went to the dairy which was about a half-mile down the road which ran along behind our two cottages. All of them had banana splits. I had a hot fudge sundae with nuts on it and I did, actually, spill a little ice cream and fudge sauce on my tie.

"Still, I was scared out of my head that Dad or Mother would see the stains. I didn't want that—even if I didn't know quite why. I wasn't even sure then whether what we had done was bad or what it was, but, I guess I knew somehow that something about it my folks wouldn't like—and even if it wasn't bad, I still had gotten stains on my new tie and I knew that that wasn't nice or good and I knew Dad would be disappointed in me for it. God, I was trembling. I didn't know what to do.

"'Will water get the stains out?' I asked.

"'Sure,' they all said, and laughed. 'Be gone in a jiffy.'

"When we got back to their cottage, they went in. We didn't kiss or shake hands or anything—just kind of said 'see ya' and they were gone through the screen door. I watched till I couldn't see them anymore and then I walked as casually as I could—I was dying inside—down to the end of their pier and, trying to make it look like an accident, I jumped into the water and scrubbed the daylights out of my red tie. I knew I'd catch it when I got to our cottage, but for falling into the lake, I didn't mind. I'd caught it for that plenty of times and this time I knew instinctively it would be a punishment for a lesser offense. I did catch hell, sure enough, but it didn't matter. I felt good—and I knew I'd gotten away with something that was something I wanted to go back for again and again. I didn't do it anymore though in the few days left because their parents were always home and then it was Labor Day and everybody left and we didn't even say anything about the time we did do it. And then—that was all. I never saw any of them again."

"Never?" Janelle said. Gardner shook his head no.

"What was her name—the older one—do you remember?"

"Snow White White."

"Good God."

CHAPTER 8

"I know," Gardner said. "Still, she was my---"

"<u>Snow White</u>? *Was she* the fairest of them all?"

"Pretty enough, as Mrs. Webb says in 'Our Town.'"

"Good God, Sam. You are square squared."

"My folks to this day have never mentioned sex—except my mother always used to say, 'Be a good boy;' and my Dad would say, 'Harry knows. Boys just know. Harry can be counted on to do the right thing.'"

"If today's any indication, Father was right."

Gardner held up his paper cup in a toast and wondered privately what had happened to Snow. To whom he was grateful. "To Snow—who taught me to screw."

"You ought to put it on your gravestone."

"No, I've got something else for that."

"What?"

"Oh, I can't tell. It's a secret. I don't want anyone to steal my epitaph."

"Stop that dancing up there is going to be mine," Janelle said. She toasted also. "To Snow White White—who knew how to thaw." They both laughed and sipped at their drinks and thought within themselves.

"What about you? Who was your Snow White?" Gardner asked.

"Wouldn't it be funny if I said it was Snow White for me too?"

"I don't think she did it with her sister—not that day anyway."

"Oh, no, I'm sure that came much later—when she was a ripe old fifteen."

"Yeah. What about you?"

"Nanook of the North."

"No, come on."

"Mine was nicely depraved also. How do you stand on incest, Harry?

107

You can't really disapprove after your friends at the lake. Don't look so shocked. It wasn't always taboo, you know. The Homeric Greeks didn't seem to mind it. Or the Inca kings. They had to marry their sisters—that was the law. And the Pharoahs traditionally had to marry incestuously. It's only later we got hung-up about it. Though, old Snow seemed pretty cool on the subject."

"What about Oedipus? He suffered plenty."

"That was later. Sophocles was 700 years after Homer."

"Time really goes fast when you're having fun."

"Henry VIII also hung that rap on Ann Boleyn—along with the rest. Said she did it with her brother."

"Tails he wins, head she loses."

"That's the worst joke I ever heard."

"I'm sorry. I didn't mean any—you know—"

"Oh, I don't mean because I'm sensitive or identify or anything like that. It's just a lousy joke."

"I've got worse."

"So have I—true life."

"You don't have to tell me."

"You don't have to listen."

"I want you to—tell me."

"It's your old father-daughter-step-mother bit. I wonder if Freud had any idea how little he'd make us feel by categorizing us so? Making us all seem so small and repetitious. Anyway, my own mother died when I was very young—about eighteen months or something like that. Very bad scene. I never get it out of my thoughts. Course, I don't have a first -hand memory of it. Were you in the war--?"

"I was in the Army. But I didn't see any action. I was in the PIO in Washington—designing posters."

"Loose lips sink ships?"

"Like that—yes. Why?"

"I don't know. Just curious. I envy men who've been to war. Anyway, I've seen it all a million times—the thing with my mother. She was driving a group of women home from a church affair—that's what ruined it forever between me and God. It was raining and where the street T-intersected with the lake—there are three lakes in Madison—where we usually make the turn, she drove straight on—into a wooden barricade and through it into the water. Three of the good church-going women of God met their Maker sooner than they figured—my Mother among them. One lady got out. She was a young teacher in the high school—English--very big on literature—and she taught swimming in the summer-time for the city park department. She survived. She tried to rescue my mother, she always claimed. That was the family mythology. My father used to say so too—when he talked about it at all. And it was said my mother refused to leave the other ladies. Imagine that? I don't know. Oh, Christ, I supposed Florence did try to save Mother really. It's just so hard to—and the part about Mother staying. I've never understood that. I just never could believe any of it. In fact, I always imagined Florence holding Mother under, making sure she drowned good and proper. It was natural for a child to think that, considering the way things turned out. Less that a year after the accident, Florence married my father, and, in another year after that, they had a baby—a boy. That completes the cast list.

"My father was a very stern, pious, Bible-Belt, Calvinistic kind of man. His father had invented a fountainpen with the, you know—little rubber tube inside and it fills with ink when you manipulate a small lever on the outside? The Donaldson Write-right? It was very big for years—till the ball point came along. Still, he did all right. But he said the ball point would never catch on. Funny, fountain pens are catching on again. Like Tiffany lamps. Anyway, my father was all hung up sexually. I found out. I don't know what his relationship with my real mother was. Like your family, I guess. We never shared any of that kind of knowledge with each other. Nobody ever said anything really personal. Anyway, Florence, the school teacher, and I never did hit it off—from the start. I guess she never had a chance with me, with what I could blame her with. I used to compete like crazy with her. I always felt so righteous too doing it; telling myself I was defending my dead mother's memory and position. Not that there was much affection in my father to compete for. There wasn't much of that for anybody. Me or Florence. He was so rigid. Though later I got to him. Did I ever.

Florence was totally devoted to him. Her mother ran a rooming house and was smotheringly bourgeoisie and respectable. Still, they were far below us in the social scale. My father was a leader in the town and a millionaire and in those days being a millionaire was really something—especially in a town that size. And he was a college graduate and had been to Europe. Which he hated, of course. Still, he was quite a catch and Florence was very grateful. And he was willing to let her be grateful too. She did everything for him and he liked it that way. She quit teaching and fired the help and did all the cooking herself and cleaning. Even the floors and windows.

She even cleaned out the goddamned rain gutters in the spring. Not that she excluded just me. She didn't give much more to her own child. Just everything went for my Dad. So I hated her, right? That's clear enough, Sigmund.

"Then, I don't know why—didn't then anyway—Florence stopped cleaning and doing and just took to her bed. I was sixteen or so at the time. A senior in high school. And her "illness" was such she began sleeping in a different bedroom and it's funny—while my Dad was the most earnest, punctual, hard-working, tightest-ass man I ever knew, he never smoked or drank—he loved Joe McCarthy, there was one thing: he just couldn't get himself awake in the morning. (My shrink said that was withdrawal) Alarm clocks, nothing worked. He had to be shaken awake and talked to till he was really awake or he'd go back to sleep. And Florence, of course, was too weak--"too poorly"--they used to say—to wake him. Later, I found out why she wouldn't go near him. So, I got the job. Fantastic, huh? That was like lighting a blow torch in a dynamite factory. Jesus, what repectable people don't know about the needs of their own drives and bodies. Till denying them backs-up and explodes.

"My father was a, physically, beautiful man. He wasn't that tall, but tall enough, and in very solid good shape. He was an excellent swimmer—that's ironic, isn't it?--and golfed a lot and went hunting and fishing constantly and he had a beautifully proportioned body too. The scale of his arms and legs and torso was perfect, I thought. It stunned me—his body—the very first morning I went in to wake him. I must have sat on the bed just staring at him for at least fifteen minutes before I shook him awake. It was May and warm and he was wearing just pajama bottoms and one leg had gotten caught up above his knee so that you could see his whole foot and ankle and calve on that leg. And it was magnificent and the hair grew just right—that part is like you—yours--and I was absolutely enchanted. I couldn't take my eyes off. When I touched him—to wake him—I went wild inside and didn't see how I could stop from screaming out loud.

"When I touched him to wake him my whole insides—just splintered and fused—like glass in fire. I only touched his back and shoulder that first morning and the next few mornings and he hardly acknowledged me at all when he would wake up. Once though he did look at me—really look at me deeply—in the eyes—the way a lover does. Each morning after that I stayed longer and took more time and touching to wake him. I was even late for school a couple of times. And then I'd have these wild, erotic dreams about him. I wouldn't shake him, which I should have, but just rubbed him and stroked him. I always believed he was awake but I never could be sure, because he always seemed to stay asleep until finally I would shake him and call his name, 'Daddy,' 'Daddy,' 'come on now.' 'get up.'

"His name was Howard, though I never called him by it—till one morning. It was raining and had stormed fiercely just before dawn. The thunder had shaken the house and had wakened me scared to death. It's so elemental—thunder and lightning—and mysterious. To this day I'm awed by it. Attracted and repelled at the same time. That morning—the rainy one—when I came in, Daddy was on his side, his back to me when I sat down on the edge of the bed and I began rubbing his back and I kept it up for a long time, slowly and really touching, feeling him fully, and my own skin too, and feeling the soothing warmth of his body and I remember feeling my vagina getting moist and then he groaned—a great, deep groan like I had never heard before and he rolled over to me and onto his back and my hand just followed the arc of his body and there it was—his giant, beautiful penis, erect and nosing out of his unbuttoned pajama pants and my hand was touching it—just touching it at first and then holding it and then squeezing it and manipulating. And I wasn't afraid or anything. Not ashamed at all. It seemed the most natural, beautiful event that had ever taken place. And I just kept it up until he came—all over my hand. And then he turned, still sleeping or pretending to anyway, back onto his side and I said, 'I love you, Howard. I love you.' And I got up and left and went to school. Then I got scared—all through the day. But not guilty-scared. Just excited-scared and uncertain about what would happen or what he'd do. But also, I could hardly wait for the next morning to come and I felt so superior to Florence and more powerful than she could ever be. I knew she had never done anything so good for Daddy. I didn't know then how right I was. He didn't say a thing at dinner that night; though, maybe it was my imagination, he seemed happier, I thought. I was thrilled with our secret. And I exalted that night when we all said good-night and I said I'll see you in the morning.

"The same thing happened the next morning and every morning after that for a month. Then one morning I—ruined it, I guess. I pulled his hand to my vagina and began caressing myself with his hand and when I got really excited I began talking and calling him Howard and said 'you're awake, Howard, I know you are. Wake up, wake up. Show me you're awake. Make love to me. Look at me. Look at us. Love me. Love me. Love me.' His eyes came open and he pounced onto me and shoved into me and he started crying and loving me and he was strangling and shouting, 'Oh, God, God, forgive us. Mary Lou, I love you. Forgive us,' he said.

"Mary Lou was my mother's name. When I heard him calling her, that ruined it for me. When he said her name while he was loving me. It just confused everything.

"He pulled out of me before he came and when he had, he ran to the bathroom and—I don't know—vomited, I think—and then he came back and beat the hell out of me. I thought sure he was going to kill me— actually he didn't hurt me that much—and kept calling me 'damned' and 'Satan' and 'whore' and hitting me. I put a pillow over my face and if I hadn't he'd have really mangled me. We were both crying and screaming and finally he gagged again and ran to the bathroom again and didn't come out till after I got dressed and left for school."

"Jesus," Gardner said.

"Now do you wonder why I go to the shrink five days a week?"

"You don't have to tell--"

"I want to. You don't mind?"

Gardner shook his head no.

"The next morning after that morning, before daylight, it stormed again and the storm woke me again and I started playing with myself in the dark and pretending it was Daddy loving me and finally I couldn't stand it anymore and I got up and went to his room and I wanted desperately to be in bed with him, but when I got there, he wasn't in bed. He wasn't there at all. I hated the thought that he might be in with Florence but I didn't really believe he was, so I went downstairs looking for him and he wasn't there either. I went into the kitchen to get some orange juice and from in there I could hear it—the garage was just off the kitchen—dully at first, because it was still raining and the thunder still sounded—off—far-away--in the East, but I knew almost immediately what it was and I remembered the whole scene in John O'Hara about Julian English and I was horrified.

"I raced into the garage and My God, there he was, slumped down in the front seat of the car with all the windows closed and the motor running. I threw open the garage door and shut off the engine—Thank God, he hadn't locked himself in—and I don't know where I got the strength or why I did it that way but I pushed the car out of the garage and into the driveway. And then I opened all the car doors and then looked at him and he was still breathing and I pulled him out and took his pulse which was still okay, so I guessed he hadn't been there long—maybe the storm had got him up too and he had got to thinking; he was still in his pajamas—and I just stayed there with him in my arms till it started to get light and he started gagging and coughing and stirring and finally I believed he was okay and when he moved again, I ran back into the house and up to my room. I could see the driveway from my window and I got Bud's—that's my half-brother—binoculars and I just watched that car solid for about an hour and I was crying the whole time and praying and being angry at myself for praying since I didn't believe in God and finally I saw my Daddy get out of the car and walk around it a couple of times and shake himself like a wet dog and then leaned against the fender for a long time and it looked like he was crying—he kept pounding his fists against the fender. And then he got back into the car and started it up and drove it back into the garage and I thought sure as Hell he was going to do it all over again, but then I heard him downstairs coming in and heard him coming upstairs.

"Neither of us said anything and the next few mornings when I went to his room, he had put a lock on it and I couldn't get in and within a week after, he and Florence sent me to visit a cousin of Daddy's who lived on a farm near Gettysburg in Pennsylvania for the summer and that September they enrolled me in St. Mary of The Woods at Terre Haute, Indiana—a God-forsaken little backwoods Catholic girl's school.

"In December, Daddy beat a whore to death in Milwaukee and then drove all night to our hunting lodge in the northern part of the state where he shot himself. He left a note saying there was a beast in him and he couldn't control it—and the beast was an offense to God and to the better part of himself and etc..." Janelle began to cry.

Gardner got up quickly and got her another drink and sat down again beside her.

"Here," he said, "Drink it, Janelle. Quickly. Straight down." She did so. Gardner put his arm around her and held her, silently and strongly, for a long time. At last, her crying stopped. She looked at Gardner and forced a little smile.

"How's that for a Snow White?" Janelle said, getting up from Gardner. She found a cigarette and lit it. "I came back to Madison the following year and finally graduated at Wisconsin and then went to the Royal Academy for a year. I don't know why I thought I wanted to be an actress. Oh, yes, I left out the part about trying to seduce my brother by getting him drunk one night at the country club. He was such a god-damned self-righteous sonofabitch. But he wouldn't have any of it and he slapped me and called me a whore and said he knew the whole story about Daddy. Seems he had seen us one morning on his way to the bathroom to tinkle—which I told him was all his dong'd ever be good for. That's why he slapped me. Poor bastard. He's a faggot."

"My God, Janelle." Gardner said.

"The worst kind—when he is. He hides it. Hates it for public consumption. He's always talking about red Commie faggot bastards. He's a nocturnal nelly—and Super-American by day—and a neo-Nazi in the bargain. All that American Legion manhood crap. He marches in their parades—and organized a committee against gun control. God. I don't know if his wife knows or not. If she did, she wouldn't say anything. I'm sure she'd be happy not to have to bother. She's so dumb though, I doubt if she does know. But old Buddy boy makes frequent trips to Milwaukee and Chicago—for 'his business.' He comes in here too—two or three times a year. Beating up pansies after he's had them. He's beautiful. Ex-president of the Rotary Club, School Board, country club. A Deacon of his church. You could puke. He's the perfect embodiment of everything I loathe—about people-and this country. The cruelty and hypocrisy—the twisted anal stiffness."

"Where is he?" Gardner asked.

"In Madison—rancid and respectable. He's a Republican member of the state legislature. His big bill this last session was trying to get capital punishment re-instated. We've come a long way from LaFollette."

"How bout your mother—step-mother?"

"She's in what's fancifully referred to as a 'rest home'--near Milwaukee. She's crackers. Went off right after Daddy did himself in. Talks to Jesus and all that—personally. Buddy claims her 'illness' in the first place came on cause she wouldn't do sexual tricks for Daddy. I guess I was right thinking I'd done more for him than Florence. She wouldn't suck him for instance. According to Buddy. He heard them quarreling about it one night."

"He was very busy, wasn't he?" Gardner said.

"Buddy? Yes—a regular FBI. He told me all that one cheery Christmas Eve party—party?--when the tattered little remnant of our family tried to get together and feast on the dead carcass of our little Christian, middle-class rituals. God, what a piece of night on earth, good will toward man that was. His wife is the world's champion bad cook. Absolute worst. Everything starch from start to finish. Mountains of white bread and lumpy mashed potatoes, and undercooked apple pie. No wonder he's getting obese."

"Fat is murder for a homosexual," Gardner said.

"She's a tea-totaler too. Though not Buddy, thank God. That's the one bearable thing about him. We both got through the night by getting stoned out of our heads and, all the while, the plastic virgin was harping, 'You've had enough, you've had enough. Both of you! What would Father think?' 'They don't make enough, housewife! In all the distilleries of the universe'--(I wonder, Sam, if there are distilleries in other planets)--'is not so much whiskey to drown you out. And fuck Father,' Buddy would say. He had a touch of the poet, you can see."

"Where was Buzz?" Gardner said.

"In New York. He never joined me for my little odysseys back home. I didn't want him anyway—after the first year. Then, he was great—the first trip home. He loved everything. Why not—I was a millionairess. Wept over the weepy things. Laughed at the funny ones. He made me show him every site that had had even the slightest significance in my life. I pointed out the garage especially, of course.

"Buzz knows about--?"

"Everything. I used to confide in him—way back. We met old boyfriends, and he was touching and riotous later on describing them and imitating them. Solicitous and kind to old aunts and teachers. The perfect husband. Which later I found out in a fight was the goddamned role he'd assigned himself. 'Like in a play, darling, that was all.' He was fantastic at the factory. Even with the workmen. God, even Buddy was totally taken with him. Gave him the whole goddamned advertising for the company right on the spot. Four million a year. That's probably all the bastard wanted in the first place. He got a raise out of it and a promotion two weeks later. He really picked me over pretty good in those early days—when he needed me. I had a beautiful trust fund and he lived in a much better league because of me—more than he could afford in those days. Jesus, if only Florence had sucked Daddy's cock, how different things might have been. Poor man. He probably wanted so desperately sexually and got nothing from that Antarctica. Poor Daddy. Him dead—with a gun in his mouth—a little misspent erotica there, eh what?--Buddy a fag. Florence around the bend—and me—me. What a piece of work are we. The paragon of animals."

"What about—yourself," Gardner said. "How do you feel about--?"

"A comedy of errors—erotic errors. A self-indulgent, hedonistic absurdist. Part-time drunk, sexual vagrant. With an enormous Protestant-Christian hang-over...and the beginnings of a crepey neck."

"Aren't you being a little rough on yourself?"

"Not really. I get all my hair shirts at Bergdorf-Goodman. Harry, dear Harry, doesn't sucking a cock seem such a little thing to screw up so much? Poor bitch. She should've had a go at it. She might have liked it."

Gardner heard Janelle burst open with a crazy kind of laugh, like a horse whinning in a stable fire. It shook him.

"When I was drunk that Christmas Eve at Bud's, after the story about Florence, when he told me that, I—I said, 'He should have asked you, Buddy Boy. I'm sure you'd have been happy to indulge Daddy.' Isn't that funny?"

"In front of his wife?"

"Oh, God, no. She was long gone—to her kerchief and bed—waiting for Santa Claus. Silly bitch probably still believes in Santy."

"What'd he do?"

"Knocked me across the living room. All the men in my family are very affectionate that way. I started throwing Christmas ornaments at him off the tree. Can you imagine? I never had much sense of weapons. I almost threw the whole damned tree at him, but he stopped that by nearly breaking my arm. It was sore for a month. That's when he reminded me about having seen me in the kip with dear old Dad. It was wonderful, warm night of family confession and recollection. A typical, warm holiday get-together. Christ! Finally, though, we ended up crying like babies holding each other and comforting ourselves and our self-pity and loathing. Such sweet, perverted sentiment. I got the first plane out the next morning. I just couldn't stick around for the Christmas Day mash potato orgy or any more exorcism. So. That's America to me. Travels with Janelle. America, America. A suck, a suck—my republic for a suck! Oh, Harry, what happens out there? Out there from sea to polluted sea? To all those good Christian folk? They betray their own best mythology and hate their drives and deny their bodies and end up hating and killing each other—and loathing life. There's a whole nation-hood out there—just--holding its moral breath—just to please the dead soul of—what--who--of Cotton Mather? And now, today; this fine, scientific, atomic day we wake up and find out Cotton's Christ was no more divine that Richard Nixon—and we see our frail little umbrella of faith whip off into the wind, somersaulting down the gutter of our real condition, and so even it's gone now, our little Jesus umbrella which used to justify us and protect us—and--and--here we are wrinkled wet and nearly drowning in a deluge of indifference—in a universe that takes no heed or interest in our coming extinction. And so we stop holding our breath and out it comes, fetid, in a wild rush of drugs and sex and killing Vietnamese self-righteously—and probably blacks before it's finished, and maybe, after that, all of us, everything—as simple as ABM. Is there any Scotch left?"

Gardner nodded and then looked at his watch. "Holy God," he said.

"What?" Janelle poured herself another drink. "You want one?" she said.

"No, I've got to go. It's after six," Gardner said.

"Right now?"

"Yes." Gardner got up and began to gather together his clothes.

"Have another drink."

"I can't. I've got to go."

"Mama gonna scream if you're late for supper?"

"It's not—I've just got to go."

"Well, sure why not?" Janelle said. "You got fucked and sucked and you heard my sad story. What else is there?"

"I don't feel that way, Janelle."

"Don't shit me, pal. You're all alike."

"Janelle, that 's not so. You know it. Nor fair. I don't feel like that."

"Fair? What's ever fair? Jesus, you just don't give up, do you?"

"And you've had enough to drink. Both of us. Please, let's go. We can meet--"

"I never have enough to drink, Harry-Sam Stud."

"Come on. You're getting--"

"No, we've got a lot to discuss yet. Really important shit—like we haven't said one word about Liz and Richard yet. Not one goddamned word. Do you think he's faithful to old Liz?" Janelle laughed. "I'll bet."

"Janelle, I've got to go."

"Why? You lose your allowance or something if you come home late? You'll have to stay in your goddamned room for a week, I betcha."

"Janelle." Gardner could feel the warmth and sympathy he felt in himself for this woman begin to turn color, and a kind of alarm starting to pollute his good feeling; and he heard her natural Mid-Western accent coming back.

"I'm really disappointed in you, Sam," Janelle said. "Just when I thought maybe you were a man, you turn out to be--"

"That's enough now. No more."

"Oh, yes, lots more. It's never enough, you goddamned boy scout."

"If I am that, I'm beginning to wish I hadn't helped you across the street."

"Don't call me an old lady, you sonofabitch."

"Jesus, what gets into you?"

"You for one, Harry-Sam. You got into old Janelle, hunh? Didn't you?"

"Janelle, don't—don't ruin—matters."

"Matters? Matters? This isn't a goddamned sales presentation. Oh, shit. Okay. Was I very, very good to get into, Harry Sam? What's the market research say? Was I technically A-OK? How was the package? How would the computer read-out my humping?"

"God, Janelle, My God."

"My God" Your—God? Your God, your god, your god. Don't you listen?" Janelle advanced on Harry, who tried to pull away from her, but she seized him by the shoulder with her free hand. He decided he had better not resist her. In her other hand she clutched her scotch and she spilled some of it on him as she grabbed him.

"Janelle, watch, be careful."

"God is dead, Harry-Sam, hadn't you heard?" Janelle said, in an exaggerated whisper. "He shot himself in the fucking mouth, etc! Don't try reviving him! Christ, are you something. A dreamer in a room full of people having nightmares. God has been kicked in the ass out of here."

"Janelle, please—look, we're all spiritual amputees one way or other, but--"

"God is mother-fucking, stone-cold dead. Kaput. It's mechanics. Now. That's what's in. Technological Theology. Technology is tops. T.I.T. To the new God—TIT! Hail affluence, full of transistors. Hail comfort. Now and at the time of our death. Tomorrow Playboy merges with Mechanics Illustrated. The gospel accordingg to Werner Von Hefner!"

"Janelle, let's go. Please. You're getting rough."

"Don't you sometimes, boy? That's what I hear? And that's the price you pay in this house! You gotta pay the whore her price, whatever it is. You're a gentleman, aren't you? Pay the whore. Have another drink. Don't stiff the whore. Another lot of drinks."

"Why? Because your comfort-seeking leaves you feeling so comfortable? Like now?"

"Oh, go fuck yourself."

"Baby—if that should ever become technically possible, I'm sure you'll be the first one to try it."

Janelle let go of Gardner's shoulder and took a step back from him. She could not focus very well, Gardner noticed, but as well as she could, she stared into him. She turned the paper cup of Scotch upside down and the contents poured onto the floor. She wadded the cup in her fist. Then she dropped it. She stopped staring at him and began to gather up her clothes.

Gardner took his clothes and went into the bathroom. He washed himself off and tried to sober up. He had difficulty dressing, especially in trying to get his pants on. Finally, he pulled himself together with a major and exhausting effort, enough to finish the job. He looked into the mirror on the back of the door and tried to see if anything showed. Nothing. He looked to himself like the same familiar Harry Gardner, except a little out of focus. Foke you! More nothing! Even here, with this, there ought to be some sign. Something ought to show or to be different!

Suddenly, Gardner felt his guts congeal. What about Norma? And Kathleen? Buzz? Would he be late—too late—getting home? What about the Scotch on his breath? Would Norma have called the office? Were the children all right? Had the waiter recognized him? Maybe Jerry Novack had tried to reach him at home. Was Janelle going to go ape out there—here--and make a scene? She might. She really could. She was on the edge and he wasn't out of this thing yet. God, she might even slash his painting. Remember that in "The Light That Failed?", he told himself. Or call Janelle. She might do that. Or tell Buzz. He suddenly saw his name in a Daily News headline.

No, no, steady, boy. Steady, he told himself. Don't panic. Just—just pull together. Use everything you've got to get that woman out of here. And don't be seen. And then, forget her. Steer clear. She's murder. Really wacked up. Get her out, and out of your life. That's all. Just do that. And things'll be okay.

Gardner came back into the room. He saw that Janelle had fixed herself up very well, and on her too, it looked as though nothing had happened. She appeared to be so untouched, except that she was swaying some from the liquor.

"You stay and lock up," she said. Her voice was very quiet now, flat and empty, Gardner thought. "All right? I'll go down and get a cab. No—don't say anything. I know. Maybe you're new at this, but I'm a veteran. I know you don't want to be seen with me. Obscene, sure, but not plain seen. A Boy Scout could lose all his merit badges for that, hunh?"

And then, she was gone.

After a few moments, Gardner got up and out, got a cab, got home and there were no problems. No one had called and the children were fine and he explained the Scotch on his breath, which Norma did notice and mention, by saying that he had had a couple of drinks after work with Jerry Novack who was worried about an account. Norma did not question it further; and he was pleased about that, and that his voice sounded normal to him as he talked about it.

Gardner was very good with the children through the whole evening and so warm to Norma that she commented on it. Gardner explained that he had just got to thinking carefully about what a lucky man he was. He was very grateful, he said and he meant it.

Norma was grateful for that and they had a lovely time of it. They even made love, and just before he fell asleep, Gardner promised himself once more that he would never see Janelle again, and meant it deeply.

After that, he saw her regularly at least once a week.

CHAPTER 9

"Nancy—I just can't believe you haven't seen 'Oh, Calcutta'?" Toni Carpenter said.

"It it really sexy?" Nancy English said.

"Well, it's the first time I ever saw <u>that</u> on stage." Toni said.

"What?" Nancy said.

"Everything," Toni said.

"What?" Nancy said.

"Cocks and balls and cunts and humping." Janelle said. "Good old soixante neuf."

"Oh," Nancy said. "They actually show--?"

"Yes, and between a man and a woman. Sorry, Duane," Janelle said.

Duane shrugged. "What's the 'Calcutta' have to do with it?" he said.

Slowly, Gardner became aware of the voices around him and he realized that he had just come back from the long journey of his thoughts. His eyes caught on Janelle. She looked back at him directly.

"Harry hasn't heard a word we've been saying," Janelle said. "Have you, Harry?"

"Well, he's been looking fascinated," Madelyn said.

"Oh, he's good at that—I hear. He's famous at the office for smiling and nodding and frowning in all the right places. He's a very practiced listener—without hearing," Janelle said.

That was true, Gardner thought. He was able to do that. He was extraordinarily gifted at following any conversation in perfectly parallel, quite socially-acceptable responses and yet without—absolutely--any nerve end of him getting aroused or any brain cell recalling for more than the instant of transmission what the person talking to him had said. They might ride the trains of their thoughts and words over the track of himself and, while the freight was upon him, he would make the same polite, acceptable responses as rails bowing under the passing weight, but when their trains had rolled on, he would be as untouched, noticeably, as the rails are—except that perhaps like them—worn down over the years—though still imperceptible to the casual eye, he would simply one day finally be removed from the line; but even this merely because in some undramatic millimeter of his measure of himself he would have been frictioned away.

Had he always been—so lifeless? Good Lord, Straight Rail Harry Gardner didn't even have a speck of rust on him, Harry Gardner decided. Where was his human feeling or at least even corruption? Or indignation? Spent on a touch football field in Central Park? Screwing Janelle? Was that the sum of his participation in caring?

Janelle, maybe. That showed some spark, surely. No, not a chance, he contradicted himself. He had been as organized and prosaic and careful about his relationship with her as he would have been going to a therapist once a week—or a dentist. And, after her, he got going with others. Lots of others. By this time, Harry-Sam was a big swinger.

He was great in bed, he had to grant himself. And creative. And outside himself. And giving. "I hear you're trying to over-throw the government with your cock," Janelle had said. But that and then alone was _it_ for him.

Everything surrounding _it_ for himself, Janelle and the others was ordinary, bloodless, matter-of-fact. No scenes, no running off, no found hot love letters, no unexplained Tiffany receipts. Though they all grunted and rooted and licked and sucked and fucked, they never—not once— touched another.

He saw Norma staring at him. She looked very confused, he thought. Maybe she was wondering about how his AMERICANS THE BEAUTIFUL idea had gotten full-blown into the head of Ralph Wright, without any credit going to himself. He'd think of some lie to cover that. Blame Billingsly. Something. Jesus, he hoped she wouldn't say anything to anybody about it being his idea. Wright, especially. I don't want any trouble tonight, he thought. I just want a nice, quiet time of it with Norma when I get home. I want the love-making I'm owed from the bathroom earlier. Christ, I deserve that. Is that so much? It is my birthday!

Gardner looked away from Norma and began talking quickly, jumping right into the conversation at his end of the table. He didn't know for sure if he had interrupted anyone, but he knew exactly what they had been talking about—wasn't that his maestro-talent, being able to flow with the sense of a conversation without his mind even being there?

"I liked Portnoy's Complaint," he said. "I thought he hit it perfectly."

"Including his ball glove, his sister's bra and his mother's liver." Janelle said.

"I haven't had a chance to read it yet," Nancy said.

"You know what it's about, don't you?" Janelle said.

"Sort of," Nancy said.

"You know about the whacking off then," Janelle said.

"The what?" Nancy said.

"You know—whacking off, beating your meat—masturbating," Janelle said. "I love all those expressions. He left out a good one though. <u>Pounding your pud</u>. I guess that's midwestern. "Did you fellows jerk off all that much when you were young?"

"I did," Gardner heard himself say out loud.

"Hurray for Harry. Let's give him a big hand," Janelle said.

"He's got his own, apparently," Toni Carpenter said.

"You all are—just--not to be believed," Duane said.

Janelle said, "The truth's the truth—Duane--and it's good for you to get it out. That's the wisdom of the Catholic Church and Sigmund Freud and you can't go against that."

"Well, <u>everything</u>?" Duane said, "all over <u>everybody</u>?"

"Isn't that good, Harry?" Janelle said, and Gardner heard her tone changing, zeroing in on him. "Telling the whole truth?"

"I think it is," Gardner said.

"Well, you seem a little more with us, Harry. What happened?" Janelle said.

"I remembered it's my birthday and I've decided to enjoy it—wallow in it."

"Good for you, Harry," Toni said. "I will too."

"More wine, Mister Gardner?" Gregory said, walking up.

"Yes, please—good, Gregory—fill it up. Thank you." And hold the spit, Gardner thought.

"Everybody, Gregory," Janelle said. "Maybe we ought to all tell the truth tonight. All of it. Have you ever heard of the truth game? They play it at parties in Paris all the time. It's marvelous. Everybody takes a turn and says what he really thinks of himself and of the other people in the room—and what he knows about them. Wouldn't that be fun?"

"<u>Gawd</u>, no," Duane said, "In this crowd? Not me."

"Well, if we play," Toni Carpenter said, "You'll have to, Duane."

"I think it sounds fascinating," Nancy English said. "I read about a place in California—Insulin, I think—where they do something like that.

"Esolon, I believe it is, dear." Cleve English said, spinning into the conversation again. Pretty good, Gardner thought. The sonofabitch is not bad himself at listen/no-listen.

"Yes, that's right," Nancy said. "Esolon. They have some interesting psychological tests there—telling the truth."

"Not half what we could do here," Janelle said. "Let's play."

"Janelle," Gardner said, "I think you ought to drop it."

"Why? I want to play." Janelle said. "Come on, Harry, just think—how delicious. The secrets we could tell."

"I'm ready," Toni said.

"I'll try," Nancy said, "But mine'll probably be boring."

"It's not a nice game," Gardner said, "Especially boozing. I've seen it played. It can be mean and very dangerous."

"Whoopee—just like life," Janelle said. "I WANT US TO PLAY IT," she said.

"Are you going to force it—because you're the boss's wife?" Gardner said. "You can. Can't she, Duane? You and me—all of us. You do have power over us, Janelle. I'm not sure abut Ralph Wright. Can you make him play your games? Or Toni? Through commercials, I suppose. And Cleve? And your husband—what about him—on his birthday?"

"You are a sentimental shit, aren't you? Janelle said. "Oh—fuck it."

Duane got up. "Excuse me," he said.

"Did I say something tasteless?" Janelle said.

"No more than usual," Duane said, "<u>Darling</u>."

"Don't pout," Janelle said.

"I've got to make a front naughty," Duane said.

Janelle laughed and so did Toni. Nancy smiled. She would smile at the announcement of plane crashes, Gardner thought, so little did she listen and so hard did she try to please.

"Duane talks like Blanche DuBois's mother," Toni said.

"Look at that gait," Janelle said. "Margot Fontayne walks butcher than that."

"Janelle," Gardner said.

"Well, hell—I didn't turn him gay." Janelle said.

"He's your guest—we all are," Gardner said.

"Oh, yes, that is absolutely correct. Harry-the Saint is right again. Do forgive me everybody. The hostess will try to remember her manners. I am the hostess—or is it—the Madame?"

"We could do with some more wine," Toni said.

Janelle motioned for Gregory, who brought more wine and, when he had poured it all around, everybody drank. Gardner lit another cigarette and tried, through the gathering smog of the alcohol in his brain, to get his thoughts to connect. They would not. His head was a mess. He tried, but the words in his brain raced like a crowd who's been told the theatre's on fire. His thoughts were jamming up at the exits. He felt his rage at Janelle swelling to include everyone at the table. But Norma. He dragged on the cigarette and realized that he was smoking continuously. He could just see his lungs! Withering in, black as prunes! Drying out for cancer! That's it, boy. That's how you'll get it! Cancer killed Harry Gardner! Fitting disease for a modern man! What could be more appropriate than that parasite feeding on his impotency, contained rage, fakery, anxiety and finally the disrespect for himself which the body had to know about and in its last honorable act confront by consuming itself?

Gardner smoked, inhaling to the Tierra Del Fuego of his lungs, and stared into the color of the wine in the glass he held. He closed his eyes and drank it down, down to below where even the smoke could get, and began to hear Norma's voice from along the way down the table.

"I can justify the expense of the moon program—even with our social problems. At least, it's a positive expenditure—and ultimately some good will come from it. That's the history of all great experiments and adventures. Already, in fact. But the money wasted in Vietnam. That's obscene totally. Besides, the horror and indecency of it all."

She was such a good woman, Gardner thought; intelligent, strong and morally serious. Realistically compassionate. How dark and beautiful and historic she looked right now, he thought, opening his eyes and openly staring at her. 5000 years of scattered, struggling Jews stood illumined in her face and he believed he could see the desert in her skin, burned in by long ancestral exposure and he wondered upon the begettor who begat who begat who begat in that dim untraceable line which finally placed her here tonight—the thousands of days and nights—the ten thousands of days and nights of desert and pain and death and faith and the unconscious repetition of a million daily acts that came down through the sperm and genes and countless wombs to her. Daughter of Daniel and David and Ruth and Esther and dark nameless, faceless Hebrews from Egypt and Israel and the millennium days of The Diaspora and he could see her in the rough cloth of Bible times or dressed in black on the steppes of Russia or making tea in the backroom of a German tailor's shop or huddling in the cramped hold of a steamer or sitting with the patience of a statue on the hard, bare benches of Ellis Island or amidst the fire-escape jumbled architecture of Orchard Street on the lower East Side. The whole tough, tenuous line was sculptured into her look and carriage and invisibly into her character and he knew she knew from all of this without thinking, in a corpuscular kind of knowing, about dignity and pain and trying and pride and earned joys—with a wisdom he would never attain.

God (?) be praised, Gardner told himself, that Norma had been spared that lately New York Jewish corruption of "Schtick" and "Boobala" and peroxide wigs and football helmets and Great Neck and country clubs and phallic automobiles and accountants with love beads around their necks and their sun-scorched wives with the crapey boobs pushing out of the sequined dresses—and the wheeling and dealing and going to Bar Mitzvahs at the Plaza, exchanging alligator wallets for floral centerpieces and going to theatre benefits to be seen rather than even entertained.

How grateful suddenly he was for her. What careless Egyptian or cossack, sated with rape and killing, had he to thank for sparing the bloodline of this child? Out of what tangled cloth of sand and suffering, of hideous fright in the endless cruel night of the desert and the pogrom had this tapestried girl been allowed to be woven and brought forward to him? And to be joined through him to his own long and laboring line of heritage. It was such a precarious and uncertain conjunction that the mere fact of its existence made Harry Gardner feel that it must be something beyond. And yet—he could not convince himself. It just lingered on—the other thought—seeming all too likely to himself, that rather than ordered by design, they had arrived at each other by the merest stumbling chance. On the whim of man and nature were they joined. A Cossack filled with killing had spared a great, great grandmother. A drunken Great, great, great etc., had come home and runted just the right sperm into his wife against her will and slobbered out drunk asleep after the grunting deed. Whim, chance, accident, action and inaction and the beasty deeds of unthinking men. These were the gods of their destinies. These. Not Old White-beard working from His script.

Still, Norma impressed him mightily and he regretted deeply that something in him found it necessary to cause her so much pain. Though even this he knew he could forgive himself, and certainly she did, as long as he reached towards her, no matter how clumsily. It was the newer stain that broke her heart—about him, and, in a larger way, about life: He was turning her away from her joy in being alive.

She had caught the death from him and he had it good. It was on him like mildew. He felt as though he had nothing to give—to himself nor to her. Their life was over, he felt, and they were simply living off the days like a jail sentence. It sat there in him, on its great haunches, constantly, staring holes into everything he did. Even the children were no relief to him or joy or hope. They would grow, graduate, marry, visit at Christmas time and then finally he or Norma or some one of them would consummate the act and die and that would begin it, until they were all dead.

The beast had stirred and shifted somewhat tonight—earlier back there in his bathroom when they had started to make love. He knew it wasn't staring at him then and he had genuinely wanted to love her. But before then, he knew, weeks had gone by in which he did not make love to her nor want to. It had seemed—well, just unnecessary. He had had absolutely no physical desire for her. Even to kiss her seemed a kind of profanity, it had been so much done. Everything seemed to him to have been so much done and yet, he wanted desperately to get over this feeling that things were over. God, what plagued him? He wondered. Had he finally to admit that he was incapable of being a man? Were only the joys of being a boy the only joys he could experience and, with these gone, wither? Perhaps men lived too long, he thought, and erosion worked you down if you lived past 30. What about those kids who said don't trust anyone over 30? Is this what they were seeing and were they right? Did they smell the defeat and the death? And, if so, what would become of them when they reached that age, bringing with them that terrible self-condemning knowledge? No. No, he said to himself, there were many people his age who had energy and purpose and joy and hope about themselves and their work. Still, so many did not. What was wrong with them, that, like himself, they could not sustain the clean mountain of the dreams and drives of their youth?

What had happened to gully him out? Was it simply psychological? Norma thought so certainly and she blamed his family; and then him, for not seeing a psychiatrist and thus exorcising his bad weather for once and forever. Could he be so scarred? And, what could he do? See a doctor? End the marriage? That, for the first time, was a real possibility, he believed. He had thought about it a lot lately and Norma had threatened him with it plenty of times and he knew that she was no longer bluffing.

"It's something you just have to go through I suppose, but I don't like it. I understand how these things can happen. But you do nothing about it.

You refuse to see yourself or get help. That's what I hate. I have absolutely no respect for that. Maybe you should leave, if you have to. I hate you like this. It's such a waste." That's what she always called it. The waste! Then why did she stay? Gardner wondered. Social pressure? The children? Those were involved, he supposed, but those weren't the true reasons. She was simply a decent woman, he thought, who had seen the good things in him once and was, despite his floundering, hopeful that they might return. She was that good. And constructive. She would stay for that—hadn't she promised "for better or for worse" (and to her the words were solemn)--but even so, he knew, even if he could "find" himself—and he doubted that he could now—it would never be the way it had been, with the knowledge and experience of his having stumbled so badly.

Oh, Goddamn her goodness and her genetic strength and her hope and her resiliency and her and her doctors! Let her go. Who wants to live the rest of his life being grateful and guilty? They'd both be better off apart. He just wasn't built for marriage. That happened sometimes, he told himself. You made a mistake, that's all. Why be so gloomy and constipated about it. They'd have money; they each had personality resources. They'd be fair—about each other and about the children. They'd even stay friends probably. They were too far along and mellowed for melodramatics. She wouldn't have to carry around the dead-weight of him all the time and he might actually—have some fun again. (He thought about all the women he would have and enjoy). It all made sense, finally. He was thinking all right now, he thought. All right. All right, tomorrow he'd have a sensible talk with Norma and they would separate—and he'd break off with Janelle also. A clean, fresh, spring of a start. Oh, Christ, am I out of my mind? Norma's seven months pregnant! You don't run out on a woman at a time like that! Okay, okay. So you stay now, until the baby comes. Then later you tell her. Later you leave.

"Did you hear about Teddy's favorite song?" Garve Shoaley said. "Like A Bridge Over Troubled Waters."

There was much laughter, Gardner heard. He saw that Norma did not laugh. He had heard that joke and he did not laugh, now or the first time.

"He's washed up," Billingsly said. "And good riddance too. I'm sick of the whole bunch." Gardner remembered that yesterday Billingsly had only praise and sympathy for the Kennedys while talking to a liberal Democrat, who was head of sales for a network.

"I never liked any of them—all the way back to Joe," Ralph Wright said. Billingsly knew his market, Gardner thought.

"I always thought they were more interested in power than principle," Buzz Billingsly said.

"You ought to know," Janelle said.

"What?" Billingsly said.

"Well, you just can't live that way and not get caught. The Lord works His punishment," Ralph Wright said.

Gardner wondered where the Lord would be later on tonight when Wright got together with Honey O'Hara.

"Maybe he just didn't want the damned thing. Maybe he just down deep somewhere, since the bloody thing had killed two of his brothers, wondered about the merits of winning it, and decided to stick it, but good," Gardner said.

He was surprised to hear himself talking and to hear the stridency of his voice, but he didn't want to stop. "Maybe he knew the presidency had turned out to be a Moby Dick for that family; and he was trying his damnest not to be a candidate. Maybe in his deepest-most recesses he was nauseated by this nation and its tender, murdering response to what his family tried to do. So he drank and screwed around and tempted the Gods to take him out of the running and, at the same time, save his life from some psychopath panting to close the circle. Teddy may have just chosen to live."

"He was livin' it up, don't you mean?" Ralph Wright said.

"He got caught that's all," Garve Shoaly said.

"He's a weakling. Mary Jo. The cheating at Harvard," Buzz Billingsly said.

"You cheated at Harvard," Janelle said to Buzz.

Janelle's remark stopped Billingsly for a moment but he ignored her, Gardner saw.

"Buzz shaved his legs and wrote the answers on his calves under his socks," Janelle said.

"Kennedy's a weakling," Garve Shoaly said.

"He was very brave and fine when Bobby died," Norma said. "He gave the whole country dignity and the courage to--"

"He was probably on tranquilizers and Sorenson wrote the speech," Billingsly said.

"God, how we delight in the fall of a good man," Gardner said.

"Good?" Billingsly said. "You're kidding? The drinking and—the other."

"Everyman at this table is half-bagged and so is half the male population of this country this Saturday night. And as for the others--we haven't been caught," Gardner said.

"Speak for yourself, Harry," Garve Shoaly said, in a tone, Gardner thought, that was more brag than denial.

"We don't want to be President, son," Ralph Wright said.

"The hell we don't. I'll bet Buzz does," Gardner said. "He'd run in a minute if he thought there was half a chance--"

"Harry's right," Janelle said. "Buzz is always fantasizing about if he were President."

"I suppose every American boy dreams of being President," Cleve English said, exposing his own ambition, Gardner thought. "It is sort of promised to us."

"Oh, nobody believes that—after he's 10 years old," Billingsly said.

"We don't believe in Santa Claus either, but there's one on every street corner at Christmas," Gardner said. "If you buy deodorants and shampoo you'll get laid. If you buy the right toothpaste you'll be successful in business. What is that? If we didn't believe in lies, advertising'd be finished. We spend more here on myths and dreams than reality."

"That's true everywhere," Madelyn said.

"Well, we sure got sold a bill of goods on Teddy Kennedy. All that image-making got washed away when that girl drowned," Shoaly said.

"Did it make you a better person, when she did, Garve? Did you feel good about it?" Gardner asked.

"No one felt good about it, Mr. Gardner," Ralph Wright said. "But it did keep Teddy out of the White House."

"Yeah," Gardner said, "and Chavez and Mrs. King and the kids in Viet Nam."

"We ought to just crown them Kings and be done with it!" Ralph Wright said, "the way you talk."

"No," Gardner said, "but we ought to stop killing them and questioning their motives and so the Kennedys are interested in the use of power. I wouldn't want a President who wasn't"

"I still wouldn't want Teddy Kennedy sitting by the red phone," Ralph Wright said.

"Maybe," Gardner said. "But a lot of good things about the country got the wind knocked out of them with him. We belonged to each other—the

Kennedys and America, in a strange way. They represented the best of us, and made us feel better things were possible. If they didn't triumph always, at least they showed us what we could be. Joe wanted that from his boys."

"God," Billingsly said, "old Joe Kennedy was a tiger—ruthless as they come."

"I don't know," Gardner said. "Maybe Kennedy did start all pride and ambition. Most of us use America that way—don't we—as a private feeding ground for all our appetites, but that's not what he taught those boys—or Rose taught them or what they learned. They were learning to want to put things back. That's the difference. They had everything we thought we had when we were young—physical beauty, charm, wit, the will to try—the need to win—without destroying. And to enjoy living. That's why the poor and the young and the alienated rallied to them. If we all conspired to endow Teddy with qualities he might not truly have or hasn't found yet—where's the crime? In refusing to keep our eyes in the gutter?"

"Mr. Gardner," Ralph Wright said, "That's gibberish, if I may say so. I still don't want him to be my President."

"Did you _ever_ want him to be President—even before Chappaquiddick?" Gardner said.

"That's beside the point," Ralph Wright said.

"No it isn't," Gardner said, and his voice was insistent and pressing. "Did you?"

"Well, no—I sure didn't. So what?"

"So—everything I said. For the young and the poor and all those people trying to get some decent share of this society. You're for politics—Mr. Wright—with the draw-bridge up. Haves keep and to hell with the have-nots. Which is the greater indiscretion—Mary Jo Kopechne, or the ABM?"

"The point is he should have been home with his wife," Ralph Wright said.

Gardner held his laugh in, looking at Honey O'Hara. Norma smiled and Janelle guffawed. "Maybe—and maybe Melvin Laird should go out more," Gardner said. "That's human at least."

"Young man, I disagree with you strenuously. I think your thinking is very confused," Ralph Wright said. "You've been away from Indiana a long time."

"You're being ridiculous," Buzz Billingsly said to Gardner. "The wine's got you, Harry."

"Whatever it is, I don't think much of his ideas," Ralph Wright said.

Gardner stood up. "Mr. Wright," he said, "may I tell you what I think about <u>your</u> ideas and <u>your</u> life? And your vaginal deodorant?"

"Harry," Cleve English said. "Sit down, won't you?"

Norma knocked her glass over and the wine bled across and into the white tablecloth as though from a bull's mouth in the kill moment.

"Oh, God, look at that," she said. "How stupid! Janelle, I'm sorry. Mr. Wright, look at what I've done. Now what? Do I throw salt over my shoulder? Or have seven years bad luck? Will my baby have warts?"

Gardner saw she was making funny, vaudeville gestures with her napkin towards the spilled wine, then dabbing it at her eyes and behind her ears and under her arms even. She was playing the court jester, the distractor; the old Jewish humor was coming through to get out of a rough spot. She had spilled the wine deliberately, he was certain. "Janelle, I'll come and clean for a week," Norma said. "I'll buy you a new tablecloth— don't tell me this one's an antique family heirloom. I'll knit one or whatever you do."

"I could have used something like that on my wedding night," Janelle said, looking at the red stain. "Forget it."

"Pour salt on it, Dear," Ralph Wright said.

"Will that break the curse?" Norma said.

"It absorbs the wine and cuts the stain. Mrs. Wright taught me that trick. See?" Ralph Wright poured great quantities of salt on the spilt wine, which began to disappear into the salt.

"That's fantastic," Norma said.

"It really does work," Ralph Wright said.

Gardner felt as though the wine could have been his blood which they were sopping up. Why did she stop me! Why didn't she let me say what I thought of this pious old poulet and shoot him down?! That isn't wine she's mopping up! It's my blood. Gardner looked at Ralph Wright and hated him.

That wide lapel, maroon sock, nasal speech, 2nd table-from-the-left-in-a-business-convention-8X10-glossy-photo face! That bastard! He could make you think he was a vegetarian in this carnivorous crowd, but Wright can tear flesh with the best of them! And'd say Grace before he devoured you! Gardner knew him: one of those middle-western middle minds with the button on the brain, that could be switched from icy business decisions in favor of anything that spawned an extra buck to the tepid platitudes of the simple and rigid Bible belt code that ruled out against everything he did when the button was in the first position. It was a grand button to have, if you were Ralph Wright, Gardner thought. How convenient, the way it whisks away those smudgy little question marks in the corners of life--"get yours today" "Don't let the left hand know what the right hand is doing." His dogma of "dawg gone it" and "God helps them that helps themselves" could eat you alive! I know that pious panther! He belongs to the Chamber of Commerce, Rotary, the NAM and The Republican Party; and to Heaven: (one of a drowsy dozen sects of polite Protestantism) and both Caesar and God are his pals. He's the most dangerous animal alive!

And what are they doing to my world? Wright would ask. Gardner imagined. What's become of it? That's why I speak of returning to the principles of our forefathers, and everybody knows the principles of our forefathers means life as it was lived under Calvin Coolidge! It's not easy to be a man who wanted Robert Taft and was forced to accept Eisenhower, who thrilled to Goldwater and has had to settle for Nixon. And, my God, why had't Thou forsaken us to a Kennedy and nigger-lover Johnson who couldn't even win a lousy little war! And a communist Cuba? You tell me one good reason why we can't go in there and wipe out all those smarty little Red spicks. Cuba, Russia, China—all of them? We've got the hardware, by golly—and that's the only way we're ever going to get peace on this God's green earth—is to kill them all. We won World War II, didn't we? (Gardner did not know but would have been pleased to have been informed that Wright saw World War II in the newsreels and from the food rationing board in his home town.) We made the bomb and walked the moon. And don't tell me about <u>Atomic Holocaust.</u> I have a fall-out shelter and besides, they'll probably only just bomb New York and that would be good for the whole country. I agree with Senator Richard Russell: If it comes to an atomic show-down, let it; just so long as the last two people left are Americans. (How bout Eldridge Cleaver and Angela Davis, Ralphie—They're Americans)?

There's no problem on earth that can't be solved if we just allow some nice, sincere, patriotic Christian folks to run things. We could cut taxes and put the niggers in their place and do away with welfare—that kills initiative. (This last idea struck Gardner with particular irony since he was sure from having read Wright's story that he had inherited his business from his father and grandfather, which was all the initiative any man would need). But still he would say, Gardner imagined, look at me—I'm a self-made man. Oh, sure, I went to Ohio State, but I got my real learning in the school of hard knocks!

And, with it all, oh yes, Amen, see the sampler on the wall: THE FAMILY. Hiya, Ralph boy, how's the family? The family, the family, tra la, tra la. How's the little woman? Oh, Mother's fine—that's her over there with the screwed-up face and the screwed-out body—from starches, not fucking. The one with the turquoise tortoise-shell glasses hanging on her bust on a gold chain. And that's why I have to come to New York every once in a while and find a Honey O'Hara. I don't even have to stick it into her if I can just be around her and smell her and look at her for a little while. You see, Mother hasn't been too well lately (for 30 years) and we don't sleep-well, the doctor advised us to get twin beds and then we made our two children while Mother had her clothes on and I had to shove her skirt up over her head to get into her and, when I did, I came right away, so, as you can see, sex wasn't a very large part of our relationship, but I don't mind because it really is sort of dirty anyway, don't you think, and Mother gets all the sex she needs from forcing our son to sleep with her till he was fifteen and by smothering him; and by douching a lot. It's not very exciting I suppose but it is healthy and moral and that's very important, don't you think? I think excitement's bad for a person. Interferes with business. No, as for myself, I don't think very much at all. You see my hemorrhoids keep me pretty well occupied, sexually anyway. The children? Oh yes, the children. I'm sorry, I forgot; usually people ask about them much sooner in a conversation and then I'm all primed with photos and stories about their schooling and honors, but you waited so long I nearly forgot them. Isn't that something? Oh, it's a wise man these days who knows his children. Gardner imagined for sure that Wright didn't know his children worth a damn. Beyond words about general health, weather, sports and obituary items, he hadn't said anything to them freely or clearly since they were six years old—and probably they had given up trying to talk to him about that same time. Oh, he probably had remembered to damn Franklin D. Roosevelt to them a few times, but even so, one of the little bastards had probably grown up and become a Democrat. What were children coming to?

No dreams, Mr. Wright? No flights of fancy? Oh yes, sure-- things like Honey O'Hara and, one of these days, Mother and I will probably retire to Arizona. We used to think California, but, with Goldwater, I think we'd be happier in Arizona. We'll be even richer then because of you, Mr. Gardner, because you will design beautiful ads for my insert vaginal deodorant and carry the solemn message of my cosmetic surgery to—to a society dedicated to turning all of its citizens into odorless, tasteless, sightless, soundless, thoughtless, touchless, wrinkle-proof automatons of consumption! That's right nice of you, son. I couldn'ta done it without you!

"I don't know what things are coming to," Ralph Wright said. "I really don't. I tried to take my grandchildren to see a moving picture last week and there just wasn't anything—except Patton. All these other movies are just filth."

Duane re-entered the room and started to sit down.

"Everything come all all right?" Janelle said. "I've been meaning to ask—do you sit or stand?"

"I'm sure you stand," Duane said.

Janelle threw her head back and laughed.

"Sounds like you all are having the time of your life down there," Ralph Wright said, from the other end of the table. Gardner had been watching Wright pick his teeth with his fingernail.

"We are having the time of our life, Mr. Wright," Janelle said. "If you'll pardon a little strong language—the goddamned time of our life."

"Well," Wright chuckled, "damned if I'm not too." It was the most democratic swear word Gardner had ever heard. They do insist, these midwesterners, on trying to be liked, Gardner told himself.

CHAPTER 10

Janelle stood up again, with her wine glass in her hand; with her other hand she reached for the table. Otherwise, Gardner saw, she might have fallen down. "And, you, Sir, are—a goddamned Christian gentleman." She fell back down into her chair, her wine glass in hand, cutting the arc of a toast above her head.

Wright smiled, a bit uncertainly, and he looked at Billingsly to see if everything was all right and still friendly; Billingsly shifted in his chair and smiled back a tight smile, Gardner saw.

"Well, thank you, Mrs. Billingsly," Wright said. "And thank you for this wonderful dinner. It was just wonderful. I've never had duck before—and I was just telling your husband--"

Suddenly, there was the noise of a loud argument in the kitchen, Gardner heard. He could pick out Gregory's voice, but he didn't know the other voice. It was masculine, he heard, but thin for that. Everyone looked towards the kitchen door and saw it swing open.

"Mother, you've got to come out here—now! Gregory's impossible," Kirk Billingsly said. The boy had pushed in from the kitchen as quickly and gracefully as an animal in the circus.

"Kirk—I thought you were out marching," Janelle said.

Gardner looked at the boy. He was fourteen and already nearly six feet tall. His hair was very long and wiry and brown. He had Billingsly's eye coloring, but Janelle's features. He was wearing cowboy boots, the heels rundown, and bell-bottom trousers, very tight and dungarees. His shirt was wine-colored, red, and like one that Errol Flynn always wore in sea pictures. It closed with criss-cross lacing at the neck and had full, blousy sleeves, gathered at the wrist. He wore an Indian beaded-band around his head and a suede waistcoat. On the coat were two pins; one, Gardner knew was the Peace symbol. He couldn't make out what was written on the other.

"God, just look at you," Billingsly said. "I don't know. Mr. Wright, this is my son, Kirk, who's obviously forgotten his manners bursting in like this. What do you want?"

"I want to speak to mother about Gregory," Kirk said.

"And I want to speak about you," Gregory said, who had entered now just behind the boy.

"I'd like a word with you, Mrs. Billingsly."

"Well, what the hell, let's have it—right here—open forum. Folks, you know Gregory—and this—pouting pile of rummage is our son Kirk. He's what's known as a hippie. Have you ever met a hippie, Mr. Wright?"

"Mother!"

"Well, aren't you? We hired him from Hertz-rent-a-hippie—just for your visit, Mr. Wright, so your trip'd be complete."

"What's up, Kirk," Billingsly said.

"Gregory has grapes in there, Man." Kirk said.

"What?" Billingsly said. "And don't call me that."

"Grapes! He has grapes in the kitchen! He's going to serve them!"

"So?" Billingsly said.

"He can't!"

"I will," Gregory said.

"Kirk, we're trying to have a party!" Billingsly said. He stood up. "We'll discuss this--"

"Mother promised me there'd be no grapes in this house until the strike is settled. Now this--"

"What the hell are you talking about?" Billingsly said.

"Cesar Chavez," Janelle said.

"Who?" Billingsly said.

"You know—that Mexican grapepicker," Janelle said.

"He's a Saint!" Kirk said.

"He's leading a strike in California and--" Janelle said.

"What the hell's that got to do with me?" Billingsly said.

"Dig it, Man," Kirk said. "You have grapes in your house."

"Don't call me Man! I always have grapes in my house—whenever I damned feel like it! Now you go to your room—we'll settle this later!"

"They're Peruvian, Darling," Janelle said. "Relax."

"I don't buy that."

"No, you get everything free around here," Janelle said.

"Mrs. Billingsly, either he goes out or I do," Gregory said.

"Isn't the new politics fun, folks?" Janelle said.

"Mother, you're stoned."

"You're so observant."

"Kirk, you keep a civil tongue in your head," Billingsly said.

"At least mine's not slurred."

"See-what Gesel and Dr. Spock did?" Janelle said.

"Janelle, you're not helping," Billingsly said.

"She's drunk," Kirk said. "Again."

"Kirk, I warned you," Billingsly said.

"Hail, Mayor Daley—now and at the hour of the revolution. Let them eat grapes!" Janelle said.

"Screw all of you," Kirk said. He turned and ran out of the room, through the door that opened on to the front corridor.

"Kirk—come back here!" Billingsly said. He ran after his son.

"I'm leaving," Gregory said. "I can't live in the same house with an anarchist." Gregory turned and bolted back into the kitchen.

"Woops," Janelle said, "there goes dessert."

"I don't believe--," Ralph Wright said.

"Sit down, Mr. Wright," Janelle said. "The supper show is over."

Wright sat down and everyone looked very embarrassed, Gardner saw.

"Poor baby," Janelle said, "he must have had a terrible time with his analyst today." Janelle got up and aimed for the kitchen. She was walking wildly. "Excuse me a minute. Looks like Marie Antoinette has to serve the cake herself." Janelle disappeared. There was heavy silence.

"Janelle told me the boy's taking the grape thing very seriously—he's been picketing Gristede's," Norma said. "I'm all for it really."

"I wanted to be a flower child, but I have hay fever," Toni said.

"That young man needs the strap," Ralph Wright said.

"Is he really in analysis?" Nancy said.

"I think they all are," Madelyn said.

"The daughter too?" Toni Carpenter said.

"Maybe they go on a group rate," Madelyn Shoaly said.

"It's so hard for young people today," Norma said.

"Too easy, if you ask me," Ralph Wright said. "They handled them in Chicago. That's the way to do it. Not coddle them."

Janelle came back in from the kitchen. "Gregory's decided to stay," she said, "if we give him shares in the agency. Can you imagine? Him—a

Socialist—and anti-union." Janelle had great difficulty in getting back to her chair. "Thank God, Kirk hasn't found the Saran Wrap yet—he'd immolate himself."

"What's wrong with Saran Wrap," Nancy English asked. "They're one of Cleve's sponsors."

"Dow Chemical makes it," Janelle said.

"Oh, the napalm people," Norma said.

"Precisely," Janelle said.

Gregory came in, carrying a large white cake with lit candles. At the other door, Buzz Billingsly re-entered.

"He must have—run out of the house," Billingsly said. "I can't find him. I'm sorry."

"Never mind, darling," Janelle said, "You can't have your cake and beat him too."

Billingsly came back to his chair and sat down. "God, teen-agers. I just don't know. I'm sorry, Mr. Wright. What can you do?"

"Ever consider military school?" Ralph Wright said.

"Cut him off without a penny," Norma said, smiling.

Janelle started singing. "Happy Birthday to you, Happy Birthday to you;" The others picked up the song. "Happy Birthday, Dear Buzz and Harry--(the others didn't hear Janelle singing this next, but Gardner did)--"Happy Goddamned Birthday to you." Cleve English started up some applause. Gregory put the cake in front of Buzz at the table.

"Help him blow it out, Harry," Duane said.

"Now, Duane, don't talk shop," Janelle said.

"Buzz can manage," Gardner said.

"If he does, it'll be the first good blow jo--" Janelle started to say.

"Did you make a wish?" Norma said.

"Yes—that Kirk was Neil Armstrong!" Billingsly said.

Cleve English jumped in. "These guys don't look a day over 30, do they?"

"Did you make a wish, Harry?" Norma said.

"Oh, sure," Gardner said, smiling and lying, he knew. He had tried, in some old motor response, when the cake first came in, to make a wish, but the machinery for that was all rusted locked. You had to believe in the possibility—even on a long shot—that wishing things might make them so—like it had been as a kid when he used to write in to all those contests and actually think he would win them. Well, all right, he said to himself, wish that: Wish that you could believe in wishing, and that—finally—you can do something nice for Norma.

"Don't tell," Nancy English said.

"What's your wish, old blower," Janelle said to Billingsly.

Billingsly again ignored Janelle, Gardner saw, and blew out the candles. Cleve English got the applause going and Gregory removed the cake to a sideboard, sliced it and began serving it around.

"Speech, speech," Cleve English said.

"Amen," Janelle said, "Give us a little 'seven ages of man' for our money, gentiles—I mean 'gentles.'" No offense, Buzz."

"Come on, Buzz," Garve said.

Billingsly stood up. "I'mmm—I'm grateful," he said, "to know such wonderful people as are gathered here tonight—and--"

Janelle belched out a laugh. "Radcliffe rides again."

"—and—I wish Harry, whatever he wishes for himself." Billingsly sat down; English began the applause.

"What a mean, goddamned thing to wish on anybody," Janelle said. "That's worse than <u>not</u> getting what you wish for."

Billingsly smiled, after a fashion, Gardner noticed.

"Your turn, Harry," Cleve English said.

"Come on, Harry," Garve Shoaly said.

Gardner looked around quickly at the faces, which were swimming in his vision. "All right. Okay," Gardner heard himself saying out loud. He was surprised when he felt himself getting up. He was standing now, as well as he could, he realized, and again he was taking in the faces. He saw them all, through the gauze of his gin. He tried to focus on Buzz, who he thought was looking at him as though he were something he had bought and paid a lot for and which suddenly didn't work anymore. And, <u>goddamn</u> it, that was about to be true! He, Harry Gardner, was going on the blink! His motor was busted! Hang a sign on me—goddamn it—"out of order!"

"Well, come on, Harry—speech," Garve said.

"Tell it like it is, Baby," Toni said.

"Don't be the shy one," Duane said.

"How bout '4 score and seven years ago'?" Janelle said.

"Were you there for the original, Darling?" Madelyn said.

"No, why don't you tell us about it?" Janelle said.

"I never read Lincoln, I just drive them," Madelyn said.

Gardner looked once more at Norma. He saw that her head was lowered and that she was looking into her empty wine glass.

"All right—tonight," Gardner began, "is my birthday—okay—and as I stand here—as well as I can stand, considering—for the 43rd celebration of my decay—in this annual rite of running to seed—I, like the other natural-feeling men of my generation, am a little bit drunk. And I smoke too much. And I think too much about dying—and life looks like—mostly recollections."

Norma started to get up.

"No, wait, Norma, sit!" Gardner said. "They asked me for a speech!"

Norma sat down and lit a cigarette.

"Let's see. I know more and I understand less than I did when I was 20. It's not that I've done so much. I haven't tried incest or folksinging, for instance."

"Don't knock it till you have," Janelle said.

"It's just that I have this sense of knowing everything, and how things work and how they end. The limits of our possibilities and the depths of our culpabilities. I think I know when a man's in trouble—and you don't help him, that you're responsible. An accomplice from then on. Granted, there are guys who don't want to know when a guy's in trouble. Who can etherize themselves. Well, bully for them! They're the survivors in this paradise—they preach democracy while they're spraying Mace. Do I do anything about it! No, I don't do anything about it. I'm paralyzed too. I severed my soul from my mind and body and it's wandering in the long darkness of my American lifetime, searching for the missing parts. Am I making any sense? You all were cashing your paychecks and missed Icarus as America falling—and I saw it—and you think I'm insane when I try to tell you about it. Well, I've seen Icarus shattered, melted wings and all and I can never be the same again. And so, on my 43rd birthday, I ask you for asylum—from your sanity—from what in our country passes for sanity—and I forgive you all." Gardner sat heavily on his chair but sprang up. "Oh yes, one thing more: When I die. On my tombstone. I would like it said: 'This space available for advertising.'"

He held up his glass in the manner of a toast, then drank down the wine in it and slumped into his chair.

Garve Shoaly made a long whistling sigh, if Gardner had heard it.

"Me thinks the drink has made him mad," Madelyn said.

"Find out what he drinks and give it to all my guests," Janelle said.

The others were silent. They began to eat. The cake was very good and full of rum and everyone but Gardner finished the piece in front of him. Gregory served them coffee—"Sanka for me," Ralph Wright said—and then brought in some cheeses—Brie, Camembert, Port de Salud—and served the grapes. Everyone ate grapes but Norma.

"Let's go upstairs—or out in the garden," Janelle said. "My ass is absolutely numb. I think it's pretty outside. Gregory, see who wants brandy—I do."

Everyone got up. Billingsly took Wright's arm and was really talking to him. God, Gardner thought, when it comes to business, Billingsly has the single-mindedness of a sperm!

Janelle opened the French doors which formed one wall of the dining room and which opened onto the garden at the back of the house. The cool air, coming through the doors, rushed in and it felt good, Gardner thought. He breathed deeply and walked, as well as he was able over to Norma. He took her by the elbow and steered her into the garden.

"Oh, Harry," Norma said. "You promised."

"Promised what? What'd I do wrong?"

"You're drunk."

"What the hell did I do wrong?"

"I want to go," Norma said.

"We can't go. We just ate dinner."

"I know you. You're going to give one of your famous performances tonight."

"What performance? I made a little speech. It's my birthday."

"Let's go. We can say I don't feel well."

"Do you?"

"It doesn't matter. I want to go."

"I don't want to. Aren't you all right?"

"Would it make any difference? Please, Harry, take me home."

"No, we just got here."

"I can't take it again—not tonight."

"Will you please tell me what's wrong? What'd I do so terrible?"

"Don't hurt me, please. Please, Harry."

"Hurt? Jesus! It's my birthday. They asked me to make a little speech and I did. What's so wrong about that?"

"Why didn't you tell me about AMERICANS, THE BEAUTIFUL?"

"It came up. I—needed to give Buzz an idea."

"That's your painting!"

"I needed an idea."

"But that was private. Away from the job."

"Oh, what the hell difference does it make?"

"It was your <u>painting</u>."

"My job is my painting. That's my life."

"He didn't even give you credit."

"I get very well paid. He didn't give himself credit. Wright thinks it's his idea."

"But it's yours. Away from the office."

"There's no away from the office. That's how dumb I am to think there is."

"You are dumb. Let's go."

"Unh, unh."

"I'm going. With you or without."

"Please, don't. Don't go."

"You ruin everything."

"I wonder why?"

"What does that mean?"

"Nothing. I just—"

"If you want a divorce, just say so."

"I didn't say that. Jesus Christ, everytime I—"

"Please, Harry, let's go home."

"Can't we have any fun?"

"You don't know how to."

"So I talked a little. Is that so horrible? Let's just have a drink and a little fun."

"Do you have to agree and laugh at everything that bitch says? Are you going to stick it into her next?"

"Who? What laugh? What the hell are you talking about?"

"You know perfectly well who. Janelle is a bitch and she's all over you! I'm not going to sit around here and watch. I'll go myself!"

"Oh, God, you're crazy."

"Take me home!"

"Forget it."

"All right. I will, Goddamn you."

"What's the matter with you?"

"What's wrong with you, Harry? All that talk about responsibility and knowledge and—why don't you show a little to me and your family? You're so sick and full of shit."

"Oh, sure. The boy in the crash was perfect. I'm sorry he got it. You should have married him."

"I didn't say that. If I hadn't spilled the wine—you just don't see yourself! You were ready to attack that poor boob from Cincinnati. Buzz was furious."

"So what? Screw him."

"I wish you meant that. You'd die if he fired you."

"That'll be the day."

"You're pathetic."

"You did spill the wine on purpose, goddamn. I thought so."

"You ought to thank me."

"Why the hell did you do that? Will you stop all the time trying to save me?"

"One of these days I won't."

"Is that a threat or a promise?"

"If you want out just say so. Oh, Harry."

"Then why stay if I'm so useless."

"I don't know."

"Nobody's begging you."

"Sh'hhh. Are you coming. Darling? Please."

"Not a chance. And you're not going!"

"Yelling won't—Harry, I hope you die one of these nights like this."

"Thanks a lot—loving wife of mine."

Janelle came through the French doors and into the garden. She bumped against each side of the door frame and staggered up to Norma and Gardner.

"There you are—Helen and Paris," Janelle said.

Gardner lit a cigarette and walked further into the garden.

"Janelle, I think we'll go on home," Norma said; "I'm not feeling well and—"

"You can't leave now. We're just beginning. You want a pill of some kind? I've got a cabinet full."

"No—I just think—"

"I forbid it. I haven't even had one dance with your old man yet."

"Really, Janelle, we have to. It was a lovely—"

Gardner turned around and faced the two women. Suddenly, he felt crazed and powerful, dazzled by the whiskey in him and its swelling armies of self-assurance. He felt intensely aware that he would do big things tonight. He would be magnificent and menacing. Triumphant and seminal events were about to transpire and he would husband them. He felt brilliant and indomitable. (He didn't realize he was barely able to stand). Two women here, he thought, and he had banged them both! It was a fortuitous omen on the eve of battle! The trumpet sounded and the whiskey charged around in him, calling him beyond himself, into the bloody triangle at Gettysburg, the moist and bloody triangle of womansburg! The whiskey reared up on its back legs and he held on! Against the sky! The earth! The universe! He challenged it, reining in the fire! (And tried to find his legs). A man among men! Prevail! Dominate. Dominus. Dominum. Spiritus Sanctus. Sex and the sinews of his man's strength! God head! Give head! Lux et Veritas. Any old piece of veritas! Yuk. Yuk. And no sniper wife of a woman would bullet him off his high Gin horse or pierce his flesh— impossible—impenetrable—immortal! Man—and man alive!

"We're not going any damned place. It's my birthday."

"Is Norma always this much fun?" Janelle said.

"She used to be," Gardner said, and laughed, "when she was young."

"You bastard," Norma said, and she tried to slap him. But he backed away before she could reach him.

"Norma, relax," Janelle said. "Let him have a little fun. That's all he wants. A little good time."

"With you?"

"Why not," Janelle said.

"I'm sure he'd love to," Norma said.

"As a matter of fact, he did," Janelle said. "He's terrific."

Norma's mouth fell open and she looked at Gardner, who looked away and then at Janelle who stared back.

"Oops. Didn't you know?" Janelle said.

"Harry?" Norma said.

"Norma, she's only kidding. She loves to say things like that," Gardner said.

"My ass," Janelle said, "if you'll pardon a figure of speech."

"Norma! You know Janelle."

Janelle laughed in a pitch that hurt Gardner's ears. She laughed and laughed in her whole body—which stumbled backwards until she fell-sitting on the edge of the rock garden wall that lined the fence of the yard, and doubled over and held her stomach laughing. The laugh came close to breaking the alcohol on the battlements of Gardner's brain. His guts collected, close as cattle in the cold.

"Yeah," Janelle said, finally, still laughing, "I'm only kidding. I'm always only kidding. I just wanted to see your face, Norma. You always have everything so worked out straight. I just wanted to see you—different."

Janelle got up and tried to put her arm around Norma, who pulled away.

"Come on, Norma, honey. I was only kidding. It was just a joke. Let's have a little drink and play some games and then you can go. Come on. Maybe we'll all go. There's a new discothèque in the Village. Everybody gets bare-assed. Okay?"

"Send him home when you're finished, but I wouldn't keep him too long. He spoils." Norma said. She turned and walked through the French doors.

Janelle turned to Gardner. "Jesus. Is she really going?"

"Sure," Gardner said. "It's not the first time."

"Shouldn't you get her a cab?"

"She's a big girl. She's got $20"

"She's so pregnant."

"Get her a goddamned cab yourself, if you're so concerned."

"I don't care. Anyway," Janelle said, and she walked towards Gardner with her arms stretched out to him, "now I'll have you all to myself."

Gardner shoved her away. "You don't look out for anyone, you callous cunt! Jesus Christ. Right out—telling Norma we'd made love."

"She didn't believe me. Nobody believes the truth."

"Norma does. That's all she knows."

"If she's such a saint, why do you shit all over her?"

"Cause I'm a prick—just like you're a cunt."

"They go together, don't they—nicely?"

"If that's what Daddy taught you."

Janelle slapped Gardner. He hit her back, even before he felt the pain. Janelle stumbled backwards and finally fell, thump on her ass, on the stones of the garden floor.

CHAPTER 11

"Janelle," a new voice said, Gardner heard. He looked up and saw a man silhouetted in the French doorway.

"There you are, you mother-fucking angel. What the fuck you doing on the floor?" the voice said.

"Otis, you big hick, you came," Janelle said. The man moved forward and helped Janelle get up. "What the fuck happened?" the man said.

"I tripped—on my tongue."

The big man—he was very big, Gardner saw—in the shoulders and chest and back, though not too tall, embraced Janelle and lifted her off the ground. They held each other tightly and energetically and hugged-kissed. Gardner thought the man looked familiar, but he could not name him and had not caught what Janelle had called him. He was wearing a turtleneck sweater and Levis and a buckskin jacket and he had a beard.

"You fabulous old fucker, I love you," the big man said, "I wouldn't miss your party for the world. Who's here?" The man saw Gardner. "Who the fuck is he?" He continued to hold Janelle tight in his arms, but stared—so Gardner guessed in the darkness—right at Gardner.

"The fuckee," Gardner heard himself saying.

The big man let go of Janelle like a sack and she almost fell down again and the big man began laughing, though he started coming towards Gardner. Gardner didn't care. He felt the adrenalin shoot through him and he wanted to take the big man. I'll kill the sonofabitch with my knife if he tries anything!

"He speaks my language," the big man said.

"Otis uses fuck for all parts of speech when he's drunk," Janelle said, "Which is a good part of the time. Noun, verb, adjective—conjunction even. He learned it in the Army. Didn't you, Otis?"

Fuckin'-A right," the man said. He shook Gardner's hand like a politician on the first day out and jolted his whole body.

"I'm Otis Price," the man said.

"I'm Harry—<u>Otis Price?</u>"

"I don't owe you any fuckin' money do I?"

"My God."

"You know me?"

"Well, sure."

"This mother either hates my fuckin' work or loves it. I can tell."

"I love it. I know everything you've done."

"You do? I'll be fucked."

"There's a sure bet for the 70's," another voice said. Gardner looked again and standing in the doorway now was a silhouette that looked blacker than Price's before. A woman. Against the backlighting from the dining room, Gardner couldn't see her face, but he sensed that she was beautiful. There was just something about the way she stood, he thought, and it was in her voice too.

"Hello," Gardner said.

"That's Naomi X, my wife," Otis Price said. "She's a fuckin' Black Panther or something. I don't know. Anyway she'll murder me in bed one night. She's almost fuckin' killed me there a few times already, if you know what I mean." Otis Price laughed his big laugh again. She was beautiful, Gardner knew, even if he could still not see her. He had seen her in photographs—with Price in <u>Vogue</u>.

"I'm sure he does, Whitey," Mrs. Price said. She came forward out of the doorway and into the garden and practically disappeared in the darkness. "What's happenin', Janelle?"

"Hey, Naomi. Come on in. The blood is fine."

"Another quiet evening at the Billingslys, hunh?"

"Normal as the Nixons," Janelle said.

"Where you from, uh--? Otis Price said to Gardner.

"His name is Harry Gardner—and he's from nowhere," Janelle said.

"I don't want to know from your fuckin' lovers' quarrels, Janelle," Otis Price said. "Where you from, Gardner?"

"Indiana. A little town called Lancaster."

"No shit? I'm from Sherman, Illinois."

"Yeah, I know. I used to drive through Sherman. My grandparents lived near Charleston."

"Yeah?"

Gardner nodded.

"He sounds like a fan, Baby," Mrs. Price said. "Here's another evening down the toilet."

"She hates my fuckin' fans," Otis Price said. "And me. You know how they are now. She hates everybody but Eldridge Cleaver. You know that runaway fucker?"

"He's coming back—to get you," Mrs. Price said.

"I've read 'Soul on Ice'," Gardner said.

"Whoopee," Mrs. Price said.

"Hear that, baby?" Otis Price said. "That and a 'Free Bobby Seale' button, maybe my wife'll spare you when they take over."

"You'll still be up against the wall, baby," Mrs. Price said; "the first ratatattat is for you."

"Another happy marriage," Janelle said. "Love is everywhere."

"So you're from fuckin' Indiana," Otis Price said.

"We gonna hear that Midwest WASP crap again all night," Naomi Price said. "I better get stoned."

"Baby, you're on the outskirts now. You got any grass, Janelle?" Otis Price said.

"Does a whore have towels?"

"Hallelujah," Mrs. Price said.

"That's a girl. Where's your old man?" Otis Price asked.

"Upstairs. Sucking away at some new client."

"Good old fuckin' Buzz. He never quits, does he?" Price said.

"He better not. I couldn't keep buying your shit if he did," Janelle said.

"My shit? How do you like that? Gardner, say somethin'. I thought you were my fuckin' fan," Price said.

I've seen the things Janelle's got of yours. They're fantastic. Jesus, I didn't know she knew you."

"For a thousand years. Before Black-is-Beautiful of course," Price said.

"I used to feed the poor sonofabitch. He'd have starved if it hadn't been for me," Janelle said.

"You should've let him." Naomi Price said.

"When?" Gardner said.

"In New York. After the war. He couldn't sell a pot-holder." Janelle said.

"Speakin' of pot," Mrs. Price said.

"Yeah," Janelle said. "Come on. I'll get it."

The four of them moved through the French doors—Janelle and Otis Price hand in hand—and across the dining room and through the door to the corridor and to the elevator. Janelle got off at the second floor where her bedroom was. The others went on up to the fourth floor and the main room.

There, Gardner saw Wright at the center of an attentive group—Billingsly, English, Shoaly and Honey O'Hara. Madelyn Shoaly was on the couch talking to Nancy English. Toni Carpenter and Duane were dancing. A Herbie Mann record was playing, but not too loud.

"Buzz, you old fucker," Otis Price said. "How's your hammer hangin'?"

Billingsly stopped in mid-word, as though someone had grabbed his throat, Gardner saw. Everyone in the room stopped and looked towards Price. Gardner watched Wright go bloodless and he saw Madelyn Shoaly whisper something to Nancy English, who nodded. Price marched up to Billingsly and shook his hand—arm, shoulder, body—before Billingsly could work his own lateral grip.

"Otis, uh," Billingsly said, "What are you---?"

"How the fuck are you?"

"Uh—you're drunk," Billingsly said.

"Drunk? I'm beyond that—into fuckin' mummy cloth," Otis Price said.

Gardner was loving it. He had never seen Billingsly so paralyzed.

"Uh—this is Ralph Wright from Cincinnati—Wright Shampoo?" Billingsly said.

"You one of that fuckin' Silent Majority I been readin' about?" Price said.

"This is Otis Price, the famous painter and sculptor," Billingsly said.

"And dirty talker," Madelyn Shoaly said.

"He lives in Paris," Billingsly said.

"Is that French he's talking?" Ralph Wright said.

Price laughed his big laugh and grabbed Wright's hand. "Hey, pretty good Mr. Wright on," Price said.

"We don't say you-know-what in front of the ladies." Ralph Wright said.

"What ladies?" Price said.

"All over the room, Mr. Price," Ralph Wright said.

Price looked around and saw Duane. "Oh—there—hi. Sorry," he said.

"Otis, for God's--" Billingsly said.

"I'll bet you love old Spiro, hunh?" Price said to Ralph Wright.

"I do," Wright said.

Otis Price said, "I had better brains for dinner last night."

Ralph Wright's whole face compressed, Gardner saw. He was boiling. And he stared at Billingsly.

"Otis is a famous artist and he loves to shock people. He's as coarse as Russian toilet paper. Now, behave yourself, Otis," Billingsly said.

Otis Price roared a mighty laugh.

"Well, he certainly does know how to shock, and he is coarse," Ralph Wright said.

"Say hello to my old lady—that ought to bust your shock meter altogether," Price said, and he was still laughing.

Naomi Price came towards Ralph Wright with the spiraling power of a black tornado funnel, Gardner thought.

"Que pasa, Bwana," she said to him.

"You're Mrs. Price?" Ralph Wright said.

"Ungawa," Naomi Price said.

Wright looked to Billingsly, then to Price, Gardner saw.

"That means 'dig yourself, baby,' or 'fuck off' or something. I never could pick up on Swahili," Otis Price said.

"Do you have to use that word, Mr. Price?" Ralph Wright said.

"My government taught me how to talk 30 years ago—in the South Pacific—in defense of liberty," Otis Price said.

"Otis, please, these are my guests," Billingsly said.

"We all know the word, Mr. Price," Ralph Wright said.

"Good. Then I think I'll have a fuckin' drink and celebrate," Price said. He walked towards the bar.

"How bout you, Indiana?" Price said to Gardner. Gardner looked back and saw Billingsly—a 100 words a minute—talking to Wright, and the others.

"Baby?" Price said to his wife.

"I'll wait for the shit," Naomi Price said.

"I thought it had arrived," Madelyn Shoaly said, loud enough.

Naomi spun and turned towards her. "Say what?"

Gardner felt sure Naomi had heard it. He had.

"I said—I thought you'd arrived—yesterday—from Paris?" Madelyn Shoaly said. "I read it in Leonard Lyons."

"Yeah," Naomi said. "Dig yourself, baby." She turned away and joined Gardner and Price at the bar.

Billingsly came over to them. "Otis, for God's sake, behave yourself. Wright's an important new client."

"You amaze me, baby. Ambition's really got you by the ass," Price said, but not loud.

Billingsly smiled his full salesman's smile, Gardner saw. "Look, Otis," Billingsly said, "I love you, but lay off. I'm just beginning to work on him. He's very square."

"But not powerless, pal. He's just why I left this fuckin' country."

"Please, Otis, let up on him."

"Is he important to you, Indiana? Price grabbed Gardner in a hurting hug around the neck, but Gardner liked it and took some of the power of the arm into himself.

"He's full of shit. The enemy in brown socks," Gardner said.

"Harry, Jesus," Billingsly said. "You stoned? You know what Wright means."

"Yeah—intestinal corrosion," Gardner said.

"Now, look, goddamn it, I won't have you two drunks louse this up. Now get with it or get out. And, Harry, I'll see you Monday. Happy Birthday." Billingsly walked away, back to Wright who had moved, along with the others, to the far end of the room.

"What do you say, Hoosier?" Price said.

"Let's go," Gardner said.

"Naw, man, that's too easy," Price said. "I gotta study that mother. You said yourself he's the fuckin' enemy. I ain't seen him for awhile. Let's infiltrate."

Gardner saw Janelle enter the room and come towards them.

"Here's your ticket, Otis—first-class," Janelle said. She put a marijuana cigarette into Price's hand. Price looked down at it. Janelle gave Naomi one, too.

"Jesus, it's got a filter," Price said.

"Only the best, baby," Janelle said. "Here." She held one out towards Gardner. He took it. In that moment, Gardner decided to go all the way. Whatever happened tonight—happened. He'd do what he wanted to do and say what came to him. No brakes, blocks or edits. Cut free. Snap the leash. Fuck all.

Gardner lit the point that looked like a cigarette and took a drag of it, deeply, and held it for as long as he could. He tasted the sweetness in his mouth and savored it and reluctantly let the smoke out. He smiled at Naomi who was staring at him. Her eyes were flat and she did not return his smile. Her face was non-committal, but there was something about her overall which was menacing, Gardner thought. Well, so am I, baby, he said to her, without saying it aloud, so watch it. The words must have gotten into her head somehow, because, Gardner saw, the slightest frown began to pull her mouth down at the corners and then one shoulder shrugged up and she broke off their eye duel. She turned away to the bartender.

"You gotta ginger ale, there, brother?" she said to him.

Gardner was glad he had out-stared her. He could outstare anyone tonight. She is beautiful though; my God, beautiful, dangerous... I've never made love to a black woman. Maybe tonight's the night. Maybe her. Gardner took another deep inhalation of the joint and looked at Otis Price.

He listened to Price tell Janelle about his one-man show at the Guggenheim Museum which was to open Wednesday of next week for 2 months.

That's who I wish I were, Gardner said to himself. Famous. A working artist. Lives free, anyway he wants to. Great drinker, brawler and he's always saying something outrageous. He knows Norman Mailer! Gardner remembered Price's horrid-beautiful drawings from the war (nothing as good since Goya's grotesques) that began appearing in Life and Collier's from New Guinea and Saipan and Iwo Jima and Okinawa and told you all you had to know about war and he remembered that Price had been wounded at Okinawa and saw in his mind Price's drawings from the hospital which told you all you had to know about getting broken and full of pain. And now he remembered photos he had seen of Price's first important work after the war—a sculpture in Hiroshima—of a child, all fragile arms shielding against the sky. It was so good, so simple and had been made from the steel that had been left in the ruins. It was the most powerful and moving work he had ever seen. He would ask Price about that, Gardner told himself. They would talk about that. And art. And Norman Mailer. He was grateful Price was here.

"I'd love to turn on that old honkey," Naomi said, looking at Ralph Wright.

"Fantastic," Janelle said. "I'll bet we could. Hey, you want to play the truth game?"

"Dig yourself, baby," Naomi said.

"Jesus, no," Price said. "The last time you were in Paris and we played, what a fuck-up." He talked to Gardner now.

"Two friends of mine—French painters—one accused the other of being a Nazi during the war. They almost killed each other."

"And wrecked the apartment," Naomi said.

"They paid," Price said.

"Let's play," Janelle said.

"She has a natural gift for demolition," Gardner said.

"Turn old Whitey on first," Naomi said.

Gardner looked up and saw that Billingsly was going out of the room—to the toilet, he supposed.

"I'll do it," Janelle said. She walked over to Ralph Wright who was talking-- "They've destroyed all the old values—these kids—no respect for any--" he was saying.

"Mr. Wright," Janelle said, "have you ever smoked pot?"

Gardner watched Ralph Wright's face. His expression turned hard.

"Excuse me?" Ralph Wright said.

"You know," Janelle said. "Pot-grass. What the kids use."

"Marijuana?" Wright said.

"Close enough," Janelle said.

"Good Heavens, no," Wright said. "It's illegal."

"I have," Honey said. "It was scrumptious. I giggled for hours."

"I'm surprised to hear that," Ralph Wright said.

"You'd be surprised about a lot of people in this room," Janelle said. "You see, as a parent, Mr. Wright, I've got to be very careful about pot. It's in all the schools, you know."

"Not in Cincinnati."

"I'm sure. But in New York, you can't be safe. So this doctor friend of mine—said the best way to know if your son is experimenting or taking it is to try some yourself—in moderation, of course--

"All things," Ralph Wright said.

"Exactly. Then you'll know the symptoms," Janelle said. "So, you know what he did? He gave me some."

"You have it—here?"

She nodded. "Right here." She opened her fist and looked down at the five joints she held there.

"But if the police found out. We could all go to jail. We'd be ruined," Ralph Wright said.

"No--" Janelle said. "How would they know—a respectable house like this."

"Oh, we could try it, Ralph," Honey O'Hara said.

"It's against the law," Ralph Wright said.

"Oh, who'll know," Honey said.

"I would," Ralph Wright said.

Janelle lit one of the joints and inhaled it.

"See," Janelle said, "there's nothing to it. Here."

She held out the cigarette to Wright, who backed away from it.

"Mrs. Billingsly, I guess your doctor knows what he's—but--"

"Try it, Mr. Wright. Everyone does. I've had it at the Shoalys. And Cleve English and his wife smoked here last time."

"Just to try it," Cleve English said. "A couple of puffs. Nothing."

Honey said, "All my friends smoke it."

"Honey!" Ralph Wright said. "This is strictly forbidden by law."

"So's adultery, Mr. Wright," Janelle said.

Honey O'Hara laughed, and Gardner saw her blush. Wright looked at her fiercely.

"What's that mean?" Ralph Wright said.

"Nothing." Janelle said. "Should it?"

"You're really embarrassing me, Mrs. Billingsly," Wright said. "I don't mean to be a spoil sport, but—"

"It's harmless," Janelle said. "Just makes you feel good."

"Harmless?" Ralph Wright said. "Not according to J. Edgar Hoover."

"But see," Janelle said. "No fangs, no horns, no warts."

"Oh, try it, Ralphie," Honey O'Hara said. "Just for fun—once--for me."

"Mrs. Billingsly, I--" Ralph Wright said.

"I'll try," Honey O'Hara said.

Janelle passed the cigarette to Honey, who giggled, and then inhaled it—very knowingly, Gardner saw.

"Honey!" Ralph Wright said.

"It's sexy—for me anyway," Honey O'Hara said.

"Here, Mr. Wright. What can it hurt? You'll relax yourself and all the rest of us. Everyone's dying to have some," Janelle said.

"Don't be a party pooper, baby," Honey O'Hara said. "I don't want to go home with a party pooper. That gets me very upset." She giggled. "Do it for Honey."

"I see no reason to insist," Cleve English said, "if he doesn't--"

"Here's one for you, Cleve," Janelle said. "Remember how much you loved it?"

"We could smoke one, Cleve—just to test," Nancy English said. She took the cigarette from Janelle—fast—and lit it and took the first drag.

"I'm sure the whole thing is nothing," Ralph Wright said.

"Of course—then try it," Janelle said.

"Well—this is ridiculous," Ralph Wright said. He took the cigarette from Honey and put it in his mouth as though it were bad medicine. He made a face and puffed on it, without inhaling. "There. Nothing."

"You're right, but you've got to really inhale and hold it—almost swallow it, Mr. Wright." Janelle said. "Like this." Janelle inhaled the cigarette.

"All right," Wright said, and he did as Janelle showed him, coughing just a bit.

"It's the whole life that's bad. The attitude. You have to want it to have an effect," Ralph Wright said.

"I guess we may as well experiment too, Madelyn," Garve Shoaly said. Madelyn nodded and smiled and looked, Gardner thought like a kid about to lick the fudge bowl.

"Again, don't you mean, Garve," Janelle said.

Wright took another drag and held this one even longer, Gardner saw.

"It absolutely has no effect, if you don't want it to," Ralph Wright said.

"Who wouldn't want <u>sexy</u>," Honey O'Hara said.

"Holy shit, she did it," Naomi Price said. "Janelle is supin' else."

"Fuckin' dynamite," Otis Price said, watching from the bar.

"Ralphie, you are right. There's nothing to it. It just relaxes you a little. Not as bad as sleeping pills even," Janelle said.

"But it's the life—not giving a damn about things," Ralph Wright said.

"Isn't that nice for a change?" Honey O'Hara said.

"Got one for us, Janelle?" Duane said. He and Toni moved in and Janelle handed Duane a joint.

"Does Mrs. Wright take sleeping pills?" Janelle asked.

"Does she ever," Honey O'Hara said. "<u>All</u> kinds."

"Honey," Ralph Wright said.

"Well, that's what you told me."

"Now," Janelle said. "I have a wonderful game. Everybody sit down. Do you like games, Mr Wright?"

"I don't play very well, but I like them. Like 20 Questions?"

"Not exactly," Janelle said.

"I'm really not good."

"It doesn't matter. In this one you just say what's on your mind—the simple truth."

"Janelle, no," Billingsly said, entering the room. "I forbid it."

"Buzz, it's just a little game," Janelle said. "Why get so excited?"

"I love games," Honey O'Hara said.

"Of course, you do, Honey—me too," Janelle said. "They're just so uptight, pay no attention. Now, all you do--"

"Janelle, I'm warning you," Billingsly said. He pulled her aside and said: "Is Wright smoking pot? You didn't, Janelle."

"Yeah, he's loving it and leave us alone." Janelle rejoined the group.

"We ought to just smoke and rap," Otis Price said.

"Sure," Janelle said, "we'll do that, Otis, but first we'll play my little game—or get out."

"Perhaps we should end this," Cleve English said.

"I want to play. I want to play," Honey O'Hara said. "What do I do?"

"All right, Honey, you can go first. Just say what you think about people—here in the room and about yourself."

"That's all?"

"That's all," Janelle said.

"That doesn't sound like much fun."

"You'll see. And the most honest wins. You'll love it," Janelle said.

"Anything?"

"Anything that comes into your pretty little head," Janelle said.

"Janelle, really," Billingsly said.

"Shut up! No go ahead, Honey. You start it. Then Ralph can go."

"Well," Honey said. "I think—I think this is a swell time tonight. And—I wish—I wish I was pregnant. Oh, where'd that nice pregnant lady go? I'd love to have a baby."

"Happy to oblige, M'am," Otis Price said.

"In rehab heaven, mother--" Naomi said.

"And--" Honey said, "I think Ralph is very smart and successful. Everybody here—and talented. But you know what surprised me about Ralph? He likes to have his feet rubbed. That's all he wants most of the time. Isn't that--? That always just makes me laugh, a big corporation president who likes to have his feet rubbed and he likes to rub mine, but I can't stand it. I really can't, Ralph. Don't be mad, Ralph. It's the truth. Uh, wow. Let's see. I think Mrs. Price is very beautiful and I think he's cute." Honey O'Hara pointed to Harry Gardner. Gardner was not surprised, not tonight. He thought he was pretty cute himself. "Wow. That's all."

"But you didn't say a word about yourself," Janelle said.

"Oh, I'm nobody. I'm just—nothin worth mentioning," Honey O'Hara said; and she seemed to mean it, Gardner thought. He'd make her think she was somebody! But he had to lay Naomi Price first.

"Okay, Ralph, your turn," Janelle said.

Ralph Wright stood up and looked down at his shoes, Gardner saw.

"Well, I'm—I do like to have my feet rubbed. I don't see what's wrong with that. It feels good. After a hard day. It even feels good after an easy day. And, I think you're somebody, Honey. I'm very surprised about myself tonight. Smoking one of these—things. And about your son," Ralph Wright said, looking at Billingsly, "Maybe I shouldn't say it, but I'm surprised at his lack of respect and discipline. That's what comes of progressive education I think. And I'm not impressed by Mr. Price's language, no matter how famous he is. And I'm—I'm just a little taken aback by all your—cleverness—in this room. It's a little fast for my speed. Cleverness frightens me. I don't trust it. I have to tell you that. Eugene McCarthy was clever. And Adlai Stevenson—the worst. I think a man ought to plod more. Those punks in Chicago were clever. And—I always feel uneasy in New York. It's not quite us—America. And, Mr. Gardner, I'm troubled about you. I liked you at first. I could tell you were from my country, but then later—you seemed, well, I have to say it. You seemed foreign. I, uh, like Buzz very much. And Garve. And I admire Cleve English about as much as you can. And I think you're—very forceful, Mrs. Billingsly. Uh. That's all. I'm not very fast on my feet."

"Give 'em a rub, Honey baby," Naomi said.

Gardner watched Wright sit down and take out his handkerchief. He wiped his face and continued to look at his shoes.

"Very good, Ralph," Janelle said. "Very good. Otis?"

"Not a chance, baby," Otis Price said. "You fucked me once already with this game."

"Ditto, okay," Naomi said.

"Chicken," Janelle said.

"Shit," Naomi said.

"Duane?" Janelle said.

Duane sprang up. "I love everybody here," he said. "Myself included. It's a marvelous party. Oh yes, I wish Buzz would give me a raise." Duane sat down and laughed, as though, Gardner thought, he thought he had said something witty.

"That's it?"

"Yes—and beautiful John Lindsay should be mayor forever."

"And week-end at the Pines," Janelle said. "Toni?"

"I should have a hit record. And a Dean Martin booking. I—no--that's all. That's cool. I'm not going to dive into this tank of piranha."

"Cop-out," Janelle said. "Buzz—darling?"

You could clean an oven with the way Janelle said <u>darling</u>, Gardner thought.

"I pass. I just hope we all behave ourselves, that's all," Buzz said. "Where's Norma?"

"She wasn't feeling well," Gardner said. "She said to give her regrets and she got a cab." At least, you think she did, Gardner said to himself. <u>She did. She did.</u>

"All right, birthday boy. Come on, Harry," Janelle said.

"Later."

"You can't duck it."

"I won't. Just let me think," Gardner said.

"Cleve?"

"I guess my biggest fault is golf. I spend too much time playing golf. Can't help it. I love my wife—though I wish she wouldn't worry about me so much or come to the studio all the time. I think Ralph Wright is very nice—and creative. Toni's my favorite singer. And Janelle is a naughty Elsa Maxwell. Oh—I wish Otis Price would be on my show. Would you?"

"With his mouth?" Janelle said.

"The boob tube's not my fuckin' bag, pal," Otis Price said. "Sorry."

"Well, think about it. We could bleep you. Buzz is—the most energetic, brightest man I know. And Madelyn does write dirty books, though I love every page. And—let's see—uh--once I had an erotic dream about Shirley Temple."

"Cleve," Nancy said.

Cleve English laughed; and looked embarrassed, Gardner thought.

"Whatever made me remember that?" Cleve English said. He sat down, looking, Gardner thought, sincerely puzzled.

"Nancy?" Janelle said.

"Oh, I wouldn't dare," Nancy English said. "I wouldn't know what to say.

"Don't be anal, dear," Janelle said.

"Garve?"

"There is one thing I've been thinking," Garve Shoaly said. It's you, Madelyn. I've never told you."

"Watch it," Madelyn Shoaly said. "I'll have you deported."

"I detest the way you eat popcorn every movie we go to. That's it," Garve Shoaly said.

"Better be," Madelyn Shoaly said. "I've got loads on you."

"Well, tell it," Janelle said. "Christ, no one's playing the game. Not one word about sex."

"Fuck," Otis Price said.

"Well, it is one word," Janelle said.

"I dig it," Naomi said.

"You silly savage," Janelle said. She laughed.

"Dig it, baby," Naomi said. "Humpin' and ginnin' and singin' and dancin'--all the live long day."

"Do da Do da," Otis Price said, singing it.

"Come on, Nancy," Janelle said, "you've got to play. You must think of something!"

"Well, I believe in—the spirit world," Nancy said. "Astrology too—it's important. We should pay more attention to all those things. And, lets' see-well, all right—I--I think Cleve is the nicest person—the very nicest kind of person. And has been very successful. I never dreamed he's be this successful. And—I like going to see his shows and meeting famous people. Don't you really want me to come to the studio?" Nancy looked at Cleve, Gardner saw, genuinely puzzled and hurt by what her husband had said. She kept looking at him.

"I don't know what Cleve sees in me," Nancy said. "Maybe he's just always felt—obligated, cause we went together since high school, but—I don't understand why everyone is so unhappy. Things are so good in this country. We have so many blessings and nice things. The moon and appliances. And if all the colored--" Nancy stopped and looked at Naomi. "I'm sorry," she said and she smiled, "Blacks—were like my Eunice--"

"Who?" Naomi said.

"Eunice," Nancy said, "who thinks it's just terrible all the trouble her people are causing."

"Is Eunice your maid, baby?" Naomi said.

"Why, yes."

"Sheet," Naomi said. "Sheet, sheet. The maid! And Sammy Davis got rhythm, right?" Naomi said. "You dingaling bitch."

"Now just a minute," Cleve English said. Gardner was surprised. He had never seen English react with such heat. "Seems to me there's no reason to--"

"This mother-grabbin' country's going backwards instead of forward," Naomi said. "Excuse my black ass." Naomi dropped her cigarette into her drink and walked out of the room.

Nancy looked around into all the other faces. "I'm sorry."

There was silence, "Give me another drink," Otis said to the bartender. He looked at Nancy, "You don't know it but you sound like a fuckin' racist."

"That _word_," Cleve English said, "do we need it all the--"

"Racist? Me?" Nancy said and her lower lip was giving way, Gardner saw, and he heard the tears coming into her voice. "I didn't mean any harm—I--"

"Of course you didn't, Nancy," English said.

"--Harry Belafonte's been to our house. And Godfrey Cambridge. Lots of color—_black_--" Nancy began to cry, openly. "Tell them, Cleve. Tell them. Tell them I'm no racist—I'm--I'm a Christian."

Cleve English went to his wife and held her in his arms and gave her a handkerchief and pattered her on the back. "Of course you're not, honey—there, there," he said. "I do think you and your wife owe my wife an apology. If anything she said was offensive, I'm sure it was all in innocence. She meant well—and I've done my part for Negroes."

"Putting on Black girl singers?" Otis Price said. "Aw—fuck it. She'll be back."

"In case you didn't notice," Janelle said, "_that_ was the apology."

"Really, Otis," Billingsly said, "Don't you know any other word? Let's all say it—like children and be done with it."

CHAPTER 12

"Where were we?" Janelle said.

Nobody answered.

"Let's end this stupid game too," Billingsly said.

"Absolutely not," Janelle said. "We're just warming up. And you got off too easy—love-of-my-life. You're the only Jew I know who'd pass up a chance to talk like this." Janelle looked at Ralph Wright, who looked surprised. "Surely, Mr. Wright, you knew Buzz was Jewish? No, you didn't, did you? I can tell. He never told you?" Janelle looked at Buzz and a slow, slicing smile opened her mouth. She looked back at Wright, then back and forth between Billingsly and Wright.

Gardner knew Janelle was delighted as a maggot to come onto this bit of pus.

"I can't imagine why." Janelle said. "I'm sure it wouldn't change your view of him," she said to Wright.

"Why no, course not," Wright said.

"See, Darling? What's wrong? You look paralyzed. You're not ashamed, are you? Is that why you changed your name from Berstein to Billingsly? And joined the Racquet Club?

Gardner had seen that Billingsly really was punched by Janelle saying he was Jewish, but as he watched him, he saw Billingsly recover himself quickly. He had seem him do that too—often.

"Janelle," Billingsly said, in a doctory-condescending kind of tone, Gardner heard, "Are you feeling quite all right? You seem—disoriented."

Janelle belched out an enormous laugh. It went on and on, more like a scream that laughter.

Buzz looked at Wright and smiled. "She did complain this afternoon," he said, "of—female problems." Wright was nodding in real need, grabbing for this information, Gardner thought. He needed all the reference points he could get, Gardner figured.

"Female problems?! You bastard," Janelle said, still laughing. "Mr. Cool—nothing cuts through that ice. If you want to know the truth, Mr. Wright, I do have a female problem—not getting laid! In bed, Mr. Billingsly-Berstein is not exactly King Kong. He keeps his penis locked in the safe at the office, and he's thrown away the combination."

Cleve English was quietly manuvering his wife towards the stairs, Gardner saw.

Janelle turned on them. "Where are you going?"

"Just—I have an early date—don't want to break up the party. Go ahead." Cleve English half-whispered.

They both waved and Cleve English and his wife kept on walking. They disappeared into the stairwell.

Gardner eyed Billingsly. He was waiting and wanting him to fall apart, but, no, he was playing it with tolerance and dignity. You'd think he was her shrink, Gardner said to himself. He watched Billingsly whisper something to Ralph Wright, who was really in there nodding heavier than before. Janelle spun around and saw them.

"What? What are you telling him?" She screeched.

"Nothing, dear," Billingsly said, "just—explaining."

"I don't need any goddamned explaining! Don't explain me! Explain yourself!" She started to falter, Gardner saw, but then she righted herself and got new strength from somewhere and she stumbled towards Billingsly and Wright.

"Better idea," she said. "I'll explain you—you scared closet Jew. Desk humper! How bout if I start with how you married me for my money? Let's tell Mr. Wright everything about this emotional igloo we live in. Still so cool, Darling? And your soft-ons?" Janelle stopped talking and fell down. Flat out.

Gardner looked at Billingsly and saw that he was making no move towards Janelle. No one did. Gardner went to her, knelt and lifted her a bit. Duane came over and bent down on the other side of her.

Janelle shook her head like a punched fighter. She looked up at Gardner and Duane and slobbered, "Jesus—talk about the Odd Couple." Gardner and Duane lifted her to her feet. "Who pushed me?" Janelle said.

"Are you all right?" Duane said.

Janelle nodded. "I just wanted to see if I could still do that."

"I'm sorry Janelle isn't herself tonight—obviously," Billingsly said, "perhaps we ought to--"

"They're staying," Janelle said. "They'll go when I tell them to!"

"Mrs. Billingsly," Honey O'Hara said, "maybe we should—split."

"Call me Mrs. Berstein, dear."

"Janelle, you're drunk—and making an ass of yourself," Madelyn Shoaly said. "Let us go, and do yourself and us a favor."

"So you can run to '21' and tell all our friends about me?" Janelle said.

"Oh, Janelle, kiss off," Madelyn Shoaly said. "If Buzz won't tell you, I will. I'm not the gentleman he is."

"No," Janelle said, "but still very masculine, darling, so don't be so hard on yourself."

"Oh God, you're insufferable," Madelyn said.

"Ooooh, I know an even better story," Janelle said. "Stay, Madelyn—the gang'll love this. The true account of how one Hungarian photographer named Garve Shoaly—what was your real name, Garve?--met one American dirty book writer lady on the French Riviera and married her so he could get to America and--"

"That's slanderous! Buzz!" Garve Shoaly said.

"--be a citizen—and screw all the American ladies he could get—the original little Buda-pest."

"She's a witch!" Garve Shoaly said.

"Relax, pal. You'll break something," Otis Price said.

"You don't like that story?" Janelle said. "All your friends do."

"Poor Janelle," Madelyn Shoaly said. "I'd heard you were psychotic, but--. Buzz, you'd better sign the papers. Your wife should be committed. I'm sorry."

"Don't patronize me, you cun—"

"Good-night, Janelle. May bands of angels carry you to your padded cell," Madelyn said. She went to Buzz and kissed him on the cheek. "Call, Buzz, if we can help. I really am sorry. How you put up with...Come on, Garve." Garve shook hands with Buzz. They didn't speak, but Garve gave Buzz a friend-at-the-funeral look, Gardner saw.

Janelle coughed up that searing, terrifying laugh again. Then she fell—lump--onto the couch. Madelyn and Garve Shoaly walked towards the stairs.

"Go—go. I'm sick of you," Janelle said. "Go type another 300 pages of mouse droppings—uck."

Gardner looked at Madelyn Shoaly, who had her back to the room. She stopped. A kind of nerve gas seized her. The back went rigid. Then finally it rose in a deep breath and Madelyn Shoaly turned around.

"I suppose it's true afterall," she said. "They always said insanity ran in your family. And didn't your father commit suicide?" Madelyn Shoaly turned around and with Garve went down the stairs. Gardner felt that Madelyn thought oxen would be coming to drag away the carcass.

"That dumb bitch," Janelle said. "She thought that was cutting."

"I apologize—to you all," Billingsly said. "You see—but, I'm sure you'll be sympathetic."

Janelle looked at Billingsly and stuck her tongue out. "You ass kisser," she said. "I'm sure you'll be sympathetic," she said, imitating him. She heaved with laughter. "Mister-rise-above-it all. Play the great man. Never lose your cool. Me and the children? We could be trapped in a great burning building and you'd be outside charming the firemen."

"It's true, isn't it, Buzz?" Otis Price said.

Billingsly turned around quickly.

Price said. "Somebody ought to knock you on your fuckin ass—but good."

"You ought to drink some black coffee—or get group therapy with Janelle and stop getting it out in decent people's homes," Billingsly said.

"Don't get cute, ad man. I will put you on your ass."

"Duane," Janelle said, "tell us about being homosexual. I want to know—seriously. What's it like?"

Duane had been inhaling a cigarette at that moment. He choked and coughed on the smoke, Garder saw and heard. Duane tamped out the cigarette in an ashtray, but he kept coughing. He took Toni Carpenter's elbow and walked straight up to Billingsly.

"Gracias, Buzz," he said. "It was—different. See you Monday."

"Good-night, Duane—I'm sorry," Billingsly said. "Toni."

"Courage, baby." Toni said.

"Nighty-night all," Duane said. "God bless. Ciao."

"Toni," Janelle said, "are the rumors about you true?"

"Forget it, Lady MacBeth," Toni said. "You're tuned out." She and Duane got to the stairs, and disappeared.

"They say she's a Lesbian," Janelle said.

Billingsly dropped his head and shook it back and forth slowly, Gardner saw.

"Ralph," Billingsly said, "I'm sure you want to leave. I'll see you to the door. And Miss O'Hara."

"Miss O'Hara. Jesus, isn't he good at it? Ralph doesn't want to leave, do you, Ralphie? He's fascinated. This confirms everything old Ralphie ever thought about New York. Right? Didn't Barry Goldwater tell you we ought to be lopped off the country and floated out to sea? New Yorkers aren't Americans—not Ralphie's kind. We're savages to old Ralphie—aren't we? Like in National Geographic. I'll bet you wish you had slides even—to show the folks back home. Hey—aren't the women topless? Here, Ralphie, I'll go topless like the savages." Janelle started fumbling at her clothes. Billingsly grabbed her by the arms.

"Janelle," Billingsly said, "stop it."

Janelle tried to resist at first, but was too drunk to have the strength. She relented and relaxed into the couch.

"All right, missionary—I won't bare my boobs. Let go." Billingsly did.

Janelle was absolutely right, Gardner was thinking. He hadn't been able to figure out why Ralph Wright had stayed through this whole evening in which so much must have been repugnant to him, but Janelle had hit it. He was fascinated. We're a show to him—shock theatre. He wouldn't miss this freak spectacle for the world. Now he'd have New York nailed for sure. He could hear him telling it at home: "Why, you just can't believe it, Mother," he'd say, "how they carry on...those effete snobs. Spiro's right, Mother—they're degenerated. Perverts. Sick. They're what's wrong with this country."

"Shall we--?" Billingsly said, indicating the door. "Then I'll see she gets to bed. It'll be all right. I'll take care of her—and call the doctor in the morning."

Wright and Honey O'Hara moved towards the stairs.

"Wait!" Janelle screamed, and Gardner heard the desperation in her voice. "Harry, please, baby, the game, the truth! Tell it! Now's your chance. Don't lose the chance. Tell us what you think of Ralphie."

Ralph Wright turned around and looked at Gardner, and smiled. It was a confident smile, Gardner thought. He saw that Wright could not imagine that he would say anything but good things and too, in the smile, there was a signal of shared indulgence about Janelle's drunken screaming. One good fellow to another. Two mid-west regular guys. Gardner figured in the first instant that Wright was right about him, but then he listened and heard what his voice was saying.

"I think he's a dangerous sonofabitch," Gardner said.

"Harry—you're joking," Billingsly said. Gardner didn't take his eyes away from Wright who was staring right back at him. Wright's eyes didn't flinch, but, Gardner saw, he had splattered the smile off his face.

"No, I'm not," Gardner said. "He is. He's a menace. His kind of thinking. His America. Oh yeah, just for the record, 'Americans The Beautiful' is my idea—and it's not for sale. It's a painting I did and the idea is not for sale to Ralph Wright. And I think—I think I'm drunk—Ralph Wright is my greatest enemy—conquering all the have-not bastards of this world with a rotary bell! He's a racist, imperialist, self-righteous murdering sonofabitch!"

"Harry," Billingsly said, "for Christ's sake!"

"You're drunk, young man—and very out of line!" Ralph Wright said.

"And you're treacherous. I despise and fear everything you stand for— from your pious hypocrisy to your napalm-loving little heart. I hate your brown socks too. And your foot rubs."

"Harry, shut up!" Billingsly said.

"You don't believe in America of the Constitution or of its people— you're scared to death of the people."

"Let's go, Ralph—don't mind him," Honey O'Hara said. "He's stoned."

"No!," Janelle said. "We're just getting somewhere."

"Can't you stand the truth Mr.Wright?" Gardner said.

"You don't own any, boy! You're what Agnew was talkin' about! You're talking garbage."

"And your solution is a bigger and better cunt spray!"

"I don't care how drunk you are! You'll never work on any account of mine—ever! And if Billingsly wants my business you won't even be in the building!"

"Amen—dinosaur!"

"Harry, shut up," Billingsly said, "You're fired!"

"I quit," Gardner said. "And fuck both of you—from sea to shining sea!" Gardner ran towards the stairwell and looked as though he might physically attack Wright, who put his arms up to defend himself; but Gardner pushed him aside and ran down the stairs, two at a time, and he was crying, and he was stumbling forward, banging against both walls, but he kept on his feet and kept going, down, down, down. Get away! Escape! It's a brothel—full of lies and venereal ideas. While there's time.

The collapse is coming. The rotting crumbling, compromising order of things. I'm free. I've westled my balls back—they're out of Billingsly's cupped hands and back between my legs—where they belong. Feel them? Feel them bouncing like church bells—announcing good news. And—and away from Janelle too. That great evil Madonna of a black religion, who's held you trapped in sexual addiction and laziness. You're free of her too—of them all. You can go—go to Norma, your true Church, nestle in the wet heat of her good sanctuary and love yourself clean in that shrine of decency. You can mount that altar with your guilty penis and find the penance for all of your sins. You'll be clean and new and innocent. And tomorrow. Tomorrow you can begin again—born once more from the kiss of her womb and you'll recapture the Harry Gardner who mattered who counted for something—for--for something! His thoughts stopped. For what? Gardner stopped his physical running and looked around him and realized dimly that he was in the garden again. What can I count for? He was choking for breath. WHAT? He screamed. Say something! Voice it! What is the WORD? I have to count! It had to matter! I set out to! It's in me! WHERE? WHAT? Gardner's head exploded with light shows and heavy drums and his thoughts squeeled like an amplifier feeding-back at highest volume. His leg muscles twitched and finally gave way. He blacked out and fell down and hit his head on the low brick retaining wall that separated the fieldstone floor from the flower beds. He didn't know it, but he cut himself in the fall and his head was bleeding. He moaned, turned on his side, stretched out and lay there with his head in the dirt of the flowers, his blood soaking into the soil.

Gardner didn't know it, but Naomi watched him fall. She had been sitting in a metal chair at the far end of the garden smoking a cigarette, when Gardner had run in. She had heard him shouting "what" and "where" and "the word" and had wondered what it meant. When he fell, she didn't move, since she expected him to get himself up. But, after a moment, when he didn't stir, she realized that he was unconscious and might be hurt. Still, she didn't hurry. Why should she, she thought, for some drunken whitey. She dropped her cigarette on the stone floor and crushed it out deliberately with her boot heel. Silly drunken bastard, she thought to herself. She got up, slowly, and went over to him. She stared down at him. She jostled his body with her foot.

"Hey, man," she said, "come on. That's no place to <u>dormez.</u> Shake it up. Come on. Aw, sheet-who needs this mother?" She knelt down beside him and shook him. "Hey, man, pick it up. You'll freeze your ass off here.

Go on inside." Gardner didn't move or make a sound. Naomi turned him over and her hand brushed against his forehead and she felt the blood streaming down his face.

"Sheet, man, he did a job on hisself." Naomi took her thumb and forefinger and tried first one eye, then his other, to open them, but they closed shut each time she let go. She moved his head off the brick wall and onto the stone floor. She walked back to the chair she had been sitting on and picked up the seat cushion. She carried it back to Gardner, and kneeling down again, she put it under his head.

"Don't go way, 'fay," Naomi said to him. "I'll be right back."

She got up and went into the house with the idea of telling someone what had happened. She heard Janelle screaming.

"Harry—Harry!" Janelle was yelling. "Where are you?"

Naomi saw Janelle and Otis Price emerge from the stairwell.

"You seen Harry?" Janelle asked.

"He's in the garden--" Naomi said.

"Oh, good, he didn't go," Janelle said.

"--flat on his ass," Naomi said. "the dumb bastard's bleeding all over the place. He fell. If he got any on me, he's gonna pay for a new outfit."

"Florence fuckin' Nightingale," Otis Price said, "couldn't have put it better."

"Up yours, Jack," Naomi said. "I'm not that ofay mother's nurse."

"What happened?" Janelle said. "Is he all right?"

Janelle stumble-ran through the dining room, knocking into a tea trolly and sending two cups crashing to the floor, and out through the French doors.

"I'll get some towels," Naomi said. "The dingaling really did hurt himself." Otis Price nodded and followed after Janelle. Billingsly came walking along the hallway, from having taken Ralph Wright and Honey O'Hara to the front door. He saw Naomi.

"Where's Janelle?" Billingsly asked.

"In the garden—with that Harry cat," Naomi said.

"He's here—still?"

"He's gonna be—for awhile."

Billingsly pushed by Naomi and rushed towards the garden. When he got there he saw Janelle sitting down on the stones and Otis Price kneeling over Gardner's unconscious form.

"Get him out, Janelle!" Billingsly said, "Now!"

"He's hurt," Janelle said. She was holding Gardner's head in her lap.

"I want him out!" Billingsly said.

"The mother-fucker cut himself," Otis Price said. "He's bleeding like a bull."

"I want him out of my house! Out. Out, do you hear me?! Get him out!"

Naomi returned with two wet towels.

"Buzz, shut up," Janelle said. She took one of the towels from Naomi and placed it on Gardner's forehead. "Here," she said to Otis Price, indicating the other towel, "put this on his wrists. Naomi, honey, in the medicine chest—smelling salts. Get 'em will you?" Naomi nodded and walked back into the house.

"I don't want that ruinous, crazy sonofabitch in my house," Billingsly said, and, coming up, he started to kick at Gardner's body.

"Hey, can that shit," Otis Price said, springing up to his feet. He pressed his body against Billingsly's, driving him back, and he locked Billingsly's forearms with his big hands.

"I want him out of my house!"

"My house, godamn you. I paid for it, remember?" Janelle shouted.

"You're insane, all of you," Billingsly said, trying to break loose from Price's grip. "You don't give a goddamn about anything—proper!"

Naomi came back into the garden. She stopped and watched.

"Oh, fuck off, Buzz," Janelle said. "All you care about's your goddamned account. So you lost one. How rich do you have to be, for Christ's sake? Stop sweating, and show a little concern for Harry. He's your friend, or supposed to be, you jerk. He's already made you more dollars than you can do with. Help him. He's in trouble."

"I hope he bleeds to death," Billingsly said.

Janelle didn't say a word, but she got up and came straight to in front of Billingsly. Otis Price let him go. Janelle looked at Billingsly and though he couldn't see the look in her face, he could feel it, and he was afraid of Janelle.

"Do you mean that?" Janelle said.

"Yes—I do," Billingsly said.

Janelle nodded. "Yes, you do," she said. "I hope he doesn't You want to know why? I love him. I love him. He's my lover. He makes beautiful love to me. Better than you did—ever. I want him to live and love me and—you--you can die—where--you stand—Jew." Janelle began beating on Billingsly with her fists and he shrank back and protected himself from the blows and turned and ran through the French doors. "Jew, Jew, Jew!"

Janelle said, chasing after him. But Billingsly got inside the house and locked the doors and ran over to the switch and turned out the dining room lights.

"--Jew--worse than Jew! You Jew-hating Jew coward bastard prick!"

"Janelle, Janelle, baby, cool it—cool-_it_," Otis Price said, coming to her. Janelle was pounding on the glass of the doors and still shouting at Billingsly. Price picked her up bodily and carried her away.

"You'll break the fuckin' glass. Hey, don't hit _me_, for Chris' sake. Hey, kid, relax. Cool it," Otis Price said.

"You white cats sure are civilized," Naomi said.

"Lay off, Naomi."

"I sure is learnin' a lot."

Janelle fell her full weight against Otis and began sobbing and she cried and cried and cried—huge mounting waves of crying convulsed her and she cried for her mother and her father and her brother and her Gardner and her marriage and her life until, finally, she had no more tears. Price held her through it all and could feel the depth of her quaking and was awed by it and, at the end, gently, he sat her down in a chair and, going to his knees, stayed by her and held her and kept muttering, "it's okay, baby; Janelle, baby, it's okay," but he did not believe it.

"What about the goddamned patient," Naomi said after awhile. "We gonna let him bleed to death?" Naomi walked over to Gardner, knelt down beside him and waved the salts under his nose. Gardner groaned and twisted his head back and forth. Janelle shot up off the chair and ran to him.

"Give me those," she said, snatching the salts from Naomi. "Harry, Harry—hear me? You're gonna be all right. Harry—Harry, please, hear me!"

Gardner felt the bad odor in his nostrils and tried to shake away from it, but couldn't. It wouldn't go away.

"Harry, Harry! Come on, baby!"

He heard his name being shouted from far away but couldn't tell from where—but it seemed, the voice, so dist—oooh, his head. He felt the pain and throb in his head and he reached up to find the spot.

"Don't, Harry-don't touch it. You're hurt," Janelle said. "He's coming to, Otis—isn't he—coming to?"

"He'll come around," Price said. He was at the French doors now trying the handle. "That fucker locked us out. We'll have to scale the fuckin' walls."

"A great, shitty night this is," Naomi said.

"Harry, Harry, can you hear me?"

Gardner opened his eyes and saw the blackness and thought he had gone blind. He closed his eyes, opened them again—blinked several times and then opened them. He coughed and the spasm hurt his head. He moaned, but now he could make out the blacker form of a person bending over him. He could see. "Nor—ma?" he said.

"It's me, baby. Janelle," Janelle said. "You fell. You hurt yourself. It's me."

Gardner came to. He knew the voice and he realized where he was. But it was so dark and his head hurt so. What had happened, he wondered. He made a move to sit-up. Yes, and to run. He remembered. Too quick though, and the pain in his head pushed him down again and he hit the back of his head on the stone floor.

"Unnh," he said.

"Easy, baby," Janelle said. "Harry, are you all right? Be all right, honey."

Gardner tried again to lift himself when he heard Janelle's voice. Carefully though this time, and he brought his head up and, putting his hands behind his neck, raised himself to a sitting position.

"Jesus," he said.

"Harry—you all right? Tell me you are."

He nodded. "For a dead man," he said. "Christ, my head. What happened?"

"You blacked out, pal," Otis Price said.

"And fell on your ass—and head," Naomi said.

"Jesus," Gardner said and he touched his head and felt the blood. "I'm bleeding."

"He's gonna need stitches. Did you look at that gash?" Naomi said, matter-of-factly.

"Otis, help me," Janelle said. "Can you get up?" Janelle tried to lift Gardner.

"Yeah, I think."

"Where the hell are you," Price said, "I can't see a fuckin' thing."

"Over here," Janelle said.

Price walked towards the sound of Janelle's voice.

"It's blacker than a bastard," Price said.

"Or me?" Naomi said.

"Ouch, watch it," Janelle said. Price had kicked into her. "How'd you survive the jungle, you blind--"

Price knelt and grabbed Gardner under the arms and lifted him to his feet.

"You okay?" Price said.

"I feel like shit," Gardner said. "Whew—am I pissed. Oh, Christ, my head."

"We've got to get him to a hospital," Janelle said.

"Yeah, but your fuckin' old man has locked us out," Price said.

"Not for long," Janelle said. She found a rock in the flower bed, pulled it up and walked to the French doors. She felt for the handle and touched the glass pane next to it. She backed off a step and threw the rock. The glass shattered and you could hear the rock hitting on the dining room floor. Janelle reached through and turned the key, unlocking the door.

"Come on," she said, "let's make a break for it."

CHAPTER 13

Otis Price put Gardner's left arm around his shoulder and steadying him, they and Janelle and Naomi walked through the dining room, along the corridor and out through the front door into Beekman Place. The night was clearer now and the sounds of the city seemed remote. Down the block, a taxi cab had stopped in front of an apartment building and an older man and a young blonde girl in a maxi-coat were getting out.

Janelle spotted the cab and she, who could whistle through her teeth—something else her father had taught her in Wisconsin—did so. "Taxi," she yelled.

The cab rolled up the street towards them and stopped. Janelle opened the door.

"How many?" the driver said.

"Just four," Janelle said. The driver's hair was long and blond and was held back by an Indian headband. He was young, Janelle saw, and he had a full beard and wore a handwoven Indian vest. Janelle nodded and Otis Price helped Gardner into the back seat of the cab. Janelle and Naomi got in after him. Price sat up front.

"Where do we take him?" Price said.

"Lenox Hill," Janelle said.

"Where?" the driver said.

"Lenox Hill—Hospital," Janelle said. "Park and 77th. Go up 1st or 3rd and across 77th. The emergency room's there."

Gardner groaned.

"Is he—okay?" the driver said.

"Who?" Janelle asked.

"If he's shot I'm supposed to report it to the pigs. I'm not sayin' I would," the driver said. "Is he?"

"Just a cut on the head," Otis Price said, "nothing for you to sweat—just hurry."

"I wouldn't tell the pigs anyway," the driver said, nodding. "Even if he is shot." he put the car in gear and pushed down on the accelerator. "Pigs are pigs," he said.

Gardner's head was hurting intensely now, but he tried to forget the pain by trying to remember what had happened. He thought he remembered that he had been running and had been trying to get to Norma and away from Janelle, who he knew was sitting next to him; and now he was heading for Lenox Hill Hospital where Norma had given birth to their two children (what grades where they in)? And where she would be coming in two months to have their third. He felt bad about that and decided he wouldn't think about it. Instead, he tried to remember what he had said and done before blacking out, but he couldn't get it clearly. He did think he remembered quitting his job, but then that didn't seem possible.

"Did—did I—quit tonight?" Gardner asked.

"After you got fired," Janelle said.

"Fired? For what?"

"Telling Mr. Middle America he was a racist, murdering capitalist bastard. Something like that," Otis Price said.

"Who?" Gardner asked.

"Sheet—he's got amnesia," Naomi said.

"Ralph Wright," Janelle said. "You broke it off in him."

"Oh, yeah, Wright. Good," Gardner said.

"You told him and Buzz to go fuck themselves," Price said. "You're out of work."

"I did?" Gardner said. He enjoyed this news immensely and began laughing; anyway he meant to laugh but it came out in a rack of coughs.

"You sounded like the Chicago 7," Janelle said. "It was one hell of a performance."

"You didn't do so bad yourself, baby," Price said.

"You like Abbie Hoffman?" the driver said, to no one in particular, but finally looking over at Price for an answer.

"I sketched him once," Price said.

"You did?" Whad'ya think of him?" the driver said.

"He's a fuckin' idiot," Price said.

"Hey, man," the driver said, his mouth drooping into a pout. "What about Judge Hoffman?"

"Ditto, pal. A mirror image," Price said.

"How don't you like either of them?" the driver said.

"By thinking. It's easy," Price said.

"I think Abbie's groovy."

"If you like self-centered, self-righteous mental masterbators," Price said.

"Shit, man," the driver said. "He tells it like it is."

"Not even close. He or the judge. They both hate America."

Gardner tried to follow the conversation but couldn't. He couldn't stop coughing and the paroxysms jerked his head and bolted the pain. He couldn't fit his thoughts together or focus his eyes. The lights in the street and in the buildings and on the cars went blurring past him; his stomach began to roll and he thought he was going to vomit.

"Janeh—the window—some, some air," Gardner said.

Janelle reached across him and lowered the car window.

"We're almost there, baby," Janelle said. "Hang on." She put her arm around him.

Gardner let himself lean towards her and he closed his eyes and, without meaning to, began to think about the first time he had met Norma.

In his mind he saw the Mittersill Inn in Franconia, New Hampshire, which was half-way up the side of Cannon Mountain and which was a copy of an alpine resort in the Austrian Alps which had the same name and was owned, both, it was said, by an Austrian Count; and he saw the mountain covered with snow and the roof of the inn, and huge icicles hanging from its brown wooden eaves and it was February and it was cold and he was there to film a commercial for a man's hair oil and it was all about skiing and how this famous skier kept his goddamned German blond hair all beautiful and groomed with this hair oil and laid every girl in the lodge at night because of it, and, he, Gardner, who had never skied and had never even been to a ski resort hated the whole idea and the German especially. He remembered how badly the filming went and how the camera kept jamming from the cold and how the German's hair would not stay in place while he came slashing down the mountain on which Gardner wished he would fall and break his ass, and how it started snowing and how the wind blew and how it would not stop snowing, and how when it finally did, it was the lunch hour and the cameraman refused to shoot then because he said that he had to have hot soup and his lunch or he would get a headache and Gardner had pleaded that it was the first decent weather they had had in three days and that they were over budget and that the cameraman could have his hot soup later and the cameraman saying, "no, I have to have my hot soup now and the filming can wait. I get bad headaches if I don't get soup," and how, he, the cameraman, had stalked off the mountain where they were waiting to film and headed down to the lodge, with him, Gardner, chasing after, yelling silently against the mountain and the wind, and running into the path of a girl racing down one of the gentler slopes and colliding with her and sending himself and her spattering—a windmill of skis and legs and screams and curses—into the snow, and he remembered the German yelling, "Achtung—dumkoff" and himself thinking that the German was right—he was stupid—and that he had probably killed the girl who lay motionless, and feeling himself to see if anything was broken, and watching the German skiing, smooth and fleet, over to the girl and bending to her, saying something soft and certain.

He remembered seeing the girl stir and rise up on her rump and look at the German and smile and Gardner remembered thinking that the German would probably lay this one too that night, but had his thought broken off when he heard the girl say "Just tell me one thing—is this good or bad for the Jews," and that he had laughed and liked her and was glad that she was not hurt and felt that he had to meet her and that he thought her beautiful.

He remembered her getting up from the snow and coming to him and saying, "I thought you guys were going to leave us alone after World War II," and skiing off; and he remembered trying to follow her, but losing her and finding the cameraman instead in the dining room eating his hot soup, and how he had argued with the cameraman until finally he was in such a fury he had picked up the soup bowl and poured the remains into the cameraman's lap, and how the cameraman had jumped up and swung at him and then he at the cameraman, several times, both of them, and both of them missing mostly, until they bear-hugged each other and wrestled till they fell onto the floor and knocked over two tables and grunted around this way until the waiters separated them—he still on the floor, the cameraman getting up and yelling, "You're crazy, crazy! I'm going to New York and you can take you hair oil and shove it. I've—I've got a headache!" and how he turned and started to get up, then saw the girl at the table directly in front of him and she was smiling at him. It was her and she said, "I'd hate like hell to be your Blue Cross representative."

He laughed and they introduced themselves. Her name was Norma

Spector and she asked him to join her for lunch. She told him she was a magazine writer and that she was there from <u>Holiday</u> magazine to write a story on the Austrian Count who had not yet come in from Europe, although he had been scheduled to arrive two days earlier. Her father was a doctor and lived in the Bronx and she had graduated from Barnard. She lived in an apartment on 10th Street in Greenwich Village with a girl named Laura, who worked at <u>Time-Life</u>.

He and Norma had dinner together that night and had drunk Scotch and Liebfraumilch and had played ping-pong in the small tavern off the lobby of the Inn. They had danced too, in the same room, to the music of a small band—a piano, drums and an accordion—and they had fitted very well together. He had always believed himself to be a good dancer— women he knew said it too—and Norma had followed him fluidly. There, in the tavern, they had drunk stingers and had danced and had got happily drunk. She wore beautiful clothes—tight-fitted black ski pants and apres-ski boots and a bulky white Norwegian sweater which, even so, showed her breasts. They laughed at his outfit—a suit and tie, even out on the mountain, and cordovan military boots, which there in the tavern were dry and curled from first the cold and snow and then the heat. A very handsome friend of the handsome German had come over and asked to dance with Norma, but Gardner had said, stiffly, he remembered, "I do not allow my wife to dance with other men," and when the handsome man had walked away, with a strange look on his face, Norma had roared laughing and taken his hand in hers and said, "You're some jealous husband—and so <u>new</u>. I had dinner with <u>him</u> last night."

Later, a young, timid man from Boston had sat next to them and bought them a drink and had asked Norma if she were foreign and had said it was his first time skiing and Norma had said yes, she was French and that it was her husband's first time too, although not hers. "True," Gardner had said, "My wife is an Olympic champion—she won in 1956—the woman's giant slalom." He loved that expression "giant slalom" and, although he had read it many times on the sports page, had never until that night said it out loud. He loved saying it and repeated it many times to the man from Boston, who had seemed very impressed and went away when the tavern closed at 3:00AM never knowing that Norma was not a ski champion.

When Gardner and Norma had left the tavern, they walked outside and, under a full moon, saw the shimmering, pearly bulk of the mountain, and above it and all around, a cascade of stars which in the clear, clean night not even the moon could dim. "Let's go up it," Gardner remembered saying, "Mach Schnell, Fraulein!" and they had climbed up the bottom slope of the mountain, tripping and sinking and regaining their footing in the snow as they climbed. The whiskey made them warm in the cold night and they held hands to keep from falling. When they had climbed a hundred yards or so, they stopped, turned and looked back at the Inn. Smoke lifted straight up from its chimneys in wispy strands of an old woman's grey hair and the lights from its windows gauzed up towards them like luminous moths. There was no wind and the stillness was something you could hear. Above them, the trunks of trees, marching up the mountain along the ski trail, which where they were not thick, looked like a child's keeping count on white paper—1111 and at one place a fallen tree marked a five count—1̶1̶1̶1̶.

"Zey vil nevah zuzpect vee are heir," Gardner had said. "Vee will attacks zem mit zurprize." And this had started a game where they both pretended to be German ski troopers about to invade Austria and kidnap the Count. They kept this game going until Norma fell into a drifted snow bank and laughed and said, "To tell the truth, as a Nazi, I'm not so hotsy. Winter—schminter; give me Miami Beach." They both laughed and Gardner remembered feeling very good.

When they came down from the mountain, Gardner's feet were aching from the cold and they hurried through the lobby which was quiet and deserted and where the fire in the high fireplace was ebbing. He didn't imagine that she'd say yes but he invited her to his room for a nightcap and when she accepted he was physically aroused. He remembered that clearly. In the room, Gardner lit the paper, kindling the log which had been arranged in the fireplace by the maid and from the bottle of Scotch he had, he poured two drinks into the waterglasses he took from the bathroom. He took off his shoes and socks and rubbed his feet with a towel and then wrapped a second towel around them. They drank and talked and she told him about the Bronx and her family and about the boy she would have married except that he got killed. He was from Virginia and she had met him at a USO dance and he, when the war was over, wanted to be a lawyer. In 1945, in April, on the way to New York City from Fort Dix in a used car he had bought the day before, he drove himself and two other soldier-passengers head-on in a fog into a semi-trailer truck which was carrying a load of medical supplies to Camp Kilmer. For a hundred yards in every direction, after the crash, the ground was covered with aspirin and gauze and the boy from Virginia was dead and so were the two soldier-passengers who had come along to witness his wedding to Norma which had been the reason for the trip. Just the same, their names went up in their home towns' public squares to the gold star section of the honor rolls and they were thought of as having given their lives for their country. Gardner told Norma about Indiana and his family and about advertising, until finally he reached for the bottle to pour them another drink and saw that it was empty. "I'd better go," Norma had said, "It's late. My God," she had said, "It's getting light." And it was, Gardner remembered. They walked out onto the little balcony off his room—he had put on clean dry socks—and they stood there watching the coming sun backlight the black line of mountains to the East. Norma had broken off an icicle and was licking it and neither of them spoke until the sun came up where you could see it and spilled its bright orange and gold over the jagged mountains and showed them white with snow and black with trees. "God, it's so peaceful and beautiful—and awesome," she had said. "I feel—religious." She had turned to him and they kissed.

Gardner remembered that it was good and natural like the dancing had been and he immediately had gotten an erection, which embarrassed him and, as he later learned, surprised and puzzled her. That had never happened instantly to any man she had ever kissed, she had told him; and, when he had thought about it, he realized that it had never happened to him either.

She had come in off the balcony after the kiss and had gone to the door. "Good-night—my husband," Norma had said. "It was a pleasure bumping into you." Gardner remembered it as the happiest day of his life.

The following day, a new cameraman had come on from New York, Gardner remembered, and the weather had lifted and he had got his shots, but he had called his office—it was Thursday—and had said he wouldn't be back until Monday.

Late in the afternoon he and Norma had driven into Littleton and had shopped for him. He bought a heavy sweater, a parka and warm boots and corduroys; that night they slept together and Gardner was voracious. They made love five or six times before sun-up and twice he fell out of the bed from the wildness of it all. They made love every night from then on until they married in June, and for a long time after that. And the Count never did show up, as far as they knew.

"How you doin', baby? Janelle said.

"Perfect. It was so beautiful and perfect," Gardner said.

"What?" Janelle said.

"Slalom, a giant slalom." Gardner said.

"He's got a concussion, I think," Naomi said.

"He'll be all right. He's fuckin' stoned—is part of it," Otis Price said.

"Yeah. Yeah," Gardner said. He rolled off Janelle's shoulder and leaned the opposite way against the car door. He looked out the window and saw that the cab was on 1st Avenue, headed uptown and that they were going through the neighborhood of the "singles" bars—Maxwell's Plum, Mr. Laff's, O'Sullivan's, Alice's Restaurant went blurring by. Coming out of one of these was a man who reminded Gardner of himself: Slightly balding, older than he should be to be here and drunk and lost-looking. His tie was loosened and his coat collar turned up. He was carrying an attache case. Probably from out of town, Gardner thought, as the man vanished behind him. Or he quarreled with his old lady and walked out of the house—looking now for revenge and for his youth. Gardner remembered how he himself had stalked these bars, after his affair with Janelle got him started, looking for girls and validation—adventure. Imagine: He had drunk himself crazy along this street 40 nights or more over the last year, weaving in and out of these bars like—like a giant slalom--(Great word for a drunk—slalom. Even sober you sound drunk saying it)--through snow and rain and cold, believing in his drunkenness that, each time, in the next bar, would be the one—the single girl who would understand and take him home and love him and hold him and take away the fatigue and the defeat and give him life once more.

He recalled the monstrous insanity that gripped him on those "nights out." He remembered being thrown out two different times from one Irish joint along here, where both times he had pretended to be a policeman. The first time it had worked—sort of. Anyway, they had taken him out gently, but the second time he had tried it, the guys who ran the joint had remembered him and they had picked him up flailing and had thrown him sprawling onto the sidewalk and one of them had hurled Gardner's attache case after him, hitting him in the back with it. He was sore for a week. Two other times he had had long running arguments with squad car cops, who finally let him go. Each time they had asked him if he were a lawyer (he talked bigger words when he was drunk) and he had always taken pride in this. Other times, he had believed he was being followed and he would go through elaborate maneuvers to avoid his tail. He'd hide for half-hours between parked cars and walk blocks out of his way to get to a bar that, until he saw it, he had had no particular intention of going into. One night he had gotten sarcastic in a bar and was really in danger of being beaten up, and somehow he had known it, and quickly had pulled out the business card of a junior member of the Russian consulate with whom he had had lunch that day, explaining American advertising, and had pretended to be him. The card had confused the man he was arguing with just long enough for him to get out. He had run across the street and into another bar. In a moment he looked out and saw a squad car in front of the bar he had just left. He had loved that. Nobody wanted an international provocation—especially with a Russian. He always thought when he was drunk how clever he was.

But he never found the girl; not that he didn't find girls. There were plenty. They were pretty enough too, but, in his mind Gardner heard again their endless, deadening speech and saw the anxious, suspicious faces, tight with wanting love and some piece of undefined glamor. They were ready to trade sex for any shard of kindness and excitement. These bars were a sort of whorehouse foyer where one wants to choose and to be chosen. The language is brittle and tries to be sophisticated but it comes from men and women who really don't like each other because they don't trust each other and don't believe each other because they cannot be clear themselves about what they want. When they do get together it is harsh and combative—two dehorsed warriors runting in the dirt in the armour of their lies. Gardner remembered how he had got through it in his drunkenness and had sat for hours listening to the tin conversation about where they skied last winter or swam last summer or where they'd go this year and how many they were sharing a house with and what they saw on television or bought at the sale at Bloomingdale's or about the dog they had (with photos) or the cat that died or the smutty little double entendres or smears about their roommates' sexual proclivities or Jackie Kennedy or Mia and Andre and wasn't Dustin Hoffman just the most sensitive? There had been an X-ray technician, a couple of nurses, several secretaries, one kindergarten teacher and a squadron of stewardesses. He remembered one of these—a girl with a big sensuous mouth and blank beautiful eyes who came from Newport News, Virginia. He had taken her home to her apartment which she shared with three other girls and had screwed her while sitting on a chair in the kitchen while one of her roommates was getting fucked on the living room sofa, and he didn't even have his pants off (they were around his ankles) and the Johnny Carson Show was blaring on the television set in the living room and the stewardess (what was her name)? was ticklish and giggled, and he could barely sustain an erection! After that only night, he had bought lunch for her once and had gotten her two tickets for the Johnny Carson Show through an account executive at the agency, for which she sent him a very proper thank you note, and about whom he never heard again. He recalled riding down in the elevator with the fellow who had been fucking the roommate in the living room. He too, Gardner remembered, had been wearing a wedding ring.

And he recalled another night, so drunk he could barely walk, clumping into a phone booth at 4 AM, after striking out in the bars, and calling a receptionist from the agency whom he had never met and had only said good-morning to and whom he didn't even actually find very attractive, but who was the only one at the moment he could think of to call and whose name he couldn't remember except that it sounded like Appomattox and which he finally figured out and found in the phone book under A. Maddox. Amy was her name. Good old Amy Appomattox--"I surrender, dear!" he sang to himself. When she answered the phone she had been surprised, but she had recovered quickly and efficiently and had said if he wanted to come over he could because she had always admired his brain—all the people at the office did, she said—and she would just love to have the honor of a conversation with him and so would her roommate probably since she was an illustrator for ads at Macy's and would he be wanting coffee and was he celebrating something or other? Was that why he was out and calling at 4 AM? He, his brain—even he could realize—pickled practically beyond functioning, had said, Jesus—no--no celebration and I'm sorry—It's so late—and--maybe another time. Yes, another time—soon--and he had gone home immediately and had beat off in the bathroom and had cried—just a little—and had come, dryly. He nor the receptionist ever mentioned the phone call, but after that she always smiled warmly at him when he came in or went out.

Norma, Norma, where am I, Gardner said to himself, then aloud, "Where am I?"

"Baby, it's okay," Janelle said. "We're taking you to Lenox Hill."

"To be born," Gardner said, "child of my children."

"Sheet—he's flipped," Naomi said.

"Never mind, Naomi," Otis Price said.

"You all right, Harry?" Janelle said.

"This it?" the cab driver said. He stopped the car. They were parked in front of the hospital.

"Yes," Janelle said.

Otis Price paid the driver while the women helped Gardner out of the taxi. The four of them entered the emergency receiving room.

The lights from the florescents in the ceiling caught everything at its worst. There were no shadows. Although there were stand ashtrays around, cigarette butts were crushed out on the floor. To the left, as you entered, was a glass window with a small circular opening. Through it Gardner could see two women, one seated behind a desk, and the other standing just beside her and smoking; behind them stood a man with a big belly dressed in some kind of policeman's outfit. None of them looked up when Gardner and the others entered.

Opposite the window on a couch along the far wall sat a drunk, half-sprawled out and unconscious, his pants wet in the crotch and his right hand hanging limp. It was wrapped in a dirty rag of some kind that blood had been soaking through. He was muttering sounds that almost made words. Diagonally from him sat an elderly man moaning and being comforted by a woman who must have been his wife. His head was bandaged in the back and he had on glasses, but one lens was missing and also a temple shaft on one side. There was dried blood on his nose and a high strawberry on his upper cheek. He and his wife both were wearing orthopedic shoes and she had on a yellowing mink coat, with worn spots near the buttons and pockets. Across from them sat a Puerto Rican woman with hairy legs, holding in her lap a baby who cried without let-up. Next to her sat a man in a T-shirt and open windbreaker and baseball cap. He was holding his right side and he kept telling the Puerto Rican woman that his appendix had burst. Standing in the corner, near the entrance door, was a woman in her 60's probably, but slim and weirdly attractive, who paced and smoked nervously and looked at the baby and then at the drunk and back to the baby with real hatred in her eyes. She was wearing a vintage silver fox coat and her hose drooped. As Gardner and the others had entered, this woman had rushed to the glass window and yelled at the women inside, "Is the doctor going to see <u>anyone</u>?" The women did not answer her nor did she seem to expect them to. She retreated back to her corner without waiting for an answer and lit another cigarette off the butt of the old one and she started pacing again.

"It's like a fuckin' barbershop," Otis Price said, "out of Samuel Beckett."

There was no place to sit and the four who had just come in seemed at first unable to decide what to do. But, after a moment, when the silver fox lady had left the window, but said nothing—apparently she believed that her presence would be enough for the women to take notice and to do something, Janelle rapped on the glass window and said, "Hello." Still the women did not pay attention. (They ignored her.) She rapped on the glass again, harder this time, and said, "How bout a little goddamned service, angels of mercy?"

The two women stopped talking and looked up. The woman seated behind the desk reached into a middle drawer and pulled out a form. The uniformed man took a step forward. The woman with the form picked up a ballpoint pen and held it over the paper which she smoothed out on the desk. She stared down at the paper.

"Name," she said.

"Holy Christ," Janelle said. "Get his name later. He needs a doctor."

"Name," the woman behind the glass repeated.

Otis Price said, "His name is Harry Gardner, please, and he is badly hurt. He needs a doctor. Can't the paper wait, please?"

"How do you spell Gardner?" the woman said.

"G-A-R-D-N-E-R, I think," Otis Price said.

"As in Adam & Eve," Janelle said. "Shit, I don't believe this scene. Will you get the goddamned doctor," she said, "before I tear this place apart."

The uniformed man disappeared.

"Address," the woman behind the glass said.

"What's your address, Gardner?" Otis Price said.

"Wha?" Gardner said.

"Your address? What is it?"

"Oh. 170 Central Park West," Gardner said.

"170 Central Park West," Otis Price said, repeating it to the woman behind the desk.

"Will you stop playing office and get a doctor," Janelle said to Otis Price, "before I shove that pen up her ass."

The uniformed man emerged from a door in the wall opposite the entrance door and near the side wall where the glass window was. He walked up to Janelle.

"Lady, please, you gotta hold it down," he said. "This here's a hospital." His breath was acrid with garlic and beer and he smelled all over of pizza.

"Get a doctor and I will," Janelle said.

"Doctor's busy. So just s'hhh. You gotta s'hhh. There's people waiting."

"No kidding?"

"Just fill out the form, hunh?"

"Screw the form. He's hurt. He can't wait."

"Lady, shush. I'm tellin' you."

"Shush, shit. I want a doctor."

"I'm gonna put you out, lady, if you don't behave—for causin' a disturbance. There's rules."

"Rules, my ass. My husband gave $5,000 last year to this—abbetoire and I want a doctor."

"M'am, I ain't kiddin. You been warned. Mister, please," the uniformed man said, turning to Otis Price, "tell her. I got my duty to perform. And mind her language. There's ladies and children."

Price nodded. "Janelle, shut up. Officer, our friend is hurt. He needs a doctor. His head is busted. See for yourself."

"Was the nature of this injury a police incident," the uniformed man said.

"No—he--just fell," Otis Price said, "but he's hurt. He needs stitches."

"There's others."

"I see, but this is an emergency."

"So's their's. The Doc'll get to him."

"5,000 dollars and no goddamned doctor," Janelle said.

"Age," the woman behind the desk said.

"How old are you?" Otis Price said to Gardner.

"43—today," Gardner said.

"Yeah? Happy Birthday." The uniformed man said. He smiled.

"Holy Christ," Janelle said, "why don't you sing it to him?" She walked over near the lady in the silver fox coat.

"I'm 30," the lady said.

"Can I steal a cigarette?" Janelle said to her.

The silver fox lady nodded and gave Janelle a cigarette and lit it off her own.

"What do you expect," the silver fox said.

She has had money, Janelle thought, and decided she was determined not to end up like that.

"Social Security number?" the woman behind the glass said.

"Gardner—come here. Can you?" Otis Price said. "Answer the questions if you can. What's your social security number?"

Gardner weaved over to the window and began giving the woman the information required by the form as she asked for it. Over her shoulder, a young, dark man appeared—Indian or Pakistani, Gardner figured—in a doctor's hospital whites. He took up the bottom form from the wire basket which rested on top of the desk.

"Rodriguez," he said.

Janelle came back to the window at the sound of this voice and said, "Are you the doctor?"

"Are you Rodriguez?" the doctor asked.

"Madame Nehru—would that help?" Janelle said.

The Puerto Rican woman with hairy legs and the baby stood up and came forward. "Rodriguez," she said and nodded.

The woman at the desk behind the glass pressed a button and a buzzer sounded in the inner door. The uniformed man opened it and motioned to the Rodriguez woman to come through. The doctor turned and started walking away from the window.

"Hey, Gandhi, wait a minute," Janelle said, but the doctor was gone.

"Ma'am, I'm tellin' you—quiet or out you go," the uniformed man said. The Rodriguez woman went through the door and the man in the police outfit followed her.

"Do you believe any of this," Janelle said.

"Sheet, man, it's just like in the ghetto," Naomi said. "Who'd of thought? Equality at last."

"You're not funny," Otis Price said.

"I can wait," Gardner said.

"You won't," Janelle said.

"Please, Janelle," Gardner said. He walked over and sat down heavily where the Puerto Rican Rodriguez woman had been.

"My appendix has busted," the man in the T-shirt said to him. "They won't see me. I'm gonna die right here—and I've got Medicare."

"Yeah—I'm sorry," Gardner said, and meant it sincerely.

"Goddamn communists—and Lindsay," the man said.

Gardner nodded to the man and suddenly felt very tired. His head throbbed hotly. He closed his eyes, but only for a moment because, when he did, everything began to spin. He opened his eyes and pulled his head up as though he had had a bit in his mouth. Then, after another moment, he fell dead asleep or unconscious at least.

The little plane took off nicely and the day was clear. Gardner was really pleased about the trip. The Earth was vivid and the objects on it were becoming toys as the plane rose and you could see the horizon crisply in every direction. He breathed in deeply as the plane leveled off and he closed his eyes to closet the good sensations he was feeling. Suddenly, the little plane hit a downdraft and dropped like a foul tip at the plate. Gardner blinked open his eyes and felt the tossing of the plane as it tried to regain inner control. It bobbed like a ping-pong ball on a shaft of air and Gardner hoped that the air would keep blowing. That no one would turn it off. Finally the plane relaxed and sped along again smoothly, but then Gardner looked ahead and there right in front of him were the highest mountains he had ever seen. He couldn't possibly avoid them. He looked back the way he had been coming and there were mountains there too. Mountains ringed the plane on every side. The biggest, boniest, most frighteningly beautiful mountains imaginable. The plane was going to crash for certain. He looked forward again and was ready for the impact. Suddenly, exactly at his altitude, there was an opening and the little plane aimed for it and just got through this narrow space between two enormous peaks. Even so, the plane would not have made it except for the fact that the wings folded up on themselves like those aircraft carrier fighter planes in World War II. When the plane had come through the mountain pass, it made a quick landing in a huge meadow. A large van was parked near where the plane stopped and Gardner got into it. The van pulled away and it moved through a small town, when, quickly from the rear of the van, a tiger sprung full into the front seat and began tearing at Gardner and at the driver who was Naomi. It ripped with its paws and mouth at both of them, but, after a moment of this fierce attack, Gardner realized that neither he nor Naomi was cut or bleeding and he could feel no pain at all. When he got to the meeting in the high school gymnasium, there was a very large crowd seated on folding chairs set on the playing court and there was one angry, snarling dog and as he made his way through this crowd someone grabbed him by the arm and told him Naomi was dead. By the end of the meeting he was drunk and when he came out of the gym he climbed into the back of the van and somebody locked the door behind him and the van began to move and when he looked up front he saw that Naomi was driving him to the university where he put on his jersey and he and the football team rushed onto the field and there, at the 50 yard line, was an immense medieval castle. Gardner and his teammates joked about how phoney the castle looked and about how easy it would be to take it. They put on their steel helmets and they rushed it confidently. Gardner was there first and the first one to see the moat with real alligators in it. One alligator bit his toe, but he pulled back in time from that bite, although another alligator got in a good snap at his knee. Fortunately, Billingsly rushed up to save him just in time and he, Gardner, was astonished that such a fake castle would be surrounded by real alligators. When he looked at the film of it on the moviola in the cutting room in the basement of the Tecumseh County Bank Building in Lancaster, Indiana, Janelle, who was there, said, "You're very talented, Harry."

"Harry? Harry—come on, baby," Janelle said, "the barber's gonna see you now." Janelle jostled his arm gently.

Gardner stirred and opened his eyes and saw Janelle and was not surprised. "The film really okay? He said.

"What film?" Janelle said.

"The film—in the bank," Gardner said.

"What?" Janelle said.

"He's been dreaming" Otis Price said.

"Are you all right, Harry?" Janelle said. "The doctor's ready."

Otis Price came forward and he, on one side, and Janelle on the other, lifted Gardner from the couch and began walking him toward the inner door. The uniformed man was holding it open. Out of the edge of his vision, Gardner saw Naomi and was very surprised and pleased. He stopped and turned towards her.

"Naomi--. It's wonderful to see you—really," Gardner said, and he smiled at her.

Naomi frowned at him and looked quickly to Otis and then back to Gardner. She smiled through the frown. "un, yeah, man, you too. Keep cool, hear?"

"Right through here," the uniformed man said. He nodded toward the door he was holding open.

"I'll hang out here," Naomi said.

Janelle and Otis steered Gardner through the door and slowly along a corridor with blank walls and many door openings, which were covered by curtains you could slide back.

"This one," a nurse said, who was standing by one of the openings and who pushed back the curtain as Gardner, Janelle and Otis approached.

Seeing the nurse, Gardner freed himself of the others' support. "I can make it. I'm okay," he said. "Hello," he said to the nurse and managed to smile. He thought she was pretty—enough.

"Hello," the nurse said. "Now just lie down. Right here. The doctor's coming."

"Finally," Janelle said. She and Price followed Gardner and the nurse into the room.

Gardner stretched out on the examining table and felt very good about lying down. He remembered that he had been dreaming before and he tried to recall the details. Mountains came back, and the low-flying plane and Lancaster and Naomi dead, then alive, driving him in a van. What did it mean? And the castle with real alligators? What had the meeting been about?

The nurse came over to him and helped him loosen his tie. She removed his glasses. Next she washed the wound on his forehead and then swabbed it with an antiseptic of some kind. As she did so, her breasts were only inches away from Gardner's face and he liked them immediately. They looked so clean and ample, he thought, pressing against the nylon uniform she was wearing. He looked at her. She was young, very young-looking, and big, but not fat-big. Her forearms were large and chocolate. She seemed very certain, Gardner thought, and almost masculine in her movements. Even so, he wanted very much to touch her boobs.

"Whew, you really did yourself," the nurse said. "What happened?"

"You have beautiful breasts," Gardner said to the nurse.

"Harry—for Christ's sake," Janelle said.

"He's taken a turn for the nurse," Otis Price said, imitating W.C. Fields.

The nurse said, smiling, "You're cute yourself."

"Clara Barton was a camp follower," Janelle said.

The nurse was okay, Gardner thought. She had a good overbite too, he noticed. The nurse turned and walked away from Gardner, to across the room to a cart with medicines and gadgets on it. Gardner looked at her legs and ass. They were strong and molded-well, he saw, and the nylon sizzled as she walked.

"Where the hell's the doctor, Nurse Goodfront," Janelle said. The nurse turned to Janelle and her face was serious.

"Campana, M'am," she said.

"What?"

"My name is Campana."

"Where is he?" Janelle said. "We've been damned near an hour."

"In the next room. It's busy tonight. Saturdays always are."

"The stored-up passions of the week," Otis Price said, continuing to mimic Fields.

"Yeah," the nurse said.

"Stop that stupid imitation," Janelle said.

"And even more when the moon is full," Price said, going right on.

"I'll say," the nurse said.

"You believe in that theory, my dear?" Price said.

"I see it. Right here."

"Why, here's the noble surgeon now," Otis Price said.

The doctor entered and quickly looked at Janelle and Otis Price. He looked down then at the form on a clip board he was carrying. He looked up at Janelle.

"Hello. Are you Mrs. Gardner?" he said.

Janelle shook her head <u>no</u> and did not speak.

"Friends of the loved one," Otis Price said.

"It's against our procedure really—for you to be here." the doctor said. "I'm going to ask you to please go to the main waiting room."

Janelle started to protest but Price grabbed her arm and started leading her out.

"Thanks a lot, Sabu," she said. Price pushed her through the curtain.

The doctor walked over to Gardner and bent over the wound, looking very serious, Gardner saw. The doctor pushed at the bridge of his glasses which were slipping down his nose from leaning over.

"Hiya," Gardner said.

The doctor nodded and said, "It needs stitching." The doctor began taking Gardner's pulse. "Do you have a headache?"

"Excedrin 1000," Gardner said.

"Novocaine, Ann," the doctor said.

The nurse had already prepared a hypodermic needle and she handed it to the doctor.

"You been in America long?" Gardner said to him.

"A year," the doctor said. He aimed the needle point along the perimeter of the wound and pushed. The Novocaine spurted onto Gardner's forehead.

"Another, please," the doctor said and the nurse prepared a second syringe and traded the new one to the doctor for the old one.

"Do you like it?" Gardner said.

"Yes—and no," the doctor said.

"Like tonight is <u>no</u>, hunh?"

"It is not so bad. That is the work."

"I'm sorry about—her remark."

"Oh, I have been called worse. At home they know the words that really hurt. Here, it is mostly 'nigger' they call me."

"Really?"

"Of course. I am not white, so—people do not make fine distinctions."

"I'm sorry."

"No. There are many good things. It is not everyone. Just a few. And they are disturbed or ignorant. It is worse sometimes where I come from. The castes, you know."

"Oh, yeah, is that on color?"

"It's different. And more rigid—formalized. There is no mistaking your position. Here, nothing is fixed. One is nice, another hateful. It creates much confusion, don't you think? Never knowing where one is exactly. This freedom is very exhausting. How is your head?"

"It feels numb. The pain—feels gone."

"This one may hurt. I'm injecting it into the tissue."

"I don't have to know everything."

"How is that?" The doctor pushed the needle point into one side of the tear, and then into the other.

"I'm already pretty numb—from the booze."

"Good. I can stitch now." The doctor turned away from Gardner to the nurse and Gardner closed his eyes. He thought about the nurse. He did not notice the doctor turn back to him, but he could feel, vaguely, a pulling in his forehead. He opened his eyes and saw the doctor over him stitching the wound.

"But freedom, of course, is illusory," the doctor said. "You have very definite patterns here, but they are hidden and nobody admits to them. Your myth is that you are free. You do have more choices than most people in the world. I see much harm in that. People are so uncertain about who they are or what they should be."

"I know what you mean." Gardner said.

"You have a lot of people waiting, doctor." the nurse said.

"Miss Campana thinks I am verbose," the doctor said.

"Whatever that means," the nurse said.

"And quite dull," the doctor said. "She says I think too much."

"You complicate everything," the nurse said.

"Things are complicated," Gardner said.

"Not for me," the nurse said. "I'm Catholic."

"Isn't that complicated?" Gardner said.

"No, you just—well, it's gotten—crazy--with all the changes. It's a lot different than I was raised," the nurse said.

"Things always are," Gardner said.

"In my village, it is not so different yet, from when I was raised. Though it will come." the doctor said. "Methods and beliefs last there for a thousand years. Here, not a month even."

"But you're all starving," the nurse said. "What kind of place is that?"

"No, not all. Only some," the doctor said, "some of the time. The breed always goes on. The famines used to regulate population. We submitted to nature, because that was right. We never tried to conquer it as you have. And where has that come? To bombs and DDT and carbon monoxide—and to the knowledge that you have nearly vanquished yourselves, yes? But since Independence the same is coming at home. Now all will live—and for what? Our women too will take the pill and our men end up on assembly lines."

"You can't be against science. You're a doctor," Gardner said.

"No," the Doctor said, "But I am not all together for it either. Its ends are as paradoxical as the mysteries it solves. Finally I believe that for every gain, there is a concommittent loss. It is always, in life, beyond our reach. Ah, but I talk too much. You came to get your head sewn."

"Will you go back—to your village?" Gardner asked.

"No. That is no longer possible. I could not go back as I could not bear to see it change. Here it is different. One accepts the change as the way of life."

"The pay is pretty good too, you know," the nurse said.

"Miss Campana is pragmatic, to the exclusion of all else," the Doctor said. "She is very American in that; and money is the determining factor."

"You told me you like the money. You did," the nurse said.

"I do. But I regret it also. There we are. 9 stitches. Very nice."

"Thanks," Gardner said.

"I enjoyed it," the Doctor said. "You are good company. So few here in this circumstance are." He began bandaging the wound.

"You did all the talking, you know," the nurse said.

"One can be a good conversationist as a listener, as this gentleman is," the Doctor said.

"I'll get hurt more often," Gardner said.

"I would suggest," the Doctor said, "you drink no more tonight."

"Yeah, I suppose."

"Go see your personal physician on Monday to check. There should be no complications."

"Don't count on it, Doctor," Gardner said.

"Yes. I know. I have to go now. Others are waiting—for Sabu." He smiled and made a small bow as he backed out of the room.

"He's such a drag," the nurse said. "If he don't love it here, he ought to leave."

Gardner and the girl stared at each other. She smiled at him and he smiled also and looked at her good breasts.

"Well, like—I gotta go," the nurse said. "Happy Birthday."

"Hunh?"

"I saw it on your admittance form."

"Oh, thanks. I"ll call you sometime, okay?"

"What for?" the nurse said.

Gardner shrugged and smiled.

"Okay. A. Campana. I'm in the book. I hope you feel better."

"Thanks."

The nurse smiled again and turned and left.

Didn't I see you in <u>Farewell to Arms</u>? Gardner said to himself to the nurse. Oh, to hell with it! <u>What</u> <u>for</u> is right.

Gardner put on his glasses and stood up. He had to steady himself against the bed because his legs sagged. Bloody legs, he said—forward march—you drunken beauty of a beast. Move your ass, nature's noblest!

He stumbled out of the room, getting hung up as he went on the curtain, like a novice matador confounded by his cape. Then, some raw effort. And along the corridor. Through the door. See Janelle—and Price and Naomi—hump <u>her</u>—and a new-faced flock of assorted sick and wounded.

"You all look like the cast party for Marat-Sade," Gardner said.

"I need a fucking drink." Price said.

CHAPTER 14

They got their first drink in the East Village in a place called the New Blues, near the corner of Third Avenue and St. Mark's Place. Price and Gardner remembered it as a jazz joint and both had heard Thelonious Monk there. Now it was operating on a discotheque policy and the records played so loud on the stereo that you had to shout to hear each other ear to ear. There were many blacks in the room. Lots of male ones with white girls and some girl ones with white males. A few couples danced on a small floor clearing in the center of the room. It was dark and full of smoke and whiskey odors, and the crowd looked beaten-back and tough, Gardner thought. The crowd did not look as young or graceful as the one at the Electric Circus.

The Electric Circus was a rock hangout halfway into the block on St. Mark's Place where Janelle had wanted to go and that's why they had ended up in this neighborhood in the first place. The Electric Circus was in a former Polish Club meeting hall, and there, live on a stage, in a blur of manic light, an acid rock band was making electronic noise that hurt your ears; and the room was jammed and you couldn't buy a drink.

"Screw this," Otis Price had said and they had left.

They were on their second drink in The New Blues when a hard, threatening argument broke out between two men. They both were white, or looked it to Gardner. One of the men pulled a knife and aimed it at the other man, but didn't attack him. It was the first time Gardner had ever really seen someone pull a knife on another person. He was not more than four feet away. It startled him, but it didn't frighten him as he would have expected it to.

Almost immediately, two police officers entered, one black, one white, and took the knife away from the man. The white policeman hit the knife-man over the head with a nightstick and, as he went down, the knife-man called the policeman a pig and then the two policemen took both men out and the other people in the room started dancing and drinking again. At that moment, Gardner realized that his hand was in his pocket clutching hard on his knife.

"Let's blow this place, man," Naomi said.

Gardner got up and found the waiter. He paid for the drinks and they left.

Outside, the night air was clear and caressing at the ground level and the street was crowded. There were no stars that you could see and a light smog hung higher in the sky towards uptown. A bus groaned away from the corner, spuing out fumes from its exhaust and a cab driver blew his horn at the driver in from of him just at the instant that the light changed. At the corner, there were scraps of young people eating pizza slices and Italian sausage sandwiches with peppers and onions, served from a small food stand that opened onto the sidewalk. A black young man in a cowboy hat walked by, brushing Janelle and said, "Wanna play Nigger and Indian, baby?" He kept walking and Janelle did not speak.

They started walking west, with the light, across 3rd Avenue. Janelle and Naomi walked together in front and Gardner followed side-by-side with Price. They walked past Cooper Union.

"Lincoln spoke there," Otis Price said, "and got hot as a presidential prospect."

"'Let us, to the end, dare to do our duty as we understand it'" Gardner said. "He closed with that."

Price nodded. "How do you know?"

"Who knows," Gardner said. "My great-grandfathers were in the Civil War—on the North."

"You understand your duty?" Price said.

"Clearly. To find a safe, quiet room to drink in."

"Let's dare to do it," Price said and laughed. "You're all right, you fuck." He threw his arm around Gardner.

Janelle and Naomi had gotten ahead of them and had reached the modern sculpture which sets on a small island in the middle of the traffic through Astor Square. The sculpture was a large black-painted steel cube, resting on one of its points and, if you pushed it, it rotated. Gardner looked ahead and saw Janelle pushing it. Hippies went by him and Price as they walked, thick as insects in the lights of a summer night car. He watched Janelle spinning the sculpture and saw her laughing. Two teenage boys were passed out at the base of the sculpture and there was heavy litter around it. When Price and Gardner got up to the women, a young boy with long hair, wearing an Aussie soldier's hat, asked them for money. Gardner gave him a quarter and the boy said "Peace, brother."

"It turns," Janelle said, "like a square world. I'll bet it's a symbol." She turned it again.

"You like it?" Gardner said to Otis Price.

"It's fun. For a playground. But it's no fuckin' piece of art."

"Let's go to the Gate," Naomi said. "Miriam Makeba is there."

They found a cab and went to The Village Gate on Bleeker Street. The room was dark and smokey and nearly full. They got a table just inside the entrance and far away from the music and the stage.

There were many blacks here too, Gardner saw, and mixed couples, but there were dresses now and shirts and ties and more money and many suburban whites. Janelle and Naomi began talking about clothes. Janelle said she would refuse to stop wearing the mini skirt, even though she had bought some midis. Naomi told her about a new boutique in Paris.

"What'd you think of the Circus?" Gardner asked Price. "And the kids?"

"They look so fuckin' morose and worn-out. At sixteen that's horrifying. They don't laugh much."

"There is something appealing about them."

"There always is about the young. But these young seem so old. Fucked over, fucked out."

"No, I mean—their vulnerability."

"In ten years, they'll be insurance salesmen—if the companies'll take them."

Gardner nodded. "These kids are arming, you know—some of them."

"The Weathermen?"

"Yes."

"What the hell's happened since '45 and now?" Price said. "I don't know this fuckin' country anymore. I know it's falling apart physically. I see that every time I come back. But what the hell is happening?"

"Christ, can't we get a drink in this joint?" Gardner said.

"Yeah," Price said. A waiter was going by. Price reached out his big arm, grabbed the man and stopped him immobile in the single gesture.

"A round for everybody—doubles, gin and a twist," Price said. The man nodded and seemed cowed by Price's physical authority.

"Jesus," Gardner said. "Freud belittled us, God died and deserted us and, hard as we tried, "I Love Lucy" couldn't fill the void. So what's left? Impotence, a sense of gullibility—some golden guilt? What's that to give a child? Then, of course, we end up hating their guts and fearing them cause we gave them money instead of meanings. Trinkets instead of time. And we know they know it. So they suck a weed, pop a pill, shoot a vein, ball a chick, put on the Stones and turn up the sound and drown it all."

"I just don't get the fuckin' message," Price said, "of turning off reality that way. I like to drink, and smoke occasionally and get an extra-curricular fuck now and then—but not to saturation. Not to blank out. And I—I still don't really dig pot. Do you? There's no hangover. I love my hangover—and my sex guilt. I like to feel fuckin' guilts and pay the price for pleasure. Norman talks about that. Mailer. What the hell's the use of sinning, if there's no sense of sin? I hate fuckin' things stripped of their mystery and fear."

"My God, you may live in Paris, but you never got rid of Illinois, did you?"

"I hope I never do. You think I ever want to get over saying 'fuck' and feeling kind of wrong about doing it?"

The waiter brought the drinks. "Bring another round," Price said. Price and Gardner picked up their drinks and gulped at them immediately. The women went on talking.

"You know," Gardner said. "It's absolutely frantic here. We're really on the wire between chaos and fascism."

"Is there gonna be a revolution?"

"No. From the right maybe. If we could just get out of that fuckin' war. Even that won't change the really gut problem."

"What gut problem?"

"Oh, it's complicated. Let's just juice and be good Germans and to hell with it."

"Aw, don't give me that fuckin' shit. You care, you little WASP bastard."

"That's the problem."

"What is?"

"WASPS."

"Whadya mean?"

"Us. WASPS. Nobody's got a single view of America any more. What we think it ought to be."

"I don't follow you."

"We were the Americans—you and me—WASPS. And everybody

bought that. Everybody's standard. Sure as hell the WASPS did—and so did the outs and the immigrants."

"Everybody wanted to be—us?"

"Right. The blacks conked their hair. The Jews changed their names and noses. Everybody wanted to be American—and what they meant by that was WASP. The style was always WASP, no matter where you turned."

"Fucked up model, if you ask me."

"Otis, I'm not saying it was right. Christ, it wasn't right at all. But it did have cohesion."

"And a Depression and World War II. Those goddamned Naziis were Anglo-Saxons too, you know.

"Maybe it was Hiroshima, we started doubting our assertions and assumptions about America. Right in there, somewhere, the WASP began to lose his way. He came home from the war and lost his nerve. Didn't you? Were you so sure after that of what you believed in?"

Price nodded and took a heavy swallow from his drink. "And our kids learned from us. We started sending out static, and the minorities couldn't get the message clearly anymore—about America. They lost their standard. They couldn't judge how they were doing. They think 'Jesus, if the kids of those who've made it are dropping out, what the hell is it all about? Or for? What the hell is the American Dream, and where's its mystique if those who have it don't fuckin' want it?' That's why the hard-hats are so pissed off at these middle-class kids of ours."

"Yeah, but the WASPS still run this fuckin' country. All the corporations and the White House."

"Not like we used to. Nixon feels left out too. Jesus, he even created a new minority out of his majority: 'The Forgotten Man' 'The Silent Majority.' That's defensive language. Those aren't the words of a class who knows what it is—or still thinks others want to be. Nixon's living off the bones of the old ideal, but he doesn't trust it anymore. Otherwise, he wouldn't be so scared. He's got the White House guarded by air born troops—from children carrying candles."

"I thought you said they were carrying bombs now."

"They are—cause the WASPS forgot how to change and grow. WASPS used to be the doers in this society. No more. We're managers now—and consumers—not innovators. We're at the end of WASP America—the way we knew it."

"So?"

"So, the melting pot idea is finished. Just look—we've become a nation of tribes, each with a single view of what America ought to be. Even our goddamned women have become a group. The Jews keep their names and now they've taken over our literature—and the Blacks our revolution. They didn't usurp it; they filled a vacuum. The Blacks don't even want to integrate anymore and they've let their hair go Afro. And the biggest defenders of the old way are the Irish, Poles, Italians, Greeks—Spiro's Greek remember? And the poor southern whites. They became a minority too after the Civil War. All of them. Cause they were getting close to making it and they're mad as hell the game may be over before they get their chance."

"The WASP hasn't exactly rolled over dead, for Christ's sake."

"Oh no—he hasn't given up at all—trying to keep what he has. But he's scared now. His confidence is gone. Sure, he still owns the army and the police and the means of production. And he can still rally enough of the outs with the old hollow cries about America, but what'll be the quality of the victory, if he does win? Not the America we knew. Not the old WASP vision that was self-assured enough to unite us."

"Well, Jesus, I don't know, but what the hell happened? The WASP ain't exactly failed in this country. What fucked him up?"

The waiter brought the second round of drinks.

"I don't know. Technology I think. Bigness. They cut him off from Zenith and Grover's Corners. Winesburg, Ohio, was a universe, goddamn it, where everybody knew everybody and everybody counted. We don't have that anymore. Now we have chain reactions and chain stores and transfers from one town to another and they all look alike. And groups and committees running things. Nothing individual gets done. That's what dries up your courage and confidence about yourself. You want to know what I think America's going to be? Anonymous technologists and soldiers in the street."

Gardner made a toast with his drink. "Happy New Year—1984."

"You're so boring when you're drunk," Janelle said. "We come out to have a good time and you get drunk and boring. Do you know you're boring? I mean do you have any sense of how really, truly, absolutely boring you are?"

"Oh, for Christ's sake, Janelle, let up," Otis Price said. "Stop bitching him."

"You're as boring as he is," Janelle said.

"Don't start on me, baby," Price said.

"Whydn'tcha all cool it, hunh? Naomi said. "I'm trying to groove on the music. You blancos talk the ass off everything."

"I'm getting so bored with that 'Black is Beautiful' bull shit," Janelle said.

"Baby, you're bored with everything," Naomi said.

"The brotherhood of man," Price said, going into his W.C. Fields imitation again.

"I want to go," Janelle said.

"Another drink?" Price said.

"Yah," Gardner said.

Naomi looked fiercely at Price, "You gonna get pissed and pass out again, white knight?"

"Why not?" Price said.

"Cause I ain't been laid in two weeks, Picasso," Naomi said.

"Don't call me that," Price said.

"How's 'Stud dud'? Naomi said.

"I said I want to go," Janelle said.

Gardner looked at her, or tried to. His eyes were spinning.

"Then—go," Gardner said.

"What?" Janelle said.

"Go. I'm not stopping you," Gardner said.

"We're going together—now," Janelle said.

"Not me, baby," Gardner said.

"You're drunk, Harry," Janelle said.

"No shit?"

"I said we're going."

"Aw, shut up," Gardner said.

"It's not Norma this time, Harry. You don't piss on me," Janelle said.

"No need to. You're a cunt that pisses on itself."

Janelle jerked up from her seat and swung a fist a Gardner. He pulled away from it and Janelle missed, and went sprawling onto the table top, knocking over her drink.

"For Christ's sake, Janelle," Price said, pushing her back into her seat. "What the hell's matter with you? Sit down. Sit down, goddamn it. I'm trying to have some fun, not a fuckin' brawl."

Naomi said, "For a change."

"Janelle'd of made a wonderful Lesbian," Gardner said.

"You sonofabitch. I'm going to call Norma. I will, goddamn it. You want that? I will call her—and tell her everything."

"You need a dime?" Gardner said.

Janelle came forward as though she'd been punched in the stomach. Her mouth dropped open.

"Janelle," Gardner said, "why don't you go home—and grow old gracefully."

Janelle began to cry, without sound. She stood up, turned around and stumbled off through the tables and the crowd, pushing and crying harder as she went—noise too now—and almost falling down after one collision. Gardner wanted her gone. To hell with her, he thought. To hell with his weakness for her, for his wanting.

"You happy with your exhibition?" Gardner said.

"I don't know," Price said. "We'll see when it fuckin' opens. I like the early stuff. Lately—it seems pretty thinned out. It gives you the fuckin' willys to see your whole life hung up there. You wanta come to the opening?"

"I'd love to."

"Giv'me your address. I'll send you a thing."

"How's the wall art film work? I read about it in <u>New York</u>."

"Gimmicky."

"I mean—mechanically--how does it work?"

"Oh, you shoot a film of someone—head-on—a long time. Like Warhol did in his movies. You know, just static. All they do is blink or smile a little. But then you put the film on a loop and light it from behind and frame the fuckin' thing. It's a kind of living portrait. It's got a small motor and lens to project it. It ain't cheap."

"I'd like to see one."

"You wanta?"

"I'd love to."

"I got one of Zelda, the Zulu here—where we're stayin'."

"Oh, sheet, Otis. Not tonight. You said--"

"He wants to see it."

"Sheet."

"I want to show him my thing."

"Show him your other thing, baby. I ain't seen it in two weeks."

Price turned and looked at Gardner. He was smiling. "Why'd we ever free them?" He said.

"What makes you think you have?" Naomi said. She wasn't smiling. "Free this, baby."

"Come on," Price said. "Let's go to our place. You can't get a fuckin' drink in here anyway."

"You sure need another one, don't you, Dude?" Naomi said.

"Look," Gardner said, "maybe tonight's a bad time to--"

"Great time," Price said. "No time like it."

"But your wife doesn't seem to want to--"

"She's okay. Ain't you, baby? Come on, let's go." Price got up, though he had to steady himself on the table, Gardner saw. Naomi unwound from her seat.

"May as well," she said. "He's no fuckin' good alone anyway. Or should I say no good fuckin'."

"All ready?" Janelle said; she was back. "I paid the check—on my way from the ladies room."

She was back, and seeing her, Gardner felt dropped and broken—like a mean aunt's good vase. What was she doing here? She was over, he told himself. Finished. He'd decided that. Done with—and now she was back. As though nothing had changed. Leechy. He thought he'd put the cigarette on her. But she wouldn't pull out. She was still in there, sucking his blood. Jesus, she was smiling even—cry puffed around the eyes, he could see that, but smiling and handling it. Jesus!

CHAPTER 15

They got in a cab right away or it seemed so to Gardner. His judgment of time and space was dead in the Gin. For vision, everything was like opening your eyes underwater—dirty water and speeded-up for that. He could hardly breathe and his heart was punching against his chest. But—he'd get rid of her somehow. He had to. He still could think that much.

"Josh loves your house in Paris," Janelle said. "I had a letter from him yesterday."

Bitch. Out. Don't talk like normal. Like I hadn't erased you. This is no normal night.

"He did say for you not to make bombs in his basement," Janelle said.

Bombs. Kids. S.D.S. Stormy Wathermen, can't pull my poor self together. Nam De Viet. Oh, say can you see by the dawn's early violence.

"Yeah," Price said. "Jesus. I walked by there the other day. What a fuckin' mess those kids made."

"I know Boudin." Janelle said--

Is there anyone you don't know, bitch.

"--Never met his daughter though."

"They're learnin', baby," Naomi said.

Blacks. Bad. Wichcraft. Scared in the dark. They know. Why did we ever import slaves?

"It's in the same block as us, you know." Price said, "only on 11th Street."

"I know," Janelle said. "Dustin lives next door."

The Midnight Cowboy. Everybody's talkin' at me.

"You know Dustin Hoffman?" Price said.

"Just through Josh. Met him at parties," Janelle said.

"Good actor," Price said.

I'm gonna throw up. Can't breathe.

"How's Josh's house?"

"Good," Price said. "He did a good job."

If Gardner had been able to notice he would have seen that the cab had come around Washington Square, up along lower 5th Avenue and had now turned into 10th Street. It stopped in front of a townhouse.

"This is it," Price said. He paid the driver.

This is what? Where were they? Someone said 10th Street. I know someone on 10th Street. I do. Who?

"Come on, Hoosier, let's get a fuckin' drink," Price said. He put his arm around Gardner, who was glad to have it to right himself, and he led Gardner down two steps and to the door of the house. The women followed. Price fumbled in his pockets, searching for keys, but couldn't find them. "Where the fuck are my keys?" Price said. He wobbled as he stood.

"Here, Massa," Naomi said. She handed Price a set of keys.

"Those mine?" Price said, as he grappled with the lock. Finally the door swung open, taking Price with it. The others followed him and Price turned on a light. As well as he could see, Gardner saw a very expensively decorated kitchen. All brick and built-in and show-roomy. He saw a large circular staircase winding up to the parlor floor level. My head. My head.

"Get the ice, hunh, Topsey?" Price said to Naomi. She growled lowly but without words and walked to the refrigerator. Price headed for the stairway, pulling Gardner along. They started up. Janelle stayed with Naomi.

"No love like that of two drunken friends," she said.

"Bastard," Naomi said.

"Come on, Indiana," Price said. "Hey, do you know him? There's a painter named Indiana. Robert? He's from there. Wears big hats and did that LOVE poster everybody's got. Jesus, they've copied it all over the joint. I saw the same motif the other day with the word SHIT instead of LOVE. You'll see upstairs. Josh's got it on highball glasses. LOVE, LOVE. Jesus, they'll put Guernica on toilet seat covers next. Come on."

Price helped Gardner up the stairs, which were rough to make drunk, Gardner thought, and they came into the living room. Modern, modern, Gardner thought, looking at it—rich, white leather—posters--paintings--and over there—a big bar. Gardner made out one of Price's paintings hanging over an off-the-floor fireplace. It was of a man who looked like

Hemingway lying on a bed and you knew he'd just shot himself in the mouth. The rifle was still between his legs.

"That was in my romantic period," Price said. He walked to the bar and pulled out two LOVE glasses.

"See?" Price said. "Gin okay?"

"Yeah," Gardner said. He had found a beautiful hard-cover book, coffee table size, of Price's art. It must be new, Gardner thought, since he had never seen it. He turned through it, though he couldn't see for much, his eyes were carouseling so. "Jeez, this is beautiful."

"Oh, yeah," Price said. He came up to Gardner and handed him his drink.

"Thanks. Jes beautiful."

"Pretty good. The plates are made in Switzerland. Abrams does a good job. It's brand new. They're gonna sell 'em at the Guggenheim first—for the show."

"God, that's great."

"Yeah, it's a good feeling."

"God, jes look at all the work."

"You want it? The book's yours."

"Oh, no, I couldn't. It's--$25."

"Fuck it. It's yours. Here I'll sign it."

"No, really."

"Come on. I want you to have it. We're friends. And you—understand."

"Jesez—that's fantastic."

Price took the book from Gardner and walked over to a desk and sat down. He picked up a pen and began writing in the front of the book.

Gardner sipped at his drink and felt very grateful.

Price came back to Gardner and gave him the book. "There, paly, it's yours."

"God, I don't know what to—it's just great. Thank you."

"Ain't you gonna read it?"

Gardner opened the book and there on a blank white page in the front, Price had written: "To mon ami—a Hoosier WASP who sees more than he looks at. F. for fondly, Otis Price."

"Thank you, Otis."

"Fuckin' movie business is good, hunh?" Price said, as he moved away into the room. He found a cigarette in a box on a coffee table. "Old Joshie does all right. How's your drink?"

"Great, just great," Gardner said. He fell into a chair to keep from falling onto the floor. Price leaned on the stand-up bar.

"How'd you get stuck in advertising?"

"H'mmm," Gardner said. "I wanted it since high school."

"What kind of fuckin' ambition is that for a kid to have?"

"I don't know. Anymore. It seemed so right then. When my talent first showed, when I was six or seven, I guess, I used to copy illustrations out of magazines—ad illustrations. Started like that. That was the only model I had in Lancaster. I got damned near all my images of America from ads—from the start. And that was okay with my folks too. Who the hell in a town like that wants their kid to be an artist or a painter? You know what their idea of that life is like."

"Garrets and whores and all that shit." Price said. "I was lucky. I got raised by my grandmother. There was a good old boozer. She'd get into the cider so, she didn't much give a damn what I did. She'd try some, but had no control over me. I was a wild little bastard. I just grew and free. I never did meet my old man. I don't know for sure if my old lady even knew who he was."

"Where's your mother now?"

"Dead. Got it in a tornado—can you imagine? Leveled the fuckin' house right down on her. The houses on either side—weren't touched. Not a scratch. I was at school when it happened. Didn't get the school either, damn it. What'd your old man do?"

"Ran a clothing store. Still does." Gardner said. "God, I used to lay out his ads for the local newspaper. And I was art editor of the school year book. All that crap, you know."

"What was your first ad—you remember?"

"A sketch of a horse and the caption I wrote said 'Clothes horse? Maybe at other stores, but we clothe people.' Jesus. I was twelve."

"Copy writing at twelve too. That's pretty good. A double-gaited talent."

Price laughed at his own joke and pulled at his drink.

"Do you know I really consciously, earnestly planned for a career in advertising." Gardner said. "I majored in it at college. Figure that out. And I had very good skills as an artist. Still do, technically, but, God, I, you know, never saw a real oil painting till I got to college."

"Where'd you go?" Price asked.

"I.U., down at Bloomington. I could've been a painter or an architect even. Good God, even a cartoonist, for that matter; but it just never occurred to me in those days. I just wanted to be, yearned even, to be an advertising illustrator. I was fascinated by magazine ads and the art work. I still see America that way—sometimes. I had such a pretty vision of it. I thought it was really the way it was in the <u>Saturday</u> <u>Evening</u> <u>Post</u>. And nobody in my hometown or home ever told me any different."

"I see you waited," Naomi said. She and Janelle were up the stairs and into the room.

"I poured yours. It's here," Price said.

"Forget it. I'"m gonna smoke. You want one?" Naomi said.

"Naw," Price said. "I really don't like that shit—next to booze."

"Gardner?"

"No—thanks."

"I'm going to have both," Janelle said. She flopped down and stretched out on a long, low, black leather couch. "Bring me, Naomi? Please?"

"Sure, the nig'll get it." Naomi walked over to the bar and, as she approached him, Price put out his hand to touch her shoulder, but she pulled away and looked at him as though he was George Wallace. She set down the ice bucket and pulled out a handful of cubes. She plopped two of these into Price's drink--

"Hey, easy," Price said.

--and she put the others in a glass of Scotch on the bar. She took another handful of ice and the glass of Scotch and walked first to Gardner. She put the ice in his glass.

"Thank you," Gardner said.

She took the Scotch to Janelle.

"Here you go, Scarlett. Move your ass," Naomi said.

Janelle took the drink and pulled her legs up towards her body so Naomi could sit down next to her on the couch.

"You want a smoke?"

Janelle nodded and Naomi lit a joint, took a puff and then handed it to Janelle.

"Are you drunk?" Gardner said to Price. Gardner knew that he himself was very drunk. Everything was going around and he had to stand up or be sick. He stood up and moved over to the bar.

"Pissed," Price said.

"I'm past pissed" Gardner said.

"What's past pissed?"

"Pussed?" Gardner said. He looked at Price's painting over the fireplace; he squinted trying to bring it into focus. "Suicide. Doesn't seem so unreasonable as it used to. He looks so calm. Is it Hemingway?"

"Sort of," Price said. "Just any strong man—who quit."

"Did you know him?"

"Yes—some. In Paris. Couple of evenings I don't remember any marble quotes if that's what you want. We were both pretty loaded both times. I was anyway."

Gardner thought he saw Naomi put her hand on Janelle's leg and begin to stroke it. She was, but it didn't matter to him.

"I'm so out of it," Gardner said.

"Come on, Hoosier, the night's young."

"I don't mean that. I mean—exhausted. I—I envy you so. I feel so empty. And—just—tired."

"Christ, kid, don't envy me. I'm pretty fuckin' used up myself. <u>Zeitgeist</u>. It's the spirit of the times."

"But you've got everything. Your work—fame. You're in the mainstream and on your own terms."

"Bull shit. The mainstream? Cause I"m in Leonard Lyons' column and Saphire over there gets her picture in <u>Vogue</u>?"

"But your show at the Guggenheim and being able to get away with punching that art critic I read about. I can't do that."

"You gave Buzzy pretty good tonight. Shit, I gave my thing up years ago. Or the chance of it."

"What do you mean?"

"Going to Paris. Copping out—as the kids say."

"But you didn't," Gardner said. "You've never stopped working."

"That's not work," Price said. "Not the way I was taught. There's no guts in it or fire. It's all up here. Technical. Cynical. Fucked. I'm like a goddamned fighter who can still throw a punch even after his eyes are beaten shut—or—Jesus, like a guy I saw the other day at 55th Street and 6th. An old fart. He's out in the street directing traffic, but nobody pays any attention. They go when the light's green, but he acts like he's making them go. And he's good—he's got the form and the style—probably a retired cop who's gone crackers. Whatever. He's good at it, but it doesn't fuckin' count. It's just gestures. Jesus, I watched him for a long time."

"Then it counts. At least he had an audience," Gardner laughed. "But I don't believe that about your work," he said.

"It's true, paly. Just gestures. I got the form, but it doesn't mean anything. I don't know. It just fell apart. I couldn't hold onto it. And Paris was part of it. I'm not a Parisian, goddamn it. I'm an American. From Illinois. What the fuck am I doing in Paris? I should be out on the fuckin' prairie."

"But the stuff here isn't much. Except George Segal. I like him," Gardner said.

"I know. The work here is bad, but it does reflect," Price said. "Warhol and Rauschenberg and those guys are disposable, but they're right. They are reflecting the scene. We're a junk, quick-use, disposable culture. I know my stuff's just as good—or bad—and sells for as much, but theirs is authentic fake at least. It comes from really walking the streets and dodging the dogshit and the fuckin' muggers and opening plastic wrappers. Andy even got shot, so he knows about violence too. Mine's all second hand. I steal ideas and innovate. I get my America out of The Times and Time magazine, which I have delivered. Everything I produce is hunched out, thought through to capitalize on the fads and 'will they like it,' 'will it sell.' Not, 'do I want to make it,' 'have to say it and tell some truth from my own senses and feelings.' I haven't made one fuckin' personal statement in my work since the early 50's. Oh, shit, what's the point? Who needs artists anyway in this society? A good computer programmer's more important. I feel cut off totally. I don't belong to France, sure as hell and here, I missed it all. Every fight, every feeling. I was at Iwo Jima, right? I should have been at Selma or at the Pentagon with Mailer or in Chicago. When America's soul was bleeding out in Dallas, I was having dinner at LaSerre and laughing and getting drunk."

"Why'd you go over there?" Gardner said.

"To work—isn't that funny?" Price said. "I didn't want to fight anymore. I'd had enough of that in the war. I just wanted to be an artist and work. And where do artists go? Paris, right? I'd read all the books and plays and seen the movies. Jeez-us, how conditioned we get against our natures. Paris was okay at first. For a long time. I did some pretty good work in those years. Then. I don't know. When Max died, I just—that was the end of it for me."

"Who?"

"Max Wolfe. He was my teacher in Chicago. The greatest American painter of his generation—and I mean painter—not a kindergarten diddler. He could paint faces you wanted to kiss or touch or talk to. Only inspiring man I've ever known. He was a German Jew who had to leave cause of the Hitler shit. Tough little nut. Very definite. And the best kind of man. Reserved, confident, just. I never heard him use an obscenity. I have a feeling he was the only genuine intellectual I've known. He loved thinking. And his joy—his active joy in every moment of life. And he had such deep feelings. He suffered more than most men, I'm sure, cause he felt things so deeply. But he always controlled them so gracefully and strongly. I never heard him whine or bitch like the rest of us. It was as though long ago, in a way most of us never can—he matured. God, what a foolishly abused word. I wish I could be more precise.

"He loved art and he made me love it in whole new ways—as discovery and intellectual ordering of things and intense sensuality. God, these poor darling kids with their pot and speed. Max was my mind-expander. Comforting and stretching and exciting my sense of myself and the world. Seeing beyond seeing. Seeing touch and listening to sight. Not dead, distracted; not mindless of life's plan and irony and indifference and chaos, but awake to it, confronting it like a mine face, from which your honest working of it could extract peace, love, courage, order. His life was so good for me; and his death taught me nothing. The mine face metaphor was his. Work your mine face, Otis, he would say. Do not turn from it. Ever. No matter how hard.

"Jesus, a man learns nothing when you kill things he loves. Nothing but hatred and impotence. His death—my reaction to it wouldn't have pleased him—made me turn away completely. And it just showed me how far I'd drifted in my work. He got killed down south. He went on one of those freedom buses and some red neck bastard blew it up. Can you imagine a little 60-year old German Jew artist riding a freedom bus?" Price's eyes filled and he began to cry, Gardner saw. He wiped his eyes on his coat jacket. "He wrote me about it before he went. Saying it might be dangerous but he didn't think so really, but in any case it was something he had to do. He felt very strongly that he'd run from Hitler and should have stayed to fight him. He didn't want to repeat it here. After Max, I, well, you know, turned to the pop crap and said to hell with it. Turned it out like taffy and made a bundle. Mine face? Shit, I didn't even report to the shaft after that. Just to the salons and Shor's and April In Paris balls and Cannes and Bill Paley's house and Easthampton with encrusted old bitches who read <u>Suzy</u> and <u>Woman's Wear Daily</u> and think Leonard Lyons is a literary giant—who buy paintings and pieces of junk sculpture like they were boutique items. That's me. Shit. What kind of fucking world can you expect if the artists are all lying? If, going in, he's outsmarting critics and dealers and taste-purveyors, the whole goddamned society fails. If the artist doesn't tell the truth, how can anyone else? They wouldn't even know how to recognize it. He can fail, but, Jesus, he mustn't lie. Oh, fuck."

"No, fuck," Gardner said. "Fuck is your sheild. Your goddamned self-contempt."

"Fuck you, ad man," Price said.

"Otis—why don't you come home?" Gardner said. "Back to America."

Price shook his head no and looked away. He looked at Naomi and Janelle. Naomi had her hand up Janelle's wide pants leg and she was masturbating her. Janelle had her eyes closed and was squirming and making little gargle sounds.

"Naomi, for Christ's sake, what are you doing? Cut it the fuck out," Price said.

Gardner looked over and saw what was happening. Janelle smiled at him. He was surprised that he felt nothing.

"Stop it, goddamn it," Price said.

"Gotta do something, baby," Naomi said.

"We're just playing till the boys come home," Janelle said. She laughed, but she did push Naomi's hand away and she sat up and turned and put her legs on to the floor.

"Jesus," Price said. He went behind the bar and made himself another drink. "What kind of shit is that?"

"Come back, Otis, please," Gardner said. "We need you."

"With my fat and my exhaustion and my dyke wife?" Price said. "No, America's too fuckin far gone and so am I."

"Yeah, why don't we come back, Otis?" Naomi said. "What are you scared of?"

"Jesus, why'd they have to kill Max?" Price said. He had tears in his eyes.

"Sheet—why didn't you tell me you had no guts without him 'fore I married you?" Naomi said.

"You were gonna be my new guts, baby. And energy. As bizarre as that may seem now."

"Sheet, I could've worked in a nursing home here. They're always lookin' for good niggers. I didn't have to move to Paris to be your nurse."

"Why'd you marry me, love? Let's talk about that."

"I thought you were a man."

"Sorry to disappoint you, ma coeur."

"You sure did, Dude. You're a fake. A fuckin' fake and you won't come home cause you're fraid everybody'll find it out. In Paris, it don't show so much that the famous Otis Price is a fuckin' fake."

"I just told my friend here I'm a fake, luv," Price said, "but what about you? Let's tell out friends about you. You ran out too, baby; you left your fuckin' people and the fight and sold your high black cheekbones to every designer in Paris. You read Cleaver and talk revolution, but you lay your black ass down on silk sheets 5,000 miles from the front. At least, I'm an honest fake. I was famous right? And Paris was safe. And you're the darling there. Nobody says "nigger" or puts you down. It's easy, huh, baby? You sold out too, who you kiddin'? So don't say fake to me. Huh?

"Why your balls in your tongue, white boy?" Naomi said.

Price grabbed the book from the bar counter and came around the bar and rushed over to Naomi and pushed the book in her face and screamed out, "Look at this, you goddamned panther bitch. That's the balls in that book, baby! More balls than in all of Harlem!"

Naomi slid aways from him and rolled off the couch and stood up. She was laughing. "Lot of fuckin' good it does in a book, sport," She came at Price and reached out with her hand and got him squeezed in the crotch. He yelled. "What's down there, baby? Nothin'. Nothin'."

Price pushed her away and, bent over in pain, came back to the bar and his drink. He slammed the book down on the counter. Naomi followed him.

"You're so fuckin' out of touch." she said. "I don't need no passport to visit <u>my</u> emotions! You're up against the wall, you bastard. What did I ever see in your white ass? Integration in sheet. To be like you? Uptight and scared sheetless. Fuck off, paleface."

Gardner couldn't believe it. Price was weeping and not saying a word. He couldn't stand what was happening. It was like seeing Chartres get hit by a wrecking ball.

"Leave him alone," Gardner screamed.

"You want your balls clipped, white boy?" Naomi yelled. "You better stay clear."

"Don't talk to him that way," Gardner said. "He's a genius, you stupid--"

"Genius, my ass," Naomi said. "He's a fuckin' has-been, cryin' the blues in a bottle."

"You stupid bitch," Gardner said.

"Hey, hey, don't call her that, paly," Price said.

"But, Otis," Gardner said, "listen to what she's saying. What she did."

"But don't call my wife a bitch, boy," Price said. "I'll have to knock you on your ass."

"Knock her on her ass," Gardner said. "That's what you ought to do."

"Don't interfere, boy," Price said.

"But," Gardner said. He was very confused. "I won't let her talk that way to you. I love you."

"A faggot," Naomi said, "just like I figured. Couple of goddamned faggots. You deserve each other. No wonder I go for Janelle. Ain't a man in this whole room."

"Shut that woman," Gardner said. "Shut her up. She's you wife, goddamn it."

"You probably are a fag, you fuckin' farmer," Price said to Gardner. "Why don't you get your fag ass out of here?"

"I'm not a faggot and you know it," Gardner said. "You asked me here. We're friends, goddamn it. I want to be your friend. I love your work."

"What's a faggot, fuckin' advertising man know about art? My work is shit. It stinks, you dumb ass."

"Why do you piss on it?" Gardner said. "Why do you let her? Shut her up, goddamn it. She's your woman. Shut her up or I will."

"Try me, white ass," Naomi said.

"You touch her and I'll kill you," Price said.

"You'll have to if you don't shut her up," Gardner said. He seized the book off the counter and clutched it to himself like a halfback with the ball and he backed off, getting ready to defend himself. He was reaching in for his knife with one hand. Price took a couple of steps towards him.

"Give me that stinkin' book back. It's not worth shit," Price said. "And you're worse."

"You gave me the book. You signed it. It's mine and I want it."

"I don't want you to have it," Price said. "Give it back!"

"You'll have to take it!"

"Harry," Janelle screamed.

Price lunged at Gardner. Gardner got caught with his hand in his pocket and he couldn't get the knife out. He side-stepped quickly though, at the last and right moment, and the big man couldn't stop his momentum. Gardner put out his foot and tripped Price and, as Price went down, Gardner clopped him in the neck with the spine of the book. Price lay in a heap on the floor and he did not move. Quickly, Gardner looked to Naomi, expecting her to come at him, but she wasn't he saw. She was rigid and looked surprised. Gardner ached and began to cry. He threw the book at Price's body.

"Take the book," Gardner said. "I don't want it anymore! You're yellow, you fat fake fuck. I hate you. You're no better than the rest." Gardner started for the stairs. Naomi was in his path. She moved out of the way fast as he came towards her.

"You sonofabitch," Naomi said. She tripped and fell onto the couch.

"Harry," Janelle said, "Don't leave me."

"Gardner, don't! Come back," Price said. He rolled over and started to get up. Gardner stopped and turned and looked back at him. "I want you to have it. Please."

"Let the faggot go," Naomi said.

"He's not a faggot," Janelle said to Naomi. "You're the faggot."

"No," Price said, getting to his feet. "He loves me. He knows me, my work. He understands."

"No, keep it," Gardner said. "It's no good to me now. You shit on it. You turned your back on your own work. On your best work. I don't want it if that's how you feel."

Price stumbled towards Gardner. Gardner was uncertain. He thought it might be a trick. He got ready again.

"Gardner, please. I—I want you to have it. I don't give everyone a book. Look inside. Read what I said."

" I read it," Gardner said. "You don't mean any of it."

"I do. I do," Price said. "You understand. Take it. Please." Price rushed Gardner and pushed the book into his stomach and he embraced him till Gardner's back hurt, as Gardner clutched the book between them. "I want you to have it." Price and Gardner were crying and sobbing.

"Jesus," Naomi said. "Look at the squalling queens."

"Shut up, Naomi," Price said. "Just shut up."

"Don't tell me to shut up, you drunken impotent bastard. You are. You're impotent. The great man is one big limp dick."

Price released Gardner and walked heavily and quietly, back to the bar. He picked up his drink and sipped on it. Price looked up at Gardner and Gardner saw the tears on his face.

"I'm—sorry," Price said. Gardner wasn't sure what he was sorry for, but seeing Price like this made him furious and Gardner suddenly hurled the book at Price with all the force he could summon and his aim was good and Price did not move, even though he had been looking right at Gardner and saw what was happening. He stood in place as though he expected it to happen and he was resigned to it. Deserved it even. He made absolutely no move to protect himself or to get out of the way. The book slammed Price hard on the neck and skipped up and hit him in the temple and then bounced off, arcing downward, its pages spread and fluttering like a great bird shot in take-off--till it bellied along the floor and died. As he watched it, Gardner believed truly that it was a living thing killed. Dead, he told himself. That too. He had admired Price so deeply and had responded so strongly to his work and now, in one horrid night of lightning, he'd seen the rot in Price and the stench of pretense coming off him and the stretched-out suicide of his life and he mourned for it all and he mourned for the feeling he felt getting killed in himself. All the good things dying and deceitful.

"It's a lie," Gardner said. "You're dead and you know it—full of worms!"

Gardner stared at Price who just stood there at the bar crying and he hated him and he wanted Price to rush him and he wanted to kill him with his knife. "Liar!" Gardner said and he heard his voice. He was screaming and he could feel the tears on his own face and he thought of choking them back, but decided finally to let them come. What else could he do? But he felt ashamed and deceived and he wanted out. Right now. He'd identified a corpse he'd thought could never be killed. That was enough. He had to get out of this morgue, he told himself. "Liar!" Gardner bolted for the stairs and took them down two at a time for four and then missed the curve on the force of his momentum and fell, bam, whap, out of control for the rest of the way until he flat-crashed onto the kitchen floor.

"Harry; Harry, wait for me," he heard Janelle saying. The words fell like small attendent rocks just before the avalanche of himself.

But now everything was very quiet and strange. At first, Gardner was afraid to move. He was sure that something was broken in him. But, after a moment, he made little tests of himself; first, his feet—and legs. Then his hands and arms. Then his back. And now—his neck. Everything seemed to work. Nothing was cracked and not much hurting either. God takes care of drunks. It would hurt though. Tomorrow will hurt hard when the booze has said good-bye. And the battered parts reported in. He knew that. But that was tomorrow. Gardner tested some more and finally got himself up to being on all fours, when Janelle reached him.

"Harry—are you hurt? Are you all right, darling?" she said. She got down on her knees beside him and put her arms around him. He pulled away and pushed her back. She fell over on her side, spread out on the floor.

"Get away from me," Gardner said.

"Harry—don't—please--I love you," Janelle said.

"Don't use that word." Gardner's head was hanging limp between his arms now. Everything was spinning. He thought he was going to fall off the floor.

"You have no right to use that word," he said. "None. It's still-born in your mouth. Your love leprosy." Gardner, in a great effort, got up from the floor and staggered towards the front door. I've got to get out of here, he told himself. Away. From her. From place. I got get out. He wrestled the handle with both hands and finally undid the lock and flung open the door. He ran through it and up the two steps and out along the sidewalk. He stumbled as he ran and fell to his knees and he tore his pants leg and, although he didn't know it, the flesh beneath. Janelle was right behind him when he fell and caught up to him.

"Harry, don't leave me. Please. You can't."

"I'm gone."

"Harry, don't. Don't say that. I'm sorry. Please. I need you. You're all that's left."

"Nothing's left. Nothing was."

"No—we are, us."

Gardner struggled to get up and finally he made it to his feet. He was rolling heavily. He tried to look Janelle in the eyes.

"I don't want you in me!" he screamed. "Disease—terminal. And I—I want—be well! I want live!"

"Harry, look—look. Here's your book. I brought your book. I brought it. He wants you to have it. Here, darling, take it. He's good. You love him. It'll be okay. I will. I'm—sorry. We'll be okay, you'll see. Let's get a cab. Okay? We'll go to the studio and I'll love you. You'll see. Everything. I'll suck you and everything.

"I don't want you! You don't suck, you syphon. I don't want you! Can't you hear that?"

"No, I won't! I won't! I'm not going to lose you! I've lost enough!"

"Give me my book!" Gardner jerked the book out of her hand and took it to his body like a pet or a baby and jostled it, every so gently. He looked down at it and began to coo.

"It's dead, you know; it's dead, Janelle."

"There's a cab. Look, Harry. A cab is coming. Come on. It's okay." Janelle tripped off the curb into the street and she almost fell. She recovered herself and flung her arm up to signal a taxi that was coming along the block. It stopped, just about hitting her. Janelle opened the door and then went back up on the sidewalk to Gardner. She put her arm around his waist and she started walking him towards the cab. "Come on, baby, we'll go home. And be all right. Honest we will." Gardner allowed himself to be led into the cab and Janelle followed him, closing the door behind. Gardner felt very hot now and thought he was going to pass out.

"64th Street—between Broadway and Central Park," Janelle said to the driver.

The cabbie moved the car forward in a jerk and Gardner let his head fall back against the rear of the seat. He closed his eyes and everything in his head came loose. He was spinning out into space and there was nothing to hold onto. He was going to die. He knew it. Then, something threw him forward.

He opened his eyes. The cab had stopped at the end of the block for a red light. I got get out. Gardner grabbed the door handle and threw open the door. He jumped out and whammed the door shut behind him—and he ran, back up the block, in the direction they'd just come from, clutching the book like a football. He ducked behind a parked car and almost ripped his lungs trying for a breath. He slouched down against the fender and put his face to the metal. Cool. Cool. Feels good. Then he saw the taxi backing up, coming towards him and then going by him. It backed all the way up to Price's house. He watched as Janelle started to get out. Gardner looked around behind him and saw steps leading up to a brownstone house. Up there. He bolted for the stairs, staying in a crouch as he ran, and got up the steps and inside the front door. She didn't see me. She didn't see. Gardner was in a small vestibule and immediately he sat down on the floor and slumped into a corner. He told himself to be very quiet and everything would be alright. Be quiet. But he couldn't quiet his heart and he thought the noise of his pounding heart and breath would give him away.

He heard her out in the street yelling, coming along the block. "Harry! Harry! Where are you? Come back. Please."

S'hhh. S'hhh, he told himself. Just be s'hhh and she won't find you and she'll go away and you'll be safe. S'hhh.

"Harry—come out. Please. You've got to---I'll kill myself!"

Good. Good. Gardner thought. That's very nice. That's good solution.

Very considerable for everyone concerned. Not such a bad girl, after all. Yes, That'll do very nicely. You go kill yourself. You go kill yourself.

Gardner closed his eyes and fell asleep. When he woke up, he remembered everything and quickly he listened carefully. He wondered how long he'd slept. But it was quiet. So lovely and silent. She must be gone. Oh, yes. There was one thing. He wondered if Janelle had killed herself. Probably not. Damn it. She exaggerated everything. Gardner pulled himself up, in a crouch, bracing himself against the wall of the vestibule. He rose full and fell forward. He put his arms out front and broke his motion and he leaned against the opposite wall. Just stay this way, for a minute, he told himself; then look out. But be careful. She might be there. Hiding. Waiting. She very smart. Careful. Gardner shook his head to clear it and then he looked straight ahead at the wall in front of him . He jerked his head back to clear the dizziness and saw a backwards number 10 on the glass above the door. Number 10, number 10. 10, 10th Street. I know a 10th Street. Patience, Patience. From the checks. Patience Cromer. For baby-sitting. English Patience. Where does she live? "You live in Village, right?" Gardner remembered saying. "I do, yes. 18 West 10th Street. Not at all Bohemian." 18. 18. Gardner hurled open the door, ran down the steps and along the block. 12, 14, 16, there is 18. 18. He found himself standing over a row of mailboxes; and each box had a name on it and a little black button. He closed his eyes again and opened them again, trying to get them in focus. That's better. He read the names. Solomon. R.Dill. Horan. Patience Cromer. That's Patience! Good God! Oh, Patience, Patience. Save me, save me. Love me. Gardner pushed the small black button next to her name and held his finger on it. Patience virtue. Patience virgin. Patience.

CHAPTER 16

"All right—stop that bloody ringing, won't you?" Patience's voice said. It was coming through a small speaker and sounded thin and metally.

"Who is it?" she said.

"Mr. Gardner. <u>Me</u>. Harry Gardner."

"Who?"

"Mr. Gardner. You baby-sat there tonight."

"Mr. Gardner, is it?"

"Right. Him. <u>Me</u>. "

"Patience. Let me in. I need you. Can I come in?"

<u>May I</u>.

"What?" I can't hear you."

"I need you. Mr. Gardner from Easthampton."

A buzzer sounded in the door and Gardner pushed himself off the wall and free fell over to the door and opened it. Inside, he stopped—lost. Where was she? Which floor? Jesus, I forgot to ask. I don't know where to go.

"Up here," Patience said.

Gardner tried to straighten himself at the sound of her voice. He looked up and there she was—at the top of the first flight of stairs—all blurred and beautiful—in a shorty night gown of some kind, blue it was, light, and she was bare-footed, and her hair was all soft and long and hanging down around her face. Face, face, mouth, breasts, look at those legs, pure Botticelli. I got to get up there. Climb. Go to her. To the legs, ligaments, loins, tra la.

Gardner put a foot on the first step and stumbled up the steps, crashing between the banister and the wall, back and forth, and almost falling forward each time he took a step.

"Mr. Gardner—be careful," Patience said.

Got to get there. See her boobs beneath the silk—or rayon or whatever the hell kind of slippery, crinkly stuff you could see through it was. I see the shadow where her cunt is hiding. Go. Go. Get there. Goddamned banister keeps moving. Made of rubber. Cheap landlords. Never fix anything. Smile. Look okay, will you. How's your breath? Wish I had some toothpaste—or mouthwash. Climb. Get there. She'll understand. Don't need that shit. Just reach up. That's it. Now you're getting there. Hold your breath back. Don't breathe so hard. Not out of shape. No. Don't show her that. Goddamned cigarettes. Few steps. And. And. Gardner was there. He stretched his arms out and dropped them on her shoulders like bags of cement. She buckled under the weight of them and took a step or two backwards, but she held him. She held him.

"Patience—I need—you."

"What's happened, Mr. Gardner?"

She's got me. She's okay. She's recovering. She's putting her arm around my waist and she's leading me along a corridor—dark in here, goddamned landlords put 25 watt bulbs in the hallways to save their crummy mummy—money—and there's a door. It's open. Must be her place. Place. Place. My place is your place. The place is familiar but I can't remember the—

"Are you all right—are you? Don't mind, please. The flat looks a fright."

Dying, bleeding, done and she's worried about the bloody flat. Goddamn women. Can't measure things. Can't—no. sis okay—trying please you. Good instink. She's okay. Got me inside. Heard door close. She good—good-night. Here' I go.

Gardner fell forward, hard, tree chopped down. On the floor. Silent. Not out. Just down. Lie still. Rest. Fight again some other day. One. Two. Three. Floor feels good. Four....

"Mr. Gardner! What is it? What's wrong?"

Five. Six. Seven. Eight. Do something. Don't no knock out. "What? What's it? Where?" Gardner rolled over on his back and saw Patience's legs disappear—all four of them—into the darkness under the nightgown. Goddamn, what a referee! Prettiest ever saw. Where" Respond. Get Corner. Trainer fix you up. "Oh, yeah." Seem clear. Smart. Responding. Funny. Ten. Tenth Street. You live there. Patience. Want you. Want up. Everything is. It's not—ish desperate."

Here she comes. Getting down side me. Don't put mirror over my mouth, bitch, to see if I live. I live. I live. Oh, not bitch. Nurse. Good. Woman. Tender. Give. That's her arm under my head now.

"Mr. Gardner, are you all right? Please. You haven't hurt yourself, have you? Mr. Gardner, talk to me. Please. Really."

Yes. She right. Must. Talk. "Birshday. Mine. Drank. Drink. Hippy Birschday to me." Look at that. Look what's right there—staring you in the face. "I see your birsh. Birsh in the hand worsh screw in the brush." Touch it. Reach. Just right there.

Gardner put up his hand and placed it on Patience Cromer's crotch. "You have lovely cunner, Mish Comer."

"Mr. Gardner, really," Patience said, but she didn't take his hand away.

"I like very mush, Mish Cunner. I have the Harry for you, if you have Patience for me," Gardner said—and laughed. "Isn't that punny?"

"Your head. Whatever happened to you? Mercy."

"I want to live you. Love." Gardner began stoking the mound beneath her pubic hair and he began pulling the leg of her which was nearest to him up over his body so that she would be strattling him.

"Mr. Gardner, please," Patience said. Then—she was strattling him.

"I want your Patience—and your nurses and medicine. I need. Medicine. Very sick. Need whole resources of hospital. Need hard transplant. Hummmp. I'm Christian. You're Barnard girl. Play it Cooley. Cooley, man."

"Mr. Gardner, really, you mustn't. You've been drinking. Something's upset you."

"Stinking, finking. Sinking, blinking, shrinking—and Blitzen." Now. Now.

Gardner pulled himself up and put his arms around Patience and began kissing her nipples through the cloth.

"Ummm—good nurses. Very good nurses. Here, Lenox Hill." Hold on. Hold on.

Gardner could not sustain sitting up in the position and he fell back to the floor, bang the head, ohhh the what the—pulling Patience down with him, on him. His head was rolling back and forth, left and right. Life of its own. I've got my troubles, you've got yours.

Are you kissing sweet?

Gardner kissed her and tongued right in. There for your cruddy toothpaste and mouthwash! Just go like man. Kissing sweet, my ass. I kissing Gin-and-smokey-sour. So what? I'm kissing. Kiss her head off.

That's the commercial. Gargle on this, baby. Tongue on WASP—and hold the mayo—as long as you can—and find the nurse. Where'd that nurse go? Push the button and the nurses'll turn up. Turn up, little nurses all starched and plump. Reach your hand for the gentle Nurse Goodbody. Rub her gently—ohhh, so gently, but firmly. Be in charge. Oh, I'm in charge I am. In charge at Bloomingdale's, Bonwit's, Bergdorf and Saksman's and then some. Whoops, feel the thermometer rising and starting to probe the scene. The scene and the obscene. Hello, Doctor. What a bedside manner you've got, old internist. You're pressing her abdomen. Me shacka ab-do-men. Ab-do-men. Sounds like Arab church or Mosque or whatever those fruit of the loom dressers call their house of worship. Yes, Mosque. Well, we're just gonna have a little mosqueraid right now. Right here, nursie. Tell me if it hurts. Just a little exploratory operation. Nothing to get hung about—strawberry yields forever. South of the belly—down Mexico way. Dingaling. Dingalong. Longadong. What's this? Is this a dagger I feel before me? Farewell to Arms, nursie, the nursie is giving you a belly rubdown, belly to belly, bella, bella. That's a good nursie, rolling over in the foyer—these field operations are always tricky—and reaching for the incision of the zipper. That's funny. I thought I was performing the operation. No matter—we'll do joint surgery. Ha, ha. Joint surgery. That's a good one. How convenient you're cutting me open just where my zither was—zipper is. What a handy incision to have for the future. What's that you say? Dreadfully swollen, Mr. Gardner? Very dangerous operation? Vital organ and all that you know. Terribly inflamed, wouldn't you say? Oh, yes, rather. It's got to come out, Mr. Gardner, that's all there is to it. Yes, all right, I'll sign the waiver. The sooner the better, Mr. Gardner— there's always the danger of complications. There now. Doesn't that feel better? Ooooh, yes. Kiss it and make it well, nursie? Ooops, don't be hasty. A cursory examination first. Don't curse, son, it's not gentlemanly. Nursie, dear, nursie, I feel you getting a first-hand report. Yes, then we'll see what has to be done. But what about me, Doctor? I have this frightful gash between my legs and it just won't seem to heal. Whatever shall I do? Perhaps, we can give you something for it. At least temporary relief. Oh, anything, Doctor. A hot compress maybe or splint—some chicken soup on it. Anyway, let's have a look at it. I'm sure it's nothing serious. My God, that is a proper wound. Can you treat it, Doctor—can you? Oh, yes, of course, my dear, to the best of times and the worst of times. We'll just roll you over on the examining table—sorry I'm out of stirrups at the moment—and have a look-see and touch-see and a kissey and an entry. Screw your Patience to the sticky point!

"Mr. Gardner---ooh, ooh, baby."

"Ummmmm." I have performed this operation many times, my dear; even in Vienna under the famous—under, on top of, sitting up, backwards, in an elevator, upper berths, lower berths, sour breaths, in the shower, for an hour, in the corn—or a morn noon nite and also on Sundays— once in the basement of the Presbyterian Church in Lancaster, Indiana, the Reverend Donald C. Chapman officiating. Well, not <u>officiating</u>, of course—not intercourse. I mean it was his parish (he thought) and we only borrowed it. (Let's do it in the road). Afterall, one good rite deserves another. Right? Wright. <u>Wright!</u> Oh, Jesus C. Chapman. What have I done? Doing. Screwing. I'm insane. You're not insane. You're in Patience. I have no Patience. I have Norma. You're abnormal. I'm not sick, I'm just disturbed. It is a far, far better fling than I have ever flung. What afterall is Norma these days? What with the <u>Bomb</u> and the "Bums" and the thousand nauseous toxics flesh is air to. Wright? Wrong. Twat's that you say, outrageous fucking? Lay on, Macduffer. Give her your slings of error rather than fly to those you know knot of. Knot of. Ha, ha. Terrible. Well, shit I can't be funny and fuck at the same time. Oh, unfair, oh feel ya! What the hell am I doing? Screwing is what you're doing. At any price. Price. That lousy prick. What about your own lousy prick? What price is that? She gets a $1.50 an hour for baby-sitting. You call this sitting? Good idea. Sit up. Give her a little razzle-dazzle. She'll like that position. You know, don't you. Doctor-Mr. Hyde? See though, see; the Patience is responding. Dat's right, Kingfish. De Patience is responding good. What you like bestus, Rastus? I like ass-bestus. Yuk, yuk, yuk. Buzz me, Miss Blue—care of the United States of America, Continent of North America, Western Hemisphere, The Earth, The Solar System, The Universe, the Mind of God and—and Occupant Unknown—and you never got over playing The Stage Manager in high school. Oh, Emily Gibbs, I loved you so. I so loved Our Town that I named my only begotten daughter Emily. Hello, Emily. Hi, Daddy, where'd you go? Out. What'd you do? Got laid—by your baby-sitter. Naughty naughty Daddy. No allowance for you this week. Honey, you got give me allowances all the time. No, Daddy. Go to your room—Mama's room. And stay there till I tell you to come out. I'm coming out. Don't care what you say. Jesus, I am coming out! What the Hell? I was going great. Soft now—what light through yonder window breaks. Shit. I've gone soft. Soft as. Why'd you have think at all? Is the light in the window? What the hell time is it? Dawn? Must be? Stop. Stop thinking. Put it back in. It won't go back in. It wants to go to its room. Like a good Daddy. It's been naughty and should be punished. Oh, shit. Grow up and get it in there. Where's her hand? Make her work it. That'll get it going.

"Nurse. Nurse! Medic!"

"Unnn, What?"

Call the fucking nurse. You're having trouble. You have a right. You've got major medical. There. That's it. Healing nurses' hands. Yes, Emily, this is what Daddy wants for you—screwing any drunk in the middle of the night who comes along. STOP! You're soft in the head! No, I'm soft in the dick. You wouldn't if you'd stop thinking. Just feel her hand. Concentrate on the hand. The hand that took your son Andrew by the hand to bed and tucked in Emily and took the baby-sitting check from the hand of your wife. Is that the hand you want me to concentrate on? Shut up—off! Stop it. Your cock's lying there like a handful of cold manicotti and you keep cogitating when you should be copulating. What's she gonna think? You're impotent. That's what. So what? A lot of what. You don't want that. No guy wants a girl to know he's impotent. I'm not for Chriss' sake. Just for now. She doesn't know that. It's the first time. Kiss her. Anything. Do something for Chriss' sake. Don't just hang there. Kiss her something. And she's looking right at you now. Wright at you. Fuck Wright! Fuck fucking Wright. Fuck her. I can't. I don't want to. I change my mind. Change your mind? What kind of dumb, selfish bastard are you anyway? Get out of your head and—head. Head. That's it. If she'll suck your head, you'll get hard again and you could do her too, in the meantime. Do something. She's looking! Kiss her tit for a start. Easy. Don't be an ape. They like it gentle. They do? All of them—are you sure? I read about some who like it rough. Beatings and all. Maybe her. No, and don't worry about others, damn you. You can't even handle this one. Oh, I can handle her. I just can't fuck her. Gardner soft on Come-ies. Yuk. Yuk. Yuk. There. Hey, the tit thing worked. She's going. Okay. Then keep at it. Now. That's it. She won't even notice something wrong. Ah, ah—see—something is wrong though. I caught you. I knew. It's just not Norma to be the way you are. Not that kind of wrong, dummy. I mean your cock! It's soft! Can't you feel it? Doesn't that worry you? So what. She won't notice if I get busy. Show her your tricks. Change-up. You got more than a fast ball. Try the knuckler. It's all in the way you place your fingers. That's it. Good. It's working. She went for it. Now the spitter. Right down there in the pocket.

U'mmm, good stuff. Good control. That's it. Now turn her around. Lay her down. Don't balk. There. You're on the mound. Now the wind-up—and the –delivery. Wow—feel her. A regular Leo-the-lip. What's the score? 6 to 9. Fantastic! What a game! Yeah? This is good you think? Forget it. You're still a no-hitting pitcher. Can't even get your bat up. Who needs it? This is fantastic. You need it, you jerk. Get it up. Put your funny where her mouth is. Mouth to mouse resuscitate. Stop thinking, for Chriss' sake. Stop it. Feel. Just feel. Concentrate. I can't. The booze and cigarettes. The <u>Bomb</u>! Screw the bomb. Screw her! Get your high, hard one back. I can't. I can't. Nothing's happening. I lost it. The slider's all I've got left. You said a mouth-full—not even. Look out though—here she comes. Here she comes. Oh, thank God! Ah, you won on a forfeit, you bastard. Anyway, I won. Now try for a double-header. No, I can't. I don't want to. That's all. The game's over. I'm over the hump. There was no hump, idiot. I don't care. It's—ummm-my ball and I'm taking it home. Bush leaguer. Mouth fucker. You <u>are impotent</u>. Oh, bull—what's it matter. And, wait a minute. Feel that? <u>That</u>? That's nothing. You're not gonna do that in her mouth—and limp the way you are? You just met her. I'll—I'll have –to. I can't—the other way. Too much on my mind. Oh, damn, okay; come on. I give up on you. Let's go home. Well? Come on!

Patience swallowed and coughed a little. And the game was over.

She turned around and put herself on top of Gardner. She looked down at him and smiled He tried to smile and look back into her eyes, but he could not focus.

"No, really—I—am—sorry—about coming here like—this. And—about—about—"

"You had me frightfully worried, luv," Patience said. Are you sure you're all right? Is your head? What happened to it?"

"My birsh—<u>birthday</u>—and I just drank too—I'm sorry—really."

"S'hhh, Luv. It's all right. S'hhh."

"But I'm sorry I---"

"Really you needn't keep apologizing. I'm terribly pleased that you wanted to come to me."

Gardner nodded and he smiled a bit and he remembered how really it was that he happened to be here and he felt very bad.

"I did. I wanted to see you," Gardner said.

"I'm so glad. I've thought the same about you. I'm certain you noticed it."

"I'm sorry I went—let you down."

"Nonsense. Really. It's perfectly all right."

"Firsh—first time is always so—"

"You probably just had too much to drink, didn't you? I understand. With it all, you're super. Very tender, you know."

"I wish we'd of—well, that I, you know. I'm sorry."

Patience embraced him and put her head on his chest.

"So full of sorries, aren't you, lamb? Don't be. Please. I'm not. You're not sorry you're here, are you?"

Gardner shook his head no but he was wishing otherwise.

"Wanted you earlier—back at house," he said. "Thought bout you all evening. Then—drinks gave—"

"Well then, there you are. Not so bad afterall, if they brought you here. Do you want something, Luv? Coffee? Juice? I have grapefruit juice, if you like. It's very good."

"No, thanks—uh—cigarette maybe."

Patience kissed Gardner's chest, then his mouth, lightly, and his nose and his forehead and then she got up and went out of the room. Gardner rolled over on his side. He zippered his fly and looked at the light gaining in the window. God. Must go. Get out here. Fore children get up. Jesus. Insane. But God. She really did number. Went down. Got her. How bout that? How bout what, impotent schmuck. Go. Get out. No business here. Yes. Mustn't seem abrupt though. Not nice. Impolite eat and run. Oh, Jesus. Words. Puns. Everything dirty these days. Patience came back and knelt beside him. She was carrying the cigarettes and the grapefruit juice.

"Here we are then."

"Uh—thanks. I—I feel bad I—"

"S'hhhh, please."

She lit a cigarette for him and handed it to him. She unbuttoned his shirt and put her hand inside it and rubbed his stomach and chest.

"I'm glad it's—started, at least," Patience said.

Gardner nodded and tried to think of something good to say and get out. Haul ass, boy. It's late. It's over. The party's ended. It's day after birthday. Drunk as he was, he knew he was holding his stomach muscles tight while she was touching them.

"You—I—have to—"

"Yes, I know, Luv. I can feel it—in your body."

"Hunh?"

"You've become very tense. It's all right."

"It's just so—late—I realized."

"I understand. Really I do."

No good way. Just do it. Do it. Go. Gardner pushed her hand away, grabbed the book, and got up quickly—standing but weaving.

"Jesus, Patience, I—what to—say."

"Don't worry, Luv. I'm very—close-mouthed—and glad."

"I don't mean that. Oh, God. I just such uh—I was so out of it and you—being—our sitter—I've got to go. I'm sorry."

"Yes," Patience said and she nodded. She got up and came to him. She put her arms around him. "Luv?"

God, woman, let me go. "Yes." Gardner put his arms around her.

"Am I your first—English girl?"

What Hell's that got to--? "Yes."

"Oh, good. I'm so pleased."

"Dawn. I'm—sorry."

"Go then. Be careful. Good-night."

"Yeah, good-nice."

"Will you be back I wonder?"

Gardner nodded. Patience leaned back and looked Gardner in the face.

"I know I'll see you again at least."

"Course."

"I mean tonight. I'm sitting. Didn't you know? You and Mrs. Gardner have theatre tickets with the Whitakers."

"Do?"

"Isn't it odd? You and Mrs. Gardner made love on this same block I suppose. Didn't you? She told me once she used to live here. Before you were married."

Jesus, that was so! And now! Oh, go. Go. Get. Vanish. Wrong. Must.

Gardner let go of the girl and stumbled back a step. "Good-night. I—good-night," he said and he turned and he staggered out on the run. Out the door. Down the steps. Into the street. Drunk. Very drunker than he'd ever been—and feeling bad. Still—I made her. Had Patience in bed. Not bed, but in body. Not bod. Bad. Same thing. Same thing. Scored. Floored and scored. Okay. Look out now. Very drunk. Can't see. Stumbling. Muggers' choice. Easy mark. Try walk straight. Pull gether. Get cab. Quick. Go. Avenue. Cab. Get. Don't get rolled. Killed. Look tough. Where's knife? Put knife in hand. Be ready. Sober. Ah. There. 5th!

Be okay. Get cab. See. Look. Focus. There. Comes one. Don't wobble. Audition. Smile. Citizen. Be respectable. Thank God. Nut. Black. Those poor bastards. Wave hand. Nice. Stand straight. Don't weave. Good. Good. Working. Cab stopping. You know game. You spectable. White. Solid. No-off-duty for you. There. Stopped. Open door. Take time. Get in. Know New York. No wonder success. Be nice. Gentleman. Get way. Style important. Speak.

"170 Cenral Park Wesh-t."

"Whuh?"

"1-7-0 Cen-tral Park---West."

Did it! Cab moving. Won. Safe. Got laid. Powerful. Clever. Relax. The Whitakers! My God! Middle class terrible couple. And her. Uck. Who'd want to lay her. Who'd want---Good-night. Sweet Dreams---ssssss.

CHAPTER 17

"Hey, mac. Pal. Come on, hunh?, the driver said.

Wake. Man talks. Far off.

"This is 170, okay? Be a good guy, hunh?"

What? Oh, cabbie. Spectable. Right. Be spectable. Look. 170. He did. Apartment. Home. Dawn. See dawn light. Oh, say can you—oh, pretty late. Bad. Terrible. Pay. Be good guy, hunhh, Pay. Get out. Uh. Stumble. Fall. In street. Not bad. No hurt. Okay. Not bad. Fell very well. Now get up. There. Pay. Big tip.

"Birshday. Celebate. Brate. You unnershtan. Here." Give im money. There. Look. There's money. Picture Lincoln. Know that's money. Don't carry Lincoln's picture my pocket. Lincoln 5. Too mush. Oh, screw. Give im. Wazza diff. Jez pay. Never see gihn. Bye, bye, cabbie. Jez. Didn't even thank me.

Oh, Doorman. That's counts. That's the sonofabitch. Pull gether. Get pashit doorman. Fuckin' doorman. Modern man conscience. There. Good. Up steps. Careful. No muggers. Get in. Safe. Live. Look spectable. You up steps. So good, so far. Where fuckin' doorman? Sleep. Drunk. Bastar. Ring bell. Say work all night. Cut film. Why explain at all? Bastar. Who he? Fuckin' drunken doorman. Don't have please him! Where fuck is? Ring gihn. There comes. Smile. Be nice. Look sober. Right? Spectable. Open it, sonbitch.

"Hello—how are ya? Workin'. Film. Cut. Good-night," Gardner said.

Bastar. There. Think I'm drunk. I showed you. Bastar. Didn't even look me eye or speak. Just nod. I look him eye. Not drunk. He won't know drunk. Walk straight now. Follow line in floor. Bastar, he's watching. Look at me while walk to elevator. Straight. Straight. Casual. Slow. Digny. Human digny. There. Made it. Prez elvator button. Good. Stand rect.

235

Bastar, still looking. Turn slow now. See mirror. Hallway. Mirror. Check look okay. Not bad. Look pretty good. Not bad looking bastar, you are. Here. There. Elvate come. Good. Walk digny. In. Made. Good. Baser doorman. Not say me drunk. Pless 12. 12. Press. Good. Up. Up. Now get pash. See Norma. Polzgize. Splain. Unerstan. Birshday. She good. Love. Eleven. Twelve. Prez one when get out. Nobody know you in late. Ha, ha. There. Get off. Keys. Got. Need keys. In pocka. Dig in pocka. Geh kays. Ah. There. Good. Stand still door. Hit hole. There. Put key hole. Ah. Bing. Good. Good drunk. Funshun. Always able funshun. Turn. Sheee. Stomach. Whazat? No sick. Please no sick. Got ac straigh. In. Made key work. In. Light on still. Still. Very quient. You and place. S'hhhh. Good. No one up yet. Good. Made it. Succhess. Know New York. Know everything. Funshun. Good. Get way with. Walk bedroom now. Very Indian. Tippy-toe. S'hhh. Sun up over park. Daylight. Safe though. Safe. Cept stomach. Oh, God! Get bedroom fast—bathroom. See. See. Make it. Kids sleep still. Hallway. Bedroom straigh head. Don't falter. Don't fall. No. Don't. Don't puke. Can't. Floor tilting. Can't make Falling. Going. Going. No! Gone. U'mmmm. Carpet good Warm. Stay. Sleep. Okay. Forgive. She forgive. You live. Safe now. Home. Safe. Sleep. U'hhhhhh. Oh, no. Don't do that. No. Don't throw up.

"Get up, goddamn you! Don't sleep there. You bastard, get up. Don't let the children see you," Norma said.

Why she kick me? Luv her. Came home. Birthday. Not fair.

"Norma, love. Save. I home. U'mmmmm. Don't kick me. No. I—love—you."

"Love? You scum," Norma said.

"What's a matter, Mommy?" Andrew said. He came around the corner from his room.

Andrush. That's Andrush.

"Andrush. Hi. I love you. World's no good, honey. Must tell you what I know."

Norma was tugging at Gardner, trying to drag him into the bedroom. "Daddy's sick, Andrew," She said. "It's all right. Go back to bed, sweetheart. It's nothing. All right? Daddy just ate something at the party and—he's got a stomach ache. He fainted."

"Andrsuh, Billsingly's a bastar. Did you know that? World ish evil. I'll tell you bout it in morning."

"Is Daddy drunk again?" Andrew asked.

"He just doesn't feel well," Norma said.

"Looks drunk to me," Andrew said.

"Mommy—what's matter?" Emily said. She walked up, yawning.

"Nothing, baby. Daddy just got sick. That's all. Now go back to bed. He'll be all right."

"I'm hungry," Emily said.

"Daddy's drunk again," Andrew said.

"He gonna sleep there?" Emily said. "I can't find the sugar pops."

"Not drunk. World sick," Gardner said.

"Harry, get up! Get up!" Norma said.

"Can't. Sleep here. Children unnerstan. Don't you, kids?" Oh, Jeez, stomach. Gonna puke, throw up. Guts going! Can't. Can't help it! Right now! Nowwww. Uhhhhhh.

"Harry, no. Oh, Christ! Andrew! Emily! Go back to bed! Go on! Go!"

"But, mamma, he looks terrible." Emily said and she began to cry.

"It smells," Andrew yelled.

"He's just sick. He ate some bad food. Can't you see? Go to your rooms! Go!" Norma yelled. She began to sob and slumped against the wall. The children backed off, Emily clinging to Andrew and crying. They disappeared around the corner of the hallway but they did not go to their beds. They waited, just out of sight, listening and confused. Andrew was angry.

"Oh, Harry, for Christ's sake, get up from there," Norma cried. "You're in your vomit!"

Cool. Cool. Vomit feels cool. Liquid. But face in. Get heat off face. There. Good Nicsh pillow. Vomit. Good-night.

Gardner was asleep and knew none of it, but felt himself try to help Norma as she dragged and pulled him out of the hallway and into their bedroom. He remember her seventh month belly and felt worse. He felt her get his suitcoat off and loosen his tie and he felt her make sure that he had not swallowed his tongue. He fell asleep on the bedroom floor.

CHAPTER 18

"I've come to help you, not exploit you," Gardner said. He was wearing a pith helmet and talking to a group of black natives. It was very hot and he was sweating and he realized that this was the first time he had worn a pith helmet since he was a little boy and his father had bought him one as a souvenir at the Indianapolis 500-Mile Race. Wilbur Shaw won it that year and Floyd Roberts got himself killed.

"I'm not here to push the American way of life; you've got to understand that. Bwanna hates colonialism. I only want to help you—to till the soil, lay bricks, make buildings."

Unh! What was that? Bloody jungle! Something tugged in his groin and Gardner reached inside his pants to find the thing that was growing there. He pulled a ten-penny nail out of his penis. He was very surprised, of course, but it didn't hurt at all. It did, however, wake him.

A dream. I've been dreaming. Hold onto it. What was it? Tanzania or someplace and I was in the Peace Corps. The Peace Corps? Yes—why not? That would be good. Kennedy and—but what could you do? Till <u>soil</u>? You don't know the first thing about it. <u>Or</u> laying bricks. You've never built anything in your life. A birdhouse once! Wonderful, Harry. Course, you could show them how to mix a good martini or—layout an ad—but would anyone in Tanzania care? They'd probably rather have a poultry expert. <u>Why would a nail be in my penis?!</u>

Gardner turned on his side and looked down at his crotch to make sure he had been dreaming. He saw that he had his clothes on, and that he was lying on top of a bedspread. Where am I? He stared at the brown spread. Oh, thank God. That's ours. I'm home, at least.

He relaxed a little and fell back flat spread-out and he stared at the ceiling. Suddenly, he felt the immense size and weight of his eyes and, in his brain, he felt the blood rushing and jamming against his skull and he felt the veins in his temples pounding, and his heart was punching on his chest and his chest felt like it was shrinking and his lungs felt like rusted and broken chicken coop wire that he once cut himself on. His tongue felt like a carcass, some dead thing left out to bloat in the sun. His teeth felt algied. His knee bones ached, one especially, and his feet were swollen and his right arm was asleep. He felt sweat in his shirt collar and his neck and in his hair and on his forehead.

And it was Sunday, he knew and, oh yes; God—now I remember—I was so smashed! He tried to remember details and he thought about Norma first thing, but nothing else came and he knew that nothing would be coming as long as he hurt so much.

Pills, pills, he thought. Get the pills. Gardner tried to sit up, but he got slammed right down by his pain—and now there was a new one in his forehead. He remembered the hospital and falling down and the cut and the stitches. But—but--he couldn't remember more. I've got to get the pills! He thought. He got up and walked to the bathroom fragily. He fumbled around in the medicine chest until he found the pills. He took one Darvon and three sodium bicarbonate pills. He had a rule about taking these before going to sleep on nights when he had been drinking in order to head off a hangover and he was angry now that he hadn't done it last night. A jazz musician he met one night taught him this trick.

He turned away and to the toilet and unzipped his fly and felt for his penis. He was afraid he'd find a ten-penny nail in it. But he couldn't find it at all. Where is it! Who took it! My cock! His stomach jumped and he tried with both hands to find the opening in his boxer shorts. There was no opening! God, I know it's there! It's gotta be! Gardner unsnapped his waistclasp and pushed his pants down and then his shorts, which were all twisted, and—oh, thank God—it's there! He touched it and he looked at it and he saw that it was shriveled and that the head was hiding in the foreskin, but he didn't care. It's there! That's all that matters! Gardner pulled back the foreskin and, continuing to look at his penis, urinated. It came out spurty and at an angle and some got on the carpet. He moved a step and he took his other hand and widened the opening and he saw it now hitting right and into the bowl and he saw that it was very cloudy and very yellow and he wondered why it had spurted. It's like that after I come. Jesus Christ—Patience! Patience! How'd I end up with her? And what happened? Oh, God, my head! I can't think!

Gardner flushed the toilet, pulled up his pants and saw that he had banged his knee and torn the suit fabric in front of it. He walked back to the bedroom. He lay down on the bed and tried to remember what had happened last night and how he had behaved. He couldn't do it.

What time is it, he wondered. It feels late. If you want to know—get up—go over and look at the clock-radio on the dresser. I can't! I want to stay here! It's safe here! If I get up—I've got to hear what I did last night. And I can't remember! I've got to think—to defend myself! It was bad! I know that. This is a good suit. Ruined.

He listened for sounds in the apartment. Nothing. Norma isn't there. Yes—she is. She's somewhere—in that big orange canvas duster dress she always wears on Sundays. She's doing something in the kitchen or sitting on the floor in Andrew's room, playing "Trouble" or "Candyland" or whatever those games are. Forget it. Maybe she's keeping the children quiet so I can sleep late. She's very nice that way. Maybe she left you—how bout that? She wouldn't leave me! Oh, no? No, no! Oooooooh. My head! Damned Darvon hasn't done a thing yet! Gardner looked down at his hands and saw them trembling and now he felt the nerve ends all over his body palsied in that same kind of involuntary tension. He remembered a suspension bridge caught in a high wind which, he had seen once in a newsreel and he saw it now in his mind, the roadbed buckling like nylons whipping dry on a clothesline and the cables finally snapping, collapsing the whole into a deep gorge below. That's me. That's me, he thought!

That's not you! You're somebody, son; you're a Gardner, he heard himself saying to himself, but then he realized that it was not his own voice talking, but his father's. How was he—them--his sister? He hadn't written any of them or called in weeks! I'll bet your father isn't hung-over this morning!

A siren sounded—<u>Whoop, whoop, whoop</u>—in the street and Gardner came back to himself. I've got to get up, he told himself. He did and, everything aching, he walked over to the dresser and squinted at the clock. 2:15. He felt bad that it was so late and sensed it would get worse. <u>Whoop, whoop, whoop.</u> He started to walk to the window to see whatever it was that had a siren on it and was going by, but he stopped himself when he remembered that he wouldn't be able to see anything without his glasses. He walked back over to the bed to get them off the end table. He fumbled around for them but couldn't find them. <u>Where were they? In the bathroom, maybe.</u> He started walking towards the bathroom when he stepped on something and stopped. He bent down and picked it up. His glasses. One temple shaft was bent and the lenses were smudged and he saw something dried and solid on one lens. Vomit.

A piece. Then he remembered that he had thrown up and he felt worse and his hands started trembling worse than before. He flicked off the vomit piece and shuddered and walked back to the bed and cleaned his glasses on the sheet. Did I do it in the toilet? I can't remember. I didn't smell it there.

Gardner went to the window and opened the shade. The light was soft but it pinched his eyes at first. When he looked again, he saw the day—pure, clear, blue and bright. It was spring. The way you want to remember spring.

He could see as far as the candystriped stacks of Con Edison in Queens and he could see that they were quiescent today, with no smoke coming out, and closer in, across the way, he saw the east side buildings standing cleanly defined in rank and file and crest and drop, appearing to him like natural objects, beige and grey mountains of a sort, and they were beckoning and satisfying and remote at the same time, but still, today, not threatening in the way they were usually when he thought about them as people-made, and about the people in them. Then they became something to beat, overcome and get the better of—or be beaten by or worn out on. Today he didn't want to get the better of them. Gardner looked down into Central Park. The boat lake looked like a huge plaza of shimmering, aging bronze; there must be a hundred boats on it—dots of blue and red and yellow and green and he saw one boy with no shirt on standing up in his boat and the boy dived into the water, which until then had looked like a solid, Gardner thought, and he supposed, seeing the boy jump, that it must be warm. In the trees Gardner could see spring visibly. Those trees close to the lake were fully leafed and darker green while the green in the trees farther away paled lighter into lime, until there was no green at all on the trees farthest away, because there were still no leaves.

His eyes caught on four boys playing war on a rock out-cropping, just inside the park, along the bridle path and then he looked some more and saw a boy kicking a soccer ball and a man walking a poodle which was stopping to pee and he saw a woman tucking in a blanket in a baby buggy and, on a bench, an old lady sat with her legs spread and she was feeding some pigeons and next to her sat an old man who had his pants legs rolled up and Gardner knew the man was showing his varicose veins to the sun. A young couple holding hands passed in front of the old people—laughing, talking, slow in motion—and now, two girls on horseback came into view and they broke their horses into a canter and disappeared into a tunnel and then he saw a covey of bicycles—girls on them and in short shorts—and then suddenly, birds—against the sky on his eye level. Blue they were with white wings. And speckled ones. And lower down, lead-grey pigeons. Solid Black. And now the white of two gulls arcing by—in from the ocean they implied.

He heard the music of children's voices and he looked down and saw a file of children coiling and uncoiling on the path along the lake and he saw two or three grown-ups prodding them along and then he heard the bongo drum again and a steel band now and again the rock group in the bandshell and he recognized a song from "Hair," and he saw a kite and saw the sun catch on a jet high up and the jet looked thin and silver and fine and all at once Gardner felt overwhelmed by the scene, by the sights and sounds and the park and the idea of the park and the buildings and the idea of the buildings and New York City and the idea of New York City on such a day and at such a distance. From up here or from a plane or from across the rivers or from high up in one of its buildings you could remember why you came to New York, he thought, and why you went on living there and why, when you left it, you always wanted to come back to it and you could forget about the noise and the dirt and the mostly ghastly weather and the danger and the menace in the crowds—the hatred and fear in the ethnic and religious tribes shouldering up against each other—and the fumes and the filth in the rivers and the neuroses and the ambition and the deceit and the power and the loneliness and the unforgivingness. You could love it with a physical filling up, with a passion you could feel in your head and your stomach and your heart and Gardner was feeling it that way now. And he loved Norma and wanted to see her and he knew that he had done something very bad to her and he wanted to find her and make it up to her and to be as good as this day was, which now seemed to him like an indictment against himself. Go, get her, find her, love her and make her love you back. Do it. Don't be afraid.

But he _was_ afraid—suddenly—terribly. He was alone. And Norma had left him—he knew it! And his children were lost! And Billingsly—Good God—and Wright! I lost my job too! I did it all! Destroyed everything! Oh, my God, I am afraid! Alone and afraid and—I'm going to die! I know it! I've always known it! Even at 10 and in Lancaster! That was physical fear of dying, fear of the pain—but this—this is annihilation! I'm disappearing! I won't be! I've got to find Norma!

Gardner showered and dressed and started out. He took his knife as usual. Coming out of the bedroom, he saw the stain on the carpet in the hallway and remembered now that that's where he had thrown up. And he remembered lying in it and that the children had been there. Oh, no! What have I done? I've got to find them! <u>I'll bet they're in the park.</u>

CHAPTER 19

Gardner came out of the apartment building and ran past the doorman, who was Puerto Rican and wore white socks and pants too short and a uniform coat that was too large. The coat had formerly been worn by the big Irishman who died in the winter and had been the last of the imperious Irish doormen at their buildings. They were all Puerto Ricans now and looked more like loiterers in from the weather than doormen.

He crossed Central Park West at 75th Street and moved south on the parkside towards the entrance at 72nd. The street was jammed with cars and the sidewalk was crowded. The sun was warm and there was a good breeze and all the people looked happy, Gardner thought, but there were so many and he felt threatened by them.

He almost tripped over a child on a trike. And there was a drunk asleep on one of the benches. Jesus—that could be me. Thank God, I got home. A section of the Sunday <u>News</u> blew along in the gutter. Goddamn litter.

Slow down. Eat something. It's going to be all right. At 72nd Street, Gardner stopped and bought a coke and two hot dogs with sauerkraut from the woman who had the pushcart stand with an umbrella. She was Italian and wore a black dress and black stockings and had a moustache. Why the hell do they let themselves go? Don't they know about <u>Neet</u>? He always ate lots on days when he had hangovers. He thought it cut the booze and the cokes made him belch, which made him feel better.

He put his napkin in the litter basket, which was overflowing, and he went into the park. The benches along the entrance street were lined—full up—with old people and there were many more old women than old men. <u>Women outlive men</u>. He started hurrying again.

He decided to look for Norma and the children at the Bethesda Fountain. They often went there together on a Sunday afternoon to lunch at the Fountain Café. The Café was next to a plaza with a large round fountain in the center. The fountain had a replica statue of Winged Victory in the middle of it. The plaza faced into a lake, and had become a hippy hangout.

Gardner looked at the hill closest to him. He saw a young couple lying in the grass and they were kissing. Up from them, partly hidden in a clump of bushes, was an old man watching them. He was beating off. <u>Good God</u>. But - <u>why not</u>?

Gardner got to the mall area which overlooked the fountain and had stairs at either end of it leading down. The area was crowded, he saw. But no sign of Norma. The scene was a jumble in his eyes and not pretty.

The hippie scene had been pretty at the beginning, Gardner thought. When they were fewer and they carried flowers and the force of a loving idea. They were very pretty and they gave you hope.

Now, Gardner resented them. He hated their filth and isolation and smugness—and their clothing, which, at first, had seemed so original, but now looked like the tattered uniforms of an army in retreat.

These people were his enemies, he decided suddenly, and still, faced with George Wallace and Spiro Agnew and the Chiefs of Staff, they might be his only allies. Oh, God, where is she? Where's Norma? She's the only ally I've got!

Gardner went to the steps, hurried down them and entered into the mob. It was like being in a drop of water under a microscope.

He came to the edge of the lake and stopped.

"Get your nigger ass in here," Gardner heard someone yell. He turned to his left and saw a young black motioning out to a boat in the lake. The boy was motioning for it to come back to where he was, Gardner saw. Looking out, Gardner saw two more blacks, shirtless and flat-stomached and solidly muscled, in a boat about fifteen feet away. One was standing and he yelled to the one near Gardner, "You cocksucker. You had the boat for a fuckin' hour." All of them wore black silk bandanas tied around their heads. The one rowing in the boat gave a high, sudden tug on the oars and this threw the standing one off balance. He almost fell into the water. "You motherfucker," he said, and he slapped the rowing one across the head with his hand. The rowing one laughed. Then they both laughed. The one near Gardner yelled, "I cut your ass if I get my hands on you. That's my boat." Gardner slipped his hand into his pocket and gripped his knife. The two in the boat, still laughing, ignored the one on shore and the rowing one took the boat farther out. Gardner looked at the black near him and then his eyes followed the blacks in the boat, until off to the right of them, and about twenty-five feet from shore, he saw Norma and the children in another boat. Andrew was rowing and Norma was in the stern, leaning back. Her eyes were closed and her face was turned up to the sun. Emily was sitting in the front of the boat and she was trailing her hand in the water.

Gardner felt good, but gutted in the same moment. "Norma, Norm," Gardner yelled. "Andrew! Here!"

Norma opened her eyes and she looked towards Gardner and so did both of the children.

"Norma. Hey, Andrew," Gardner said. He motioned to Andrew to guide the boat towards where he was standing. Norma, Gardner saw, motioned to Andrew to steer the boat in the opposite direction and she turned her face away from Gardner. Andrew began to row farther out, but Emily had seen Gardner and she leaned over to her brother and tugged at his sleeve, pointing in the direction of her father. Gardner couldn't hear what they were saying but he saw Andrew and Emily struggling until Andrew finally slapped her and she slipped back off her seat into the bottom of the boat. She began to cry. It was like watching a horror movie with the sound turned off. Norma leaned forward and was saying something to Andrew, who was shaking his head no and was continuing to row the boat away from where Gardner stood. Emily sat up and pounded her brother on the back. He was ready to hit her again, but Norma reached forward and grabbed his arms. She started to stand up to take over the rowing. The boat was rocking and Gardner thought it was going to tip or that someone was going to fall out. Gardner yelled, "Sit down. Be careful." Andrew resisted his mother, Gardner saw, but finally gave in. He moved to the back of the boat, with a push from Norma. She sat herself in the middle and began to row. The boat turned around and was heading towards Gardner. Emily was smiling and she was waving. He waved back and felt afraid and relieved at the same time. It would be all right, he said to himself.

Norma brought the boat to the steps, which it hit against, and Emily was shouting, "Daddy, Daddy, Hi, Daddy."

"Hello, baby," Gardner said. "Hi there. Give me the rope."

Emily did and he slipped the rope through a metal ring anchored in the step and he tied it.

"Daddy," Emily said, "Mamma let me row and everything. I row good."

Gardner lifted Emily out of the boat and he squeezed her in his arms very tight. "Oh, good, baby, good. I'll bet you do."

"The best. Ouch, Daddy, not so hard," Emily said, and she squirmed.

Gardner loosened his grip slightly but he still held onto her hard. "Oh, baby, baby." He thought he was going to cry.

"Daddy, whatsa matter?"

"Nothing, Darling. I'm happy to see you."

"Andrew hit me," Emily said. "Did you see 'im?"

"Yeah, but I'm sure he didn't mean—"

"Yes, he did, he did. He hit me hard. I fell. I hate him."

"I did not, you," Andrew screamed.

"A'hhhh. It's all right, baby."

"I love you, Daddy."

"I love you, sweetheart."

"I'm hungry. Can I have a ice-cream?" Gardner felt her whole body and voice tone change. She had forgotten all about Andrew now.

"What?"

"I want a ice-cream."

"Oh sure. Andrew, you want something? Wait a minute." Gardner sat Emily down and reached into his pocket and pulled out a dollar. "Here. Andrew, you hungry? Andrew. I'm talking to you."

Andrew was silent and he was staring out at the lake, with his back to Gardner. Norma had not turned around either.

"Andrew!" Gardner said, raising and tightening his voice.

"You get it, Daddy," Emily said. She rubbed up against Gardner's leg and reached for his hand. "Andie's mean. He hates us."

"Andrew, come out of there or I'll—"

"What?" Norma said. She turned around harshly. Her eyes were swollen but they were narrowed and furious and Gardner was suddenly afraid. "Leave him alone."

"I asked him to get Emily an ice cream. Is that too much?"

"You never ask much of anyone, do you?" Norma said. Her voice sounded raw as subway brakes.

"Norma," Gardner said. And he could hear the pleading in his tone.

"Norma," Norma mimicked him.

"Daddy, I want it," Emily said. She pulled at Gardner's pants leg.

"Yes—just a minute, baby. Andrew'll get it."

"Why can't you?"

"Yeah, I—I want to talk to Mommy."

"You always talk to her. I can talk."

248

"I know, honey, you can, very well, but—but this is grown-up. Important."

"I never see you. You sleep all the time or go out to parties with <u>her</u>," Emily said and she began to cry, Gardner knelt to her and embraced her.

"Emily."

"You're great at making people cry," Norma said. "Andrew, okay, go on. Get Emily an ice cream."

"I don't wanna," Andrew said.

"Please. For me. I'd like an orange too," Norma said.

"No."

"Andrew. Help me. Remember, you said."

Andrew turned around and looked Norma in the eyes. He got up and climbed to the front of the boat but he put his head down and did not look back at Gardner. Norma squeezed his hand as he went by her. "Thank you, Andrew," She said, "I know."

Gardner reached out his hand to help Andrew out of the boat, but the boy ducked away from him and jumped onto the shore without looking at Gardner. Andrew started to walk away, stiff and erect and full of anger. His fists were clenched, Gardner saw.

"Son—here's the money."

Andrew stopped. He turned around, his head still down, and ran back to Gardner and grabbed the dollar out of his hand, and he did not look up and he turned again and gave his sister a push in the back and he walked towards the line which was standing in front of a hot-dog stand.

Norma was silent.

"You know <u>what</u>!" Gardner said. He wondered what Norma had meant when she said "I know" to Andrew. That I'm no good! A rotten father and husband? Had she told Andrew that? Norma was silent.

"What's Andrew so mad about?" Gardner said. Bad beginning, boy— you've left yourself wide-open. I've got to start somewhere! It's the best I can do!

"Ever see your father sleep in his vomit?"

"Norma, I—I'm"

"Oh, God, Harry, I've heard the speech. Don't even start. I don't want your shitkicking apologies again. That cheap Jimmy Stewart act makes me sick. <u>I—I'm sorry, Norma. I'll never do it again, Norma. I promise, Norma.</u>" Norma said, again mimicking him. "The whimpering's worse than the other. You don't mean it anyway."

"I do."

"You don't. Why do you pretend?"

"Norma, shhh."

"I'll scream if I want to. You do. Anything you damn please. And I don't have to get drunk to do it!"

"Norma, please."

"Please? I don't want to please you. Why should I? No, no more, Harry. I'm sick to death of <u>Norma, please</u>. I've had it. Go shit on someone else for a change. You're a bad man, Harry, and I'm through with it. Last night did it. Do it to someone else. Janelle, maybe."

"Norma, you can't mean that."

"I do, you sonafabitch. The last time. I've taken all I can."

Gardner could feel tears coming and he wiped his eyes across his sleeve.

"Very touching," Norma said. "That's a new one."

"Norma, it was very bad I know, but-"

"I don't care anymore. Go fuck the little whore blondes and drink and kill yourself. I've had it. I just don't care anymore. I tried too hard and-"

"Norma, you can't mean it."

"I mean it, goddamn you. You just can't believe it, ego-maniac. Old Norma—always can shit on her. She'll forgive anything. Shit on Mother Courage and she'll bless you for it. Well, not this time. I want you out. It's what you want anyway. It's the way you set up the whole thing. Why not admit it?"

"That's not true. I love you."

"Oh, God, that. I stayed all this time for that. That's all I ever wanted. And no one but you. And you say it after last--. No, not your love now, Harry. I can't take it. It's too sick and, I don't know, maybe I'm too simple to understand, but—I—I don't know why you hate women so. You're so cruel. Sadistic."

"Oh, Norma."

"What did women do out there in Indiana to make you so cruel?"

"Nothing."

"It's just not fair, any of it. And I hate you for it. I don't want to be a divorced woman in this town. I know too many of them and their scene. I don't deserve it."

"Oh, Norma, what's fair?"

"Don't make that speech. I know you've told me nothing's fair, but do you have to keep proving it? I've never hurt you or if I have, ever, even a little, I've felt terrible after—"

"I don't mean to hurt you."

"But you do and I—I just can't take anymore. The drunkenness and the insults and lying awake all night—crying and taking sleeping pills and not sleeping. And you make me nasty. I never was. You're making me a nasty, bitter, angry woman. Do you want that?"

"I don't. I want your tenderness and love and sweetness and humor."

"You don't! You don't do anything for it! What's the use. It's gone. I don't have it anymore. We used it all up. I just—I feel old and I want you gone." Norma began to cry.

"Oh, no, Norma, it's there. I know. Give me a chance. Let's try. I want to. You do, Norma, you know it. For us, Norma. And the new baby. At least, for that."

"Yeah. Thanks a lot. You didn't think of that much last night. Get a taxi at midnight."

"I asked you to stay."

"There you are. Insult me and it's my fault if I get killed."

"No, but, Norma, I didn't do anything wrong. I was just having a good time."

"You must have. Who was it, Harry, till 5 AM?"

"No one, Norma." Gardner hated himself for lying again. But he had to keep going. "Just drinking and Otis Price, the painter. He came and we drank and then ate and we're friends now. He gave me a book. He invited us to his opening."

"I saw the book. Wonderful. Who'd you lay?"

"No one, I tell you. And that's the truth." Again, Gardner felt the lie. "I just drank. To celebrate. I quit my job last night."

"You did?"

"Yes! See, Norma, it'll be different now. I'll change. We'll go away. Get out of this trap."

"Really—quit—Billingsly?"

"Yes, I'm telling you."

"I don't believe it."

"That's why I got drunk—and Otis Price—to celebrate."

"And the other times? And the—other?"

"Forget those, Norma. It was the job. That's why I drank and—I was miserable, suffocating—and that's over now. We can do something we want."

"What do you want, Harry? Do you have any idea?"

"Well, I don't—know—exactly, but we'll work it out. Everything.

You'll see. We'll be all right, Norma, honestly. Believe me. I'm not bad. I want to try."

"I have—so many times. I'm worn out and–I don't believe you anymore. No, Harry, I—I'm glad you quit if that'll make you happier or more contented, but, I want you to go. I'll get a lawyer and—you'll like yourself better. You won't have the pressure and you won't have to blame me for everything."

"I don't blame you. Norma, I love you. I—I don't know how to tell you. I need you. Just now, when I woke up and couldn't find you, I got crazy desperate. I need you, Norma. God, I'm a disaster area without you. You're it. All I've got. I know how hard, but what's better? Apart? Alone? Maybe you could make it, but I don't think you want to, and I'd be finished completely. Norma, I need you so much."

"You have a hell of a way of showing it." Norma looked down into the water and she was silent for a long time. So was Gardner, because he believed he had said all that he could say. He felt bad. He had lied once more to her, but somehow, it was technically true and it was for them, and for the best, he thought. Out of the corner of his eye he could see Andrew and Emily playing tag and he was grateful they were staying away.

"Harry?"

"Yes."

"Have you—slept with Janelle?"

"God, of course not." Should he tell her, he asked himself. He wanted to—to clean the slate, to get himself good again, to make everything honest and right, but—that wouldn't help anything. It would end it all and he just didn't want that. He wanted Norma. Janelle was over. And he wanted the new baby. He'd never be with Janelle again, so let the future stand for the past.

"Honestly?"

"I told you."

"She said you had."

"She lies, all the time. You know that."

"So do you. You're the best. In this whole lying town, you lie the best."

"Norma, I swear to you."

"On what? Your word as an advertising man?"

"I didn't. Haven't."

Norma nodded and a fragile smile came into her face, Gardner saw.

"I know you're lying, but—this time I'm glad. If you have, don't tell me. Don't ever get drunk and reveal—Harry?"

"Yes?"

"Will you go see a doctor?"

"What?"

"Will you?"

"Norma, I don't need to—"

"Yes or no?"

"But I don't' need a—"

"It's the only way, Harry. Yes or no."

"Daddy, Daddy," Emily said, "Andrew hit me."

"There wasn't any orange, Mom," Andrew said. "We didn't forget."

"He killed me almost."

"I did not," Andrew said. "She wouldn't stay in line. She's a pest."

Andrew came back to Gardner but he did not look at him. He held out the change to him and Gardner took it. Gardner would see that Andrew's chin was trembling and he wanted to embrace him and apologize, but he decided against it for just now. Andrew climbed into the boat and went to the back seat and turned his face, to stare at the lake.

"There's a stand over across the lake," Gardner said. He thought he was going to cry also. "Let's go there, maybe they have an orange. Besides, it's my turn to row."

"Oh, goodie. You're a good Daddy," Emily said. She jumped into the boat.

"Yes, aren't I?" Gardner said. "The Father of The Year."

Gardner indicated to Norma that he would like to come into the boat. "May I?"

Norma nodded yes and she moved to the rear and sat next to Andrew and she put her arm around him and when she touched him, he buried his head in her shoulder and began to cry. Gardner choked back his own tears and he untied the rope and he got into the boat and pushed it away from the steps with the oar. He pulled on the oars with all of his strength and, in the act, was determined to burn the alcohol out of his system.

The day was beautiful and serene. He was together with his family and they were safe and he wouldn't have to face Billingsly tomorrow—or ever again.

You can start fresh, now, he thought. Try something new. Change your life completely. And this time something worthwhile. Solid. Something you—and Norma—can be proud of.

But—<u>what</u>, he wondered. Teach, maybe; sure—at the college in Lancaster. Or work in government. VISTA even. Or paint full-time and get a worker's job to make money. In a factory or a gas station.

That's it! It's so simple when you think about it. Just dismantle and simplify. De-emphasize all the crap and the competition and the complications. You don't need a Doctor. You need a simple meaningful life. That's all.

But Jesus; I wonder what a school teacher makes a year—even a college one? And—you've got to have a PH. D. or a Masters Degree, at least, I think. And Norma wouldn't want to go to Indiana, or the kids. They hate it. Why kid yourself? And—be honest—the time you worked in a gas station you were there two weeks and you tried to hot patch a tire and you burned up the whole goddamned thing and you screwed up even worse in a factory. You're only 43 too, you jerk. You haven't saved that much money. Your grandmother lived to be 93. Suppose you live that long? Or you get sick? Or Norma does? Or the kids need help getting started? What'll you do for money then? You can't quit! The rent on the apartment. And the help. And the schools and insurance. And the house in Easthampton. Jesus Christ, you barely make it now from paycheck to paycheck. Miss one and you're on welfare practically! But, God, what can I do? I told Norma! I said we'd have a different life! She won't stay otherwise! Wait—think it through. She'll stay. Just shape up a little. Go to the doctor a couple of times. Make the effort. That's all it'll take. Norma loves New York. She doesn't want to leave it. Her work's here and her friends and family and she wouldn't really be happy anywhere else. And Billingsly can't fire you. <u>S'hhh-Fem</u> was yours. That's right. I remember now. I was a big hero for that. Billingsly needs you. The bastard'll have to take you back. You're the best. And, really, what'd you do so wrong? He can hide you. Wright won't have to know you're there. And that old sonofabitch can have Americans, The Beautiful. What do I need it for? Just an ego trip. I don't have to paint. I'll take up golf or something to get it out. You'll probably get a raise even.

And you'll ease off on Janelle too. That'll help. Just see her once in awhile. Pick up with Patience instead. She's sweeter anyway. Not so crazy or tough. My God, wasn't she sweet though? Just like that she blew you—got to ask her about that—and—you could live without that Zodiac crap of hers, but—

"Harry, look out--," Norma said.

Whap. Their boat collided with another.

"Hey, sheet, man, you blind?" a voice said.

Gardner looked up and saw the blacks he had seen before, when he had been standing by the fountain.

"Stupid ofay sheet," one of them said; the one who had been standing earlier, Gardner saw.

I—I'm sorry. I didn't see you," Gardner said. He pushed his boat off of their boat with his oar and he did feel stupid and diminished and he felt a little clot of fear come collicking into his stomach. Suddenly, he could feel his hangover again, all over, and he realized about all the things he had been thinking and that they had led him right back to where he had been before last night. No change—nothing. Not one thing really different and he was angry at himself. God, it has to change this time, he thought. It just has to!

"Harry—are you all right?" Norma said.

"Yeah—just a little—shaky, you know. And—thinking. About us. What to do, you know. It's—a little scary."

"I'm not scared. Oh, Harry, it could be so good. You can teach."

"Yeah. Maybe in Lancaster. At the college."

"Indiana. Oh, I don't want to go out there. How about Europe? Or, well, somewhere, but not Indiana."

"Yeah, maybe."

"Italy. I'd love to live there for a year."

"I don't," Emily said.

"We'll see," Gardner said.

Andrew wasn't speaking.

"They don't have TV," Emily said.

"Of course, they do," Norma said.

"Sesame Street?" Emily said.

"No, but," Norma said.

"See? I hate Italy," Emily said.

Italy, Gardner thought! God, I can't speak Italian. And what would I do for a living? Italy? God. I've got to stay here. It's all I know. But you don't have to work for Billingsly. And no Janelle—or Patience—or any of them. You've got to get over that. You can. You can stay in New York and make a new life. You don't have to make two hundred thousand a year or try to lay everything in sight. You can make 50. Ease off a little. Go with a smaller agency. Open your own maybe. Why're you killing yourself? Or call Val what's his name. And work on his Urban Fund project full-time.

Can we manage though on fifty thousand a year? I don't think so. Well, you'll have to. Sell the house in Easthampton. Cut back. Jesus Christ— other people live on fifty thousand! You'll have to. And—maybe I'll lay off all together this summer. Take some of the money and enjoy it. Go out to Easthampton and read. Not sell the house. Start fresh in September. Or, we could go to Italy for the summer. Sell the house or sublet the house. Or a month anyway. Course, Val what's his name will need me middle of July at least for anything in the fall. U'hhh. Val—uh—what _is_ his name?

Gardner turned and looked over his right shoulder. He saw the bank and the lithesome lines of the little wooden boathouse coming closer. Under its roof he could see the old man and his refreshment stand. That was good. That was orange. Orange ahoy! He had found the passage to the new world!

Then, just off the shore, a few feet to his right, he saw again the two blacks in their black bandanas. One was rowing languorously and the other had his feet in the water and they both were ignoring Gardner, but still something about them curdled the juice in his stomach and took away from his good feeling. What though? And why? Ah. Never mind, he told himself. He rowed again, harder, but kept seeing them on the periphery of his vision, until he came even with them and began to pass them. The one not rowing looked at Gardner and their eyes caught. Quickly, Gardner looked away and wished he hadn't looked at all, but he had and he had the face as surely in his mind now as though on a film plate. He was unsettled by the face. By the black and angry eyes. And the turned-down moustache and by the goatee. Gardner's stomach filled with acid.

"Harry, careful, you're going to hit," Norma said. Gardner looked at Norma and saw the apprehension in her face. He jerked his head around and saw that he was about to strike the concrete pier that formed the floor of the little boathouse. He pushed the oars into the water hard and pushed them away from himself—once, twice, three, four times and—brump. The front of the boat hit the concrete, but not hard. Using the right oar, Gardner brought the boat around and along side the pier.

"You aren't watching," Norma said.

"Sorry. Thinking." Gardner said.

"Oh, my back's killing me," Norma said. "I'm gonna get out and stretch a minute."

"Okay," Gardner said. "Careful. I'll hold the boat."

Norma eased herself awkwardly up onto the pier and she stretched and, with the palms of her hands, rubbed against the small of her back. "He's gonna be a big one," she said, looking down at her belly. Emily jumped out of the boat and stood, bouncing up and down, beside Norma. Gardner saw the boat with the two blacks begin to drift in towards his own boat.

Pretending not to, he watched it carefully.

"You want anything?" Norma said.

"What?" Gardner said.

"You want something?"

"Oh, yeah," Gardner said. I'll have a vanilla ice cream."

"WASP," Norma said. She was smiling, and Gardner smiled back. Then, behind her, Gardner saw the black who had been standing near him on the shore back at the fountain come running out from a bush and down a small hill and into the boathouse.

"You motherfuckers—cop my boat," he said, and he hurled a rock at the boat the two blacks were in. Gardner spun around and looked. He saw the rock miss and bullet into the water, but he saw a second rock come in and hit the black, who was rowing, in the back of the head and drop into the boat.

"Yeeoow," he yelled and he grabbed his head.

"You niggerfuck!" the other black in the boat shouted. He picked up the rock in the boat, Gardner saw, and threw it back at the black on shore. Gardner jerked around and saw the rock hit Norma in the arm or breast—he couldn't be sure—and she screamed and Gardner saw her grab her arm and he heard Emily cry, "Mama, Mama." And he heard the old man with the refreshment stand begin cursing in Italian and he saw the black on the shore in the boathouse turn and run and then Gardner felt something bang into his boat and he pulled around and saw that it was the boat with the two blacks in it and the one who had been rowing, threw down the oars, scrambled up out of the boat and began to chase after the one on shore. He crashed into Norma, spinning her around and knocking her to the ground. Now the other black in the boat was coming out and yelling, "Get your white ass outa my way." Without thinking, Gardner stuck out an oar and it caught this black between the legs, tripping him, and he fell forward, dead-weight, and his head hit into a post of the boathouse and he dropped and his head hit on the concrete like a coconut. It made a loud sickening sound. He groaned once and rolled over on his back, his arms stretched up and out over his head. He was out, unconscious, and Andrew had rushed to Norma, Gardner saw, and he was trying to help her up. She looked all right. Emily was jumping up and down and screaming. Gardner started to move out of his boat to go to Norma. Oh, God, he thought. I hope the baby is all right. He saw that the other black from the boat had stopped and turned around and was looking back at his friend stretched out on the pier.

"Charlie motherfucker," he said, Gardner heard, and Gardner saw the black pull out a knife. Thup. A switchblade, Gardner thought—Goddamn—and then he saw the black coming back down the hill towards him very fast and looking very big and Gardner could feel his guts fuse and then he felt the oar in his hand still and he took it with both hands now and lifted it out of the lock and swung it around and just in time jabbed it like a lance at the rushing black. Gardner felt the oar meet the black's chest and felt the black's momentum jam the handle end back into Gardner's stomach and hurt something there, but Gardner pushed forward again with the oar and lifted the end of it and the end slid up the black's chest and caught into his throat, and Gardner could feel the soft part and he heard the black go "ugh" and Gardner pushed harder and felt the softness giving way until he saw the black stumble backwards, fall and drop his knife and grab at his throat. Gardner got up on to the pier, reached out and hit the black in the forehead with the oar, knocking him on his back. Dropping the oar, Gardner dug into his pocket for his own knife and he got it out and open and he plunged the knife into the black's chest. The black twitched and rolled over, trying to get away from Gardner and the knife and now the black was on his stomach and Gardner got it in again, high in the shoulder blade, and the black kept slithering, wanting to get away, and he reached out his hand and found his knife on the pier and Gardner jumped on to the black's back, but, with his greater strength, the black rolled to his left, taking Gardner with him—Gardner hanging on still—and he almost got over onto his side but Gardner stabbed again, down low this time and he must have caught a kidney or something vital because he heard the black scream and go a little limp, just as the black was driving his own knife into Gardner's abdomen, and Gardner didn't take his knife out this time, but pushed harder in and to the left and right and left again and up and down and right and left as though he were scraping out a pumpkin. With a great, last force the black reared against Gardner and whammed him over on to his back. The black also on his back was on top of Gardner. And the black was reaching around and stabbing Gardner in the buttocks, but not too hard because he was nearly unconscious now, if Gardner had known, and at the same time Gardner reached over the man and jammed the blade of his knife into the stomach of the black and he felt the black go slack on top of him and he saw his head droop loose to the side and he saw now that the black was unconscious and a few inches from his eyes, Gardner could see the stretched out throat of the black lying just off his own shoulder and the jugular vein was throbbing in it immense; Gardner knew that he himself was all right now and safe and he thought he would relax and get the black off of him. He really thought to do that, but he kept looking at the exposed throat of the man and the big Adam's apple there and the spasming vein and then he felt the crushing weight of the man on him and felt the pain boiling up in his butt and in his abdomen and he saw the blood on both of them and he felt the enormous pounding clamor of his heart and he thought he was dying and he considered how this man had wanted to kill him and then—he raised his knife and drove it into the throat of the black and the blood of the black spurted and splattered into Gardner's eyes and his eyes burned and he couldn't see and that scared him and enraged him and he drove the knife in again and heard a queer little gurgle sound come out of the hole he was making and he stabbed again and then got himself out from under the black with a hernian effort and he jumped on top of him, mounting him, straddling him, and he plunged his knife into the black's chest. And he did it and did it and did it and did it and did it, and he was enjoying it and it felt good and he forgot about his own pain and just kept doing it and he hit a rhythm with it and he kept it up, even though his arm was getting tired, but, it had to be done, so he kept doing it, until he heard a voice he knew. Not quite like he knew it—it was higher and screechy—but it was familiar and it was calling his name; though why it would bother him now when he was so busy, he couldn't understand and—it was Norma's voice. Of course! That's her tugging at you, at your shoulders, trying to pull you off. Goddamn, can't she see you're busy—and—and—he heard his own voice: "What? Leave me alone!"

"Harry, Harry—stop, stop, stop! O God, please—Stahahaahp! You killed him! Stop!"

Gardner stopped. He looked over his shoulder and up at Norma. Her face was twisted and the mascara was a black running blur around her eyes. She was crying and screaming and tugging at him. "You killed him! Killed him!"

Gardner looked back down at the black. He thought to himself: The eyes do stay open. I never knew for sure.

"He's dead," Gardner said. He looked up at Norma again. "You okay?"

"Yes, yes—are you? Get off, Harry! Are you hurt?"

Am I? Gardner asked himself. I don't know, but—I-I-don't think so—too much. And he felt all the surging in his body and the scorching in the wounds and the wetness of the blood coming out and he didn't really think he was too all right at that, and—he closed his eyes, passed out and fell off the black onto the concrete.

"Harry!" Norma said.

"Daddy, Daddy!" Emily screamed.

Gardner thought he had passed out, had really, he believed, but now he was conscious again. He was off the black he saw and on his back, looking up at the sky—so clear and uninvolved-- he thought, beyond the rim of the roof of the boathouse. He could feel and hear Norma over him—she was yelling for a policeman—and he could hear the children. His heart was a punching bag being jabbed on and his lungs were full of fire and about to burst and his arms ached and the right one was twitching and knotting with cramps and his groin hurt and his ass was sore and wet and sticky and he knew he had been cut there and cut in the abdomen too because he could feel the sear of heat there and the hot liquid oozing down into his crotch. He wondered if he was going to die. And thought to himself, what a beautiful day.

Norma kept repeating his name in a kind of lunatic litany, Gardner heard, and asking if he was all right and was he in pain and "police, police," and he felt her slip a hand in under his head and put her other hand on his forehead and stroke it. Looking up at her now, the bloody gauze clearing from his eyes, Gardner tried to smile and reach up to her with his hand, but couldn't, and, though his throat was very dry and his breathing racing and painful, he found some kind of voice.

"I—I'm okay. Think. Not bad. Love you. Just know that," Gardner said.

"Oh, God, Harry, yes, I love you! I love you so much!" Norma said.

"You—okay?"

"Yes, yes, yes—fine!"

Gardner nodded and then he felt a chill. It started everywhere in his body at once and he started shaking and there was nothing he could do to control it, but the pain in his groin and butt didn't hurt so much now. Hardly hurts at all, he thought; but that's where he got me. You can't die from a knife in the ass, can you? How humiliating! It'll look like I ran.

No, you can't die in the ass-but the abdomen you can. Least that's not running. No, but it can kill you. Lots of little goodies down there. And he got a picture of all those animal innards he used to see in Mitchell's Meat Market back home—lumpy little items, dark red and juicy—and he guessed they were livers and kidneys and guts and pancreases—pancrei- -and whatever—and you looked at them and just never thought about having them yourself in yourself or how bloody vital they were. Vital. Vital organs. Oh, yeah, vital. Vital vituals. Let's have some Gardner liver tonight, shall we? I hear it's very good, very fresh—and only 89¢ a pound. Ugh. Stop. You're not going to die. You could have. You came very close, old boy, but you're not, cause he got you in the unvital organs—and the ass. Funny, it really doesn't hurt at all now. Not there. Something hurts, for Christ's sake. Just the exertion. The exertion hurts. The muscles and nerves and all the strings. No wonder. You haven't moved like that in years—ever. The adrenalin's pissing through you like a fire hose flopping. You really exerted yourself. Used it all and it aches like hell. But it was there, right? It worked. It was there when you needed it. Not bad for 43, hunh? And an addict smoker. Not bad at all. And he's the dead one, not you, pal. You're hurt but you're alive. And you're gonna be!

Without moving his body, Gardner turned his head to the side and saw the black lying next to him, his face facing Gardner and his eyes, like taxidermist marbles, staring at him. The black's mouth was open and blood was slow-streaming out of it and into his goatee and it was coming out of his throat and his bandana was twisted on his head. The black looked very young now, Gardner thought, and not so big as before—he looked rather slight really. Did I have to kill him so much?

"How you feel?" a voice said. It was flat and tight.

Gardner rolled his head to the other side and saw a cop bending over him and behind the cop he saw the legs of a horse and beyond the horse he saw people standing and looking at him. He heard another voice say, "All right, all right—everybody back. Clear the area."

"What happened?" the cop said.

Gardner nodded at the cop.

"He's hurt, can't you see?" Norma yelled. "Do something! Get a doctor, ambulance! He's bleeding."

"It's coming," the cop said. "You know him?"

"I'm his wife. He's—do something!"

"It's coming, lady, I told you. You see what happened? What's his name?

"Help him, for Christ's sake!"

"Okay, lady, okay. What's his name?"

Gardner—Harry Gardner."

"Address?"

"Oh, Jesus Christ, I don't believe it!"

A second policeman bent over Gardner and said, "One's dead, the other's knocked out. Nothing much on him. No weapon. I found this." Gardner saw that the second cop was holding the switchblade in his hand, resting on a plastic bag, and the knife had blood on it and it was his blood, Gardner knew.

"He—stabbed—me--with--that," Gardner said.

"Aren't you going to do <u>anything</u>?" Norma screamed. "Just let him <u>die</u>?"

The two cops looked at Norma and stood up, but they did not answer. They were just standing there, and Gardner could hear Norma talking at them loud and fast and he could hear Emily crying. Was Andrew? He couldn't hear him. Was he secretly happy? Then Gardner heard a siren, far off at first, but closing fast, until it seemed to be on him and in him. He heard a car door slam and footsteps coming.

"Hiya, Mike," a voice said, "what you got?"

"Knife fight," the first cop said. "That one's dead. This one's cut. Another one over there's unconscious."

Gardner saw a portable bed wheeling in beside him—then two huge blacks in white uniforms leaning over him. When he saw their blackness his reflexes twitched and he moaned; then he realized that these blacks were supposed to help him, not hurt him and he watched as they collapsed the bed until it was at ground level and looked like a stretcher.

"Hurry, hurry," Norma said, "Give him something."

"Where'd you get it?" one of the blacks in white said to him.

"Down—here," Gardner said, pointing to his groin, "and in my ass."

The black in white who had spoken to him undid Gardner's belt and pants and slipped them down. "What's black and white and red all over," Gardner asked himself. Me, he said. Not a newspaper this time. Hurt. Hurt. Hurt. "Jesus, easy," Gardner said. Then the black in white took out a small knife and cut away Gardner's shorts. The other black in white handed him something and he put it on Gardner in the place where it hurt. It felt cold and wet. He then felt them put a blanket on him.

"Hold on. We're gonna move you now," the black in white said. "Get his head, Carter."

Gardner felt himself being lifted onto the stretcher wagon and he felt a pain jump up in his ass and in his groin and he moaned and he felt Norma take his hand as the two blacks in white raised the stretcher. They were moving now and suddenly he felt his head higher than his feet and he realized that they were going up the little hill to the road where the ambulance must be. He could see Andrew and Emily running along side. Was Andrew crying? He couldn't see, couldn't be sure.

The two blacks in white pushed Gardner into the back of the ambulance, which was a panel truck, he saw, and Norma climbed in beside him. She was pulling Emily and Andrew in behind her. Andrew's eyes were fixed, but they were dry, Gardner saw.

"Hey, lady, you can't go--"

"I'm in. Please! I'm not hurting anybody! He's my husband—and maybe he's a foreign body to you but he's—come on, please, let's go!"

The black in white shrugged and didn't say anymore. He got in and closed the doors. It was very crowded and very hot, Gardner felt. "I'm cold," He said. The black in white put another blanket over him and the ambulance started up, the tires squeek-pinching on the pavement and the whole vehicle jerking away into motion. Gardner closed his eyes and concentrated on withstanding the pain. He felt Norma take his hand and he squeezed it and he could hear her talking faster than he had ever heard her talk and she was giving order after order, though nothing changed and the black in white remained silent. Gardner wished Emily would stop crying and that Andrew might start. Does he hate me so much? Probably. That's too bad, if I do die now. Him feeling like that. If I die period! That's too bad!

The trip seemed very long to Gardner and it hurt harder each time the ambulance swerved or braked or accelerated and it swerved and braked and accelerated constantly. Hang in though, Gardner told himself. Hang in. Take it. Take it. Take it. Umph—and Gardner wished that he could faint, but he didn't Well—you finally made the Daily <u>News</u>, old boy.

CHAPTER 20

The ambulance stopped, finally, and Gardner felt himself being lifted out. The two blacks in white raised the wheel legs of the stretcher--"Hurry, hurry," Norma said—and they rolled him into a building and he saw the green walls again and fluorescent lights like those at Lenox Hill and--

"Where am I?" Gardner said.

"Roosevelt, Darling, but we'll get you to Lenox Hill," Norma said. "We'll move you. I'll call Greenburg and you'll be all right. I promise you. I love you. Is the pain bad? I'll get you something. I'll get it."

Gardner nodded and saw that they had pushed him into a small room. He saw a doctor and a nurse come in.

"Get his clothes off," the doctor said, and the two blacks in white began undressing Gardner.

"Is he going to be all right?" Norma said.

"Who are you?" the doctor said.

"Who do you think I am? I'm his wife, of course. Is he all right? Can't you give him something?"

"These your kids?" the doctor said.

"Yes—ours."

"They shouldn't be here. Take them out."

"I'll worry about them, you take care of him."

"Walter—take them to the waiting room."

"Doctor, we'll go when I know my husband's all right, all right?"

"Norma," Gardner said, "It's okay—do what the doctor--"

"Walter," the doctor said, and one of the blacks in white started moving towards Norma.

"Relax, Walter," Norma said, "I'm not going anywhere."

"Norma," Gardner said, "please."

"I'm staying, Harry!" Norma yelled.

The doctor motioned Walter to let Norma stay and Walter stopped. "Till I check him, okay?" the doctor said. "Then you're going." The doctor turned to Gardner, who was naked now, and he began to examine the groin.

"Will you give him a shot, for God's sake?" Norma said. "Is he all right?"

"Humm," the doctor said, "not too bad I think. Penetration wound of the super pubic area. Questionable bladder laceration and possible laceration of the small bowel. Intra-abdominal trauma. And a puncture wound in the right buttocks."

"Great, but what's that all mean?" Norma said.

"Not too bad. Surgery, but he'll be fine." Turning to the nurse, the doctor said, "Claire, start the dextrose and saline infusion right away, then type and crossmatch his blood. He's had some loss. We'll have to see how much. Take him up soon as possible?

The nurse tied off Gardner's upper left arm, got a vein and stuck a needle in it. She attached a metal post to the side of the stretcher wagon and hung a plastic bag of clear solution from it. She connected the needle to a tube coming from the bag and Gardner could see the solution begin to move down the tube and into his arm.

"Does he have to stay here?" Norma said. "I'd like him at Lenox Hill and I want to call our doctor. Did you give him anything yet for the pain? God--"

"Lady, I'm not a gynecologist and you're gonna give birth here if you don't relax."

"You don't act like you know how to do even this," Norma said.

"Will you get those children out of here?!"

A policeman came into the room and, as he did, he felt himself in the crotch like a ballplayer coming up to bat. Gardner thought he was one of those who had been in the park, but he couldn't be sure.

"Please?" the doctor said.

"It's all right, Norma," Gardner said. "Honest, I'm okay. The kids shouldn't see—really--you know. Kiss them. Stay with them. Outside."

Norma came to Gardner and kissed him lightly on the mouth. "I love you," she said.

"Me too," Gardner said. "You."

"Oh, God, Harry, if anything—happened. I'd—promise me no. Promise me."

Gardner nodded.

"Walter," the Doctor said, "take them to the waiting room. He'll be fine. And they have to get him ready."

Norma nodded and said, "All right. I'll call Greenburg—and Agnes to come for the children. I'll be here, Harry. Right here." Norma and the children left the room. Walter followed them out. The nurse came around and tied off Gardner's upper right arm, got a vein and took blood from it.

"How do you feel?" the Doctor said.

"No good. Sorry about my wife, I--"

"Sorry? I thought it was great. Most we see don't give a damn. Much pain?"

"Enough."

"You're gonna be all right. I've seen lots worse here—every day. It's like a war going on in this town. Claire, give him a 100 milligrams of Demerol."

"Thanks," Gardner said. "I'm cold."

"That's shock," the doctor said. "Carter, cover him, please. Ever been operated on before—besides the appendectomy?"

"No."

"When was it?"

"'59" The nurse gave Gardner a shot and Carter covered him.

"No problem with anesthesia?"

"No."

"Would you remember what they gave you?"

"No. I counted down though, I remember."

"Okay. No allergies?"

"No."

"Good. Diseases? Diabetes, anything like that?"

"No."

"Good. When did you eat last?"

"Bout an hour ago."

"That's unfortunate."

"Just a hot dog and a coke."

"Who's your doctor?"

"Greenburg—David, Park Ave."

"Okay. Ever bleed unusually?"

"Not till today."

"Yes, I see. How about penicillin? Ever have it?"

"Yes."

"No problems?"

"No."

"Good."

"Doctor—do you piss when you die—like the bulls? I saw that once in Spain."

"Yes. The bladder voids."

"Am I dying?"

"No, of course not."

"I feel wet."

"You're not wet now. You were. From the bleeding. You've lost some."

"Oh. But no urine?"

"No."

"Good."

"You'll be fine. See you upstairs."

The doctor left the room and the nurse took off the blanket and got Gardner into a dressing gown. She replaced the blanket and left. The other black in white left also.

Gardner realized that he didn't hurt so much now and he thought about the fact that he hadn't thought about what the nurse had looked like. Nothing like a little knifing to cool your pants off, he thought. Then Gardner remembered that the policeman was in the room. What the hell does he want? My confession? Can't he wait till I'm sewn up, for Christ's sake?

The policeman nodded when Gardner looked at him. He approached the bed. "Can I talk to you?"

Gardner nodded.

"I'm officer Donavan. I was with you in the park. Looks like you got no problem, hunh?"

"You read my lifeline?"

"Ah, I seen worse'n you pull through. I mean about killing the spade."

"He is dead?"

"And then some."

"There were two others."

"The other one's come to," Officer Donavan said. "the Doc says he's got a concussion. We're holding him. You did some job. The old Dago guy at the stand says you was great, Mr. Gardner. He's a good witness for you. Clear-cut self-defense, he said, and really ballsy. Wish they was more like you. Make our life easier. You stand up to 'em, they wouldn't act like such apes—if you know what I mean."

"What happens now?"

"Ah, routine. The detectives'll come. They'll have to book you for homicide. Then a hearing. But, don't you worry. Look, I just come by really to—well, meet you, you know, and say, well—anyway. This is yours, right?" The policeman held out Gardner's knife which Gardner recognized, except that he was surprised to see it clean.

"Yes."

"Thought so. Not much of a knife compared to his, is it? Still, if you had it concealed, that could be a bit of a problem, you know. Carrying a concealed weapon, you know. You have it in your pocket?"

"Yes."

The policeman nodded. "We figured. Look, why don't I just—well—hang-on to it for you till—you know—you get straightened out, hunh? That way—well, it won't be no problem."

"You have to, don't you? Exhibit A and all that."

"Aw, I don't mean nuthin' like that, Mr. Gardner. Official, I mean. I mean—personal. I'll just keep it till you're better. Then give it back to you. A souvenir like. And no trouble. Got it?"

"But then how'd I--?"

"Ju see him?" The policeman pulled out the plastic bag containing the switchblade and he shook the knife out of the bag and onto the stretcher. "Thought you'd be interested." Gardner looked at the knife and shuddered and felt frightened looking at it and remembering. But now he thought he was beginning to understand what the policeman was driving at. He and the policeman looked each other in the eye and the policeman smiled.

"Why don't you just pick it up for a second? Go ahead. Take it," Officer Donavan said.

Gardner nodded and did and gripped the handle so his fingerprints would get on it and he turned it in his hand and gripped it some more, several times. The policeman carefully picked it up and put it back into the plastic bag.

"What about—blood though?" Gardner said.

The policeman smiled and showed all of his teeth. "His is all over it, Mr. Gardner, don't you worry."

"I was—unarmed then—right?"

"It saves everybody a problem."

"And I did it with—his knife?"

269

"Yeah, which you took away from him. Just the way the old man said it happened."

"But it didn't."

"He's dead, Mr. Gardner, and you got him in self-defense, right?"

"Well, yes."

"Then, that's that. Routine."

Gardner nodded.

"I'll see you later," Officer Donavan said. "I got to talk to your Mrs. Get a corroborating statement before the detectives get here. You—just take it easy, hunh? I'm pullin' for you—all the way."

"The policeman smiled big and nodded and he flicked at his crotch again and left the room.

He's delighted, Gardner thought. That big blue jerk thinks I'm a solid citizen cause I killed a black kid. Cause I got rid of one of—"the apes, if you know what I mean." That racist bastard! Doesn't he know I wish to God it'd never happened? I didn't want to kill anybody. I didn't even know the poor sonof—Oh, really? For a guy who didn't want to kill anybody, you did a pretty terrific job of it. Well, hell, I was scared. Scared to death! What'd you want me to do? I don't know anything about knife fights! Is that why you've been carrying a knife? So—I—over-reacted. Leave me alone. Just one question. Suppose he hadn't been black? What's that got to do with anything? Just suppose—would you have done the same thing you did? Of course, I would. I was scared out of my—what the hell are you driving at? Oh, just that black scares you more than white; that, despite your "liberalism," you just never have made peace with blacks. That's all. Oh, come on—I didn't kill him because he was—Didn't you? No, goddamn it! Leave me alone. Then what about this just now? This knife cover-up. Playing along with the policeman. You said yourself he hated blacks. More lies, not caring—just looking to save yourself. I'm lying here with my guts bleeding out—and will you lay off? You can think anything you want to think cause anything we think now isn't gonna make sense. I'm in shock. The Doctor said so—you heard him—and I hurt like hell, damn you. All I can do to hang on, let alone think—Oh, sure, sure. But you know, don't you? You know.

"Hi," a voice said. "I won't be a minute. They want you in a big fast hurry. Rushy-rush." The voice was sing-songy and mushy, Gardner heard.

He looked up and saw a thin young man leaning over him. The man had dyed blonde hair, with black showing through, and he had vaseliney eyes and he was gay, Gardner saw. The thin young man pulled the blanket from Gardner and lifted up the dressing gown and began to lather Gardner's pubic hair.

"Ugh, that was close—nasty," the thin young man said. He began to shave Gardner there.

"While he was doing this, the nurse came back in. Gardner looked at her this time and thought to himself, <u>nothing</u>. Tough, older job. Dyke, probably. Jesus. Wonder what she's saying about <u>you</u>, boy—everything hanging on display—and nothing. That goddamned gay boy just gave me a grab, I'm sure of it.

The nurse attached another metal post to the stretcher on the right side and she hung a plastic bag of blood from it. She tied off Gardner's upper right arm till she got the vein up again and then she put in a needle, taped it there and connected a tube from the blood bag to it. Gardner watched the thin red line move down the tube and into his arm. The thin young man finished, wiped Gardner dry and said, "There. All nice and clean. Good luck, kiddo." He left.

<u>Good luck yourself, you—</u>

Two new blacks in white uniforms came in and wheeled Gardner out of the room and along a corridor to an elevator. They all went in it and up.

Here goes, Gardner thought; into the valley of the shadow of death—oh, stop dramatizing. You're not going to die. The Doctor said so. Oh, really? Remember the dentist in Lancaster who went in for "minor" surgery? Went Friday, supposed to be out Tuesday—and was—at Lawson's funeral home? And remember what Dr. Metz used to tell your father? "Wesley, anytime you cut into the human body, it isn't minor." I <u>could</u> just die up there. I could. So what are you going to do about it either way? Anymore than you help pilots on take-offs and landings? I lend a little body English each time. Okay, then do that and shut up.

When the elevator opened, they pushed Gardner along another corridor and finally through big double doors into the operating room where the light was very bright and there were lots of people in masks. They moved him off the stretcher and onto a table. One of the masks leaned over him and the voice through it said, "Okay? We're ready if you are." It was the Doctor's voice, Gardner recognized.

"Do I start counting," Gardner said.

"No, I'm giving you an intubate endotracial anesthesia this time," the Doctor said.

"Oh," Gardner said, without understanding. <u>What the hell is a---?</u> And somebody pushed a tube into his throat and he gagged.

"See you soon," the Doctor said.

Gardner nodded and decided to count anyway, to himself. <u>99, 98, 97—just don't piss, boy, just don't bull piss—95, 94, 93-----------</u>

CHAPTER 21

"You know I couldn't get much higher/Come on, baby, light my fire/ help me set the night on fire/come on, baby, light my fire."

Gardner was raised up in his electric bed and looking over his feet at the girl standing there singing and he was trying to smile. The girl was twelve years old and she was fat and wore braces on her teeth. She was smiling in a big metal smile back at Gardner and staring him directly in the eyes, really drilling into him with her eyes, he felt, and he got the idea that he didn't want to look away first so he was staring right back at her, focusing on a big pimple just below the bridge of her nose. The girl's aunt, who was the headnurse on this floor, was sitting in the plastic covered chair near the window, nodding and smiling and keeping time with her foot, except that the time she was keeping was offbeat, and she had a moustache, and it was 7 AM and it was Gardner's fourth day in the hospital.

She's never going to blink, he thought, she's too stupid; and his eyes felt like a back itch you couldn't reach, and he thought, why the hell is it so important whether I don't look away first or blink first—so blink. Gardner blinked.

"Come on, bay-bee, light my---"

She was going for the ending, Gardner heard, and he was grateful.

"Fiiiiiiii-re!"

Big, long, extended-- And horrible. Loud, but horrible.

"Isn't that beautiful---like Connie Francis, only hep," the aunt said.

Hep, Gardner said to himself. And Connie Francis?! Jesus.

"Just beautiful, honey," the aunt said. "Beautiful. Isn't she the most talented little angel you ever heard?"

Little Angel? You could sell hog futures on her.

"She's gonna be a big star," the aunt said. "I know it. Corbett Monica heard her last month at a wedding in Jersey and he said <u>very nice</u>. Corbett Monica! He said that."

"Yeah, that's, uh, something," Gardner said. The girl just stood there, smiling, and –<u>God she's still staring at me</u>!

"She's studying acting too—in the Village. What's that actor, honey?"

"Randy Wayne," the girl said.

"Yeah, Randy Wayne," the aunt said. "He's been on <u>Joe Franklin</u> and <u>As The World Turns</u>. Real professional."

"He taught me how to make eye contact."

"That's wonderful," Gardner said.

"See," the aunt said. "Now wouldn'tcha say she's perfect for commercials—singin' ones especially, hunh? That's why I wanted you to see her. I knew you'd be so impressed. Imagine? Only 12 and all that talent—"

<u>And pimples, and metal and pork.</u>

"—It's a gift. A god-given gift. It <u>is</u> from God, you know. And now you. Being here on my floor like this. It's a miracle. Oh, I don't mean I wished you trouble, Mr. Gardner, or that God did. It's just, since it had to be, you know—they could have put you on another floor."

Not with my luck, lady, Gardner thought. I <u>had</u> to get this floor, right? Especially being God's emissary now. <u>That's</u> why I'm on this earth? To get this postulant porker into show business? <u>That's</u> my mission in life? To kill a kid and get myself knifed just to launch Tugboat Angela here? The headnurse was still going on about God and his wonders. <u>That woman's crazy. How the hell</u> did she ever get to be a <u>headnurse</u>? <u>Waking me up at 7AM to listen to</u>—

"God works in strange ways, Mr. Gardner, you gotta admit."

<u>Strange? Out of his head weird.</u>

"Yes, yeah, I guess. Well, thank you, Angela, for singing for me," Gardner said.

"She's got another," the aunt said.

"I got another."

"Well----"

"I do <u>Hey, Jude</u>," the girl said.

"I'll bet. That's nice, but two is fine. That gives me a good idea, you know? This one and <u>Didn't We?</u> are—well, an upsong and a ballad shows me what you can do."

"Yeah," the girl said. She reached into a small purse she was carrying and pulled out a stick of gum. Gardner watched her claw it into her mouth. Chomp. Chomp. Chomp. Smack. The girl blew a small bubble.

"Well, what are you going to do for her, Mr. Gardner?" the aunt said.

"Wha? Oh, uh, nothing right now, obviously," Gardner said, and he realized that he was smiling and being charming. Why? Why do I do that? "And I'm—going into a new position, I think, after I get out of here. So I don't know exactly. Uh. Let me think about it."

"But you do like her? You know she's good."

"Well, I—I'm not really an authority. I don't do the actual casting for commercials."

"You don't?" the aunt said. "Your file card said you were the creative head. You told me, when I asked you. That's the boss, isn't it?"

"Yes, in a way—but about the concepts, the ideas for commercials. I don't do the casting."

"You know the person who does, right?"

"Yes, of course, but—"

"Well?" the aunt said, and now she was smiling.

"I'll—yes, I'll call her—when I get out. Okay?"

"Oh, that's terrific, Mr. Gardner. That's just great. I knew you'd love her. Everybody does."

"I gotta go, Aunt Rose," the girl said. Crummy school."

"She's gonna be a big star. Bigger than Streisand—"

Bigger than Kate Smith. Bigger than Jackie Leonard—bigger than all outdoors!

"—And just think, Mr. Gardner. Someday you'll be able to say you boosted her on her way. What a good feeling. Maybe she'll buy you a car too like she's always promising Aunt Rose. Right, Angela?"

"I don't need a car in the city." Gardner said.

"I gotta go," the girl said.

"Good-bye, Angela," Gardner said. "Thank you."

"Yeah," Angela said. She thinks she did me a favor!

Gardner watched the girl waddle towards the door and was grateful to see her going. She stopped and turned.

"Do you know Ted Mack?" Angela said.

"No," Gardner said, "I've never met him."

Angela nodded and glowered at him. "I'm sorry," Gardner said. The girl turned and left.

"Angela, wait on me a minute," the aunt said. "Thank you, Mr.

Gardner. You're just terrific. If you ever need anything—you just—well, my brother's big downtown with good connections. He knows—<u>people</u>. If you ever need anything—<u>anything</u>. Like about those kids bothering you? You know."

"Yeah, it's okay. I was happy to listen. I—I would like a shot if I could, I'm—"

"You hurtin', Mr. Gardner?"

"A little."

"Comin' right up. I'll get you it. You just lie right there." Aunt Rose, headnurse, left the room.

I'm crazy, Gardner thought to himself. Absolutely crazy! Hallucinating! I am not lying in Roosevelt Hospital like this with knife wounds and I am not a murderer and I am not getting threatening mail and listening to a fat 12 year old from Mulberry Street sing Light My Fire and her aunt promising me Mafia help and I—why'd I say I don't need a car in Manhattan? What the hell kind of response was that? Being polite and logical with that ridiculous—my God. I can't call Ruth and ask her to audition that kid. Even if I still worked there, which I don't—but I told the kid I would and she'll expect it. Battleship Rose'll expect it. Her brother'll probably have my knees busted or something if I don't—and that kid hated me cause I didn't know Ted Mack—and I apologized for it! Said I'm sorry. Why? What for? Why? What's become of my life? Why did I talk to her in the first place? Why'd I talk about my job? Why am I always so bloody polite to strangers and then clobber the people close to me? Why did she have to barge in here and get into my life and have a 12-year old niece with no talent and a Mafioso father—and where the hell is she with that shot? My gut is killing me—and the gas! I've got enough gas to get to Pittsburgh, yak, yak, yak. It's going to explode! And Gardner remembered how when they were kids they used to try to light farts with Zippo lighters and he sang to himself <u>Come on, Baby, light my fire</u> and he laughed, out loud; and the laugh hurt his stitches and moved the gas around and he stopped laughing fast and thought that he was really, truly about to go insane.

Like last night, he remembered. Right after Norma had left last night, around midnight, Gardner had gotten the notion that the friends of the kid he had killed were going to sneak into the hospital and stab him right there in bed and kill him and he would not be able to move, to resist or to do anything but absorb the blades and die. His panic had been instant and had lasted through the night. Every ordinary noise had become terrifying, he recalled, and he had soaked the bed with his sweat. Only at dawn had he relaxed and only then had he allowed himself to go to sleep, fitful, but pleased that he had made it through the night. But I've still got a week to go here. The doctor said 10 days or so and I've only been here four—four today. It could happen tonight. My room's near a stairwell! There's no security! People—all kinds of people—come and go as they want. They'll get me easy. And, if they don't do it here, he thought, when I get out, it'll be worse. They'll have a clear chance at me. How can I stop it? And if they don't get me, what's going to happen anyway? I have no job, no money, and no—. Stop it! Get hold of yourself. Where's your head? Two lousy crank letters and you panic like—nobody's going to kill you! Well, I didn't make it up! I did get two letters! He saw them again in his mind. The words had been made up of type letters cut from newspapers and magazines. The first, which came on Tuesday said, "Dig this message, Paddy Motherfucker: We goa waist you like you dun Lonnie." The one that came on Wednesday, yesterday, had said, "We goa kill you, gray ass, and fuck up your woman." That was fact, Gardner told himself. Not made-up. Not paranoia.

Gardner had shown both letters to Norma, who turned them over to the police, who did not take them very seriously. Isn't that what Donavan had told you when he was up here yesterday? Didn't he say though that the cops had gone up to Harlem and talked to the kid's friends about the letters and had told them what would happen to them if they were sending them or if they tried to bother you or your family in any way? Hadn't Donavan told you that? And hadn't he told you that things like this were routine in cases that get lots of publicity? It could be a Black Panther just messin' you up a bit, Donavan had said, or any kind of crackpot for that matter. And not to worry. Don't worry. Weren't those Donavan's exact words?

Donavan. That sonofabitch. Coming up here yesterday. Looking at me and treating me like some goddamned hero. Sir-ing me and respecting me like MacArthur, for Christ's sake. And bringing up my knife! (Gardner looked to the drawer in the little metal table next to his bed where the knife was resting now). His goddamned wife gift-wrapped it! Like it was frankincense and myhrr! Donavan's crazy he hates Negroes so much. And that stupid, hurt look in his eyes when I said I didn't (don't you?) – he just couldn't understand it.

Gardner started thinking about the boy whom he had killed, of what he had learned about him from Donavan and from the Daily <u>News</u>. He remembered when they looked each other in the eyes when they were in the boats and he saw the eyes now. He knew that his name was Lonnie Dobson and he was fifteen years old, just—his birthday had been in

February—and that he had been trouble all of his life! Juvenile courts for stealing starting at eight. Youth House three times, Wyltwick School and Warwick Reformatory. His father shot and killed in a hold-up when Lonnie was two and his mother had always been on welfare. She had served time for prostitution and for drug use. Lonnie had at least three brothers and two sisters—"maybe more," Donavan had said—"Who knows with them?"—and they and the mother lived in two rooms on West 128th Street near 8th Avenue. What could that be like? Gardner wondered. He tried to picture the rooms, but nothing showed in his mind. Gardner had learned also that the boy who had had the concussion was Lonnie Dobson's brother and he had been released from the hospital on Monday—no concussion was found. His name was Henry and he was 13. Good God, Gardner thought; they had looked so big and so much older that day! The third kid who ran away was a neighborhood friend called Cassius, a nickname given him because he fought constantly and wanted to be a boxer. Where is she with that shot?!

The head nurse, Aunt Rose, came in. "Look at this. Isn't it beautiful?" She was carrying a large red helium balloon. It was a replica of the old-fashioned gas ascension balloons and it had different colored satin streamers on it and flowers in the basket where people would ride.

"It's from," Aunt Rose said, looking at the card, "Janelle. You know a Janelle? There's a letter with it. You have the cleverest friends—all theses nice things they think up." Aunt Rose let go of the balloon and it rose to the ceiling. "Isn't that the cutest?"

"Where's the letter?" Gardner said.

"Oh, sure."

"What about my shot?"

"Mama Mia—I forgot all about it when the balloon came. I'll be right back." Aunt Rose left and Gardner opened the letter. "Darling Harry-Sam Sadface. I read about you in the funny papers. Sorry I couldn't make the scene, but I've been playing Doctor myself. I did call and they said you'd live—whatever that means. I'm in Chicago—it's a long story—in a hospital too. Nothing serious, however, just a severe attack of the liver, as in life. "Here love's damp muscle dries and dies," as Dylan said. I'll be out tomorrow. And I have this wonderful idea for a trip. I'm going around the world on a pilgrimage of movie stars' graves. Isn't that fab? You know, Turkey for Terhan Bey, India for Sabu. Rio for Carmen Miranda. Like that. Is Ann May Wong in the Orient? And where is Judy Garland? Ah so—if we knew the answer to that we might have made it, yes, Harry-Sam?

But, as Alice Faye said to Tony Martin, "You Can't Have Everything." Heal, Heel. With all my hate—Ginger."

Aunt Rose came in again. "Here you are, Mr. Gardner. This'll fix you up." She gave him the shot. "Angela thought you was real nice—very warm. She's really excited about doing commercials. Show business is her life's work. I wish I had that child's gift."

Gardner nodded. What was Janelle doing in Chicago? And in a hospital? What's happening to everything? Oh, Jesus, Jesus. Sleep. Let me just sleep.

He turned over on his side, careful not to pull the drain in his abdomen. Aunt Rose helped him reach the button that lowered and raised the electric bed. He pushed "down" and felt the bed begin to flatten out and he felt himself going down with it. He waited for the shot to make its pacific pilgrimage through his veins and tried to remember where they had buried Judy Garland. And Spencer Tracy. And Gable. And Coop. And where would Harry Gardner be—when the time came. Sleep. Sleep. "Good boy, take a nap," Aunt Rose left.

The phone rang and, hearing it, Gardner came out of sleep. He picked it up from the table next to him.

"Hello," he said.

"Harry. Hi. It's me," he heard Norma's voice say. "Were you sleeping?"

"Yeah—it's all right."

"I'm sorry."

"Sokay."

"I was going out and wanted to talk to you before. Are you awake? Harry?"

"Yeah—yeah. I'm here. I'm up."

"I've got to see Robinson about a new job he has for me and then I'm having lunch with Laura and then I'm taking the kids to the dentist after school and—"

"What time is it?"

"9:30. How do you feel, darling?"

"Oh—okay. Peachy."

"Really?"

"I'm all right. When'll I see you?"

"Dinnertime I thought, if that's okay. Margaret'll feed the kids and Patience'll come at six or so to stay with them. I should be to you around

279

then. Oh, Leonard is here. We'll have to talk about the bills and what we're going to do. You haven't heard from Buzz have you?"

"No."

"Well, at least, Leonard says our major medical's in good shape and should cover most of the hospital. We'll have to pay the first $500 though. But there is a big life insurance payment due and—"

"Jesus, Norma, you gotta talk about that now? I don't want a report from the goddamned accountant now!"

"You don't have to yell at me. I'm only trying to keep things going. Somebody's got to. Life goes on, Harry, and—oh, I'm sorry. You're right, to hell with it. I'll see you at 6."

Norma hung up and Gardner realized that he had been wrong. Why had he collapsed into self-pity? Ahg, who knew?! It wasn't exactly beyond comprehension for him not to want to discuss his life insurance, was it, when he had just barely escaped with his life. <u>Was it</u>? He'd apologize tonight. Damn. 9:30. He'd only slept two hours, he realized.

"Hello, Mr. Gardner—we have a visitor."

Gardner rolled over and saw his private nurse, Miss Peterson, standing there—The morning shift. That was all they were keeping now for a day more or so.

"Good morning. How are we this morning?" Peterson said.

She came over to the bed, pressed the "up" button and brought Gardner to a 45° angle. She fluffed his pillow and popped a thermometer into his mouth. Peterson was a big one in her early 40's, with stout arms, a solid ass and muscular legs. She had recently retired, after 20 years service, from the Army Nurses' Corps. She was all right, Gardner thought, but he hated the habit she had of using "we" and "us" every time she meant him. Goddamn it, he thought, she didn't have the gas pains or the stitches or the drain in her side and they hadn't put a catheter in her cock or a tube down her nose. It was his pain, goddamn it! She had no right!

"Well, good, we're normal," Peterson said, taking the thermometer out and looking at it. "Did you hear me? I said we've got a visitor. Distinguished looker too. Mr. Billingsly, he said. Said he was your boss?"

"He's <u>here</u>?"

"In the waiting room—big as life. Feel like seeing him? We don't seem too chipper this morning."

"I—I guess-- Yeah."

Peterson started out. "Oh, I hate to say it, but your Cubs won and the Mets lost. After he's gone, I'll bring you the papers. Okay? Hey, I checked you. You did all right on that crossword yesterday. We're pretty good in that department, aren't we?" Peterson left. <u>You didn't get a single word, fat ass</u>. Gardner pulled himself up, reached out to the table and grabbed a cigarette and lit it. "Here we are," Peterson said. Gardner saw Billingsly standing with her at the door. He was smiling that gigantic, super-colossal smile of his.

CHAPTER 22

"Hiya, Harry boy," Billingsly said. He came towards the bed and Peterson left.

"Hello, Buzz," Gardner said.

"How you doin', guy?" Billingsly shook Gardner's hand in his usual lateral way, and Gardner thought his stitches were going to pop.

"Unnh. Okay. Fine."

"That's the old spirit. Here are some books for you."

"Oh, thanks, Buzz. What'd you get?"

"Oh, uh, just some of the new—you know."

Yes, I do know, Gardner thought. He knew Billingsly's secretary had bought the books and that Billingsly had no idea what was in the package from Doubleday's. He opened it and looked at the 3 books: "Up The Organization" by Robert Townsend; "The Selling of The President" by Joe McGinniss; and "Love Story" by Eric Segal. With the first two, Gardner figured, the secretary had kept him in mind, but on the last one she just couldn't resist. Oh, well, he had read the first two anyway.

"That's really nice, Buzz. Thanks. Which one should I read first. What's 'Love Story' like?"

"Oh, I haven't read it, Harry. Who has time to read except, well, like you are. I'd just heard about it. I heard they're making a movie."

"Yeah? Well, thanks."

"Hey, I hear you've been up walking around since yesterday morning. That's great."

"Yeah. It's their version of the Bataan Death March. We're a happy little group. The man next door walks around with his waste in a bag—his brother-in-law shot him; and next to him is a guy whose wife stuck him in the ass with an ice pick."

"You've got a nice room. "I've never been here before. Hey, and an electric bed even."

"By the same people who made the chairs."

"What? Oh—yes—electric chairs. Fun-eee. When do you get out?"

"Bout a week the doctor said."

"That's great. You had some ordeal, hunh?"

"Yeah, I guess."

"I never saw such publicity. You're a big hero."

"Yeah, I guess."

"Talk of the office. Everybody sends their best."

"Thanks. They've been very nice." Gardner nodded towards all the flowers in the room.

"Hey, yeah, you could open a flower shop. That must be some job for the nurse—taking them out every night."

"They don't do that anymore. It was an old wive's tale."

"I thought they ate up all the oxygen or something."

"They just smell."

"I tried to give blood for you, old boy. Can't ask more than that, hunh? But I didn't pass the physical. That touch of mono I had last fall."

"Welcome to the club. 8 out of 10 of the people I know are not qualified to donate blood."

"You're kidding?"

"It's this good Manhattan life we lead."

"How 'bout that?"

"Look Buzz, I'd like to apologize for—for the other night."

Billingsly smiled his biggest smile. "Ah, forget it, Harry. That happens. You were okay till Otis Price came in. I didn't blame you. Who knows what sets a guy off. I do know Price has that affect—and Janelle was no help."

"No, I was out of line. I was very demeaning to you—though I guess I meant what I said about Wright. I was furious about Americans, the Beautiful. That was a painting."

"I know."

"I just shouldn't have done it the way I did."

"Harry, really, forget it. Wright is a boob and everything you said. And so who doesn't want to sound off on the boss sometimes?"

"Anyway, I apologize."

"Please—and the Wright thing's all smoothed over. No problem. I spoke to him yesterday. He knows what happened to you here. He thought that was great. Oh, and we're going ahead with S'hhh-Fem and everything.

It'll be in test markets by Monday—now that we've got a name for it. Isn't that great? The labels are being printed right now. I think it's really gonna be big, Harry. Harry, I've been thinking. When you get out of here, why don't you take a couple of weeks. Go to the Caribbean. Get yourself really on your feet before you come back to the old grindstone."

"Yeah, maybe I will."

"And this is extra—paid for by the company. Not your regular vacation."

"Hunh?—you fired me, Buzz."

"Ah, heat of the moment. I was pretty high myself that night. Forget it. Harry, what am I going to do? You're the best. I can't lose you."

"I don't know. What am I going to do?"

"You've got to solve that Clover Farm Diet Drink thing. The stuff we've got so far stinks."

"I don't think I'm coming back."

"Nonsense. You don't want to go back to Thompson, do you? They don't appreciate you. Not like I do."

"No, not that. I mean get out altogether. New York even."

"You're kidding."

"I killed a person, Buzz--!"

"In self-defense."

"—I'm a borderline alcoholic and—if I really face it—psychopathic— functioning maybe, but psychopathic."

"Who isn't? What are you going to do?"

"I don't know. Teach, maybe."

"Teach? Christ, you'd be bored stiff in a week. Harry, don't kid yourself. You love New York. And you need your job and the money. We all do. It's just this that's got you upset. I can understand how you must feel, but, I know you better than you do. Look at your apartment and the way you live. Theatre, good restaurants, clothes, travel, private schools. You love all that. And competition. You're never happier than with some new campaign problem."

"But, Buzz, this city's tearing me apart. And, oh, God, this sounds so silly, but I hate what I do in advertising. It's horrible when you think about it. Which I don't most of the time. I just do it—mechanically. Solve the problem without ever considering the moral questions."

"Moral questions. What's that?"

"See! That's like me. You're shocked there are any. But there are, Buzz. They're always there, even if we ignore them. And I can't just not think about them anymore. Acquiring things can't be the only virtue and meaning in life. My work's meaningless—if not criminal."

"Criminal? Jesus, boy."

"Criminally negligent, anyway. Can my whole life be measured by 'S'hhh-Fem.'"

"It's a good deodorant."

"It's unnecessary. People are starving and—

"Oh, Harry. There're always people starving. They have their role, we have ours."

"It's like a pilot I met in a bar one night. A Navy guy. He was telling me about his job. The briefings, taking off from a carrier deck, how to catapult off just right in a rough sea—I got fascinated by the <u>problem</u>. By the mechanics. All the gauges and gadgets he had to master—and navigation and flying in formation."

"That can be beautiful," Buzz said.

"Yeah. He talked about the aesthetics of flying and bombing runs and just how beautiful it was. Then, later on he got to bitching about the My Lai massacre and what the hell was wrong with those Army guys. And that's the first it occurred to me he was in the same business but didn't know it. He only saw the <u>problem</u> of how to do his job. He had no perception his job was murdering people."

"What the hell's that got to do with <u>S'hhh-Fem</u>? Nobody's getting killed and everyone smells good after. A stinking cunt could be a social problem."

"Oh, Jesus, Buzz. It's a lie. And the longer we push it, the harder it is to face the truth and the narrower the time we have to do something about it. We're doomed if we cling to the illusion. There's a force as awesome as the ice age moving onto this land and we'll perish before it if we don't learn how to deal with it."

"I gotta get you out of here, Harry. You're going stir-crazy."

"Maybe. I don't know. But it was all coming to me before here. Not straight. Screwed up as hell, in fact. All jumbled and short-circuited."

"Why don't you see a shrink?"

"No—that's just it! All the success freaks we know run to a shrink trying to make rational what their bodies and heads know is totally irrational and insane. You can't make reasonable the way we live. Did you ever ride a subway at rush hour in this town? Look at those people!"

"I wouldn't be caught dead in a subway."

"Oh, no, I know. We're the lucky ones. We seal ourselves off in corridors of limos and cabs and in all the right places—and hermetic offices and little fortress apartments and pretend our reality isn't out there. But it is, Buzz; there's dog shit in the streets and people talking to themselves and blood and addicts and drunks. Last time I went to Kennedy—over the Triboro—I saw one of our billboards for <u>Pro Ball</u> in Harlem—all those goddamned models and that big white stud in a tropical resort. Jesus Christ, that's not the world. It was insane seeing it in Harlem. And cruel. No wonder they hate us."

"You and your bleeding heart for the colored, again?" Billingsly said.

"Bleeding heart? I'm getting threatening letters they're gonna kill me."

"Jesus."

"Yeah. Oh, Buzz—it's everything. Our phones don't work. Cabbies go "off-duty" to save their lives. We get trapped on the 30th floor without air or elevators or lights in a brownout. And we joke it off. We take pride in New York being hard. But it's no joke, Buzz. They're out there. Especially the blacks. We're out there too, even if we pretend we're not. If our livers and adrenals and hearts or ulcers or cancer don't get us, they're going to. They're gonna rip us out of our cars and apartments one of these days—and who can blame them?

We're sinking, Buzz—we're absolutely sinking if we don't start putting first things first. That's why I made a scene at your house. That's why I've been making them right along. It makes no sense, but I was trying to fight or at least talk about for my—what—humanity?"

"Is that why you slept with Janelle? Is that first things first? Yeah, I know all about it. She told me. Oh, fuck it, Harry, don't say anything. What can you? It doesn't matter, really. Janelle and I hadn't—well—been married for over a year. I never went near her. You know I was out every night on business or some excuse and—shit—you weren't the only one. Better you than some of those European creeps she was always dragging around. I don't blame you. It's her. She's crazy. Has been for a long time. Maybe always, for what I know. Harry, stop looking so pained. Really. It doesn't matter. Happy to be out of it, if you want to know the truth. And I am. I'm going to Mexico for a divorce and to hell with—does Norma know?

"Jesus. No. Nothing."

"Well, I won't say anything, but—for your sake, Harry, stay the hell away from Janelle. She's bad business. Who knows what she'll do? She's really bananas. You know what she did that night after the party? I checked into the Plaza and the police woke me there at 6:30 in the morning. She'd come home and dragged the mattress out in the street and set fire to it! In Beekman Place! God. Then they found her on a plane to Chicago—dead out from some goddamned pills she'd swallowed. She had a ticket to Madison, Wisconsin, on her—that's her hometown. Ah, you know that, I guess. God. I still don't know if she really meant to kill herself or not. Ah. She's dead anyway as far as I'm concerned. How I ever managed to get myself involved with her, I don't know."

"The money—maybe," Gardner said. He really hadn't meant to say it but it came out.

"Goddamn it, Harry, I came here to be friends. Don't start with me."

"I—I know. I didn't meant that."

"Yes, you did, damn it. That's her shit, isn't it? Well, fuck her—and you too, Harry, if you want to think that way. Look, I want to make it work with you and I don't really give a good goddamn what you think of me. You're no Jesus Christ yourself, though you love acting like one."

"Don't you want to hit me or something—kill me even?"

"Like you are now? The picture of health. What for?"

"I can't understand it—you. Or me. I told you to go fuck yourself in your own home. You walk in here and tell me you know I've been sleeping with your wife and—you want to make things work."

"So? I don't have to love you, for Christ's sake, to want you at the shop. Or like you. You're good, a pro. I'm a pro and I'm in business. That's all I give a shit about. I don't love people I do business with."

"Or anybody."

"Oh, Christ, Harry, grow up! You're making this very difficult."

"I don't mean to. I'm—I really just want to understand."

"Then act like it, you asshole. What's to understand? You want a little punishment, for Christ's sake—is that it? All right, look, you hit me pretty hard the other night—and then the Janelle thing—but that's irrelevant—"

"Is it? Don't' you feel any anger at all at me for that?"

"What for?"

"She's your wife. I work for you. I take money from you."

"So—you earn it, don't you?"

"That's not the point. I betrayed you."

"You goddamned near lost me an account the other night, I'll tell you that. That's the worst thing you did."

"You really believe that? That's worse than Janelle?"

"Hunh—no contest."

"Don't you feel anything for her—compassion, pity even?"

"She's a crazy, fucked-up bitch. Don't' tell me you're in love with her?"

"No, but—I care what happens to her. She's a person."

"So who the hell isn't? Now are you coming back to work or aren't you? I need you for Americans, the Beautiful."

"That wasn't supposed to be an ad campaign."

"It's gonna be, Harry—with you or without you."

"You're really immoral, aren't you?"

"What the fuck do you want from me? Immoral? You're the one who goes around screwing other guys' wives. I don't."

"Just the cash register."

"Of, fuck you. I knew I shouldn't have come here. You're as crazy screwed up as Janelle. You two go join a religious order or something and pound your chests to death if that's what makes you happy. I'm sick of both of you judging me all the time. You have ever since I've known you. Well, you're in the shit, too, boy, and maybe you don't like it but I love it. Sure I used Janelle's money at the beginning. So what? She was a goddamned bird flying around in a daze till I came along. Spouting that crappy poetry and feeling like she was nothing. I made her feel important. And I paid her money back quadruple. Every cent. But she couldn't be content, ever. Oh, no—she had to have her guilt like you. Well, I'm sick to death of all you middle-class moralizers who don't do anything but drag your asses through "21" crying about how fucked up the world is. It's always been fucked up, and it always will be, and the only way not to get fucked by it is to do the fucking first."

Harry said, "That's what I'm fighting. I—"

"No, let me talk!" Buzz yelled. "Goddamnit! Keep quiet for once. Look, I started from shit as a Depression Jew Bronx boy and I've got some talent and looks and guts and I made it. Don't give me all that black, down-trodden horse shit, either. You want to hear sad stories, boy? My old man ran a short order joint in Harlem and owed money from the day he opened and some goddamned nigger shot him. You didn't know that, did you? My mother died a year after I was born."

Harry muttered a lame "No, I—"

"Never mind," Buzz continued. "My father was paralyzed till the day he died and I had to move in with an aunt in Newark in an all Catholic neighborhood. I got my ass kicked almost everyday the first six years of school for being a Jew. My old man was an idiot—a dumb Jew—poor, trapped in his obsolete God and his wheel-chair and thinking the socialist party was going to save everything. Fuck you, man, I surpassed myself beyond any dream I dared have a right to have, cause I saw how things are and I got my share and I'm proud of it. Fuck the niggers if they won't get it for themselves and double fuck them if they try to take it away from me like they did my old man. So I'm a clever, cold closet Jew copout turned on to all the American shit. So what? I like my color TV and trips to the coast and credit cards and so do you if you weren't all fucked up on your guilt. Well, no guilt for me, understand? Absolutely none. I owe nobody anything. I made it. And if they have to beat me or kill me to take it away, that's their lookout. I'm gonna be killing back. And survive. I'm a Jew, remember? And we know how to survive. Look, Gardner, if you want a job when you get out of here, call me. In the meantime, go—oh, you know." Billingsly turned around and walked out.

That callous, arrogant sonofabitch, Gardner said to himself; he even uses the Jews when it's convenient! I can't work for that man! Or the world! I can't! Gardner lit a cigarette. But what else can I do? I know so little—and too much.

"My, don't we have a handsome boss?" Miss Peterson said, coming back into the room. "He's got a beautiful tan. Here's the papers. Today's puzzle's a killer."

"Yeah?"

Peterson handed Gardner the papers, and he looked at the headline on the Times: U.S. AIDS SAIGON IN CAMBODIA WITH PLANES, ARTILLERY, ADVISORS. OPPOSITION IN SENATE. Fine, very nice, Gardner thought; but the warriors'll have their way. NIXON TO SPEAK ON TV TONIGHT. To prepare us for more, Richard? I'm sure you've got us in there already. Praise the Lord and pass the elocution. Gardner could hear him now: To defend the free world. Save American boys' lives. Protect the honor of our flag and country. We've never lost a war yet—blues.

Aren't you going to do it?" Peterson said.

"What? Oh, yes," Gardner said. He turned the paper open to the puzzle. "Let's see. Uh, one across—gardner—four letters." Buzz. That bastard. The world really is the way he said it is, boy, Gardner said to himself; you have got to face that someday sooner or later, or go mad like Janelle. Burning a mattress in Beekman Place! So later, if you don't mind. I'm trying to work on this puzzle. You better work on the other one.

All the big boys know how the world is, boy. Don't kid about that. The rest is decoration. The part you like. No. No. Man can change. Really? Better men are coming. Who—you? Come on, Harry, it's something in all of you. Cain kills Abel and Abraham wanted to do the same to Issac. And Christian Jew and Communist Capitalist. Communist communist. WhiteblackblackwhiteblackblackblackBuzzThompson whitewhite—who speaks another language or has a different way of making God or getting married. Come on, boy, don't hang back. Get on. The way you did with Lonnie. Round and round the killing goes and buries all with pose and prose. Naturally and forever. Didn't you feel your own old hunter deep in a ductless gland crying out for blood and begging the brain for excuses? You heard it that day. Come on, brain, it's a new killing season. Find us some nice reason that the other guy is different enough to deserve to die.

"See? I told you it was hard today," Peterson said.

"I got banal for commonplace and Butte for a city in Montana."

"What's gardner?"

"I don't know yet. Stride easily is lope."

"Hey, we're doing great."

But America was going to change all that. America? Yes, America! America! See, I feel better just saying the word? Remember how I used to love looking at a map of her and saying out the names of her states and towns and rivers and mountains? And from reading about her famous men? Sure, sure, Harry, we've been over it a million times, but you still leave out the Indian killings and the slave ships anchoring in, and what you did to Lonnie.

I don't care what you say. She's the hope of the world. It's all written down in black and white and nobody ever did that before! Life, liberty and the pursuit of happiness! Inalienable rights of man. Freedom of speech and assembly and religion—and due process of law. All men are created equal. What about that?

Indians, Harry. Slaves, Harry. Negroes now, Harry. Private greed, Harry. In profit we trust, Harry. Hiroshima, Vietnam, Chicago, Buzz Billingsly, poisoned water and air, Harry—you and Janelle. All right, all right! I know. I see it all. Why do you think I've been disintegrating! What do you want from me for believing my father and the text books? You think I like finding out they lied or didn't know any better? Couldn't do any better?

"Mr. Gardner, you're not even looking at it," Miss Peterson said.

"Hunh?"

"The puzzle. Don't you want to do it?"

"Oh, yes, the puzzle. I do. I'm sorry. I was just—uh, 7 down is pensive for dreamy, I think."

"That's you."

Are you trying to tell me there's <u>nothing</u> left of the sweet new man America said it wanted to make? You mean the whole beauty and magnitude of this continent were taken and laid a dream on just to learn all over that we're pathologically incapable of malice towards none and charity for all and of reasonableness and peacefulness and joy? That man is? Don't tell me that!

Poor Harry. Poor aching boy of good beliefs and sincere intentions—and profound confusions. Remember those rich old ladies we've seen in restaurants trying to hide the truth about themselves under pounds of cosmetics and insisting on sitting in the shadows because they can't take the light?

THAT'S NOT AMERICA!

Isn't it? Oh, you've made some superficial gains; I'll grant you that, Harry. But you haven't produced a fundamental change in man and your crimes are mounting on the pile of human history just like everybody else's. Ask your children. Where were you, Daddy, when the crimes were piling up?

Oh, screwing the boss's wife. Getting drunk at "21." Conspiring with my accountant to "minimize" my income tax. Nothing big, you see? Oh, and laughing at jokes about niggers and pollacks—don't get me wrong, I didn't actually tell any—I just accepted them and felt happy that I wasn't a nigger or a Pollack. I avoided you, children, because I really didn't quite know what to tell you about life, so I left you to the television set. And I thought up <u>Pro Ball</u> and I read the sports page, getting more worked up about the ball scores than I did about the kill ratios in Vietnam, but allowing myself to be governed by men who spoke of the latter as though they were the former. I watched a lot, but I never got involved. I looked away and tried not to think about it. And got depressed and angry and paralyzed and drunk.

Didn't you do <u>anything</u>, Daddy?

Well—$25.00 a year to NAACP and I wrote Hubert Humphrey an indignant letter about the Chicago Convention. I made posters to help rid the world of Hitler. And I cried real tears after Jack and Martin Luther King and Bobby.

Daddy, really. It seems so little. How do you plead?

Plead insanity, Harry—from trying to make the slogans stand for the reality. Insanity—from trying to synthesis what your senses know with what your ads say. Insanity, Harry—from thinking that you see that your children will probably repeat it all in their own time, from begat to begat to begat.

It's all very hard to face and keep facing. Everything in me works against it.

Face it, Harry. You can't get off the wheel of life anymore than your children will be able to. But, at least, you can stop pretending that it's a merry-go-round. You can stop pretending that you are better or that America is and you can stop pretending that electric garage doors or even missiles to the moon are steps up the mountain to Grace. You can stop acquiescing in the pretense that black men are sub-human and therefore can be mistreated. Stop pretending that you have a divine mandate to rule over all other breeds of life and so exterminate them and befoul the planet in any way you see fit.

Do it, Harr. Lift the rock and look underneath. See it clearly. See? Mankind. What's the word Norma's doctor would use. Schizophrenic? From the beginning. The lower drives always slightly defeating the higher aspirations. If he were just a killer, no one would mind it. Remember what Auden said—"The tiger can't help being tigery?" Or if he only built cathedrals and indoor toilets. But he keeps doing both and drives himself insane. Why? Why?

<u>I don't know</u>! <u>I don't know</u>!

You don't have to know, Harry, except to understand that it's true. And face it. And live with it.

Live with it? How? I can't go back. Back is illusion. There are no good old days, according to what you say. Back where we got the blood taste and devised the fantasies in the first place. Religion. Philosophy. Tribal Pride. Language to set us apart. Our fear of death. It's all back there.

True, but in any case, it may be over soon. Your boys have learned to extinguish everything now—the entire breed, all the breeds, the very life of the planet. And, knowing them as you do, is there any reason to suppose they won't have a go at it? The hecatomb.

What can I do about it?

Nothing probably. Go ahead.

To what? More and more megatons—till it's ended?

There might be a little time left for science to find something.

Science? Isn't that another God that failed? Haven't they all, according to you? God himself? Capitalism? Communism? Freud? Technology?

Yes, except that until now you've only used your science to alter external qualities. Why can't you use it to change your insides? Your head.

How?

A kind of mutation, some kind of chemical revolution. Something that'll work against the schizophrenia so that you're not condemned to repeat your crimes until the final one.

Good God, man, are you suggesting a pill?! Is that your big solution?

Something like that. Do you have any other choice?

A pill? All the poetry and the pain and the causes and applauses—and the sacrifice—were graven images—to a pill? We're all going to be hopheads?

Maybe that's what it meant when they said Jesus was stoned on the Cross.

You and your rotten jokes. But, even if you're right, supposing you are, what about now? What do I do the day I get out of here? I still have to make some kind of choices. Find one lie more livable than another, one town, one work, one shelter, one piece of flag, one shred of an idea. I'm not inanimate. I have to be somewhere. I have to do something. I have got to live beyond your terrible knowledge. I cannot just go to sleep unless I'm willing to die and I am not ready for that yet. Where am I supposed to live? What work will I do? How am I supposed to treat Norma and the children? Do you really want me to tell them what you tell me the world is like? Can they grow up that way—without a God or country or myth to believe in? It's never been done before. They can't live on that.

Trust them—they'll make up something to believe in. Humans do.

I can't. I've run out of things.

Don't worry. You'll choose one action over another and get to thinking it matters.

BUT WHAT?

That's for you to figure out.

"What's so be it—15 across?" Miss Peterson asked.

"Amen?"

"Oh, Lord, of course—Amen."

"Adam."

"What?"

"Gardner. Eden."

CHAPTER 23

Gardner was awake, but he lay there for a long time as though he were still asleep and listened to Norma moving about their bedroom. He felt a chiffon breeze on him coming in through the window from the park and it was warm. It looked like a clear day from what light he could see and after a little while longer he sat up and reached for a cigarette.

"Good morning," he said.

"Oh, you're awake. Hi," Norma said.

"I heard you."

"I was trying to be quiet."

"It's all right. I've slept. That's all I do is sleep."

Norma came over to the bed and sat down next to Gardner and she put her hand on his forehead and pushed his hair back, arranging it. It was Saturday, May 9th, now, and Gardner had been home from the hospital since Wednesday. Otis Price's exhibition had been open a week at the Guggenheim and to good reviews. American troops were in Cambodia and four college students had been killed on Monday by National Guardsmen at Kent State University in Ohio. Laura and David Akers were driving down to Washington, D.C. today to attend a protest meeting on the Ellipse behind the White House and Norma was going with them.

You really don't mind if I go?" Norma said.

"No. You convinced me last night. I wish I could."

"But what if there is trouble. Maybe you're right."

"Are you having second thoughts? Don't go if you're scared."

"No, you know me. I want to go. It's just Andrew."

"He'll be all right. He should see it. And remember last fall when we went down? It couldn't have been more peaceful."

"But what about the hardhats?"

There won't be any trouble. Nobody wants that today. I just wonder if it does any good."

"I don't know. We've got to do something. Remember what you said last fall about testifying with our bodies?"

"Did I say that?"

"Yes."

"H'mmm. I guess it's better than just—letting things go by."

"Are you all right?"

"Fine, I think. And you?"

"Okay. Except the baby kicked all night. It's got to be a boy."

"You gonna be able to do all that walking around down there?"

"Sure, I feel wonderful."

"Mother Courage. What time is it?"

"Ummm—7. They're picking me up at 7. I'd better go. Patience is here. Emily's still sleeping. Can I get you anything?"

"No, honey, go ahead."

Norma got up and went to her dresser and picked up her bag.

"Oh, where's the <u>Times</u>?" Gardner said.

Norma got it and brought it to him. "Here."

"Thank you."

"There's coffee on the stove, when you're ready. Oh, and answer your folks' letter if you get a chance—okay? Here it is."

Gardner nodded and smiled. Norma kissed him.

"I feel guilty running off and leaving you."

"No, it's okay. You need a change of scenery after the hospital. You were wonderful there."

"I love you."

"How do you do it, Norma? You always seem so clear about things. Hopeful and cheerful and full of action and plans. You're so good. What sustains you?"

"I have lots of energy."

"Is that all? Just metabolism and something in your genes. No beliefs? You sure you don't believe in God or anything like that?"

"I believe in myself—till lately—and us."

"Maybe that's the difference. I keep turning to other things to believe in and when they disappoint me, I have nothing to—take their place."

"Do I disappoint you, Harry?"

"How could you?"

"I think I do. I think everything does."

"My upbringing again? I'm telling you my childhood just wasn't that injured."

"Something was."

"I just can't accept it all comes down to Mom and Dad. Things happen in a context beyond that."

"Harry? Are things going to be all right?"

"Of course—what things?"

"Us. The world. It's so frightening. I get scared too, you know. We've been through such terrible things. Can you really change, Harry?"

"I hope so."

"That's all I need. I can live with the rest. Promise me though you won't go up to Harlem? It wouldn't help anything to see Lonnie's mother."

"I know. It was just a notion. Penance I guess. I thought I might be able to help the brother too, somehow."

"Well, maybe we can. We'll talk about it. But don't go up there now. It's too dangerous."

"In our own city," Gardner said and shook his head. "I won't. I'm glad the letters stopped."

"Me too. They scared me to death."

"I guess it's over now. I still can't believe what happened though."

"I know. It's horrible every time I think about it. But just—use it—try to use it to change."

"Yes." Gardner felt very tender towards Norma and felt himself wanting to make love to her. "We've had some really lovely times together, haven't we Norma? Remember Scandinavia—skinny dipping in the fjord? And New Hampshire?"

Norma nodded and smiled.

"I love our Christmas Eves," she said. "And remember the night we got high at the Four Seasons and checked into the Summit—no luggage or anything? I still don't know how you knew we could do that. I kept bumping into you all the way up to the room I was so nervous. I never could look the bellboy in the eye."

"But we were married."

"I know, but I sure didn't feel like it."

"As I recall, you had a very good time of it."

"You did all right too, boy. I love pretending I was your whore. The Summit was perfect for that."

"You were exquisite."

"Oh, Harry, we're so good."

"When I'm okay."

"I'm so pleased you're going to the Doctor Monday."

"I know you're pleased. I'm only doing it for you."

"That's all right. It makes me feel like you care again at least. That you want to try."

"I've got to find some way to live."

"Mom," Andrew called out, knocking at the door. "The doorman called up. The Akers are waiting."

"All right. I'm coming," Norma said. "You were wonderful with him yesterday. I'm so happy you made up. I cried."

"Who could resist getting an umpteenth clay pencil holder?"

"Well, I'm off to the barricades."

Gardner reached out for Norma and she came to his arms and they kissed. "Take care, Darling," Gardner said.

"You too. Bye-bye." Norma got up and walked towards the door. "We'll be back tonight by 11."

"Give my love to David and Laura," Gardner said.

"I'm saving that for myself." Norma left the room and closed the door behind her. Gardner put out his cigarette and rolled over in bed and saw one of Norma's bobbypins on the sheet and the crumples in the sheet which her body had made and he could smell her having been there and it was good and so was the warmth that clung where she had lain when he lay on the spot, which he did, burying his face in her pillow. He really wanted to make love to her.

You have had the loveliest of times with Norma, Gardner told himself, and that makes you a very fortunate man. It's time you believed in that. You have had love-making and laughter and healthy children and those are uncommon gifts. Consider them. Appreciate. Why hasn't it been enough? It could be right now, if she were here.

Gardner turned over and lit another cigarette. He saw his folks' letter and picked it up and read it again.

"Dearest Harry, We are still so stunned and worried about what happened to you. It's such a terrible thing. To think that in broad daylight and in your own front yard practically, such a thing could happen! It's just awful. But maybe now you'll think seriously about leaving New York. You know how we feel about it. The colored problem there is just sinful—and the foreigners. It's not much better in Indianapolis really. Everyday in the paper another incident. What can you do? Nothing seems to satisfy them. Your father thinks the whole thing is Communist inspired and so do I. It just doesn't make sense otherwise. Anyway, we're very proud of you, son, for saving your family from that terrible beast. It was even in the papers here. I've put in the clippings. Thank God he didn't hurt you more. Norma was very nice on the phone and said you were getting along fine (we were sure glad of that) and that it wasn't necessary for us to come. We would though, you know that, if you needed us. You can always count on that. It is hard for Dad to get away though now. Business at the store has been terrible lately what with the lay-offs in town. Higgins is down just awful since they lost a defense contract. As daddy says, there they are cutting back and we haven't even won the war yet. What can you do? And we thought Nixon'd make things better. He's still the best. I know—you don't agree! Norma said you have a good doctor and a nice room. I hope so. How's the food? Wish I was there to make you Waldorf Salad the way you like it. We bought a color TV for ourselves for our anniversary. Not as expensive as yours, but we're happy.

Elizabeth and Earl send their love. Did you get their flowers? Norma thanked me for ours. Earl's uncle William died Monday. Do you remember him at the wedding? Oh, and Cecil Updike. Cancer. Have you stopped smoking yet? Joan Morton got married Sunday. Didn't you date her mother in high school—Winifred Barnett? I'm sure you did. We went to the wedding and she asked about you. Little did I know then. Did you read about Kent State? Wasn't that awful? We drove through Kent once to visit Dad's cousin George in Warren. Remember? Maybe not. You were very little then—and so cute I might add. The good old days, hunnh? But imagine <u>that</u>—in Ohio! Course the ones who got it were from New York, did you notice? What's happening to these kids? The way they're behaving I guess they deserved what they got. Dad and I just can't understand any of it. Everything seems to be falling apart. The world we knew just doesn't seem to exist anymore. It really is a bother. Not that we'll be around to see it all. Dad's blood pressure is up again though he looks after it. I'm about the same. Dad tried to get me to go to the doctor, but you know me, I wouldn't be caught dead at a doctor's. He'd be sure to give me bad news. When are you coming home? All our love, Dad & Mother."

Gardner crumpled the letter in his hand and dropped it to the floor. <u>When am I coming home?</u> I wouldn't begin to know how to find it, mother dear. Oh, Father, Gardner said to himself, our Lancaster is as lost as Atlantis! I know. I know.

How dare the world force you to find that out. Weren't you told there was an absolute correlation between hard work and just rewards and didn't you take that as the Gospel of the Lord and live your lives more seriously than any people ever and curb your joys? Never looking for pleasure in sex or wine nor fancy buildings—and if you did take vacations they were short and in earnest and close to home. You didn't go to Europe and hardly ever to nightclubs. I know. We shaved every morning and kept our appointments and cleaned our own houses and made the beds and three meals a day for seven days a week for all our mortal lives and we built hospitals and schools and roads and farms from hard forests and we established churches and charities and freed the slaves and built great industries and corporations and we lived on our income and for our families and our communities and our nation and our Jesus. WHY HAS HE FORSAKEN US? And turned our children against us? And the nations of the world? What do you mean Africa isn't Tarzan? That you can't export democracy or use the atom bomb? What's a greenhouse theory?!

Yes, you'd probably feel that way too, Gardner told himself, if you had stayed behind. You understood because even now there was much of it in you still. No wonder they turn to Nixon and Agnew to turn back time and blame everything on the Communists. And it wasn't just Lancaster. They were feeling it the same in Queens and Cleveland and San Francisco and all the suburbs. Suddenly, Gardner felt a great and sincere sadness for them all, because they had accomplished so much and had been so good, in so many ways, and, for so long. They had seemed to be right. It had seemed to work their way. He knew it would be very hard for them to let go now and know the world was more complicated and needed new approaches and wanted some pleasures this side of their Heaven that hadn't held up. He wondered if they could let go. He was wary of them; wary of their tight mouths and backs and necks and colons that had strained so long in the harness of their faith. He knew that they still had frightening power and the White House and that they might not be able to come of age and might use it all in one last desperate, anguished spasm of confusion and doubt and self-righteousness to lash out at the cities and the citizens and the countries who no longer wanted to do things their smalltown way. Their passage was much in question and so for that was his.

You're seeing it clear now. Gardner told himself; but you've left out a lot about your folks, boy. Oh, leave them alone. They did all they could and told you all they knew. And meant it with good intentions. So what if my mother is superstitious and frightened and yelling most of the time and probably has always hated sex and is always talking about who got born or married or divorced or died. And so my father plays golf and belongs to the American Legion and The Rotary Club and never talked enough and was always reading the paper. So what? They held me much when I was little and if they told me nothing about love and sex, they never told me anything against it. Dad is a sweet and modest man and he kept his marriage vow, which is more than I can say. And suppose he hasn't seen Paris? Or the latest off-Broadway play? And hasn't got a single sliver of gossip about Jackie Kennedy. And I know he still wipes his silver on his napkin, even in restaurants. So what? I love him. He told me a lot that wasn't true, but he never lied. Gardner felt like crying but he didn't know well enough how to.

"Hello there—are you decent, I hope not," Patience said. She had knocked and entered and closed the door behind her in one gesture.

"Oh, hi," Gardner said, as he watched her walk towards him. He saw again how pretty she was—especially those damn little boy legs.

"Long time, no see—Yank."

"Yes, well—"

"Welcome home." Patience sat on the edge of the bed and kissed Gardner on the mouth.

"Patience."

"Something wrong, Luv?"

"Well, yes, I mean—not here."

"Oh?"

"Emily might walk in and—"

"She's fast asleep and I locked the door behind me. Don't you look adorable when you first wake up?"

"Patience, please. I'm not much in the mood for—"

"You're no fun. What's wrong? I thought after being cooped up in that dreary hospital you'd be hot to trot."

"Unlock the door, will you, please?"

"Really?"

"Please. It's not right—here."

"Then when are you coming to my place? I want to see you."

"Yes, me too, but—I don't think—you and I ought to—well, see each other."

"Oh?"

"It isn't right."

"It isn't? I thought it was groovy."

"Well, yes, but I mean—"

"Wife and kiddies and all that?"

Gardner nodded.

"I'll have to get you drunk then?"

"No. No more of that either."

"Oh, you've gotten religion, have you?"

"Not exactly."

"What then?"

She was so cool and relaxed, Gardner thought. She was smiling even, and playing with the hair at his neck. God, he was always frowning.

"It doesn't bother you I'm married?"

"Should it? Why?"

"Well, you're so young—and I have—so little to give you."

"I don't expect anything, Mr. Gardner."

"Nothing?"

"What should I?"

"Maybe not now, but you will. You can't help it. It's natural for people who feel something or get involved with each other to want something. And don't call me Mr. Gardner."

"What are you so worried about?"

"If we go on, you can't help wanting something from me. It's your right."

"Certainly not money, do you mean? I hope you don't mean that. I take care of myself."

"Of course not that. Love. Protection. Responsibility. Time. All kinds of obligations. And there's nothing wrong with that, I just can't—"

"Mr. Gardner—what is your Christian name?"

"Harry."

"You talk like my Dad."

"Don't you want those things?"

"They aren't necessary. I want to do it with you—that's all. You're attractive."

"But, Patience, that's either abnormal or naïve. If we mean something to each other, I owe you certain responses. And I can't give you anything. I was only using you the other—"

"I know that. What else do people ever do? But that still doesn't mean you have to pay for it. You paid, with the moment. I don't want you forever either. You owe me nothing. I want you for <u>now</u>, that's all—the way you had a now the other night. You felt like being with me and I liked it. It was exciting."

"I was stoned out of my head."

302

"But it turned me on. I'd never seen you so free—and reckless. I dug it, as they say. I'd been wanting a go at you right along anyway. And the moment happened. We both felt it and took it. No use paying for that good moment with a lot of bad ones, is there? Or being obligated. We're not obligated to each other, except for the moment—for the good feeling."

"That's all you want?"

"That's everything, luv."

"What about love—L-O-V-E," he spells. "Getting married? Children."

"In this world? We've had a bloody plenty of that, haven't we? That's precisely why I left England. All that Victorian rubbish. That's Mum and Dad and Sis—duty and suffocation. They're like zombies. I don't want to be tied down by a lot of other people's rules and habits. And if I am used, I want to enjoy it. I want to live my life. I have all this fantastic energy, Luv. I'm not going to squander my life and energy in front of the teley and a sink full of dirty dishes."

"Aren't you afraid of being alone even?"

"Good Heavens, Luv—we are always alone."

"You have absolutely no moral compunction about—doing it—here?—"

"I'll make the bed when we're finished."

"But we're responsible for our actions to other people. I have a wife. I love her."

"Who can tell if what you do'll turn out good or bad, really. I just know how I feel. And what I feel is now."

"But that's not true, Patience. We all carry around a lot of luggage from the past. Whether we want to or not. It's in our cells and our upbringing. You can't get rid of that no matter how hard you try."

"You aren't trying hard enough, Harry. Every time I feel I'm acting like my Mum, it's a downer and right away I do something I know she wouldn't do in a thousand years. I feel so much better after. When I do something, I want to feel it's the very first time it's ever been done. Mr. Gardner, the present is all we ever really have—don't you understand? And the sweet supply is limited. I want my share—more if I can get it."

"I just can't see it that way."

"Haven't you ever done anything just because you felt like it?"

"I—don't think so. Except when I'm drunk."

"Poor luv. No wonder you're so unhappy."

"Do you think that—that I am?"

"You wear it like a sign, luv…or a straightjacket, I should say. Too bad. Taurus is a very compatible sign for me."

Patience kissed him on the mouth.

"Patience, please. And that Astrology nonsense is ridiculous. Something's got to <u>count</u> for something!"

"The moment counts, luv—and you have just missed a very good one. Too bad. But, have it your way. When you feel like backsliding, call me. Maybe I'll be in the mood." Patience kissed Gardner on the forehead and stood up. "Want some coffee, luv?"

"Yes, thanks. I'd love it."

Patience went to the door and unlocked it. "You did want me that night, didn't you?" she said.

"Yes—very much."

Patience looked Gardner in the eyes and she smiled, very warmly. "Well, then; that's something, isn't it? And your hard-on now." She left. Harry looked down. He was erect.

Is that the only choice—barbarians or totalitarians?! God, she did look so pretty—delicious—and she's so cool about everything. Why didn't you just do it and be done with it? You know that's what you feel. I'm not an animal! I can reason! Reasonably, Harry? Reasonably?

CHAPTER 24

It was nearly four o'clock in the afternoon now and Gardner was getting out of a cab in front of the Guggenheim Museum on upper Fifth Avenue. His wounds didn't hurt him at all, but he did feel tired from the walking he had been doing.

He had taken Emily and Patience to the fountain restaurant in the park for lunch and he had drunk a full carafe of white wine. Afterwards, they had walked to the playground and the wine had made him very free and he had enjoyed Emily—she was a lively, extremely intelligent child, he decided—and he thought he had been very good with her. He had said nothing more to Patience that was personal and he had tried hard to ignore her physically, or to let her affect him that way. She had been helpful, he thought, by keeping her conversation directed towards Emily, though he continued to be impressed by her cheerfulness and ease—and legs.

When they had gotten back to the apartment, Gardner decided that he had definitely better not stay there with Patience during the evening. The wine was working on him and he really did want to make love, and he wished that Norma had not left that morning when he realized that he could just as easily make love to Patience as to Norma. He was angry that Patience could stir him. It wasn't right. It didn't fit his favored view of himself at all, but he knew it was true. None of his views about himself seemed to be holding up and the sex one had always been tough to handle. What the hell was it in him that compelled him towards being a sexual bandit?

Still, he had thought, no matter how much he was wanting, he was determined not to take his wanting out on Patience—and certainly not in his wife's bed. He told her that he had to meet friends for dinner and he locked himself into his bedroom while he changed into a suit. When he was dressed he left the apartment quickly. Actually, he had thought he would come here to the Guggenheim to see Otis Price's exhibition, then have some dinner alone and catch a movie after that. By then, he had thought, Norma would be home, or nearly, and he would be safe.

Gardner reached into his pocket for money to pay the driver and, feeling it there, realized for the first time that he had brought along his knife. WHY? You promised yourself you weren't going to carry that thing around anymore, no matter what! Damn. Find a litter basket and throw it away, he told himself.

Gardner paid the driver and looked up at the Museum. It looked, he thought, like some huge floating beige buoy in the sunlight and it pleased him, though he couldn't help thinking that it still looked more like a building at a world's fair than one actually set down in a permanent city. He saw the surface of it was cracking.

"Hey, Hoosier boy, how you doin'?"

Gardner looked down and saw, a few feet in front of him, Naomi coming towards him. She was wearing a new, midi-length fur coat—tiger, Gardner thought—and knee high suede blue boots. Her hair was shiny black and straight and very long. It must be a fall, Gardner told himself; still, she looks great. Following just behind her was a long-haired man in his late 30's probably, Gardner guessed, who had three cameras slung on his neck and shoulders. An older black woman in a smock walked next to him and she was carrying a cosmetics case. Two others seemed to be with Naomi, he thought. One, a man, in tight tailored pants and a cute velvet version of a safari jacket, was wearing large sunglasses and talking Italian to the woman, who was dressed in a jazzy-looking gypsy outfit. The woman made very choppy movements, but as though she wanted to give the impression that she was very sure of what she was doing and that what she was doing was very important. She was taking high, lunging puffs from a small cigar and she made Gardner think of Bette Davis.

"Hello, Naomi," Gardner said.

"How's your head, baby? All of you, hunh?--I should say. I been readin' about you."

"I'm okay."

"Yeah? Glad to hear it. Hey, that's cool on your head. You'll have to show me the others someday. Scars are very groovy."

Bette Davis with the little cigar came up in a puff of smoke and kissed Naomi on the cheek. "Ciao, baby," she said. "It was a smashing session. Superdooperoo. We'll go ahead. Your car's waiting there."

"Yeah, Tobi, stay cool, hunh? Hey, Jerry," Naomi said in the direction of the man with the cameras, "Adios."

"You too, luv—straight ahead," the man with the cameras said.

The man with the large sunglasses and the <u>cute</u> velvet version of a safari jacket came up and kissed Naomi's hand. "Grazia tante, ma bella," he said.

"Arreviderch, Luggie. I'll send the beastie back on Monday, hunh, babe?"

"My coats are made for you, ma bella. You look so luxey."

"Yeah, I'm some slick bitch in 'em, I gotta admit."

"Arreviderchi."

"Take care of business, man," Naomi said. "So long, Dinah."

"See you round, Naomi," the black lady with the cosmetics case said as she walked away towards the bus stop at the corner. The man in the sunglasses and the <u>cute</u> velvet version of a safari jacket and Bette Davis and the man with the cameras got into a limousine at the curb and drove away.

"What's happenin', baby?" Naomi said. "Whatcha doin'?"

"I was going in to see your old man's work," Gardner said.

"Aw, that's a drag. Come on, buy me a drink. I can use it."

"Is Otis here?"

"No, he's in California, the schmuk. Wait'll I tell you why. Come on, we'll take the car down to the Stanhope. They gave me a limo. Very classy, hunh?"

"You been working?"

"Yeah, baby—all day. For Lugano—his new fall furs. In May yet. For <u>Vogue</u>. He's a good wop though. Very classy. The little faggy one was him—in the bush jacket?"

"You look beautiful. That coat is--"

"Yeah? Thanks. It's all gonna be this midi crap in the fall. It's a downer, if you ask me."

"I thought tiger fur was out."

"Oh—yeah--that extinction shit? This is tiger-stenciled, they call it. It's mink."

"Really? Aren't minks a threatened breed?"

"Just us and the tigers, man. They got minks on an assembly line. Nobody bleeds for them little bastards, but them big cats gettin' it sends people uptight. It's like minks was niggers and tigers Kennedys." Naomi smiled as though she had made a joke. "Come on."

"No thanks, Naomi, I--"

"Don't be a drag, baby. Come on. I'll buy. Don't you want to hear? Otis went out there to get Janelle."

Gardner followed Naomi into the limousine and they drove down Fifth to the Stanhope Hotel, which had an outdoor cafe, on the sidewalk opposite the Metropolitan Museum of Art.

"That's where old Otis'd like to be hung," Naomi said, pointing to the Museum. "Among other places. What'll you have?"

Gardner thought about sticking with white wine, but he changed his mind and ordered a double Johnny Walker Black on the rocks and, as he did, realized that this was the first day he had had a drink since his birthday. He'd better go easy, he told himself. Naomi ordered a double rye and ginger ale.

The sunlight got in under the red, white and blue striped awning which hung over the cafe and it cut across the table so that Gardner was in the shade and Naomi was in the light.

"I could use a little tan; I been feelin' mighty pale," Naomi said. "Whew, it's a hot mother."

Her skin was radiant and smooth as brown velvet, Gardner thought. Her eyes were dark and lively and quick and the whites of them were very white and clear, he saw. Her lips and nose were definitely what you'd call Negroid but they were magnificent, Gardner thought, and the lips were made up wetly, but very well. Her cheek bones were the strongest and highest he had ever seen and he suddenly realized that he had never stared at a negro so closely before—usually he looked away quickly, the way he did with a cross-eyed person or a cripple (except for Lonnie Dobson, of course). He was fascinated by it now and felt himself getting nervous and charged-up in his body. She had his juices going and some fear too, Gardner realized. It was almost like that first time with Janelle, he thought.

"Hey, boy, watcha starrin' at?"

"Oh, I'm sorry. I didn't mean to. I was just--"

"I got sumpin' wrong?"

"No. Everything is perfect."

"I thought maybe I was losin' an eyelash or sumpin". Naomi dug into her bag and came out with a pair of big sunglasses. But you could see through them when she put them on. The waiter brought their drinks.

"Salute, baby."

"Cheers."

"So, did you hear? Janelle flipped out. I guess you know, since you and she were makin' it."

"I heard she was in Chicago."

"No, man, L.A. She's in a psycho ward out there. They called Otis. She had 'em call Otis, for Christ's sake—instead of her old man. And when Otis called him—to tell him, he said send me the bills but spare me the trip. I'm not goin'. He said he was gettin' a divorce."

"I'd heard that."

"Sheet, he still could go get her. Why'd Otis have to? She ain't his old lady."

"That's very nice of him."

"Sheet. He was goin' anyway next week. His kids is there and his Ex. And some gallery crap. Man, he jumped at the chance to leave early. I'll bet him and that bitch used to make it, that's what I bet."

"I don't think so."

"Sheet—then he's the only one from what I can see. Oh, sheet, man—no offense."

Gardner shrugged. "Why didn't you go?"

"I'm workin'. Sides, he don't need me, man, with them kids. They got enough problems. I hate California."

"It's cold and it's damp?"

"Yeah. You know where they found her, man? Janelle? In Forest Lawn—whacked out—100%. Screamin' and cryin' and yellin' <u>Judy, Judy—where are you?</u> What is that shit? She stole some lady's dog, man, and said it was her dog and it's name was Toto. She wouldn't give it back till the cops came. Sheet. That dog's name wasn't Toto. It was Zsa Zsa. That's damned near as crazy. Fuckin' people."

"Oh, God."

"She's really a crazy cunt, hunh? I always thought so."

"She's not crazy."

"Hey, take it easy, man. I didn't mean nuthin'. To me, it's crazy."

"Whatever you say, Aunti Em."

"Hunh?"

"Nothing. Look, Naomi, I've got to go. I'll get the check. Good to see you--"

"What's your hurry, baby. Wait'll we finish this and I'll drop you off. Sides, I want to hear about that brother you iced."

"What?"

"The black brother you killed in the park. Lonnie Dobson, right?"

"Yes."

"Tell me about it, man. You really did sumpin' there."

"I wish I hadn't"

"Ain't you proud of yourself?"

"What for?"

"Why, the <u>News</u> made you out a big hero."

"Well, I'm not. I was scared to death and I wish to God it'd never happened."

"Aw, come on, man—what's one black boy more or less?"

"I don't think it's funny, Naomi."

"Me neither, man."

"It was terrible."

"Worse for Lonnie. You want another drink?" Gardner saw that he had finished the first one. He nodded and Naomi called over the waiter and ordered another round.

"Why'd you kill him?"

"In—self-defense. He was gonna kill <u>me</u>."

"That figures. How come though? What happened?"

"I—oh, it was all in the papers, Naomi. You said you read it. I'd just as soon not talk about it really. What did you mean just now--'it figures'?"

"Don't you know, man? Ain't a black boy in this country can't want to waste a fay."

"I suppose. I—don't blame them."

"Yeah. I read you been getting' threatnin' mail. That right?"

"I did. It stopped, thank God."

"They ain't so submissive like they used to be—the brothers."

The waiter brought the drinks. That's odd, Gardner suddenly thought to himself. The newspapers never mentioned that I got threatening mail. The police never told the newspapers, because they said it would only make matters worse. Stir up all the nuts, Donavan had said, and you'd be getting letters from all over the place. She couldn't have <u>read</u> that—but then—how did she know? Oh, Billingsly must have told Otis, he decided. Yes, that was it, when they spoke about Janelle.

My God, she's so beautiful, Gardner thought. And wild. She says whatever she wants and I'll bet she feels it the way Patience was describing feeling, and does what she feels—only a hundred times wilder and freer and more threatening. There's a quality that's absolutely fierce about her. Oh, nonsense. Just because she's black and talks tough. She learned the language from Price probably and she's no more exotic than any other woman you know. It's just her color. That's new for you. You've never made it with a black woman and that's got you going. Nothing else. She's just a fashion model, for Christ's sake, and you know a dozen of them. No—she's not like those girls and she certainly does have me going. I can feel her difference and some kind of danger about her. And I like it. I liked it a lot that night at Billingsly's when I was drunk and feeling free. I wanted to lay her that night and made up my head I was going to. Your body made up your head that night, pal, but today your head's in charge and you're not going to get involved with her. That's really all you need! Maybe it is. Maybe that's exactly what I need. Forget it! Stop wondering what her skin would be like to touch and what she smells like! ("They do smell peculiar, poor things," Mom. "They can't help it. Most of them are nice though," Dad). And you do <u>not</u> know that she would be a savage in bed! (Them nigger bitches'll do anything," College Chum. "Nigger cunts rather fuck than eat," Army Sergeant).

"What you thinkin', man?" Naomi said.

"What? Oh, nothing. Just enjoying—the moment. I am really too, Naomi. The drinks and the sunlight. The warmth, you know. You."

"Me too. I'm glad I ran into ya. I been thinkin' about ya."

"You have?"

"Yeah. I don't know why. That night, I guess—blew my mind."

"We were all so bombed."

"I hated you pretty good that night."

"I felt it. Why?"

"Sheet," Naomi said, more to herself than to Gardner. "I've had me some bad times with that Otis man."

"I figured you'd had a fight. I didn't take it personally."

"Aw, no, man, not a fight. Just a lot of sheet. Let downs, you know. Christ, I thought he was the coolest cat goin' when I first met him. He really turned me on. But—sure a lot of bad trips since then."

"Every marriage has trouble, Naomi."

"Not like black and white, man. That's really a bad number. The worse. I sure shot me some shit with that union. Mother. I thought it'd be okay in Paris. Not all that crap you get here. But it ain't no different—just, they don't have so many of us to hate is all."

"It is bad here, isn't it?"

"Bad? Man, it's grotesque. I can't get through a day here without feeling like somebody's linin' me up in his sights takin' aim you know."

"But Otis is cool, isn't he?"

"Oh, yeah—much as he can. He talks cool. But he can't forget it either. It's worse when we come back here, but it's in Paris too. I don't know what it is quite, but like, I know I let him down, man. Like that's what he makes me feel. Just lookin' at me bein' around is like a downer for him. He gets sad, you know—heavy and sulky and sighs all over the place. You know, I think that man's ashamed to be with me—Like I wasn't such a prize afterall. Oh sheet, what's the use of jivin' this way."

"No, do—please; I want you to." Gardner didn't like his motives for saying this. It came out of those side-show feelings you get, he thought. You have no business hearing about Naomi and Otis' troubles. You're not really interested. But Gardner had never known a mixed couple before and he couldn't help being curious and besides, he felt her weakening and wanting to talk and reveal things to him and as she weakened--(She is, boy—she is. Your good old hunter instincts about women tell you that all right. You can smell that sex blood better than anybody)--Gardner felt himself getting stronger and his body liked that, whether his head did or not, and he wanted to weaken this woman, really bring her open and dominate her—suddenly, he wanted to bridle all that savagery and toughness and he wanted to get her hand out of Janelle's pants and he wanted to force her to see he wasn't any fag—you called me a fag that night, bitch—I'll show you who's a fag, goddamn it—and Otis doesn't make it so good anymore, does he, honey—you let that out that night, remember, and you're about to tell it to me again and, yeah—if black boys have such great dicks and ball so fantastically why do you want white meat anyway, and you do, don't you, baby, or you wouldn't have married Otis in the first place or be here talking to me and weakening the way you are—and I don't know yet why it isn't working with Otis or why you want it with me, but that's what's happening, ain't it, girl—and I want to find out and get it working with me, cause you're ready, baby, I can feel it—and so am I. I want to lay you good. NO! NO! Oh, yes, I do!

"You really interested?" Naomi said.

"Of course I am."

"What do you care?"

"You're a person."

"Am I? I don't feel like it. You got a cigarette?"

"Here." Gardner gave her one and took one for himself and lit them both.

"Sheet, I hated you that night. And had nuthin' to do with Otis and me. I hated you plenty for yourself alone."

"Why? What did I do?"

"You was too white, boy—and in charge. You just was doin' everything too right. Feelin' your weight and takin' your chances like you didn't give a shit for nuthin'. Knockin' Janelle on her ass and Otis—man, he's twice your strength. Tellin' that boss man to fuck off. I thought you was gonna smack me down too. You really was bad, man."

Bad is good—move in, Harry—now. "But—you like it—isn't that why you hate me?"

"Yeah, man—sumpin' like that."

Perfect. Keep going. Get it. Naomi looked down at her drink, but Gardner knew she'd look up and when she did, he'd be waiting. They were going to look at each other—and acknowledge what they knew was happening. Naomi looked up and Gardner hooked her eyes like the catcher in a trapeze act and nobody was letting go. All right, now let up a little and swing her back to the platform and make her feel safe for a minute, but wanting another somersault and thinking she's the one in charge when she goes for it. Man, she's no different than any other woman, afterall.

Don't be too sure yet, Gardner stopped himself. Don't be too sure. There's still something there you've never known before. No, just the color, man, just the color. But that color's not just in your eyes, you fool; it's in every curve and crevice of your brain—storing up there since you first had sense. And she's seeing white. You gotta figure too on what that means to her, man. You're not just Harry Gardner now and she's not just Naomi—or even just another woman. She's a black woman, man, and what do you want from that? No, it's just her. Look at her, man, she's beautiful. Who wouldn't want her—and to cut Otis down a peg. Don't lie to yourself, boy. The last part's true, you know it is. I hate him. I envy his life so. I want some of that. You know I do. And do you hate her likewise? Her freedom? Her instinct freedom that you gave up long ago? Is she gonna make you feel free and spring all your hang-ups? You wouldn't have to shave everyday with her, boy—or pay your bills on time or pay them at all, is that it? You can be lazy and shiftless and get drunk on Saturday night and dance and fuck all you want, hunh, cause nobody expects anything else from a nigger, hunh? You want to be a nigger? Is that why you're saying man and trying to talk hip to yourself. So you can let go—just LET GO. You think you'll be free to do what you feel with her and live the moment, the PATIENCE MOMENT. You couldn't do that with Norma ever, could you? She would, but you wouldn't let yourself. Oh, maybe in Scandinavia or New Hampshire—remember you make babies on vacation—but not regularly, because she was duty and responsibility and Harry Gardner harnessed up, with no threats or thrills or edge of knife; but you couldn't do it with Janelle either because she was about the same really—a little slack in the reins maybe, but no stampede. You knew the bit was still in your mouth and you kept pulling yourself up short and hurrying back to the corral. And you couldn't with Patience either, even when she offered, cause she was still of your world and white and England and teatime civilization; and so were all the others in one way or another and as much as you tried you just never got your rage and despair and frustration and lust and muscle really turned loose. You never let go, but you think you could with this one, hunh, cause she's black and that means primitive and savage and freedom and terror and LETTING GO and you know she'll understand it—all of it—the violence in you and the hatred and the self-loathing and the murder, cause she'll be feeling her own. Admit it. You don't want her because she's beautiful or chic or lives in Paris and models for <u>Vogue</u> and knows all the right people. Not because she's Naomi—but because she's BLACK. Cause you think she's the animal you ache to be. No, No—it's her! IT ISN'T HER! IT'S BLACK! Call a spade a spade.

"Does Otis make you feel like a person?" Gardner said.

"He used to. When I first met him. Man, he was the most powerful cat I'd ever known. Like, he just knew how to do things and go places and everybody did what he wanted—and they dug him. Restaurants, hotels—trains, cabs—private parties. Rich and poor. Everywhere and everybody. He didn't yell or nothin' or make scenes ever. He just had like, the power. And he knew it and everybody else did too and accepted it. I'd never known anybody could walk around free as that. He made me feel like, whole—you know, man. Like till I met him some big part of myself was absent. I just knew I had to get me some of that man. He was somethin' else. While it lasted."

"How did he feel about you?"

"Like, the same. He gave up a white wife and kids for me, man. Imagine that? I don't know. He used to talk about it once in awhile. Crazy things like saying' I gave him a second birth and I could turn around all the shit in his life and work. He said I brought new power to him. Dig that. I brought him power. That still don't make any sense to me."

"What happened, if you both dug each other so much?"

"There was a power failure. You tell me. I don't know. Like first trip back here it started. We went to a big party with a lot of celebrities and this one black cat was there—an actor. I ain't gonna name him, but Otis went ape. Said I was gonna make it with the cat. Sheet, I wasn't even close. I didn't even think about it. I barely said hello to the cat. No matter. Otis started in on him and they damned near killed each other that night. After that, he was always accusing me of trickin' with black cats. I shoulda. He shore don't any—oh, sheet."

"We're all taught they're the best lovers."

"What?"

"Black guys. Every white kid thinks all the black kids are studs. You've heard that."

"Yeah. But what else they got, man? What else? You know the other night—you remember askin' Otis to come back here—to the States?"

"Yes."

"Like I think he'd really dig that now. I wouldn't mind either, man, now the black man's gettin' off his ass a little. Paris is a drag. It's really all happenin' here."

"Then why don't you. You could easily—both of you."

"I'm ready, but—like, he's afraid."

"About his work? That's—"

"Naw, man. That was me jivin' the other night just to kick him in the ass. I do that good when I get—hung-up. I cut him down awful, don't I? Don't know why even. I just get mean-ass bad."

"Then—what's he afraid of?"

"Like you know what I think? It's me. He's ashamed of me. Of being married to a colored."

"But that's ridiculous. Why should he be? You're beautiful."

"You think so—really?"

"Of course I do. He does. He must."

"Naw, man, otherwise—like we only make it a few times a year now. I gotta tell you that. Everything else is shit if I don't tell you that. He don't want me anymore."

"Oh, baby, it changes for everybody after you been married awhile."

"Not like this, man. He's just dead. Turned off. And not just the sex shit, but like everything, but the sex most of all. And we were somethin' else. Now, goddamn it, every chance he gets we got a house full of blondes. Every party. Danes and Dutch and Swedes. English and German cunts all

over the place. Every new friend he gets—buys, I mean—they all got some
blond cunt draggin' along. And him dancin' and flirtin' and laughin' like
a sonofabitch and then I dig it. He's turned on again, like with me at the
start. Oh, sheet. I don't put him down really. Them chicks are somethin'
else. Prettier 'n me."

"That's impossible."

"Yeah? Dig it."

"I'm telling you—you're beautiful."

"I don't trust you—one bit."

"Why?"

Naomi smiled and reached over and took Gardner's hand. "Cause you
white, mother." Gardner laughed and so did Naomi. "It's funny, you know.
I just never <u>felt</u> beautiful," she said.

"I don't' believe it. They don't put you on the cover of—"

"Believe it, baby. Cept for Otis at the start. Je-sus, I remember as a
little girl. We were goin' somewhere. I don't know where, but it was extra
fancy, I remember that. And my Mamma damned near killed me gettin'
me ready for it. I thought the hair was comin' off my head, man. I guess
you know about—<u>our hair</u>. Under this fall, baby, is a kinky little colored
girl. Anyway, Mamma pressed my hair with a hot iron that day till she
burned my head. I always used to cry from it, but then I always used to tell
myself it must be pretty special if Mamma loves me enough to hurt me like
that. And that day, after the hair, she smeared me with a lot of cream shit.
I didn't know then what it was. Bleaching cream is what it was. She was
trying to make me white—goddamn her. I was in the bathroom lookin'
myself over when she finished—for burns, mostly—but feeling' pretty
sassy and pleased with myself, just the same. Then I overheard Mamma
tellin' Daddy, 'she ain't no Debbie Reynolds no how, but I reckon she looks
the best she can.' Man, I cried like a sonofabitch. I'm still cryin'."

"Gardner nodded and they looked each other in the eye.

"You wanta come home with me?" Naomi said.

"Yes—I'd like to."

Gardner paid the check and followed Naomi to the curb, where the
limousine was waiting. They got in and headed for 10th Street. Naomi
barely spoke, but, after a moment, she put her hand over his which was
in his lap and he could feel her arm against his thigh and Gardner could
feel himself getting on the roller-coaster again; except that this one didn't
have a track, he knew, or brakes or anything, just motion and stomach-in-
the-mouth and sweet, sensational speed and fear. Joyous fear of crystalline

complexion and challenging mien. It had no memory and set no sequence. Never heard of syllogisms and had no name. Or nation. Or rank. Or serial number. No address nor listing nor membership in clubs. No rules, no antecedents. It was going to be a hell of a ride!

CHAPTER 25

They got in the house and Naomi grabbed Gardner's hand and looked up at him and smiled, sort of. Gardner started to kiss her but she turned away.

"No, man, not yet," Naomi said. "But we're gonna be all right—ain't we, baby?"

"The best," Gardner said.

"Yeah." She let go of his hand and took a step away. Wanna drink?"

"I'd love it."

"Grab the ice. I wanta go upstairs a shake and get out of these good goods." Gardner nodded and Naomi started up the circular steps. She stopped. "Hey—you want some yerba?"

"What's that?"

"Pot, baby. Spick for grass. We got some new. It's good stuff."

"I—(we're riding all the way)—okay."

Naomi smiled and disappeared up the stairs. After getting the ice, Gardner went up them too, to the living room. There he saw again the suicide painting and remembered everything that had happened to him in this room. He shook his head and the roller-coaster slowed down, but he didn't want it to, so he shook off the room and walked to the bar, found glasses and mixed two heavy drinks—the same as they'd been having—for Naomi and himself. He carried them to a big coffee table in front of the couch and put them down there. He sat and lit a cigarette and picked up his drink, sipped it, and settled back into a corner of the couch. He took another sip and looked around. He saw a magazine rack next to him and, without picking any up, began reading the titles and covers of the written material in it. He didn't know what bothered him at first but there was something wrong about the material; he looked away and began to see other things in the room. Paintings. Fireplace. Bookcase. A piano. Except that he hadn't remembered the piano from the other time, nothing much caught his eye, and he looked again at the magazine rack. What <u>was</u> it? Something's out of joint, he thought. Oh, yes, that's it. Of course. Words are missing. They're cut out. That's all. He sipped his drink.

CUT OUT! THAT'S ALL!? What do you mean by that's all? What words are cut out? My God. Gardner slammed his drink down on the coffee table and grabbed up a batch of the stuff in the rack. My God—those letters at the hospital had a Greenwich Village postmark on them! <u>Get this message, Patty Motherfucker. We goa waist you like you dun Lonnie. We goa kill you, grey ass, and fuck up your woman</u>. It could be. You bet your ass it could be. Gardner told himself. The G was out of <u>Vogue</u>. And here's a <u>Post</u> with the P missing and Jesus, the P in Paddy had been from the <u>Post</u>. And it's an old paper—Monday, April 28. Jesus. Jesus Christ! Those letters were mailed from here!

"Neither hail nor sleet nor storm of night—hey, baby?" Naomi said.

Gardner hadn't heard her approach and he jumped when she spoke and he looked up and saw her standing there—right over him—grinning. She was in a black, floor-length, clingy kind of thing that defined her thighs and belly—and that her tits showed through.

"Fingered out your pen pal, ain'tcha," she said.

"Jesus Christ—Naomi—<u>you</u>! I can't believe it!" Gardner bolted off the couch and charged across to the far end of the room—"You sent me those goddamned letters"—towards the windows at the back, and he was afraid suddenly. Everything was pumping. She's going to kill you, boy, he said inside. Sure you dumb, egotistical bastard—kill you, not ball you. That's why she got you here. How could you be such an idiot? Roller-coaster, my ass. You're really on one now. He looked around for something to defend himself with and couldn't find anything and remembered the knife in his pocket and he jabbed his hand in for it and out it came—<u>oh, no, not again</u>—and he looked at the stairs-down and at the stairs-up and at a closed door he saw and suddenly he expected Otis to appear. Sure. That's it. That's the set-up, he thought, and his brain was sprinting. For that night. The sonofabitch wants to get me. Guys have killed for less. <u>Dangerous</u>! <u>Menacing</u>! <u>Unforeseen</u>! You weren't kidding were you, boy? You didn't know how dangerous. Maybe I can get out the windows—it's only a one-floor jump.

"Where's Otis, Goddamn it? Where is he?"

"Hey, baby, what's that knife shit? Cool it."

"Where's Otis?"

320

"In L.A., man—like I told you."

"I don't believe it—he's here."

"Hey, man, relax. He ain't."

"Who is then? What's behind that door?"

"A hi-fi. What the fuck's eatin' you?"

"You, you bitch. Stay where you are." Gardner moved quietly and carefully to the closed door and his heart was pounding and he squeezed the handle and threw the door open. He saw a stereo unit and a vertical tape deck. He spun around and looked at Naomi.

"Where are they?"

"Who, man?"

"Oh, come on?"

"Baby, ain't nobody here. I swear. Just you and me. In the whole house. Now put that fuckin' knife away, will ya? What's with you?"

"What's with those Goddamned letters, hunh? What's with those. You ain't gonna waste me, baby, without comin' too. Or your friends."

"Oh, sheet, man," Naomi said and burst out laughing and flopped herself on the couch. "Now I dig it. Sheet. You think I'm gonna kill you? She laughed again and laughed and laughed.

Suddenly, Gardner felt slightly ridiculous. He took a deep breath and relaxed a little and watched Naomi laughing. But still, he told himself, it was possible. She admitted she had sent the letters. Why did she, if she didn't mean it? How did he know there was no one else here? He didn't really. The letters were real enough and it was possible. Why? Why'd she send them?

"Stop that ridiculous laughing," Gardner said.

"Then you put away that silly-lookin' little knife, boy, and maybe I will. Who you gonna hurt with that thing?"

Wouldn't you be surprised, Naomi Bitch—LONNIE was.

Naomi kept on laughing.

"All right. Stop it!"

"Jes-us, you are a sensitive cat, aintcha?"

"What the hell do you expect? They weren't exactly love letters, Goddamn it. I'm taking you at your word."

"Jes-us. You're somethin' else, baby. You sure caught on fast, I gotta give you that."

"But why? Goddamn it, Naomi—why you? Why'd you send them? What the hell am I doing here if—"

"Man, I didn't know you was comin' down. I didn't plan no bumpin' into you today. If I had, I'd throwed that shit out."

"But, why—in the first place?"

"Whew—you really somethin' else. Tough stud."

"Why'd you send me those letters, goddamn it?"

Naomi stopped laughing and now she wasn't even smiling. She sat up and looked down in her lap. For what seemed to Gardner like a long time, she was quiet, then—"I knew the cat, man. Since a baby."

"Lonnie?"

Naomi nodded.

"Jesus Christ."

"Yeah. Come drink your drink, baby."

Gardner's shoulders slumped and he took a painful, deep breath and put his knife away. He walked, still wary, to the table and picked up his drink and swallowed on it, heavy.

"Did you really?"

"Yeah, man—all fifteen years of him."

"Jesus."

"Sit, baby. Aw, come on. I ain't gonna hurt you. Nobody's here. Believe it. Just us chickens. Come on."

Gardner sat on the couch, but away from Naomi, and he stayed tight, he could feel.

"Up in Harlem. Lived on the same block, man. Next building. His mother's a friend of my oldest sister. Was anyhow—when they was kids. Ruby's got five—not counting Lonnie."

"Is Ruby his mother?"

"Yeah."

"How old is she?"

"30—same as Melissa. That's my sis."

"Holy God. She was 15 when Lonnie was born."

"Yep. Lonnie was the oldest. I knew him from when he was born, man. Shore some cute baby. But, sheet—not much account later. He was a bad-ass nigger. Sheet. What else he gonna be—growin' up there. I used to keep him, man—for Ruby, when she was out."

"You baby-sat for him?"

"Like that—yeah."

"While his old lady was out workin'—God."

"Not exactly workin'. Noddin' mostly. She's a junkie. Ever since I known her. She didn't give a shit for them kids. Junkies don't give a shit for nothin'. Mamma had 'em our house most the time."

"Is your mother still up there?"

"H'mmm. She's dead, man."

"I'm—sorry."

"Yeah—me too. Fuckin' junkie got <u>her</u>. Yeah. Right in our hallway. Me too, prob'ly, if I hadn't gone for a ice cream with my girlfriend. Jes-us. Mama was a jack-leg preacher. You know what that is?"

Gardner shook his head no.

"No real preacher. Just someone who's got the callin', you know—and jives good. She had a storefront church on 8th Avenue. Jes-<u>us</u>, she was good. Some just do it in their pads, you know, but Mama had a store. She was some bad preacher. I used to play tambourine. Sheet." Naomi took a long pull on her drink.

"What—happened?"

"Aw, she was comin' from church one Sunday night with the collection and she give me some nickels from it and me and my friend split for ice cream and she bounced on home alone—oh, sheet."

It was very quiet and Naomi went a long way off. Gardner's brain felt like a bird caught in a jet fan. Finally, he said, "You want another drink?"

"Hunh? Aw, no, baby." Naomi sat up and leaned over to the coffee table. "Let's go this."

Gardner saw the marijuana joints on the table for the first time and he watched Naomi pick one up and light it. She inhaled and held the smoke for a long time and when she had let it out, she did it again.

"That's the A train, baby. Here."

Gardner took the cigarette and did with it as Naomi had done. Once. He handed it back to Naomi and she inhaled it again and returned it to Gardner. Finally, she let the smoke out, closed her eyes and leaned back into the couch.

"Did you—really—want to kill me, Naomi?"

"Aw, no, man. I guess—I felt like it, but. Yeah, that's why I sent you the letters."

"I still don't quite understand it. I couldn't help it. He came at me. I guess you do hate me, hunh? You said a while ago everybody wanted to waste a—white boy. I was yours, is that it?"

"Yeah, I did. I did hate you that night—like I said. Then when I read Lonnie got killed and it was you did it, I really despised your ass. I cried and cried. Sat up all night hatin' you thorough. And Otis. Everything. I remembered everything I used to feel on 128th Street. The hate and the fear. The useless shit of it all. All the shit you have to chew and swallow. I wanted you to have some."

"I did."

"Them letters worked in on you, hunh?"

"A lot."

"I seen it did—right now. Man, you was really uptight." Naomi sat up a little and opened her eyes and looked at Gardner. "I'm—sorry, baby. For the whole fuckin' world." She fell back again and closed her eyes.

"Does Otis know?"

"Nothin'—sheet."

Gardner took another drag on the cigarette and passed it to Naomi. "Here." She took it, barely opening her eyes.

"How'd you—get out of—Harlem?" Gardner said. "To here."

"On the A train, baby."

"But—how?"

"H'mmm. Remember the riot in '65—up there?"

"Yes."

"The Man got awful nervous about that noise. Remember? Charlie was fallin' all over himself helpin' the poor old nigger after that. Guess he thought we was gonna burn the whole fuckin' thing down. Anyway, my brother copped a camera durin' the riot and got in a camera club they started up there."

"How many brothers and sisters do you have?"

"Just the one sister—Melissa. And three brothers. I'm the youngest."

"How old are you, Naomi?"

"21"

"How long have you and Otis been married?"

"Three fuckin' endless years."

"Where're your brothers?"

"The one with the camera's in jail. Nother one's in the Army in Vietnam—and Otis got Duane a job in a gallery here. He's next oldest after Lester."

"You have a brother in jail?"

"Sure, man—every black family's got one. It's like the Irish givin' a son to the Church. Anyway, Lester got this camera and joined this club. And one night the club was goin' downtown—to the Museum of Modern Art.

Sheet. To hear some Paddy broad photographer give a class there. I went along with Lester. You know Gordon Parks?"

"I've heard of him. <u>Life</u> photographer—and he made a movie."

"Yeah. Well, he's a brother, you know, and he was there that night showin' pictures. I got to rappin' with him after, and he said he thought I could be a model. I thought he was jivin' me. Everybody was pitchin' to cool off the nigs in those days. Anyway, he give me his phone number and I called him bout a week later. He sent me to another cat—a fashion photographer—Jerry Rosen. That was him uptown today. And Jerry used me and I started getting' work 'n next thing I went to Paris with Jerry 'n—that's where I met Otis—at a party." Naomi sat up and dragged on the end of the cigarette, which she could barely hold now between her forefinger and thumb. She tamped it out in an ashtray and lit a new one. "He was shore somethin' else that night," Naomi said. She dragged on the new cigarette. "Whatcha gonna do about them letters?"

"Hunh?"

"You gonna—tell anybody?"

Gardner shook his head no and said, "No. It's—over." Naomi passed him the cigarette and he inhaled and gave it back. "I thought about going up there," he said.

"Where?"

"To Harlem. 128th Street. From the minute I read the address I've been thinking about it."

"What for, man? Jesus."

"I thought—I could maybe—do something. And I can't stop wondering about it. What it's like up there."

"Harlem? A meatgrinder, man. I ain't never goin' back."

"Is anybody you know there?"

"Naw. No kin anyway. Melissa's in Yonkers and Duane lives in the Village now. Funny bout it though. Much as I hate it, I think some good things from it. It still feels like home. That's Mama, I guess."

"Where's your father?"

"You tell me, Dad. He split long ago."

"What'd he do?"

"You white cats always ask that, don'tcha? I noticed. Black folks never do. We know cain't be nothing' good. Jes-us. He was a shoeshine boy—downtown. One of them big buildings. He did all right. Had the whole building. Cept he had to pay that bastard super a kickback to get it."

"Why'd he leave?"

"He really tried, though, you know. One time he was chewin' Duane's ass for somethin' and he was right, but Duane sassed him back—he's got a slick head on him, that one—and he called Daddy <u>Uncle Tom</u> and all that shit. Finally, he yelled at him—'who's gonna pay any mind to a shoeshine boy? The Man ain't. The Man thinks you're shit and so do I. I ain't gonna be no 40 year old <u>boy</u>. I'm gonna be a man.' Daddy didn't say nothin', baby. He just stood there. Then he went out and he never come back."

"Do you know Henry?"

"Who?"

"Lonnie had a brother named Henry. He was in the park that day."

"Sure, I knew him. Kept him, too."

"What's he like?"

"I don't know, man. I been away."

"But—then."

"He was okay. Quieter 'n Lonnie. Smarter too I remember. Always readin'. He did his school work our place."

"What's the mother like?"

"A junkie, man. I told you. And hooks. She's stretched out good."

"I wish I could meet her. Say something. Tell her how bad I feel."

"You crazy, man? She don't give a shit one way or other—nohow."

"What about Henry? Maybe I could—help him out."

"Jes-<u>us</u>. I thought you was smart. You ain't helpin' no one up there—no way. Don't try it. That's nothin' but a long row of trouble, man. Your guilt ain't gonna goose it otherwise."

"Is that what it is?"

"Nothin' else. I seen plenty of that to know it, in cats like you. And it don't help, man. What happen happened. And it'll happen again today—and tomorrow and straight on. Leave it be."

"You can't just let things—go on."

"The cops 'n Brothers'll work it out their way, man. Like, okay. Be nice if you want when you can, but stay out of it. If them brothers need helpin', they gonna have to help themselves."

Gardner nodded, but he wasn't convinced. Naomi handed him the cigarette and he took an extra long pull on it and he could begin to feel the smoke loping through his lungs and head and veins. He wasn't happy, but he didn't weigh as much, he knew, and he felt untied. He was drifting loose, at least, and there was no wind and no rough water in him; just a calm and something smooth, but saddened too, like a lake he'd known in upper Michigan once when the vacation and the summer were ending and you could feel winter getting ready even though the warm was there. It was too calm and too alone and the light was holding softer; like dying old and peacefully in bed must be, when you can't feel any pain to kill you, but you're going just the same. The cigarette was finished and Gardner crushed it out.

"I'd better go," he said.

"Hey, baby—you just got here." Naomi straightened up and pulled him back and kissed him open-mouthed and Gardner fell into a great cavern. Her mouth had no hinges on the jaws and opened like a well, but her lips were soft and moving and immense to take his mouth in, whole between her teeth. In he went like Alice to never-never land and down and down and down. He put his arms around her fiercely to help him break his fall. He pushed her down and kissed her back and his tongue went in urgent as a team of mine rescuers. His hand came around and gripped her side at the waist and felt it sinewy and the bone cage just above. He moved up the ribs like a pianist and down again and up—arpeggios—and down, and she was all bone and he reached now, his hand flat open, for her breast and he found it, flat and barely fleshy, like an ancient burial mound eroded against the bones of her earth. But she jumped when he kneaded the nipple and he needed it a lot—but who could suck on this starved child? He could. He could. He kissed the nipple through the cloth and nipped it with his teeth and it was up there—hard—and so about to be was he, and cloth felt good but in the way and his back hand worked for a zipper. She pushed his tongue back home with her tongue and sent it searching for his tonsils and he trapped it there and wouldn't let it go. She twisted and maneuvered and he forced her deeper down onto the couch and he pressed his pelvis on her pelvis to hold her and felt the bone to grind on bone and Oh, Janelle, good-bye, child, for there weren't going to be any "dies and dries" for this love muscle—cause there it is, rising over the horizon of Naomi's legged join and the sun of his pants was burning bright and today would be a scorcher! That Welshman's day was somewhere else and on another coast in mist, but on the reefs of Sam and Nigger, the day was breaking clear! Feeling the dawn, she twisted more—Naomi—and brought the zipper to him! He had it—and took it down—and touched the skin, like smoke-cured meat beneath—smooth, but filmy-smooth and thicker! That's what it feels like, Mom & Dad, and the smell is something musk. Pungent and full of weight and caring not for half-safe. Heavy sweet like swamps must be and that is where I'm going. Adios, my upright parents, being what you must. Your world is all in pieces. I'm sifting them through my fingers there, fumbling in the smoke, beneath the zipper, and now I let them fall. The Daily Life. The Bruising Recital of marriages and deaths and births and puny scandals. The little crimes of the middle class. The "How Do You Do's" that want no answer and the "Pleases" that don't implore. The "Thank yous" that feel no gratitude. My-Country-Tis-Of-Thee. Bank Accounts and Pension Plans. Estate Planning. Social Security. (Remember how you didn't want Roosevelt to let you have it anyway?) There goes the Presbyterian Church! And the College Degree for Higher Earnings but no knowledge. And the Boy Scouts—who taught me to build a fire and love the woods—and grew up to make defoliants and napalm. Good-bye, Work—and fare-thee-ill—that doesn't use my brain or courage or touch my heart. I am forgetting that I was trained to be bored and pretend it's otherwise. And Nixon cannot save it, Mom. All the king's horses and all the king's men couldn't put Harry Gardner together again. He hasn't the want and his patience is gone. Hello, Patience—but gone and good-bye! Sorry I sent you, but your MOMENT is here and simply momentous! Thanks for the present of the present and teaching me to take it! Sorry the taking's in another pound of flesh, but I'm sure you understand! It's moment to moment you told me and take them where you can—and I can here—moment on moment on moment! From cloth to zipper to flesh of back and in a flash to tit! Gardner moved his hand around Naomi's side and on to her breast beneath the cloth! He kissed her more and sent his other hand to the denseness down below—the jungle growth beneath the equator; but he couldn't feel the forest for the trees of her dress and his Stanley hand worked down the continent of her, searching for a passage to the heart of the Congo, until at the far away hem of her skirt he found his way around the horn—and Good Hope—handed North! He plunged into the bush beneath the cloth and heard the night animals in her throat moaning out the killing business of keeping alive! He worked in and out of the jungle, his finger guiding safaris, and, with his other hand, he pulled back from tit to back to out of zipper and started pulling the dress off! She helped him and when they'd finished, she put her hand on his Totum through his trousers!

"U'nnnh," his throat cried, and the panther sprung in the night.

"Let's go upstairs, baby," Naomi drummed.

Gardner got up and started getting out of his regiment's uniform. Naked Naomi helped with the shoes and socks and undid the tie. He was naked too now and they kissed standing up, pressed on each other like water against a dam! He took her up in his arms and carried her—dead, black, female Christ—up the Calvary of the stairs. And into a room and laid her down on a bed of a Cross and did what was needed to prepare the way for her resurrection—and for his! He inserted his nail into the flesh of her! And he nailed and nailed and nailed, till—forgive them, Norma; they know not what they do—and the nailing stopped! Naomi took him off of her and turned him around and took the hammer in her mouth and pulled it down her throat! Oh, Norma, Norma—why has't me forsaken thee? Can you understand—and forgive? I love thee much and more than any, but I so don't want to die that I bolt the manger and stalk the night, tracking death down where he is! Yes, it is death, see?! And that's why I called it's name back there! I don't want to wait for him and have him come and catch me unsuspecting! I've got to feel alive—and let him get me that way—if he really thinks he can! Norma—understand! Forgive me! Now and at the hour of finding death! Say then, please—and I implore you—"He was thought to have lived." –That Harry man you loved! And now I'm going murdering! To kill a black woman anti-Christ, a pagan love song of a bitch, and halve her with my knife, thus to feel me living! Down first to the swamp of primal meanings, to pounce on the living food I need to live! I don't love this meal but I've got to eat it! Gardner spun Naomi round, who didn't lose her place, and he mouthed and teethed and tongued, into the blood and secretion of the life-giving place of the wildbeast he'd captured.

I hate you, black savage witch, and I'm going to kill you, where you live—where life is made! I've done it before in other swamps, but your blackness makes me madder! And it's there, I know! Even with my eyes closed—I know it's there! I can feel it! And taste it! Your black is in me and makes me blacker—the blackest soul of both!

OH, NO! Black is why I killed him! NO, NO, NO! Yes—white, I would have hurt him if I could, but black is why I murdered—even after killing. But not his blackness—mine! He's not as black as I! Not so savage black as white, who murders black forever—and now you understand it! Forever—from the Ivory Coast to Jamestown's first unloading! And Tara! And all the other pussy plantations that murdered family—and culture—and—manhood—and virginity—and learning! And which, even after Lincoln, murdered on—lawns of burning crosses and—"boy"—and taut ropes from limbs of oak! Acquitted rape (if ever tried)! Jim Crow—and segregation—and the civilized killings of legislation and gentlemen's agreements! And the murdering must go on (they're sure to kill us if we stop)! Who that's white can halt and turn and see the bloodied road he's traveled—and face the blackness in himself!? Black is evil! Black is Devil! Black is night and danger! Black is death! Jew and Jesus Bible taught you that. (Jesus got you safe past death with a room reservation in His Father's mansion, but he couldn't bleach it out! And inventions turned some lights on to get you through the night. But nothing got rid of the evil or the Devil. There they stay—algae-walled inside you). NO! <u>You couldn't have such feelings! It wasn't your fault! Who could accept that?</u> So, turn it out to purge it and there the Blackness stands—in all his high visibility—THE NIGGER. Inside out—the ape of you! YOU! Of course, you had to kill him! A necessary right! A bath in blood to get you graced again! Oh, Lonnie, Jesus God and Ruby, Naomi's Dad and Mom! Forgive us! Forgive us for hating ourselves so much! For denying the horror in our souls instead of facing it! We talked ourselves up to Gods in status, and when we found we weren't—we took it out on you! But no—it can change! I can! It's not too late! I'm going to reverse the order of things! I'm going up there! To turn myself around! And Ruby! And Henry! I've got to change it all—for Henry! I can! I can! Oh, Naomi, quickly; die this ritual death and have it done! I've got to create some life now and make an end with killing!

Gardner came up from the swamp and turned Naomi from his cock and spread her legs and pushed it in her—knife unto a sheath. And in a moment, moment, moment—they came both into death. Spasm, spasm. Cry to cry. And then the silence—and the void. Moment of pleasure. Of drift and death. But on the third moment, Gardner rose.

"Hey, baby—were you going?" Naomi said.

"I'm 10 years older than Jesus—but it's not too late!"

"Hunh? What you sayin'?"

Gardner fled down the stairs and worried his clothes—trying to get them on, with Naomi right behind him.

"What's the matter, man? Why you goin'? What you sayin' to me? The pot got your head? You on a bad trip, baby? Let me help ya. Maybe you ain't used to it. Baby—talk on me. You actin' crazy. What the fuck a matter with you?"

Gardner had his clothes on now and was struggling with his socks and shoes.

"You fuck me like that—and just cut ass? Didn't you like me? I know you liked me. I could feel you like me. Say something, man! You did like me, you sonofabitch—now you're shamed of it. That it? You bastard! What's the matter—black pussy make you feel dirty? You cocksucker! You fay motherfucker! I hate your guts! I hate your pink, fuckin' guts—ALL OF YOU!

Naomi tried to hit Gardner, but he pushed her away—gently—and she tripped as he did and fell onto the couch. She was sobbing now.

"You're all alike! We're only good for fuckin'! I wish Lonnie had of killed you! I wish he'd kill me! I want to die...die...die."

Gardner was ready now and came to Naomi. "No, Naomi—live— we're gonna live!"

"Get you pink, sick hands off me! You're on one motherfuckin' bad trip!"

"No, Naomi—you'll see! The best I've ever known!" And Gardner was gone—out of the house—out of the street—and in a cab for Harlem.

CHAPTER 26

"A hundred and twenty-eight street? That's Harlem, Buddy."

"I know. I know. That's where I have to go! We have to go up there!"

"You, maybe—not me," the cab driver said.

"All of us! We've got to get up there!"

"Hunh?"

"I ain't goin' to no Harlem, Mac."

"Oh, come on, for christ's sake—move!"

"You move. I'm stayin'"

"You want me to call a cop?"

"Call 50, pal—I ain't going'. You can get killed up there if you want—not me. A buddy of mine got it there."

"It's seven-thirty in the evening, for christ's sake!"

"Coons don't have workin' hours, mac. They'll zetz you anytime. Why don'tcha be a good boy, hunh, and get a nother cab—hunh—okay?"

Gardner started to move forward, but saw the driver pick up a piece of heavy link chain off the front seat and hold it in his fist, ready to hit Gardner if he had to.

"Why not, hunh? Be a good boy. I don't want no trouble."

Gardner looked at the driver's name on the police department identification card: Louis Stein.

"When you gonna stop hating, Louis—how can a Jew be a racist—after Hitler?"

"Screw you! I ain't gonna get killed for no nigger-lover, no matter. Now—get your ass out of here!"

Gardner got out and yelled, "You circumcized bigot!" He started running—he wasn't afraid, but he had to hurry—back towards 6th Avenue; he could hear the driver's choking curses in his ear, but he didn't try to unscramble the words. He didn't have time!

"Oh, great, Harry boy—just dandy! You start your big love/do-good/ soul-saving mission by screaming an anti-Semitic remark! Some Jesus-Love Thy Neighbor-Act that is! He was a bigot though, Jewish or not—and don't tell me He was so perfect either! Cursing that poor dumb date tree and beating up the money-lenders in the Temple! Don't bug me with Christ, for Christ's sake! So I yelled a little! So what? So, still you're fighting cab drivers like windmills! Leave the little guys alone, Harry! "the little guys" vote in this country, brain—they have power! They are my enemies. Oh, Harry, when are you going to grow up—take ahold of yourself. Be reasonable. Why don't you just leave it and go home like a good boy. You've got it made, if you'll just look away and mind your own business. Speaking of business, you better call Buzz—then go see the Doctor Monday, I don't mind. Might be fun even. We'll have a little chat. Tell him about Mom and Dad and the office and the irksome little things Norma does around the house. We've got some great sex stories for him. It'll make you feel better. Screw the Doctor! I don't need a Doctor! I know where I am! I know where we all are now!

I am not going to let some shrink forgive you, brain, for the way you've been conducting things. I am accountable for my actions! Me! No one else! That's maturity, brain—which you're always harping about. I'm going to stop doing what's "expected of me"! Letting you push down everything I really think and feel—till I'm sick from it! I'm going to do things from now on because I want to!--and believe in them! Be reasonable, you say. I know your reasonable. Reasonable men in suits and ties and tidy haircuts signing death warrants in air-conditioned offices, commuting home to wives who ask, but don't care as long as the money's there, "Did you have a hard day at the office, Dear?" Sort of—just a few men got mutilated by the papers I signed. What's for dinner. How bout a drink?" That's your Reasonable! It's your excuse to sit up there and make a clever little mental mess of it all! Well, no more, goddamn you! We're going to feel things—and do things—right around us! Right here! What we can change! And if you want to help—fine. You're pretty good. But don't think you can go on leveling everything out with a lot of intellectual bullshit that paralyzes everything I do! I'm not gonna move up to Harlem, if that's what you think—or join the Peace Corps. Nothing like that. But I am, by God, going to do something correct about what Harry Gardner does get himself involved in! I'm going to set that straight at least! And I'm going to fight you and everyone else when you let the bullshit in me take over. We're gonna have some goddamned monumental family brawls, you and I. I'M A MAN. A HUMAN BEING!--and I'm capable of both good and evil and I'm going to understand that. And stop letting you give into the evil by putting on your mental sleeping mask from Abercrombie & Fitch! And pretend it isn't there! You're out on your ass as Chairman of the Board! You're not running this show anymore! We'll use you when we need you, but FEELINGS are going to give the orders from now on. I don't know where they are in here exactly—God, why don't you clean up this place—in the intestines maybe, or the stomach—other parts of the head; but they're all wired to you, I know that—so shape up and do what you're told! You've had it, writing those little cerebral-charities checks! You're, by God, gonna get in the shit yourself now—and face the shit—and stay conscious of the shit—and clean up the little bit you can.

So that's why we're off to Harlem, is it? To _feel_ things and _do_ things. Remember we've just come from Naomi—where we _felt_ some things and _did_ some things. Cunt and tit and tongue—you remember where I got that message from, don't you? Not very honorable, with all your high-blown talk, is it?--Oh, look, Harry, stop kidding yourself. There's nothing you can do up there and you ought to go home. If you really want to change things you can, as you say, start there. With your children and your wife. They own rights on you. Not that little lost beast, HENRY. Look, I'll make you a deal even. Give Patience a little punch if you really have to. I'll understand. I'll turn things over to my good old fellow member for awhile—he's a good sort actually—and I'll keep it discreet for him. But, Harry dear chap, Louis Stein is right. You can get killed up there. DON'T GO TO HARLEM.

That's where everything begins, you over-developed, parasitic, bureaucratic idiot! No Norma, Children, peace or America, anything— till we settle that! You're smart, brain, but you're not boss. You're just an aide now, remember? And if you'll stop shuffling messages, and burying everything in your "In" box, this Harry Gardner business might amount to something—sometime, somehow! We never will if we don't start up there! Now shut up—and I'll call you when I need you!

After all I've done for you! Talking to me like that! Naomi's right. You've got us so full of booze and pot—no wonder it's a mess in here! You _are_ on a bad trip!

SHUT UP I SAID!

Gardner hailed another cab and was relieved to see that a black man was driving it. He gave him the address in Harlem and off they went.

The cab let Gardner out in front of the address on 128th Street. The street was full of noise from voices and television sets and a horn blowing and radios and someone gunning a car engine and—downaways--beer cans hit on the pavement. Two boys ran by from nowhere and headed into a vacant lot covered with unknown garbage. A dirty sun was going down beyond the Hudson. A torn, stained mattress hunched up on the sidewalk in front of the building next door and the dead metal bones of an abandoned automobile, tireless, and looted of all personal affects, stood decomposing farther along the block. At the corner stood a group of black boys. He wondered if Henry was among them. Gardner looked up at the building and saw the iron lattice of fire escapes which looked corroded and were pitted with grime; and he thought surely they would collapse if anyone set foot on them.

Feel that? You getting the message from the engine room, Harry dear? You want <u>feelings</u>? Then feel that. Your guts are balling up and they're trying to tell you you shouldn't be here.

SHUT UP! Gardner hurried into the building and the odor hit him like a punch. Dried piss filled his nostrils—and trapped-cooking stink. Spilled alcohol of some sort. And exhaustion—of air, of wood, of plaster, of possibilities. He shuddered and started breathing through his mouth and wondered how he could know which hole here Ruby lived in.

He looked at the apartment list frame above the mailboxes, but the whole thing was rusted and the boxes had all been broken into, so that the doors on them hung open and breaking off. He turned around and, just then, saw inside, where the second set of doors should have been, the body of a black man stretched out unconscious, near the stairs. Gardner shook his head and looked at the wall opposite the mail boxes and there he saw—scribbled on it in some kind of paint--"Ruby's on 4." <u>That's your ad, is it, Ruby Hooker? A modest, but direct campaign. SHUT UP, BRAIN</u>. Too bad, Harry. You could have given her a beaut: 3 color, bleed-off lettering with mod graphics and a catchy slogan. Even throw in a logo design—just six meetings plus four lunches X 3 martinis and a falsified expense account. SHUT UP!

Harry—you never did think up anything for that Clover Farms Diet Drink, Billingsly's been bugging you about. Work on it. Let's see? <u>Fuck it and get fat</u>! How bout that, brain? Gardner laughed. That's the kind of slogan I'd like to see someday. Wouldn't that be an ad? But—advertising works—Harry—see? You know how to find Ruby because of it. You're the proof of her message. Though, of course, "you're just looking, thanks." But for what, Harry Dear? I TOLD YOU TO SHUT UP! I KNOW FOR WHAT!

Gardner stepped over the unconscious man and realized that he had never stopped at men like these to see if they were dead or needed help. He knelt by this one now and began to take his pulse, when he got a whiff of the man's breath. Booze exhaled in cubes. Gardner backed off quickly and turned away. He lit a cigarette and started up the stairs, taking the steps two at a time. I've got to see that woman and explain—tell her why I killed her son! I've got to do something for her! I'm the good guys, the cavalry come to the rescue! Hold on, Ruby, John Wayne's coming! Trumpets, boys, and show the flag! It's Superwasp!

Along the upward tunnel of chipped plaster and violated paint—of low-watt bulbs in little iron cages or no bulbs at all—between the walls—the graffitied-Guggenheim of the down and out--"Fuck you, whoever you are;" "Dorothy eats cock;" "Pigs Suck'" and lots of pictures of puss and prick—Gardner, dudutudulu, dudutudulu, dudutudula, got up to 4. He was out of breath and hurting for it. (The Duke out of breath? Impossible). He found Ruby's door right away. "RUBY": writ large and red and scruffy. Gardner tried the door. It wasn't locked. He breathed deep and pushed it open.

The room was dark, but some anemic light came bloodying in through a broken window pane. The glass around the break was fabric-thick with dirt and a venetian blind, looking like whale ribs hit by a ship, was hanging from one side only. When his eyes got adjusted, he thought he saw a form against the far wall, slumped on a plain bed of some kind. You always come in in the last reel, boy, but this looked awfully late—even for the Cavalry, and Duke Wayne.

"Is—Ruby" Is—that you, M'am? Ruby Dobson?"

There was no sound and the figure did not move.

"Ruby?"

Finally--"She ain't here. She died."

"Where could I find her—please! It's important!"

"I gave the census."

"Please. It's not that."

"Why you lookin' for?"

"Is Henry here?"

"Gone out. Dead."

"I don't believe you!"

"You Fuzz?"

"No, I'm"--who, boy, who—General Custer? Last stand, if you are.
"Uh, Harry Gardner's my--"

"Welfare? You welfare. I ain't got my--"

"I'm not from the Welfare. I'm from—from downtown."

"You got business with Ruby—or pleasure?"

"I—I want to talk to her! I've got to! Naomi Price sent me. You know
her?!"

"Hunh?"

"Naomi. She had a sister—Melissa. Your friend!"

"Turn—the light—there--by the--"

Gardner felt for a wall switch and found it and flicked it on. In the
light, thrown from a dim bulb in the ceiling fixture, which was hanging
loose, Gardner could see the woman on the bed. That can't be her, he
told himself! Ruby's only 30! That—thing—is ancient! And Hideous!
The woman's skin was pocked and her eyes were out of focus and swollen
and a huge scar knotted down one cheek onto her neck. Her hair was stiff
and sticking out. She was thin as Auschwitz. You could see the bones in
her chest and there were dried sacks of tits showing through the dirty
satiny-kind of wrapper she was wearing. The wrapper was soiled and had
a molting boa affect around the hem and where it opened in front, and it
was opened nearly all the way. Gardner turned his eyes away.

"What's happnin', baby?"

"Are you—Ruby?"

"Yeah, stud. You wantin' some fun?"

Gardner's guts spasmed and shut.

"I—I want—to--talk to you."

"Time is money, honey, and my jones is always comin'. You got coin,
dude, you can fuck or talk, I don't give a shit."

Gardner felt like he was going to vomit and thought he'd better sit
down. He looked around and saw a broken chromium kitchen chair with
the stuffing coming through the plastic. There were roaches on the floor.
He looked at the room. Everything in it was broken and torn and soiled
and thrown. The walls were painted pink—but years ago—and peeling.
The bed she lay on had a green chenille spread on it and it was dirty and
torn. There were no sheets. He decided to stay standing.

All right, Captain Marvel—this is what you've come to save!? This is
your African Queen? Your noble Black? Your redeemable Regina of the
dark continent? This scabbed, clapped liceyed wreckage? Clark Kent and
Albert Schweitzer together couldn't salvage her! Now will you get your

little guilty WASP ass out of here?! Go! Get back to Grover's Corners where you belong. NO! I'M DONE WITH THAT! THE WORLD IS DONE WITH THAT! Okay, pal—don't say I didn't warn you. Go on. Let's hear it. Go on. What are you waiting for?

"You wanna trick, babe or don'tcha?"

"I—I killed—your son."

Gardner stiffened when he heard the words come out. He didn't know what to expect. But he's said it! He had gotten the worst part out. He studied Ruby's face and waited for the words to sink in and for something to come back out. She didn't stir. She closed her eyes and began to nod. Gardner shifted on his feet and his eyes looked down at the floor and then he saw it. He had never seen it in life before, just in films and photos. A hypodermic needle and syringe—a bottle cap—and a book of matches. Stuff, Shit, H. Horse, the tragic magic, went through his head. He looked at her again. She was on it for sure, he saw—but when, how long, how much? How would you know, Rover Boy? This isn't your league. You're really an amateur, up here. You got nothing to equip you for this, Charlie! Why won't she say something?!

"I said—I killed your son! I killed Lonnie! Don't you hear me? Don't you care? I killed Lonnie! Your son. I didn't mean to! I didn't want it to happen! He was going to kill me, don't you see? But I murdered him even after that! Killed him and kept killing him! And killed him and killed him and killed him! Talk to me! I know why I did it—I want to tell you! I want you to understand! We've got to help each other! I couldn't face him! Staring at me that way! Indicting me! Accusing me! Reminding me what we've done to you! Don't you understand?! I need you to understand! I hate him cause I hated myself! All my pretty pictures of America are lies with him there! Don't you see that? You know they're lies, don't you? I do now! And damn you for it! Do you hear me? LISTEN TO ME! DAMN YOU FOR IT! DAMN LONNIE! DAMN HIM! DAMN HIM! DAMN HIM! AND KILL HIM! YES! GET HIM OUT OF HERE! HARRY GARDNER'S A GOOD GUY, IF LONNIE DOBSON ISN'T THERE! STOP STEALING MY STATE OF GRACE!!!

Gardner stumbled forward and fell on his knees by the bed and he was weeping into the chenille spread and his hands were almost clasped for praying.

DON'T YOU SEE THAT? SEE? I DO! I DO! BUT-- I CAN CHANGE! I CAN CHANGE NOW, RUBY! YOU'VE GOT TO HELP ME! FORGIVE ME! I WANT TO HELP HENRY—AND YOU! LET'S

FORGIVE EACH OTHER—AND DO SOMETHING FOR EACH OTHER! CAN'T YOU HEAR ME? HEEEEEEEEEELP ME!

"Shore, baby—come on. Right heeya to Mama."

Ruby put her hand on Gardner's head and the touch suffused his body. OH, YES, AMEN, HALLELUJAH—THE ANGEL OF MERCY HAS DESCENDED! HARRY GARDNER'S FOUND SALVATION! He has risen at last! Gardner tried to stop his crying and begin to smile and he lifted his head to look at the woman who could save him and---

"OH, GOD! NO! NO! NO!"

Ruby had pulled her wrapper off and spread her legs and was inserting S'HHH FEM into her cunt.

"NO! NO! NO!"

"Come on, baby—10 bucks. See, baby, this'll make it smell good 'n Ruby'll get your rocks off nice."

"NO!"

"Five bucks—jess 5 bucks."

"No!" Gardner picked up Ruby's hypodermic needle and staggered to his feet and he hurled the syringe against the wall and smashed it.

"Aaaaaaaaah! You grey-ass-bastard! My--'quipment! Your broke my 'quipment!"

Ruby threw the tube of S'HHH-Fem at Gardner, but it missed him and hit off the wall behind him. Her body began to jerk and she gripped the chenille spread and took it into her mouth and began tearing at it with her teeth and she burst out crying.

Gardner picked up the tube of S'HHH-FEM and felt his guts run out his ass. Oh, Jesus! Jesus Christ! He was crying too and ready to vomit!

"Where'd—you—get--this?"

"Why'dcha do that for? Why'dcha do it?"

"WHERE'D YOU GET THIS?! TELL ME, GODDAMN YOU!"

"Don't man, don't—don't hurt me. I—I didn't cop it, honest. Man give it me free sample at the A & P. (It'll be test-marketed next week, Harry—isn't that great? Sweep the market). My 'quipment. What am I gonna du? My 'quipment. 'Quipment."

"Gardner jammed into his pocket, fumbled past his knife, and wrenched out some money. He took off two twenties and a ten. He lurched over to the bed and put the money on the spread, and turned and ran out of the room and slammed the door behind him.

He leaned over the bannister in the hallway and tried to hold himself together! He couldn't! It was over! All of it! Oh—God of Jesus, Harry

Gardner! MAN! SON! You SON OF MAN. <u>Harry Gardner, Jesus-like</u>? <u>Transfigured by tragedy</u>? YAK, YAK, YAK. Forget it. That ain't your cross, baby! You're too bald and pouchy for a Passion Play. Who wants a martyr in his 40's full of childish dreams! And tin ideals! Endless moralizing and endlessly common? You stick to I pledge allegiance and Captain Midnight. Don Winslow and secret de-coder rings. God Bless old fat Kate Smith—Tom Swift that you love. Stand beside that and guide that through the million trashy movies—Hi, there—you're tuned to your stations of the Cross—easy listening all life long. TRANSFIGURATION!! For this Harry Son of Man—it's a joke—a bad—tasteless--hollow joke! Shallowed by thy name! Thy Kingdom dumb—thy will be done in mockery! Spoil earth and there is no Heaven! Give us again this day our cruel joke and lead us not into redemption but deliver us into absurdity! For thine is the prison and the impotence and the meaningless—forever and ever and ever!

Gardner heard a noise in the building, up through the stairwell, and then some laughter and then someone shushing the laughter. And then it was quiet—too quiet. It's Henry and Cassius, Gardner told himself. I know it. They're waiting for me. They're going to kill me. And for what now? S'HHH-FEM up Ruby's cunt? I've known it all along though. It's what I've been waiting for, aiming at! I want them to kill me! I came for it! Of course! And they will. They'll be very happy to do that for me. They have a whole gang probably and they're just waiting down there for me.

Maybe you could go up and out on the roof and down through another building—remember, you've read about that and seen it in films, when the kids are getting away from the cops and—but—oh, God—remember, you've read about that one kid who missed his jump and fell five flights and smashed on the—besides--they probably have the roof covered. Henry saw you come in—that <u>was</u> him—SURE--in the group of kids at the corner! How many were there? 8, at least. <u>Eight</u>! They've covered the roof, you can count on that. You'll have to face them—down the stairs. At least, by God, they'll see you're not afraid. NOT AFRAID, MY ASS! I'VE NEVER BEEN SO FRIGHTENED! Don't show them that!

Gardner slammed the S'HHH-FEM tube down the stairwell and screamed, "I know you're there, Henry!-----------You ain't gonna surprise me!----------If I go, you go!"

Gardner listened. There was no sound. But they're there! I know they're there! He looked down, squinting, into the dark tunnel of the stairwell. "All right, goddamn you—the WASP is coming! Isn't that what you want?!"

Good as dead, hunh, Henry? But watch him die! Don't worry about that!

Harry—did you pay that insurance bill?

"YES, DAMN YOU!

Well, I was only thinking of Norma.

I'M ALWAYS PAID UP!

I wonder what kind of funeral they'll give you? Think you'll draw much of a crowd? How bout a minister? You're not really going to have a religious ceremony, are you? And the music? You always wanted Ray Charles, remember—or Chuck Berry. You still want to be buried in Indiana? I always thought that was so silly—what difference does it make? Besides, you never told Norma that. She won't know. She'll stick you over in New Jersey somewhere like Harriet Ziegler and Irwin. Ugh—New Jersey! Nobody'll bother with us there. Your own kids won't come after the first time. The kids. That's really too bad. You shoulda stayed around for the kids, Harry. They coulda used you. You never got to tell them about life or get them prepared for that long series of good-byes. And the new one! You won't even know what it is! And Norma! Good God! There you'll be—plastered all over the front page of The Daily <u>News</u>—just like she told you you would if you kept it up. And it's a hell of a time to leave her, boy! Oh, sure she'll mourn you—don't worry about that—at first anyway—but then she'll hate you—all her life for this—this wastefulness. She begged you not to come up here! All she ever wanted was to love you and give you a little happiness—but, no—no, you had to go round with your stupid center not holding.

I'M DYING, DAMN YOU! LEAVE ME ALONE!

And aren't you going to do <u>anything</u> about that Clover Farms account? You're just not the good-button-down guy we thought you were. How 'bout a full photo blow-up of a great-looking chick's belly-button and abdomen, see?--real nipped-in and curvey—with a gun belt made of diamonds and a can of the diet drink in the holster? How does that grab you? And the slogan can be--"Waist not—want not." Get it? I love it!

STOP DEBASING MY DEATH!

Well—at least you've finally found a way to give up smoking.

SHUT UP!

All right, all right. You don't have to be so touchy. I didn't get us into this, you know.

Come on, damn you—we're going down there—and face them. Get the knife out, will you? Good. That's it. I can't beat them—but we'll, by

God, give them a good show. I'll bet you they're on 3. No—maybe not. That's too soon. 2, probably. The noise sounded like it was on 2—and— see, they'd think I'd think they'd be on 3—so, they're on 2. But no, if I thought they'd be on 3 and they're not, then they know I'll know they're on 2 and be ready for them. They lose surprise. So—they'll probably be on 1—or maybe on 3. Or everywhere! Zap, switch—get the WASP!

Harry—you didn't notice, but we're already on 3 and there's nobody here.

See—what'd I tell you!2! 2! They're on 2! That's where the light was out! 2's perfect for them!

This is 2, Harry. They aren't here, either, Harry.

Then 1—of course! 1 is a natural! So they can run right out. 1 is it!!

No, sorry, see? There's your drunken, passed-out friend, sleeping peacefully. And no Henry. No Cassius. Nobody. They aren't here on 1, Harry.

Outside, then! They're gonna do it outside! Of course! Then the cops can't pin it on this building! Henry'd be a jerk to do it in his own building! Why didn't I think of that!

Harry—you're standing outside. It's a hot lovely, quiet night. Just the TV sets and some car noises. See—it's lovely. Nobody's going to hurt you.

Yeah—what about that? Down there at the corner? See—that's him— them—there under the streetlight. They're playing it cool, but I know. That's them. See? They're looking this way.

They aren't paying a bit of attention to you.

There was a tremendous sound behind Gardner—Ca-rash!-- SHATTER, SHATTER, SHATTER!

He spun and his heart jammed in his throat, and he crouched, and his knife was forward, and his juice was slamming through him. Then he saw it—what the sound had been. It was a toilet somebody had just thrown out of the building two doors away and it was lying in shattered porcelain pieces all over the sidewalk.

Gardner looked at it and began to laugh—and to laugh and to laugh and laugh and laugh and laugh and laugh and laugh and laugh. A toilet! Oh, no, Harry (laugh), it was too easy your way! (laugh) Still playing for the Cross (laugh). Forget it! It is the judgment (laugh) of this high court (laugh) that Harry Gardner (laugh, laugh) has been willfully (laugh) and maliciously (laugh) seeking the easy way out (laugh, laugh)--a cowardly refuge (laugh) that he camouflaged (laugh) behind noble posturings (laugh) and weak imitations of Christ (laugh) and for extravagant shows of a soul writhing in moral pain. RADCLIFFE! You just didn't have the guts to accept life as a paradox that ain't gonna reveal its mysteries to the likes of you. So, for refusing to accept this only truth truthfully available to you, and for defying it by puking on the carpet in front of your children and lapping alien pussies and sticking your cock in where it doesn't belong—and other unseemly acts of ego and self-indulgence--(the court does recognize your view as to why you killed Lonnie Dobson so much and considers that as mitigating evidence in your crimes)--HERE COM DE JUDGMENT! Harry Gardner isn't going to die. He is going to have to live. Do you hear me, Harry? YOU ARE SENTENCED TO HAVE TO LIVE!

Gardner looked down at the knife in his hand. It was not a very impressive-looking knife, he thought; but rather oldish really and rusting slightly. And not long. The blade extended perhaps four inches. The bone sides were dark and yellow, and a small piece even had been chipped from one of these. He opened his hand flat and turned it over. The knife fell off his palm and into the dry riverbed of the gutter. Gardner turned and started walking. He was quite aways from home.

About the Author

Robert Shanks, aka Bob Shanks, is the winner of two Emmy Awards and "has been nominated almost as many times as Susan Lucci."

As an ABC programming VP, he created and/or developed *Good Morning America*, *The Barbara Walters Special* and the late-night series *The Wide World of Entertainment* including *In Concert* and the live Woodstock-type event called *California Jam*. Later, as ABC VP of News, Mr. Shanks created and developed *20/20*. Among other credits are producing *The Tonight Show*, *The Merv Griffin Show*, *Candid Camera* on CBS, several programs in the PBS series, *The Great American Dream Machine* and the first 3 years of the *Jerry Lewis Telethon*. He co-developed the *Regis Philbin Morning Show*.

His books include: "The Cool Fire", "The Primal Screen" and "Love is Not Enough", a novel.

Shanks served in the U.S. Army and is a graduate of Indiana University, which has named him a distinguished alumnus. He is married to photographer/filmmaker, Ann Zane Shanks. They have three children: Jennifer, Anthony and John and four grand-children: Tom and Patrick Kingsley and Dylan and Jackson Shanks.